A WITCH OF A TIME
WICKED WITCHES OF THE MIDWEST SHORTS 1-5

AMANDA M. LEE

WINCHESTERSHAW PUBLICATIONS

Copyright © 2015 by Amanda M. Lee

All rights reserved.

No part of this book may be reproduced in any form or by any electronic or mechanical means, including information storage and retrieval systems, without written permission from the author, except for the use of brief quotations in a book review.

❀ Created with Vellum

CAREFUL WHAT YOU WITCH FOR

A WICKED WITCHES OF THE MIDWEST SHORT

ONE

"Pick it up!"

"You pick it up!"

"I'm not the one who dropped it."

"I didn't drop it. I'm … organizing." I glanced up from the floor, my legs crossed, and fixed my cousin Thistle with an annoyed look. "We have to get some organization going in this place."

Thistle arched a dark eyebrow, her eyes flashing as she ran a frustrated hand through her blue hair. "You've made a huge mess." She gestured to the plastic bags strewn across the floor around me. "You can't organize by making a bigger mess, Clove."

I rolled my eyes, tucking a strand of my long, dark hair behind my ear as I regarded her. "If you want to organize, you have to start with disorganization." I'd read that in a book somewhere, and it stuck with me. I'm big on reading.

"What book is that, *How to Drive My Cousin Insane for Dummies*?"

I furrowed my brow. I was used to being talked down to. That's what happens when you're the meekest member of a close-knit family. Thistle always takes it to a harsh level, though. When someone is being mean to me, I like it when she swoops in and eviscerates them with her razor-sharp tongue. When her vitriol is

AMANDA M. LEE

pointed at me, I want to give her hair a good, hard yank. "No one is making you stay here," I pointed out. "We're slow today. You can go and do … whatever you want to do. You don't have to watch me."

"What are you going to do?" Thistle asked, her eyes narrowing.

"Why do you care?" I shot back. I was feeling particularly feisty today. Don't worry, it won't last. I get up the urge to fight and then wish I hadn't two hours later. It's what I do.

"Because we're exactly one week away from the summer season starting," Thistle said. "Once summer is officially here, then Hemlock Cove is going to be bustling with activity. We need this place put together … not filthy. This is how we make a living, or did you forget that?"

Since Thistle and I had shared ownership of our magic shop, Hypnotic, for three years now, her words chafed. "Of course I didn't forget," I scoffed. "Who do you think does the bulk of work around here?"

"Me!"

"You?" That was laughable. "You make candles and then pop in when you feel like it. I do all the herbs. I do all the ordering. I do all the decorating. I do all the … organizing."

"You do all the decorating because you like it," Thistle argued. "We live in a magically rebranded town. Anything 'witch' will do. You're the one who feels the need to change the decorations every season. You just like to decorate."

"People like it when you acknowledge the holidays," I retorted. "Just because you're … heartless."

"Oh, whatever," Thistle said, waving at me dismissively. "If you're insistent on doing this, though, I guess I can take a trip over to Traverse City. I need to get some new wax. The stuff I bought in the fall is almost gone – and it was a little soft for my liking."

I knew Thistle was giving me an out, but for some reason, I didn't want to take it. "Oh, are you finally going to get moving on the spring candles?"

Thistle wrinkled her nose. "Excuse me?"

"You've had months to get going on the candles," I reminded her. "You only like to work when a deadline is looming. It's frustrating."

"Not all of us are planners, Clove," Thistle said. "Some of us are more creative when we have to be. I don't like lists and … organization. I like to let my creative juices flow."

While it was true that I had never met a list I didn't like, there was something about Thistle's tone that irked me. "And where would you be without my lists?"

"Standing right here."

"Really? Because it was my lists that made sure we got the summer ordering done before the season started," I argued.

"I was going to do it," Thistle said. "You just didn't give me enough time."

The truth was, Thistle hated ordering and organizing. I loved both. I got some of my best ideas when I was doing a menial task – finding pearls of wisdom in the back recesses of my mind while I focused on something else, not that Thistle ever gave me credit for those ideas. "If we would have waited, we wouldn't have had inventory for next week. Do you know what next week is?"

"The Spring Fling," Thistle replied, her tone dry. "It's the official ending of the spring season and the beginning of the summer season – even though spring doesn't end for another four weeks. It's a stupid tradition."

"It's one of our biggest weekends of the year," I said.

"I know."

"So, how were we magically going to get the inventory if I didn't step in and do it?"

Thistle placed her hands on her narrow hips. "I … that's neither here nor there," she sniffed. "I always do what needs to be done."

"Not this time."

Thistle swiveled, stalking toward the counter so she could grab her purse. "Fine," she said. "You stay here and do your … organizing … and I'll go and get the wax. I don't feel like fighting."

She could have fooled me. "Fine."

"Great." Thistle was already halfway out the door.

"You didn't win this one," I yelled to her back.

"I always win."

No, she always has to get the last word. Unfortunately, that's a family trait.

TWO HOURS later I was almost done, and I had a great new idea for blueberry pancake wax melts to experiment with when Thistle returned from her jaunt to Traverse City with supplies. I just hoped I could convince Thistle to give it a try.

I started doling the herb bags to their appropriate spots, only stilling when I heard the wind chimes above the door jangle to signify someone's entrance into the store. "I'll be right with you."

"No hurry."

I recognized the voice. "Hi, Dad."

I was still getting used to saying that. Dad. It had a nice ring to it, although it was also awkward. My father – along with my two uncles – had recently returned to the area. Being married to a Winchester woman was hard enough, but being married to a Winchester witch was even harder. They'd left during our adolescent years, keeping in varying degrees of communication with us during their exile. Now that they were back, we were all struggling to find even footing with one another.

"The store looks good," Dad said, smiling down at me. At barely five feet tall, I'm small – and somewhat top heavy. Most men tower over me, and my father was no exception. Thankfully, he wasn't interested in looking down the vee in my shirt like the rest of his gender.

"Thanks," I said, depositing the last bags on the shelf. "We're just finishing up our spring cleaning."

"Your shelves look kind of bare," Dad said, glancing around the store.

"We don't have our new inventory out yet," I explained. "It should arrive Monday."

Dad's face brightened. "Does that mean you're free this weekend?"

"What did you have in mind? I'm not sure Bay and Thistle are up for another family dinner just now," I said, my mind involuntarily traveling back to the horrors of the last one. While I was ready to strengthen my bond with my father, Bay and Thistle were more reticent. They weren't exactly fighting the effort, but they weren't exactly embracing it either.

"Actually, I was hoping you would come out and stay at the Dragonfly this weekend," Dad said.

I stiffened. The Dragonfly Inn was my father's new business endeavor. He'd joined forces with his former brothers-in-law, and they'd purchased a dilapidated piece of property on the outskirts of town. After months of hard work, their new inn was getting ready to open – and then it would be in direct competition with the inn that my mother and aunts ran. It was a sore subject in the Winchester house. Actually, it was a *really* sore subject.

"I didn't think you were opening for another two weeks," I said evasively.

"We're not … technically," Dad said. "We're having a soft launch this weekend. We've invited several travel reporters and business executives for a trial run. We're hoping that people will consider it for company retreats, and if things go well, we should get some nice press out of it, too."

"That's a great idea," I enthused.

"This area already has a solid tourist business," Dad said. "I think we're in a good position to make a profit right away. We just want to make sure we do everything we can to make it a success."

"I'm sure you'll be fine," I said. "We don't have enough inns to keep up with the tourist population as it is. I guess I'm not sure why you want me there."

Dad searched my face, reading the fear there, even though I was trying to hide it. Visiting the Dragonfly opened all sorts of old wounds for my mother and aunts – and it made my Great-Aunt Tillie feel … threatened. And, quite frankly, when Aunt Tillie feels threatened, everyone needs to duck and cover. *Me first!*

"I understand if you don't want to come," he said.

"I want to come," I said, eager to please. "I want to support you."

"You're just worried about what Aunt Tillie will do," Dad said, finishing my unsaid thought for me.

"She's been a little crazy where the Dragonfly is concerned," I hedged.

"That woman has always been crazy," Dad grumbled.

I glanced around. In my head, I knew Aunt Tillie wasn't hiding in a corner and eavesdropping. In my heart, I wasn't sure she wasn't capable of making herself invisible to do just that. "She's just protective."

"I'm not here to argue about Aunt Tillie," Dad said. "She's been … very good to you."

"When she's not being evil," I mumbled.

"I just thought you might want to have a little fun this weekend," Dad said. "You could also get some free publicity for the shop."

That piqued my interest. "How?"

"I was hoping you would do tarot card readings," Dad said. "We want the Dragonfly branded with the town, and we thought tarot card readings – and maybe even a séance – would be a good way to do it."

"A séance?" Séances never end well in my family. They usually end up with me cowering in a ball on the floor. Ghosts are real in my world, but they're also a pain – and sometimes tempestuous.

"Nothing serious," Dad cautioned. He was aware of the witchy genes in our family, although he didn't like to talk about them. "I was just thinking something fun – something fake – would be enjoyable for the guests."

Something fake? That I could do. "I don't see why not," I said. "It sounds like fun."

"I figured you could stay in one of the rooms, too," Dad said. "That would allow us to spend some time together."

"Oh, you don't have to do that," I said. "We only live ten minutes away."

"Still, I want you there," Dad said. "This is a big deal for us. I want you to be part of it."

His face was so earnest, I didn't want to say no. Still … I had plans for this weekend, and they revolved around the new man in my life.

Sam Cornell and I had only been dating a few weeks, but the time we got to spend together was precious to us. We were still in the heady infatuation phase of our relationship, but missing an entire weekend together would be disappointing. "I kind of have a ... date ... this weekend."

I wasn't embarrassed about my relationship with Sam – no matter how much Thistle and Bay were fighting our union – but it was still awkward to discuss it with my father.

Dad inhaled heavily. I was in my mid-twenties, but I was still his daughter. "Bring him," he said finally.

I raised my eyebrows, excitement coursing through me. "Really? Are you sure? That means we'd be sharing a ... room ... together."

"I figured," Dad said, wrinkling his brow. "You are an adult, Clove. I might not see you that way, but you are."

"Thanks, Dad," I said. "I wish Mom saw me that way ... and Thistle and Bay, too."

Dad smiled. "Thistle and Bay are two of the most loyal people I've ever met."

"They still treat me like I'm a child."

"That's because you're the youngest," Dad said. "That's a good thing, Clove. You have a lot of people in your life who want to take care of you."

"What if I don't want them to take care of me?"

"I think you're in trouble then," Dad said, his eyes twinkling. "The one thing I can say without any hesitation is that you're loved. That love comes in many forms – some of it harder to take than others – but people don't stop loving you because you're ready to grow up.

"You just have to take it one step at a time," he said.

I leaned in and gave him a quick hug. "I think you just hired yourself a psychic for the weekend."

"Good," Dad said, patting the top of my head. "I don't think we could do it without you."

That was nice to hear, especially since Thistle and Bay were usually the ones people asked for help. Finally, I was going to get a chance to do something on my own this weekend.

Now I just had to convince Sam to go with me. I had a feeling that was going to be harder than it sounded.

TWO

"I'm still not sure about this."

I glanced over at Sam, taking in his strong profile as he gripped the steering wheel and stared at the Dragonfly. It was if he was trying to see the future, and the images playing through his mind were ugly ones.

It had taken some convincing, a few minutes of cajoling, and then a few seconds of outright begging – but Sam finally agreed to come with me. He was uncomfortable sharing a bed under my father's roof, but the idea of spending an uninterrupted weekend together – well, uninterrupted except for a few tasks – had finally pushed him over the edge. I think he could see how much it meant to me. He's really hot ... wait, what was I thinking?

"It's going to be fine," I told him.

Sam shot me an unreadable look. "You say that now, but you've said that before."

I worried my bottom lip with my teeth. He was right. I'd promised him Bay and Thistle would thaw – that they would welcome him – but so far, they were still being as cold as ice cream. Oh, wow, ice cream sounds good. I wonder if they'll have ice cream. Sorry, when

I'm nervous, I need chocolate. That's another family trait. "Bay and Thistle will come around," I promised. "They're just … protective."

"They act like they're your mother."

I wish that was true. My mother was going to be a lot harder to convince regarding Sam than Bay and Thistle ever would be. Eventually, I knew I could wear my cousins down. My mother couldn't be worn down by a millennium of erosion. She was immovable. Like granite.

"This is going to be fun," I said, trying a different tactic. "It will be like we're on a weekend adventure."

Sam's face softened and he grabbed my hand. "It will be fun," he agreed. "And, if things get too out of control, we can always escape to the lighthouse for a couple of hours."

When Sam had first visited Hemlock Cove, he'd done it under the guise of helping Bay's editor turn the town's weekly newspaper into a profitable business endeavor. When that had blown up in his face, he'd purchased the Dandridge, an old lighthouse that had fallen into disarray, and opted to stay in town instead of fleeing.

With financial backing from the state of Michigan, Sam was turning the lighthouse's main floor and grounds into a haunted attraction – with boat rides – and he was living on the upper floor. The work was tedious – and ongoing – but he was making real progress.

"We're not going to hope for things to get out of control, right?"

Sam smiled, the expression lighting up his already handsome face. "No. We're going to have a good time, Clove. Besides, how bad can things get? There's no Aunt Tillie here, and Bay and Thistle aren't coming, so it's bound to be better than all of the family dinners I've been to out at The Overlook."

I returned his smile. "It's going to be great."

"**THIS IS** A NIGHTMARE," I groaned, covering my face to ward off the sight across the Dragonfly foyer.

"Oh, you're here," Dad said, breezing into the room and giving me a quick hug. "I was worried you were going to be late. Why are you hiding your face?"

Sam's jaw was tense as he regarded my father. "I don't think she was expecting … them." He gestured to the far side of the room.

Dad's face fell. "Bay and Thistle?"

Sam nodded.

"They were invited by their fathers," Dad said. "We thought it would be a great way for everyone to have a good time – and make sure all of the rooms were filled."

"You didn't tell me that when you invited me," I said, fighting to keep my voice even. *I should be mad. I should be mad, right? I'm pretty sure I should be mad. Why am I so scared?*

Dad cocked an eyebrow. "Is that a problem? Don't you already live with Bay and Thistle?"

"Yes, but … ." How could I explain this without sounding like a wanton woman? "I thought it was just going to be Sam and me – and all your other guests. It was going to be like a vacation."

"From Bay and Thistle?"

Yes! "Of course not," I said. "It's just … ."

Sam sighed. "Bay and Thistle don't like me … and Bay's boyfriend, well, he just hates me."

Dad furrowed his brow. "Landon? He seems like a nice enough guy. I don't really know him. I know Jack seems leery of him, but I just figured it was because he didn't like him dating his daughter."

"He's a nice guy," I said hurriedly. I like Landon. I like what he's done for our family, and especially how he makes Bay smile. He's just … difficult.

"He's suspicious," Sam said.

Dad met Sam's gaze questioningly. "Isn't he an FBI agent?"

Sam nodded.

"Isn't it his job to be suspicious?"

Sam nodded again.

"Why is he suspicious of you?"

The question hung in the air, a direct challenge to Sam. "He thinks I'm up to something," Sam replied simply.

AMANDA M. LEE

"Are you?"

"Dad!" I was mortified.

Sam patted my back. "It's okay, Clove," he said. "Mr. Johnson, I'm not up to anything. I'm just trying to run a business, the same as you."

Dad didn't look convinced. "Well, okay then." He moved to the registration desk. "I put all three of you up on the top floor."

The Dragonfly has three stories, and in addition to storage, the top floor consisted of only three rooms. I knew our assignments were deliberate. Unfortunately, I had a sneaking suspicion that Dad thought he was doing a good thing when he made the arrangements. He had no way of knowing just how tense this weekend would be – for all of us.

I forced a tight smile onto my face as I regarded my cousins. They didn't seem surprised to see me, but they looked less than thrilled to see Sam. That was my life these days, so I was used to it.

"You guys didn't tell me you were coming," I said.

"You didn't tell us either," Thistle pointed out.

"I … I just found out earlier today."

"So did we," Bay said, leaning her blonde head against Landon's shoulder. "I think they approached us individually because they thought it would be easier to get us all here."

"So, you thought it was just going to be you and Landon?"

Bay nodded. I turned to Thistle, her head moving in the affirmative before the question escaped from my lips. They'd definitely played us. The question was: Why?

"Well, we'll just have to make the best of it," I said, straightening my shoulders. This can still be a fun weekend – as long as I don't have to spend too much time with Thistle, that is.

Thistle snorted. "You always want to make the best of things."

"Is that so wrong?"

"It's just not life," Thistle said.

Bay put a hand on her arm, stilling her. "Leave her alone."

"I didn't do anything," Thistle protested.

"You're about to," Bay said. "It's supposed to be a fun weekend. Can't we just all … I don't know … ignore one another?"

A WITCH OF A TIME

"I always want to ignore you," Thistle said, lowering her head.

Her boyfriend, Marcus, flicked the ridge of her ear. "Stop being mean to Clove."

"I'm not being mean to Clove," Thistle protested. "I wasn't even talking to her."

"Stop being mean to Bay, too," Marcus chided. He was easygoing and amiable. He rarely argued with Thistle, or called her on her crap. He was a calming influence in her life. When he did make his opinion known, more often than not, Thistle listened.

"Fine," she grumbled, lifting her head again. "I apologize for my bad mood," she said. "I just wasn't expecting you."

I was stunned by the apology.

"Have you been possessed?" Bay asked, grabbing Landon's hand and taking the proffered key from my father as she turned toward the stairs. "You never say you're sorry."

"I say I'm sorry," Thistle argued.

"No, you don't."

"Bay," Landon warned, grabbing the bag from the floor and following her toward the stairs. "Don't poke the blue-haired bear."

"Yeah, listen to Landon," Thistle said. "No one is going to be poking me this weekend."

Marcus' face fell, causing Thistle to give in. "Except you." He broke into a wide grin; that is until Uncle Teddy – Thistle's father – fixed him with a dark look from the hallway. I had no idea where he'd appeared from, or when he'd gotten there.

"Oh hey, Dad," Thistle said, not embarrassed in the least. "We're going upstairs to get settled. We'll be down in time for drinks."

Uncle Teddy didn't look thrilled with Thistle's flippant attitude. "I ...."

"See you in a few," Thistle said, ignoring the flush creeping up her father's neck.

I risked a look at Sam once Bay and Thistle had disappeared. I could still hear them arguing as they made their ascent. "It's still going to be fun," I said.

Sam's smile was watery. "Oh, I have no doubt."

"**SO, WE'RE** REALLY DOING A SÉANCE?"

Dinner had been divine. My father and uncles had opted to hire kitchen staff from the nearby culinary school, and they'd earned their money tonight. Between a delicious roast, fresh vegetables, and a decadent chocolate cake for dessert, the assembled guests seemed to be enjoying their stay. I was happy for my father – he'd worked hard for this, and he deserved some accolades. Plus, as long as the inn was a success, he would stay in town. That was a win for me – and my two cousins, even if they weren't ready to admit it yet.

The woman who had asked the question was a reporter for Michigan Travel magazine. She introduced herself as Clara Hamilton. She was in her forties, and attractive (something that hadn't escaped Uncle Jack's attention if his constant ministrations to Clara's needs were any indication).

"We are," I said, smiling widely as I pointed to the round table in the game room. My father had gone all out, even purchasing an antique crystal ball to place at the center of the table.

"Are you a witch?" Clara asked me pointedly.

I swallowed hard, unsure how to answer. For years, we'd hidden our magical gifts. Once Hemlock Cove rebranded itself as a magical destination, admitting you were a witch wasn't frowned upon – unless you were an actual witch. Most of the townsfolk knew there was something *off* about our family, but they pretended otherwise. That's the way we liked it.

"Of course she's a witch," Thistle said, stepping forward. "This is a witch town. You can't have a witch town without real witches." The smile she sent the assembled guests was enigmatic. I knew she was trying to defuse the situation, but I was still on edge.

"Are you a witch, too?" Clara asked.

"My whole family is made up of witches," Thistle answered honestly. "We're all … evil."

I frowned. I knew she was just playing it up for the crowd, but Thistle was having a little bit too much fun doing it.

Chet Corbin, a Ford executive from the Flint plant, smirked. "I love the atmosphere of this place," he said. "I like that everyone pretends they're in on the gag. It's great."

Dad cleared his throat. "It *is* great."

"And the whole town is like this, right?" Corbin said. "The whole town plays the game?"

"They do," Uncle Teddy replied. "Everyone has a great time … playing the game."

I knew three men who had disliked "the game" so much they'd fled. Sure, they were trying to make up for it now, but they hadn't seemed so keen on playing the game when they were married to our mothers.

"We all love the game," Bay said, shooting me a sympathetic look. "Clove is great at the game. She's a gifted psychic. I'm sure she can conjure up a friendly ghost or two for everyone to play with tonight."

Clara smiled. "Let's do it. I'm so excited. I've never been to a séance."

I let everyone file into the room ahead of me, and Bay stopped in the doorway long enough to give my hand a squeeze. "Just put on a good show," she said.

"And when nothing happens?"

Thistle and Bay exchanged a small look. "We'll just give them a miniature light show," Thistle whispered. "It will be fine."

My heart dropped. They were planning on using real magic. "What if someone sees?"

"They won't know what they're seeing," Thistle said. "This isn't our first rodeo."

Somehow their show of solidarity warmed me. "It's going to be fun, right?"

"It's going to be a lot of fun," Bay said, glancing over her shoulder as Landon sidled up to her and snaked an arm around her waist.

"Let's get this show on the road," Landon said. "My witch turns into a pumpkin at midnight, and I need to … ." Landon broke off, searching for the appropriate words to turn his metaphor dirty.

Thistle solved the problem for him. "Explore the pumpkin patch?"

Landon grinned. "Exactly."

Uncle Jack moved in behind us, clearing his throat as he fixed Landon with a harsh look. "What were you talking about?"

"Oh, Landon was just talking about exploring Bay's ... ."

Marcus slapped his hand over Thistle's mouth to cut her off. "They were just talking about the best way to give the guests a show."

Jack nodded, his eyes wary. "And it's just going to be a show, right?"

"Of course," Bay said, rolling her eyes. "We're not stupid."

"I didn't say you were stupid ... ."

"Oh, let's just get this over with," Thistle grumbled, irritable as she wrenched Marcus' hand from her mouth. "If we're going to perform like monkeys, I want to do it now. The longer we stand here talking about it, the more obnoxious it's going to be."

"You always were a ray of sunshine, Thistle," Jack said. "Even as a child, I could always rely on you to ruin a good mood."

Thistle blew him a kiss. "I'm nothing if not predictable."

Jack's face was grim as he regarded the three of us. "Just don't go overboard."

"Of course not," Bay said, her face bright. "That's not the Winchester way."

Unfortunately, she was lying. That was exactly the Winchester way. I could only hope tonight would break from that tradition.

THREE

The table was big enough for all of the guests to sit around, my father and uncles rounding out the crowd. Sam opted to remain standing, close enough so I could feel his presence, but far enough away that he wouldn't be mistaken as part of the show.

Bay was leaning against the wall, her arms crossed over her chest as she waited for me to begin. Thistle was next to her, and Landon and Marcus had taken up position next to their respective girlfriends. They looked relaxed, but looks can be deceiving. Landon was still getting used to our witchy ways, although he'd come a long way in a short time. Marcus was just along for the ride, his face lit with excitement as his anticipation grew.

"Everyone join hands," I instructed. "Now, everyone close your eyes and concentrate."

"What are we concentrating on?" Jim Talbot, a reporter for the travel section at one of the Detroit dailies, seemed irritated with the whole endeavor.

"A different plane of existence," I said, lowering my voice to an ominous level. "One where the dead live."

"Does it intersect with this plane?" Clara asked, excited.

"Sometimes," I said. "We have to help the ghosts cross over if we want to talk to them, though."

"What kind of ghost are we looking for?" Chet asked.

"A friendly one," Teddy said pointedly.

"Like Casper," Thistle teased.

Teddy shot her a look. "Exactly."

"A friendly ghost," I agreed, fighting the agitation bubbling up. Keep calm, I reminded myself. They weren't trying to be obnoxious. "Everyone concentrate."

There was some giggling, and the sound of people shifting in their seats as they grew impatient, so I fixed Thistle with a pleading look. She winked, and then pointed to the ceiling.

A short burst of light erupted, blue energy licking at the chandelier above the table. It was the exact shade of Thistle's hair.

"Omigod!" Clara was beside herself. "Is that a ghost?"

"Of course not," Jim scoffed. "It's a trick or something."

A quick glance at Bay told me she was offended by the assertion. She wrinkled her nose and focused on the light, and after a moment, I saw hints of yellow join the fray.

"It's another ghost," Clara said, exhaling heavily. "There are two of them."

I read the change in her demeanor. She'd gone from excited to fearful. That wasn't going to do my father any good. "It's the same ghost," I soothed. "It's just trying to take form."

For his part, Jim was staring up at the ceiling. "Where are the light machines?"

Bay tilted her head to the side, causing the table to bump. She wasn't thrilled with Jim's skepticism, and she was trying to teach him a lesson.

"Holy crap!" Chet jumped in tandem with the table.

Jim let go of the hands around him and crawled beneath the table to investigate. "How are you doing this?"

His question was met with an ethereal scream from above. It sounded like the mystical lights were in pain.

I scorched Bay with a hateful look. She was taking things too far.

Given the expression on her face, and the equally worried grimace on Thistle's, I knew they weren't doing it now. Sure, they were responsible for the lights and the shaking table, but the screaming was something else.

"What does it want?" Clara asked. "Is it trapped here?"

"It's just visiting," Dad said, shooting me a look. "Send it away, Clove." He looked ticked off.

"I … ."

"Yes, send it away, Clove," Jack ordered.

Another colored wisp – this one green – joined Bay and Thistle's ongoing light show. Bay was shaking her head when our eyes met. They weren't responsible for the green interloper. I felt Sam move in behind me. "You're not doing all of this, are you?" His voice was rigid with worry.

I shook my head.

The green light increased its pace, swimming between the other two. I saw Bay and Thistle clasp hands across the room. I couldn't hear what they were chanting, but I knew they were working against the new entity.

The green light grew in size, swallowing the remnants of Bay and Thistle's discarded magic. The table was still shaking, but I knew my cousins weren't responsible. Suddenly, the green light exploded, flaring bright, and then plunging the room into darkness.

Clara began to scream, and I wanted to join her.

"**WELL**, THAT WAS FUN," Thistle said, resting her back against the hallway of the third floor.

"We really need to work on your definition of fun," Landon said, running his hands over Bay's shoulders. "Are you okay?"

"I'm fine," Bay said.

"You and Thistle made that thing … explode, though," Landon pointed out.

"We didn't make it explode," Thistle said. "We just banished it."

"For good?"

Thistle shook her head. "I have no idea. I have no idea where it came from in the first place."

"I think it was drawn here," Bay said. "Our magic called to it. It was probably just curious."

"What was it?" Sam asked. He hadn't spoken since we left the game room. After a few tense minutes, my father and uncles had managed to convince everyone that the light show was part of the act. A few drinks later – mostly bourbon – everyone agreed they had a great time and retired to their rooms. That had given us the opportunity to put our heads together out of earshot.

"It was a ghost," Thistle said, looking to Bay for confirmation. "Right?"

"I think so," Bay replied. "It didn't take form, though. It was more like really angry energy."

"Great," Landon muttered. "Another poltergeist? The last one kept trying to kill you."

"It's okay," Bay said, gripping his fingers tightly.

"It's not okay," Landon challenged. "I don't want you in danger."

"I'm not in any danger," Bay said.

"You're always in danger," Landon said. "We were supposed to have a quiet weekend together. We were supposed to … I don't know … snuggle in a hammock and eat more food than should be humanly possible. We weren't supposed to be dealing with crap like this."

"I'm sorry," Bay murmured.

I knew she was worried. She was always worried where Landon was concerned. He said he accepted us – and our witch heritage – but he'd left once before. Bay lived under a cloud of doubt, always fearful that he would do it again. I knew he wouldn't. One look at him told me everything I needed to know. He'd never willingly walk away from Bay again, but she wasn't so sure, and I wasn't the one who could convince her otherwise. That was Landon's job, and I knew he would eventually succeed. He just wasn't there yet.

"It's not your fault," Landon said, brushing a quick kiss against Bay's forehead. "It was just supposed to be a game. You couldn't know this was going to happen."

"We should have considered it, though," Thistle admitted.

"Why do you say that?" Sam asked.

"This whole area is teeming with spirits," Thistle said. "We should have given the property a good cleaning before they opened."

"A cleaning?" Marcus was confused.

"It's a magical rite," Sam explained. "You just expel bad energy and ward the house from evil spirits."

"If that's possible, wouldn't you have done it at The Overlook?" Landon asked, his fingers working on Bay's tense neck as he pressed his body closer to hers. "How could anything evil ever get in there?"

"We do it at The Overlook twice a year," Thistle replied. "It wears down after time. With all the magic being thrown around out there, it wears down quicker. This place would be protected for longer."

"Because no real magic would occur here?" Marcus asked.

"Exactly."

Landon inhaled heavily. "So, what do we do now? Do we just hope it doesn't come back?"

Bay shook her head. "It's here now," she said. "We have to find out who it is, and what it wants."

"And what will that do?" Landon asked.

I answered for her. "If we know what it wants, we can figure out how to put it to rest. That's the only way we can be assured that it won't come back."

Well, so much for a relaxing weekend.

"WHERE ARE BAY AND LANDON?" Jack's eyes roamed the breakfast table the next morning, landing on two empty seats at the end of the dining room table.

"They're sleeping in," Thistle said, snatching a slice of bacon from Marcus' plate when he wasn't looking.

That wasn't the truth. They'd gotten up early so they could go to The Whistler and research deaths in the area. As editor of the newspaper, Bay was hopeful they could tie a specific death down to the inn,

AMANDA M. LEE

but Thistle was less enthusiastic about the possibility. The odds were never in our favor when it came to stuff like that.

Our fathers had no idea a real ghost had visited the séance the previous night. That was the good news. Unfortunately, they also believed we'd purposely gone overboard – accusing us of trying to one-up one another for attention – and they were angry. That was the bad news.

Jack made a face. "It's almost nine. Who sleeps in this late?"

Thistle snorted. "We usually all sleep until noon on the weekends."

"Why?" Jack was nonplussed.

"Because we work hard during the week."

"So?"

"So? So we like to sleep in on the weekends," Thistle said. "Bay is tired. Landon worked hard this week. They're sleeping. Leave them alone."

"Maybe they're sick," Jack mused.

"They're not sick," Thistle said.

Jack made a move to get up. "Maybe I should check on them."

I started to panic. "You're right. They're not asleep."

Thistle pressed her lips together. I can't read minds. It's not one of my gifts. I knew what she was thinking, though. I was going to be eating dirt if she got her hands on me before Marcus had a chance to calm her down.

"If they're not asleep, then where are they?" Jack's gaze was probing.

I was caught. I was going to have to tell the truth. There was no other choice. Unless … . "They're having sex."

Thistle slapped her forehead. "Ugh."

Jack's face flushed with color, and his voice was unnaturally high when he found it. "What?"

I have no idea how I always make things worse, but I do. "They're … having sex," I said.

"Oh, good, say it again," Thistle muttered, pinching the bridge of her nose.

"I heard you the first time," Jack said, his jaw clenched. "Why did you say it?"

A glance around the table told me everyone else was enjoying the show. It was kind of like having breakfast at The Overlook, only Aunt Tillie wasn't there to detonate a nuclear warhead. I kind of missed her. This was about the time she would have taken the onus of the conversation off of me.

"I … I … I … ."

"She said it because she's covering for Bay," Thistle interjected, scowling in my direction. "She's doing it in the worst way possible, but her heart is in the right place."

Jack shifted, focusing on Thistle. "Why is she covering for Bay?"

Thistle squared her shoulders. "Because Bay had to go back to The Overlook for breakfast this morning. We're taking turns putting in appearances."

I had no idea where she was going with this. I was thankful for her interference, though.

"Why do you have to put in appearances?" Teddy asked.

"Why do you think?" Thistle asked. "If we don't, they'll get suspicious, and if they get suspicious … ." Thistle left the unsaid threat hanging in the air.

"Aunt Tillie," Dad said.

"Who is Aunt Tillie?" Clara asked.

"She's just … the girls' elderly aunt," Dad said. "She's … ."

"Deranged," Teddy muttered.

"Psychotic," Jack added under his breath.

"Easily confused," Dad finished. "If she doesn't see the girls on a regular basis, she gets confused."

"Oh, that's too bad," Clara said. "Is she … addled?"

"She's just … easily distracted," I said, glancing over my shoulder. Good, she wasn't there … not that I thought she would be. What? I'm not scared of her. Okay, I'm terrified. She has ears like a cat and the personality of a ticked-off badger.

"Well, it's nice that you girls take such good care of her," Clara said.

"Yes, well, we love our Aunt Tillie," I said.

"We love her to ... death," Thistle said.

"You'll miss her when she's gone," Clara said sagely. "It's so nice you spend so much time with her. Someday, when she passes on, you'll be happy you did this."

Thistle's face was bland. "Oh, she'll never die."

"Of course," Clara said, instantly apologetic. "I didn't mean to upset you. She'll always live on in your hearts."

"I'm not upset," Thistle said. "She'll just never die. Evil never dies."

Clara swallowed hard, staring down at her plate as confusion washed over her. "Oh ... um ... ."

Well, there's nothing like a pall over breakfast to fire everyone up for a fun day.

FOUR

"Have you ever seen anything this stupid in your entire life?"

Thistle was at her wit's end, and I didn't blame her. I scanned the back lawn of the Dragonfly, unsure of what I was seeing. "It looks … kind of fun."

"They're playing croquet," Thistle pointed out, sipping from her drink and making a face. "This is awful. We need to make some chocolate martinis."

"It's not even noon," Marcus said. "I can't believe you're drinking."

"If I have to watch croquet, then I'm drinking," Thistle said, her face grim.

"But it's … themed croquet," I said. I really am a glass-half-full person. I can't help it. I want to see the best in people – and the things they try to accomplish.

"Yeah, but the course is decorated like a cemetery," Thistle said. "It's maudlin."

"It's perfect for a magically themed town," I countered. "It's kind of cute. I like the little tombstones – and that mausoleum is adorable. Oh, and look at the gargoyles."

"It's croquet, though," Thistle said. "Who wants to play croquet?"

I pointed to the handful of people on the lawn. "Everyone seems to be having a good time."

"Speaking of a good time," Thistle said, gesturing to the hammock at the edge of the lawn. "Have you talked to Bay since she got back?"

I followed Thistle's eyes, my gaze landing on my blonde cousin as she cuddled with Landon on the hammock. They were looking at an iPad, Bay's head resting on his chest as they focused on their task. They looked like they were having a good time, Landon's hands wandering beneath Bay's shirt when he thought no one was looking.

Unfortunately, Jack was watching – and he obviously didn't like what he was seeing.

"That is inappropriate," he said.

"Jack, she's an adult," Dad said. "They're not really doing anything."

"He's … where do you think he keeps putting his hand?"

"Where did you put your hands when you and Winnie made her?" Dad asked.

"Yeah, Uncle Jack," Thistle teased, sticking out her tongue. "Was Bay born to Aunt Winnie when she was a virgin?"

Jack snatched her drink from her hand. "How many of these have you had?"

"Two."

"Well … you're cut off," Jack said. "You're not old enough to be drinking anyway."

Thistle made a face. "I'm only a year younger than Bay."

"I know."

"Bay has been old enough to drink for almost seven years."

"I know."

"She's old enough to have sex," Thistle charged on.

"I didn't say she wasn't," Jack protested.

"Landon is a good guy," I said, trying to ease the tension. "He makes Bay really happy. They're just … having fun."

"They're not bothering anyone, Jack," Teddy said.

"Are you saying you'd be okay if that was Thistle and Marcus?" Jack shot back.

"Of course I would. It's a natural part of ... Thistle doesn't do that," Teddy said, changing course mid-comment.

"Yeah, she's a virgin," Jack said. "That's why that blond dude has his hand on her rear end all the time."

Teddy made a face. "He does not. Thistle is a good girl."

Uh-oh, those were fighting words.

"And Bay isn't?"

"I didn't say she wasn't," Teddy said.

"You just said she wasn't," Jack protested.

"Well, she's the one over there with that guy's hand up her shirt," Teddy shot back.

"He's just helping her with her ... ."

"Bra?" Thistle supplied helpfully.

"Shut up, Thistle," Jack snapped.

Sam leaned in behind me. "Aren't you glad they're not focused on us?"

Part of me was. The other part wished we were the ones groping on the hammock. I just wasn't that brave. "I wish they would chill out," I said. "They're acting like we're teenagers and they have some say over what we do."

Sam searched my face with a questioning look. "They're acting like fathers."

"I wouldn't know what that's like," I said, moving away from him and heading in Bay's direction. I was loath to interrupt them, but I needed some air – and that was saying something since we were outside.

Landon's mouth was pressed to Bay's when my shadow covered them. "Did you find anything?"

Landon groaned, reluctantly pulling away at the sound of my voice. "Why did you come over here?"

"I ... I haven't seen you since this morning," I said, inhaling deeply. "I wanted to see if you found something out."

"We're still looking," Bay said.

"From the hammock?"

Bay pointed to the iPad. "Landon is running files from the FBI database."

"Oh," I said. "I ... I'm sorry to have interrupted."

"It's too late for that now," Landon said, his tone clipped.

"It's just ... our dads are over there fighting," I said.

"Why?"

"Because Landon keeps sticking his hand up your shirt," I replied. I never know when to keep my mouth shut. I want to – I swear – but I just can't.

Bay's cheeks colored. "Oh. They saw that?"

"You guys are out in the open."

"So what?" Landon obviously didn't care, because he yanked Bay back down to his chest when she tried to pull away. "We're not doing anything. This is our weekend. I didn't want to come here in the first place. If they don't like it, then I don't really care."

"They're still our fathers," I said, although I had no idea why I was taking up their end of this argument.

"So what?" Landon said again. "We're adults. We do what adults do. If they have a problem with it, send Jack over here and we'll have a talk."

"Landon, you can't do that in front of their guests," Bay said, her face conflicted.

"I don't like the way he looks at me," Landon said.

"How does he look at you?"

"Like I'm corrupting a minor."

I couldn't hide the smile playing at the corner of my lips. "To him, Bay is still a child."

"Yeah? Well, she's not my child," Landon said, tickling her ribs and causing her to giggle. "If he doesn't like it, tell him to come over here and tell us. Then we'll go. I'd much rather return to the guesthouse and ... play ... there all weekend. At least we would have it to ourselves."

"What about the ... ghost?" I said, lowering my voice.

"I don't care about the ghost," Landon said. "Quite frankly, I'd rather have Bay away from this place if something terrible is about to happen. I'm surprised that Sam doesn't feel the same way about you."

His words were pointed ... and hurtful.

"I do feel the same way." I hadn't realized Sam was behind me. Landon had, though. That's why he said what he said.

Landon pursed his lips but remained silent.

"I know you don't like me," Sam said, taking my hand in his. "I understand why you don't like me. I'm here to stay, though, and I don't like you talking to Clove that way."

My heart soared at his words, and then plummeted when Landon fixed Sam with a murderous look.

"I happen to care about Clove a great deal," Landon said. "Bay loves her like a sister, and I'm pretty fond of her, too."

"Then why are you attacking me?" Sam asked.

"Because I don't think you're good enough for her." Landon's words were succinct – and brutal.

"Landon." Bay's voice was low, her gaze worried. "I don't think now is the time."

Landon rubbed the back of her head. "Clove is an adult," he said. "I'm not going to tell her what to do."

"Well, thanks for that ... I guess," Sam said, his hand tightening around mine.

"That doesn't mean I'm going to sit back and idly watch you hurt her," Landon continued.

"I notice you don't have the same problem with Marcus," Sam pointed out.

"Marcus didn't lie to get close to the family," Landon replied.

"I didn't lie," Sam protested. "I kept my mother's witch side to myself. How is that any different from what they do?"

"They didn't seek you out and try to get close to you," Landon said, unruffled. "They keep to themselves."

"I keep to myself," Sam said. "If you want me to apologize for trying to investigate them before making my past known, then I will. I'm sorry. That doesn't mean I regret coming here, and it certainly doesn't mean I regret having a relationship with Clove."

I was moved by his words. Landon? Not so much.

"I'm watching you," Landon said, returning his attention to the iPad and Bay. "If you hurt her, you'll be sorry."

Despite myself, Landon's words warmed me. It was nice that he cared – even if he was hurting Sam in the process.

"WHERE IS EVERYONE?" Bay asked, joining Sam and me in the foyer. It was after lunch, and an afternoon excursion had left the inn empty – except for a few brave souls who had remained behind. Most of them were related to me.

"They went on a tour of the town," I said. "Dad thought that showing them everything was a good way to prove how entertaining a stay at the inn would be."

Bay's face was unreadable as she slipped behind the bar and studied the offerings. "This is all … blah."

"Thistle picked up stuff to make chocolate martinis," I said. "It's in the bag behind the counter."

Bay retrieved the bag in question and then returned to the bar. "At least she was thinking ahead."

"I think we're just spoiled," I said, my gaze bouncing between Bay and Sam at regular intervals. No one had spoken to one another since the hammock incident, and I wasn't sure if I was thankful for that or not. "Where is Landon?"

"He's upstairs on the laptop," Bay said.

"Did he find something?" I leaned forward, intrigued.

"We found one thing," Bay said. "There was an odd death out here in the seventies."

I waited.

Bay sighed. "The Dragonfly was a premier inn around these parts for decades," she said. "It went by a different name, but it was popular. They had a lot of guests stay here. That's when the economy was good, before the industrial base died away. The skiing was always a draw.

"In 1975, Marian Lecter visited the Dragonfly with her husband

and two children," Bay continued. "They all had a nice dinner together, and then everyone went to bed. Witnesses say that Marian and her husband Will seemed happy. There were no outwards signs of … distress.

"Sometime in the night, Marian left the bedroom and disappeared," Bay said. "Will claimed he was asleep, and he had no idea his wife was even gone. When he woke up in the morning, he sounded the alarm.

"Marian's body was found about two hundred yards behind the inn," Bay continued. "It was hidden under heavy brush. The police were called, and they were searching, but it was Will Lecter who found the body."

"Which tipped the cops off," Sam said. "Did he kill her?"

Bay shrugged. "The autopsy said that Marian Lecter was strangled. There was no sign of sexual assault, but her underwear was missing. Will Lecter was convicted of the crime, and he spent thirty years in prison before he died."

"Do you think it's her?" I asked. The story was dark … and troubling.

"I know what you know," Bay said. "Landon is trying to see if he can find anything else, but it would fit. It was a violent death. Maybe Marian Lecter is trying to find her way back to her children. Maybe she knows it was her husband. Or, maybe … ."

"She knows it was someone else," I finished.

Bay nodded. "We won't know until we can talk to her."

"How are we going to do that?" I asked.

Bay's gaze was even. "How do you think?"

I was immediately shaking my head. "No way. We cannot have a real séance when there are guests here."

"We won't have it inside," Bay said. "We'll go outside. Landon is going to try to find a more exact location for where the body was discovered. We'll have it there."

I bit my bottom lip. "What are we going to tell our dads?"

"Absolutely nothing," Bay said. "If we're lucky, we'll be able to put this ghost to rest without them knowing."

"They think we acted up last night just to get attention," I said.

"I know," Bay said. "That's their problem. If they knew us ... if they really knew us ... they would never suspect us of something like that. That's on them."

"You're not being fair," I protested. "They didn't have the chance. Our mothers ... Aunt Tillie ... they forced them to go away." Part of me believed that. The other part wasn't so sure.

"Would you ever leave a child, Clove?" Bay's expression was serious.

"Of course not."

"Then why did they?"

I didn't have an answer. I didn't think Bay was expecting one.

FIVE

"What's for dinner tonight?" Clara asked.

Everyone had returned from the afternoon tour excited and chatty. It seemed like the weekend soft launch was going over well – even with the excitable séance from the previous evening marring an otherwise pristine extravaganza. I wasn't surprised that our fathers hadn't asked for an encore, although they were insisting on tarot card readings after dinner. For the most part, they seemed to have put their anger aside.

"We're having a brined pork loin," Jack said, smiling at Clara indulgently. I didn't miss Bay's scowl as she studied their interaction. It bothered her. I didn't blame her. It would bother me, too. I just had no idea why.

"Oh, that sounds yummy," Clara said, slathering a slice of bread with butter and chomping into it enthusiastically. "The food here is amazing."

"It's the best food in Hemlock Cove," Dad boasted.

I straightened in my chair. That was an absurd lie. The food here was good, great even. We all knew the best food in Hemlock Cove was served at The Overlook, though. Our mothers were all accomplished kitchen witches, and their food was magical. It seemed somehow ... disloyal ... to even pretend otherwise.

"It's delightful," Clara said. "I've never had bread this good."

"It's freshly baked," Teddy said. "Right here in our own kitchen. You won't find better bread in the town."

Thistle clanked her silverware together noisily.

"Is something wrong, honey?" Teddy asked.

"No," Thistle said, shaking her head. "I was just thinking about my mother's bread."

Teddy faltered. "Your mother is an outstanding baker."

"She's the best."

"Does your mother live here in town?" Clara asked, oblivious.

"Our mothers run The Overlook inn," Bay supplied. "It's out on the bluff."

"Oh, that's cozy," Clara said. "It's nice that everyone can be in the same business and not be in competition with one another. That sounds so nice."

It did sound nice. It also sounded like fantasy.

"Everyone has a nice rapport with one another," Dad lied. "There are no hard feelings."

Thistle choked on her glass of wine as she sipped from it. Marcus slapped her back and then left his hand at the nape of her neck to rub the growing fury from the tense bundle growing between her shoulders.

"Are you okay?" Chet asked.

"I just choked ... on something," Thistle said.

"I think it was a pack of lies," Bay mumbled.

I was sandwiched between Bay and Sam, so I could hear her words clearly, but I was hopeful no one else could.

"Did you say something, dear?" Jack asked, fixating on his daughter.

"No," Bay said.

Landon topped off her glass of wine. "Drink up, sweetie," he said. He didn't look any happier with the revisionist history than Bay did.

Bay obliged, downing her entire glass with three gulps. "Hit me again."

Landon eyed her momentarily and then acquiesced. "That's it until you have some food in you."

"I thought you wanted her drunk," Jim said, leering at Bay suggestively. "I bet you like her ... pliable."

Landon ran his tongue over his teeth. "I like her happy."

"So, give her more wine," Jim suggested.

"She's not happy when she has a hangover," Landon said. "Trust me."

"You've seen her with a lot of hangovers, have you?" Jake asked.

"I've seen her with a few," Landon said. "It's more fun when I don't have one with her." Landon downed his own glass of wine.

"I don't think ... ." Jack broke off, unsure.

"Where is this dinner?" Thistle asked, breaking the uncomfortable silence. "I'm starving."

"It should have been out here," Dad said, dropping his napkin on the table and moving to get to his feet.

"Oh, don't worry about it," Thistle said, beating him to the punch. "We'll check." She glanced at me pointedly. "Do you want to help?"

I nodded. I knew she needed to talk, but I wasn't sure I wanted to hear what she had to say.

"Why does it take two of you?" Teddy asked.

"It doesn't," Thistle said, walking away from the table and glancing at Bay expectantly. "It takes three of us."

"Why?" Teddy was still confused.

"Because they want to talk," Landon said. "Give it a rest."

"No one asked you," Jack grumbled.

Landon pushed Bay to her feet. "Don't be gone long."

Bay nodded. "I ... ."

"We'll be fine," Landon said. "Just check on dinner. I'm starving."

"**WELL,** THIS IS A TOTAL MESS," Thistle said the second we were in the kitchen.

"I never thought I would miss Aunt Tillie, but I miss her," Bay said. "She would have put them in their place."

"What's their place?" I asked, affronted. "They have a right to take pride in their business." Since I was angry at what our fathers said myself, taking their side seemed foreign to me. I did it anyway. Even I can't explain my actions sometimes. I just want everyone to get along. Is that so wrong?

"Their business is great," Bay said. "Their obnoxious insistence on pretending we're all some big, happy family is not great."

"They can't tell strangers the truth," I protested.

"That doesn't mean they have to lie," Thistle said, leaning over the shoulder of one of the culinary students as he carved the roast. "What's taking you so long?"

The boy looked confused. "I'm … carving."

"Well, do it faster," Thistle said. "We're dying out there."

"There's bread," he said.

"We don't want bread," Bay said. "We need something big enough to shut everyone up. Do you have something that will choke someone?"

"We have vegetables, too," one of the other students said, clearly unsure whether Thistle was joking or not. "They're spring … and they were marinated in white wine."

"Awesome," Thistle said. "Take them out to the table."

"They're not ready yet."

"Oh, good grief," Thistle said, yanking the spoon from him. "They're vegetables, not a work of art."

"I … I … ."

"Stop stammering," Thistle said. "You're driving me crazy."

The boy's lower lip started trembling. "I'm sorry."

I felt bad for him, so I stepped between him and Thistle. "Stop it. You're upsetting him." I turned to the student carefully. "What's your name?"

"Byron."

"Well, Byron," I said, forcing my tone to remain even. "My cousin Thistle has a chemical imbalance. She doesn't mean what she says.

You just have to ignore everything that comes out of her mouth. I know I do."

Byron looked unsure. "She's really mean."

"That's what keeps her skin so young and dewy fresh," Bay quipped.

"She doesn't mean to be ... cruel," I said. "She's just hungry."

"She's not going to eat me, is she?"

"You're not that lucky," Thistle said.

Byron opened his mouth to argue, but I stilled him with a shake of my head. "Let's get this food on the platters, shall we?" Dinner at The Overlook was quick and efficient. This was anything but.

"We still have five minutes until dinner is served," Bryon whined. "I was told it had to be on the table at seven sharp."

"Well, we're hungry now," Thistle said.

"Ignore her," I said, flinching when Byron rubbed his eye to ward off tears. "She's not mean because she wants to be mean. She just can't help it."

"Stop telling him stuff like that," Thistle said, doling the vegetables out onto a platter. "You'll make him think I'm evil."

"You are evil," Bay said, shrugging. "What? Sometimes you're evil. You're like Aunt Tillie."

"That's the meanest thing you've ever said to me," Thistle said, wrinkling her nose.

"It's not mean if it's the truth."

Thistle shifted, focusing on me. "I'm not like Aunt Tillie."

"Of course you're not," I soothed.

"You're lying to me," Thistle said after a moment. "You do think I'm like Aunt Tillie, don't you?"

I didn't know how to respond. It's not like it was the first time anyone had ever said the same thing. "I ... ."

"You're exactly like Aunt Tillie," Bay said. "You just don't want to admit it."

"You take that back," Thistle warned, waving the spoon in Bay's face. "You take that back right now."

"No," Bay said. "It's the truth."

Thistle shifted her gaze to me. "Tell her it's not the truth."

I was caught – like I so often was – between my two cousins. They both had polarizing personalities and big mouths. That was also a family trait. "You're not like Aunt Tillie," I said. It was a lie, but she needed to hear it. The truth was, everyone was fighting because they didn't know what else to do.

"Oh, so you're taking her side," Bay said, her face hot with anger. "You always take her side."

"I do not!"

"She always takes your side," Thistle argued. "You're the oldest. She always takes your side because she wants your approval."

"That's a lie," Bay said. "She always takes your side because you'll beat her up if she doesn't."

"I would not!"

They were both right. I hated taking sides. When I did, my stomach rolled itself into a big ball of pain, and it wasn't over until one of them won and apologized to the other. "We need to get this food out to the table," I said.

They both ignored me.

"Do you want to take this outside?" Thistle challenged.

"You have no idea," Bay said, pointing toward the back door. "I'm going to make you eat dirt."

"I'm going to make you eat dirt," Thistle countered, dropping the spoon on the counter. "Clove, take the food out to the table. We'll be back in a second."

"You can't fight," I hissed. "If you fight … ." What was I saying? I wanted to watch them fight. I loved it when they fought – especially when it wasn't with me. "Go ahead."

Thistle was the first out the back door. Her face was full of bravado, but some of it was slipping in the face of Bay's refusal to back down. "This is your last chance," Thistle warned.

I knew she was biding for time. I wondered if Bay knew the same.

Bay rolled the sleeves of her blouse up. "No, this is *your* last chance."

"All you have to do is say that I'm not like Aunt Tillie," Thistle said.

"All you have to do is say that you are like Aunt Tillie," Bay countered.

"I'm not like Aunt Tillie," Thistle said. "That's like saying ... you're just like Adolf Hitler."

"Aunt Tillie has never murdered millions of people," Bay scoffed.

"She wanted to," Thistle argued.

She had a point.

"Still ... you're being purposely obnoxious," Bay said.

"How do you figure?"

"You're trying to ruin the opening of the Dragonfly."

Thistle reached for her hair ripping a few stray strands out as Bay jerked away. "You're purposely trying to ruin the opening of the Dragonfly. Admit it! You don't like the way they're talking about our mothers."

Bay stilled, her face sobering. "I don't like the way they're talking about our mothers."

Thistle lowered her hands, conflicted. "I don't like it either."

They both turned to me.

"I hate it," I admitted, sinking to the cold concrete. "I feel like I'm being disloyal."

"Me, too," Bay said, settling next to me. "It makes me feel ... horrible."

"It sucks," Thistle said, sighing as she sat down in the spot to my left. "I thought ... I always thought that our mothers were the reason we were crazy. I thought they made us crazy."

"I thought they always talked bad about our dads because ... well ... they were bitter," I said.

"And now?" Bay asked.

"And now? Now I'm ... so confused," I said.

"Why?"

"Because ... because I love my dad," I said. "I do. I'm still kind of ... angry with him."

"We're all angry with them," Thistle said. "We all ... are struggling."

"It should be easier," I lamented. "They're our fathers."

"They're also putting themselves in direct competition with our mothers," Bay said. "And, whether we like everything they do or not, our mothers are the ones who never left."

"I want to get to know my dad," I said. "I want a father."

"We all want a father," Thistle said. "We just don't want to hurt our mothers in the quest to get to know them."

"Do you think it hurts them?" I asked, my mother's face, so much like my own, swimming in my mind. "Do you think it upsets them?"

"I think we're all so worried about them we don't know what to do," Bay said. She was always the pragmatic one, which wasn't saying much for our family. She grabbed my hand. "We can only do what we can do."

"I don't like what they said about the food," I said.

"Well, it was a vicious lie," Thistle said. "The food here is good, but the food there is ... amazing."

"I don't like that they said everyone got along," I added. "That's ... ."

"A lie," Bay finished.

"Do you think we're being disloyal?" I asked.

"I think ... we're doing the best we can," Bay responded.

"Do you think our moms think we're being disloyal?" I pressed.

"I think our moms know we're doing the best we can," Thistle said.

"Do you think Aunt Tillie thinks we're being disloyal?"

That was a loaded question, and neither Bay nor Thistle looked like they wanted to answer it. Bay was the one who broke first. "I think Aunt Tillie is going to make us all pay for this weekend."

I knew she wasn't wrong. "I guess I'd better buy some fat pants."

Thistle chortled. "I just hope she doesn't make us smell like bacon again. Marcus would like it, but it was hell for me."

"I thought it was kind of fun," Bay said.

"You hated it," Thistle challenged.

"While it was happening? Yes," Bay said. "In hindsight? It really got Landon's motor running."

"Is that hard to do?" Thistle asked.

"No."

"Marcus liked it, too," Thistle admitted. "I ... did you hear that?"

I shifted my attention to Thistle, confused. "What?"

Bay held up her index finger. "I heard it, too."

"There's someone in the woods," Thistle said.

I focused on the sounds of the night. "I don't hear anything." A sudden rustle in the nearby foliage caught my attention. "Wait ... ."

Bay and Thistle were already on their feet, moving toward the underbrush with determined looks on their faces.

"What if it's the ghost?" I hissed.

"Ghosts don't make noise in the leaves," Thistle said, jumping around the hedge that separated my line of sight with the trees. "Oh, you've got to be kidding me!"

SIX

"Who is it?" I asked.

"The devil," Thistle replied.

"Is it a murderer?" I was rooted to my spot. I kept telling myself, if someone jumped out of the bushes and stabbed Bay or Thistle, I was in the best position to get help. That would be my bravery for the day. I would be the one to get help.

"Get up," Thistle said, reaching down into the bushes.

"Get your hands off me!"

I froze when I heard the voice. It really *was* the devil. "Aunt Tillie?"

Thistle and Bay hauled a familiar figure up, forcing her to a standing position. Aunt Tillie jerked her head from left to right. "You're both on my list."

"What are you doing here?" Bay asked.

"It's a free country," Aunt Tillie sniffed, brushing the knees of her pants off haphazardly. "I have a right to take a walk wherever I want."

"You were out for a walk?" Bay asked, narrowing her eyes.

"I needed some exercise," Aunt Tillie said. "I think I might need my hip replaced, so I have to walk it off to make sure I don't need surgery."

"You don't walk off a hip replacement," Thistle said, exasperated.

"Oh, are you a doctor now?" Aunt Tillie challenged.

"No," Thistle said. "I just happen to know that when you need a hip replacement, you can't just walk it off."

"Says who?" Aunt Tillie wasn't budging from her lie.

"Says everyone," Thistle screeched, flapping her arms for emphasis.

Aunt Tillie arched a salt-and-pepper eyebrow. "Do you know everyone?"

"I can't," Thistle said, stalking away. "I just … ."

This was going to get out of control if I didn't put a stop to it. "Is your hip okay now?"

"It feels much better," Aunt Tillie said. "I think it's cured."

"Good," Bay said. "Tell us what you were really doing here."

"I already told you," Aunt Tillie said. "I was curing my hip ailment."

"No, you were here to do something awful," Thistle said, scanning the area. "What? Magical gophers? Charmed bugs? Deranged snakes? What did you bring here?"

"I don't think I like your tone," Aunt Tillie warned, extending a finger in Thistle's direction.

"Just tell us what you did," Bay pleaded, joining Thistle in her underbrush search. "We won't tell anyone what you did. Just … tell us what you brought out here because we know you brought something."

"I can't believe my own flesh and blood would accuse me of being a liar," Aunt Tillie said. "It's enough to break an old woman's heart."

Aunt Tillie only refers to herself as "old" when she's trying to get away with something. If someone else uses the word when describing her, she'll shrivel whatever part of their anatomy strikes her fancy.

"We're not accusing you of anything," I said. "We're just … . Things are already tense enough."

"Why? What's going on?"

I couldn't tell if Aunt Tillie was genuinely interested, or if she was just looking for an out. "We accidentally drew a ghost here during a fake séance last night."

Aunt Tillie made a face. "Why were you having a fake séance?"

"Because Dad wanted to impress the guests," I said. "The magical rebranding of Hemlock Cove makes people picture ghosts and witches. He just wanted them to have fun."

"And you played into this nonsense?"

"We were trying to help," I hedged.

"Well, great job," Aunt Tillie said. "In fact, I couldn't be prouder of you three if I birthed you myself."

"Thanks for that ... visual," Thistle said. "I'll be having nightmares for a week now."

"Why are you proud of us?" I was confused.

"At first, I thought you were coming out here to upset me," Aunt Tillie said. "I thought you were being disloyal. Now I know you were just pretending to be disloyal. You really had a plan to bring this ... hellhole ... down."

"What?"

Bay lowered her head, her shoulders shaking with silent laughter. "She thinks we drew the ghost here on purpose."

"She doesn't think that," Thistle scoffed. "She's just playing it that way." She narrowed her eyes, her mind clearly busy. "Did you call the ghost here?"

"That's a downright abominable thing to say," Aunt Tillie said.

"That doesn't mean it's not true," Thistle shot back.

"Well, you just moved yourself up to the top of the list, missy," Aunt Tillie said. "You're the queen of the list."

Thistle's grim features hardened. "Don't threaten me. We're struggling enough here as it is. We don't need you to make things worse. So, undo whatever spell you cast, and go home."

"Don't you dare tell me what to do," Aunt Tillie said.

"What's going on out here?"

Four heads swiveled toward the back door, all landing on Landon in unison.

"Aunt Tillie is here," Bay said.

"I see her," Landon replied, stepping out onto the back porch. "Why?"

"We were just trying to figure that out ourselves," Bay said.

Landon fixed Aunt Tillie with an inquisitive look. "Do you want to tell me why you're here?"

"Why are you here?" Aunt Tillie countered.

"I wanted to spend some time with Bay," Landon replied honestly. "She wanted to come here. So, we're here."

"You need to put your foot down more often," Aunt Tillie said. "People will say you're whipped if you keep doing what she wants."

"Well, next weekend we're going to do what I want," Landon said.

"Is it something dirty?"

Landon smiled. "It's something lazy," he replied. "Now, tell me, why are you really here?"

"She was hiding in the bushes," Thistle said. "We've searched them, though. Whatever she has planned, she already did it, or she's hidden it really well."

Landon pressed his lips together and moved toward Aunt Tillie, leaning his tall frame down so he could look her in the eye when he got close. "What were you doing?"

"I already told these busybodies," Aunt Tillie said. "I think I'm going to need a hip replacement. I was out walking to correct the problem."

Landon was obviously fighting the urge to laugh. "And you just happened to walk out this way?"

"What? That's allowed. I haven't broken any laws, agent."

Landon shook his head and then straightened. "If you can't find what she did, there's nothing you can do to stop it. Just send her back home. We're only here one more night. Let's eat dinner and try to get some sleep. If everything works out, you guys can clean this ghost up after everyone is gone."

"Send me back home?" Aunt Tillie's voice was shrill. "Send me back home?"

"You're done with your walk, right?" Landon wasn't backing down. He rarely did where Aunt Tillie was concerned. It was one of the things I liked best about him. Honestly? I think it's one of the things she likes best about him, too. That didn't mean she was going to back down either, though.

"I think I need some refreshments before I'm ready to go on my way," Aunt Tillie said.

Landon narrowed his eyes. "Refreshments?"

"I need water," Aunt Tillie said, pulling her small frame up straight. "I need nourishment, too."

"What does that mean?" Landon asked.

"It means she's inviting herself to dinner," I said, resigned.

"Can she do that?" Landon was nonplussed.

Aunt Tillie was already heading toward the back door of the inn.

"I think she just did," Bay said.

WELL, this place certainly looks better than the last time I was here," Aunt Tillie announced as she walked into the dining room.

Dad, Teddy and Jack jerked their heads toward the door, incredulous grimaces moving across their faces as their worst enemy let herself into their domain.

"Tillie," Dad said, getting to his feet. "To what do we owe the honor?"

"Well, I was out for a walk," Aunt Tillie said. "I'm trying to work out my hip so I don't have to have it replaced. I just happened to run into the girls outside, and they kindly invited me in for dinner so I could rest up before going home."

Dad shot an accusatory look in my direction. All I could do was shrug and shake my head apologetically.

"Actually, Aunt Tillie invited herself," Landon said, sidling into the room with Bay's hand clutched in his. "She's going to sit next to me."

"I don't want to sit next to you," Aunt Tillie said.

"Well, you're going to," Landon said, crossing the room. "We're over here."

"Oh, is this the great-aunt you were telling us so much about?" Clara asked excitedly.

"Unfortunately," Thistle mumbled. Marcus ran his hand over her back when she sat back down, obviously trying to calm her.

"What were they saying about me?" Aunt Tillie asked, slapping

Landon's hand away as he tried to force her into the open chair next to him.

"Sit down," he ordered.

"Don't tell me what to do," Aunt Tillie said.

"Don't make me arrest you," Landon threatened.

"For what?"

"For ... assaulting law enforcement," Landon said. "Everyone here just saw you smack me."

"Are you really going to arrest a little old lady?" Jim asked, his face flushed from the wine he was mainlining. "She looks harmless."

"Who are you calling old?" Aunt Tillie charged.

"Sit down," Landon ordered again.

"I will sit down," Aunt Tillie said. "I just don't want you to think I'm doing it because of you. I'm doing it because my hip hurts."

"Great," Landon said, settling between Aunt Tillie and Bay.

"So, what's for dinner?" Aunt Tillie asked brightly.

"Brined pork loin," Teddy said, swallowing nervously.

"It sounds gross," Aunt Tillie said. "They're serving stuffed cabbage out at The Overlook. That's a real dinner."

Bay groaned. That was one of her favorite meals. I could take it or leave it.

"Maybe you should go back out to The Overlook," Dad suggested.

"I don't think that's a good idea," Landon said.

"Why not?"

"Because she ... might have a mess here to clean up later tonight," Landon said. "I think it's best to keep her close right now."

Dad visibly blanched. "What kind of mess?"

"We're all just waiting to find out," Thistle said.

"He just likes spending time with me," Aunt Tillie said. "He keeps flirting with me when Bay isn't looking. It's despicable."

Jack made a face. "Maybe you should take him off Bay's hands? Or, I don't know, just keep his hands off Bay? That sounds like a great job for you."

Aunt Tillie's gaze bounced between Jack and Landon. "What did you do to upset him?"

Landon shrugged. "I have no idea."

"I think it was because he was feeling up the blonde on the hammock earlier," Jim said.

Aunt Tillie pursed her lips, conflicted. As much as she liked needling Landon, there was no way she was going to take Jack's side. "As long as her bra was still on, I don't see the problem. A little over-the-clothes action never hurt anyone. It can be kind of fun. Your Uncle Calvin and I used to do it all the time."

Landon choked as he sipped from his wine glass.

"Eat your dinner," Bay ordered.

"There's nothing on my plate," Aunt Tillie said.

"Someone put something on her plate," Thistle said.

"So, Tillie, you were just out here walking?" Teddy asked.

"What? Is there a crime against walking now?"

"No," Teddy said. "I've just never known you to be much of a walker."

"And The Overlook is ten miles away," Dad added. "That's a long walk for someone of your … advanced maturity."

Thistle snorted. "That was just a fancy way of calling you old, in case you missed it."

"I didn't miss it, trouble," Aunt Tillie said. "I'm choosing to rise above it. That's what a lady of proper breeding does. I'll have you know, Warren, I'm in the best shape of my life. I could run a marathon."

"When have you ever run anywhere?" Bay asked.

"Focus less on me and more on your boyfriend," Aunt Tillie said. "He's obviously feeling neglected."

Landon shook his head. "Nope. I've decided to get hammered." He poured himself another glass of wine.

"I thought you were worried about a hangover?" Jim asked.

"It doesn't matter at this point," Landon said. "This night is just going to keep going downhill. I might as well be drunk for it."

I glanced over at Sam. His face was unreadable, but he was downing his own glass of wine in tandem with Landon.

I leaned in closer to him. "Are you okay?"

"Well, let's see," Sam said, his tone flat. "We were supposed to have a romantic weekend alone, and instead we've been forced to hang out with people who hate me. There's a rogue ghost on the loose, and Aunt Tillie is clearly up to something – which means this place could explode in the next few hours.

"I'm great," Sam said, reaching for another bottle of wine. "Getting drunk sounds like a superb idea."

I pinched the bridge of my nose. This was the worst weekend ever, and I once watched Aunt Tillie do a spell that caused every underground sprinkler in downtown Hemlock Cove to go off at once and flood the downtown – in zero-degree temperatures. It was like living in a skating rink for three weeks.

"Pass me the wine," I said.

I needed to hide somewhere. Wine seemed like a viable option.

SEVEN

"This pork tastes salty."

Dinner was going pretty much how we expected it to go. Aunt Tillie was zinging barbs left and right, and our fathers were trying to dodge them without reaching across the table and throttling her. As for the guests? They found Aunt Tillie delightful. I had no doubt it was because they thought she was crazy.

"It's brined," Dad said. "It's supposed to taste salty."

"Salt is bad for you," Aunt Tillie said. "It gives you high blood pressure and heart attacks. That's why we never use too much salt at The Overlook."

"And the food is good at The Overlook?" Clara asked.

"It's the best in the state," Aunt Tillie said, guileless.

"That's funny. Warren said that the Dragonfly had the best food in town." Clara really was clueless. She was so busy flirting with Jack she'd missed every other clue tossed about the table that night.

Aunt Tillie narrowed her eyes. "Did he?"

Dad swallowed hard. "Taste is a matter of opinion."

"Really? Hmmm."

I didn't like the look on Aunt Tillie's face.

"So, Landon, do you think the food here is better than at The Overlook?" Aunt Tillie's question was pointed.

Landon's face was flushed from wine consumption, and he didn't look like he had a care in the world. "I prefer the food at The Overlook," he said. "You guys always make my favorites."

Aunt Tillie beamed, her anger with him fleeting – as usual.

"You're just saying that because Tillie is here," Jack grumbled.

"No, I'm saying it because I happen to like the food at The Overlook," Landon said. "I eat there several times a week. I think I know what I like. I particularly like breakfasts."

Landon was purposely baiting Jack. I think the wine was going to his head, and he appeared to be spoiling for a fight.

"You eat breakfast there a lot, do you?" Jack was also ready to fight. This had been brewing for a while, but it looked to be coming to a head.

"Do something," I hissed to Sam.

"What?" He was watching the exchange with avid interest.

"They're going to get into a fight," I said.

"So? I think it might be fun to watch."

"Landon will kill him."

"Probably," Sam agreed. "He might be too drunk to stand, though. I kind of want to see what happens."

"What about Bay?" I tried a different tactic.

"What about her?" Sam was clearly missing the point. "I think she'll root for Landon. Jack may be her father, but she seems to really care about Landon – although I can't figure out why."

"That's not what I meant," I snapped.

"You seem pretty comfortable with my daughter," Jack said, leaning back in his chair and crossing his arms over his chest.

"That's what happens when you're there," Landon replied, unruffled. "You get comfortable with people. Why do you think the three of them are so uncomfortable here? They don't really know you."

Uh-oh. I exchanged a worried look with Bay.

"I think we should go to bed early," Bay said, pulling on Landon's arm.

AMANDA M. LEE

"Leave him alone," Aunt Tillie said. "I think he's being entertaining."

"You should go home," Bay said. "Your hip is fine."

"I don't want to leave yet."

"Oh, let her stay," Thistle said, waving from across the table. "She's having fun. Someone here should."

Was everyone losing their mind? Why was everyone so combative? It wasn't unusual for Landon to pick a fight to protect Bay's honor, but he was being overtly aggressive tonight. Since he was the king of calm, it seemed out of character. I scanned the table, confused.

The only two people in the room who appeared untouched by the mayhem were Marcus and me. He met my gaze across the table, his eyes just as troubled as mine. What was going on here?

"Since when are you on Aunt Tillie's side?" Bay asked.

"Since she started making more sense than you," Thistle said, tapping her temple. "She's a genius."

Aunt Tillie smirked. "I'm liking you more and more tonight."

I furrowed my brow. I was wrong in my first assessment. Marcus and I weren't the only ones untouched. Aunt Tillie was fine, too. Sure, she was persnickety and mean, but she was always those things. Crap. She *had* done something.

"You're such a suck-up," Bay said, reaching for her glass of wine. "You always suck up to Aunt Tillie. You claim you're not scared of her, and you're the one who always wants to get back at her, but you're also the first one to suck up to her."

"Oh, whatever," Thistle said. "We all know Clove is the first one to suck up to her."

Bay nodded, agreeing. "You have a point."

It was the wine, I realized. Well, to be more specific, it was the red wine. I'd had wine, too, but I'd stuck to white. Marcus didn't like wine, and he'd been nursing the same beer for the past hour. Everyone else at the table had drunk red wine, and they were all acting strangely.

I grabbed the half-empty bottle in front of Bay and lifted it to my nose. "Where did you get this?"

Dad took a second to focus on me. "What?"

"This wine," I said. "Where did you get it?"

Dad shrugged. "We ordered it from somewhere."

"Where?"

"I ... I don't remember right now. I'm sure there's an invoice in the office. This crate arrived yesterday. It was an added bonus from the company for placing such a large order. It was a gift."

I leaned forward so I could study Aunt Tillie's face. In addition to being a master manipulator, and consummate busybody, she was also a renowned winemaker. She did it on the sly – and outside the boundaries of the law – but her brew was known far and wide. "Is that so?"

Aunt Tillie met my gaze briefly, her face sobering when she realized I knew. She turned her attention to her fingernails. "Well, I should be going," she announced. "I think I need to walk off my dinner."

She got to her feet and moved toward the front of the inn. "It's been a splendid evening."

"Bye," Thistle said, giggling.

Now that I looked at her, she seemed happier than she had a few minutes before. Could the wine already be wearing off? That seemed doubtful. Aunt Tillie wasn't a novice.

"I'll walk you out," I said, getting to my feet.

"That's not necessary," Aunt Tillie said, increasing her pace. "I know my way out."

"Oh, it wouldn't be fair to just let you go," I said, chasing her. "It's dark outside. Your night vision isn't what it used to be."

"I have the eyes of an owl," Aunt Tillie said.

And the personality of a stinging nettle.

For an elderly woman in her eighties, Aunt Tillie can move when she wants to. Bad hip my ... hey, where did she go? I found her on the front porch, descending the steps quickly. "Why did you do this?"

"Do what?"

"You know what," I said. "Are you that insecure?"

Aunt Tillie froze. "Insecure?"

"The Overlook isn't going to be hurt by the Dragonfly," I said. "The Overlook is already booked for the entire season. They have like two openings and those will be taken any day now. Why are you so scared of the Dragonfly?"

Aunt Tillie swiveled. "I'm not scared of anything, young lady."

I knew better than that. "Do you really think we'll like them better? That we'll love them more?"

"I have no idea what you're talking about," Aunt Tillie said.

"They're our fathers," I said, ignoring her denial. "That doesn't mean we love our mothers … or you … any less."

"I didn't say it did," Aunt Tillie replied. "I know you're loyal, Clove. I know that your cousins are just as loyal. I also know you're all worked up right now. I don't like it, and I blame them."

"So, you decided to ruin the opening of their inn?"

"I didn't know you all were going to be out here," Aunt Tillie admitted. "When I found out, I tried to take the wine back. I was going to replace it with a spider infestation. I thought that would be more festive."

"That's why you were here, isn't it? You were trying to steal the wine back."

Aunt Tillie nodded. "It was already too late. I never wanted to hurt the three of you, or Landon and Marcus."

I frowned. "What about Sam?"

Aunt Tillie shrugged. "I haven't decided about Sam yet."

"Does that mean you'll give him a chance?"

"It means I haven't decided yet," Aunt Tillie said. "Don't push your luck."

I could live with that. Still … . "Why do you hate our fathers so much?"

"You don't remember what it was like after they left, Clove," Aunt Tillie said. "They broke six hearts when the left, and I had to pick up the pieces."

"So, you just want payback?"

"It's not payback," Aunt Tillie said. "It's a lesson."

"And what lesson are you teaching them?"

"That life is full of choices," Aunt Tillie said. "One of those choices should never be running away from your family."

"They're trying to make up for it now," I argued.

"And, if they're sincere, they'll do just that," Aunt Tillie said.

"Wait ... is this a test?"

"I don't test people," Aunt Tillie said. "I teach lessons."

"Oh, I know." I blew out a frustrated sigh and pushed my hair off my forehead. "You have to at least help me get Thistle and Bay up to bed."

"They'll be fine," Aunt Tillie said. "Thistle is just getting giddier and giddier. She'll be a fun drunk all night."

"Yeah, why is that? Why is Landon so angry, and why is Thistle so giddy?"

"The spell latches on to a specific part of a person's personality, one they don't put on display very often," Aunt Tillie said.

"Landon is angry when he's around us all the time," I pointed out.

Aunt Tillie shook her head. "No, he's not. He pretends to be angry. He's not really angry, though. He finds us entertaining."

"I've seen him very angry with Bay," I said. "You saw him after we sneaked onto that boat and found those kids. He was livid."

"That was fear, not anger," Aunt Tillie said. "He was terrified something was going to happen to Bay. He lashed out because of the fear."

I worried my bottom lip with my teeth. "And Sam? Why is he so relaxed?"

"Probably because he can never relax around us," Aunt Tillie said, shrugging. "I'm not a psychiatrist. I can't say for sure. I don't blame him, though. He's not very popular in the Winchester household."

"You still have to help me," I said. "If Landon and Jack come to blows, it's going to hurt Bay more than anyone else. I know you don't want that."

"I don't want that," Aunt Tillie said. "The spell will work itself out, though. It should only be a few hours. You don't need me here. My work is done."

"No, it's not," I said, stomping my foot on the front porch for emphasis. "You made this mess. You have to help clean it up."

"Yeah ... I'm not going to do that. It's almost my bedtime, and I want to catch Jimmy Fallon if I can. He's very funny."

"Yes, you are so helping," I said, reaching deep inside of my soul to find my courage. "You have to help. We're your family."

Aunt Tillie groaned. "Fine. I'll help Bay and Thistle. The rest of them are on their own."

"Fine," I said. What? It was something. Frankly, it was more than I'd ever gotten out of her before. "Let's go and get them upstairs. Hopefully they'll all just pass out and forget this whole night."

Once we were back inside, that didn't seem like an option.

"Holy crapsticks," Aunt Tillie said, taking a step forward and surveying the mayhem. "You can't blame this on me."

Unfortunately, she was right. What was happening now was all my fault. The ghost was back, and it was putting on a show.

EIGHT

The dining room was ... a mess.

It looked as if people had tussled, and I was hoping that it wasn't Landon and Jack. I couldn't dwell on that now, though. The overturned chairs and discarded wine glasses weren't our biggest problems. No, that was the bright green light bouncing off the walls as it careened from one end of the room to the other.

Oh, and then there was the screaming. The unearthly sound emanating from the spirit was bloodcurdling.

"What the hell?"

"It's a ghost," Aunt Tillie said, pointing. "Are you blind?"

"I see it," I snapped. "What should we do about it?"

"I kind of like it," Aunt Tillie said. "It has good energy."

The spirit screamed again.

"It sounds like it's in agony," I said, glancing back to the table. Most of the dinner guests had taken cover underneath the table, including our fathers and Sam. Bay and Thistle were standing, their faces unreadable as they watched the scene. Landon hadn't bothered to get up, and Marcus was busily trying to protect an unmoving Thistle. "What are we going to do?"

"We have to send it away," Aunt Tillie said.

"What a great idea," I said, sarcasm positively dripping from my tongue. "Do you have any suggestions?"

Aunt Tillie clapped her hands loudly. "Hey! Go away!"

The light moved faster, and the keening increased in frequency and tone.

"Oh, well, that worked," I deadpanned.

"No one needs your sass," Aunt Tillie said. "If I'm not mistaken, this is your fault."

I pointed to my glassy-eyed cousins. "And that's your fault. If they weren't so ... stoned ... Bay might be able to talk to it."

"Bay isn't the only one who can talk to ghosts," Aunt Tillie reminded me.

"So, talk to it."

"Not until you adjust your tone, missy," Aunt Tillie said. "I am not your slave."

"Oh, good grief," I grumbled. "We have to do something. This is going to totally ruin the whole weekend."

"I know," Aunt Tillie said, grinning. "I wish I had thought of this myself."

"Aunt Tillie!"

She scowled. "Fine. There is one thing I can do."

"Well, do it."

Aunt Tillie widened her stance and spread her arms wide. I could feel magic being pulled to her core as it whipped past me. I had no idea where she was gathering it from, or how she was doing it without a circle – or something to anchor herself with. "Be gone!"

"Be gone? How is that going to work?" I pulled up short. The room had quieted, the only noise coming from the whimpering masses beneath the table. The light had also dissipated, although I had no idea for how long. "How did you do that?"

"I'm gifted."

I turned to Bay, whose face was a blank slate. Thistle didn't look much different. "We have to get them upstairs," I said, keeping my voice low. "They're going to be under attack, and they're in no shape to deal with it."

"They're fine," Aunt Tillie said, waving her hand dismissively.

I shook my head. "Since Thistle is your biggest fan right now, you and Marcus get her upstairs right now. I'll handle Landon and Bay, and then I'll come back for Sam."

Aunt Tillie glanced under the table. "He looks like he'd be perfectly happy to sleep there."

"Just ... help me."

"Fine," Aunt Tillie said. "You're such a worrier. That's your worst quality. You know that, right?"

"Get them upstairs!"

"WHAT HAPPENED?"

It had taken work, but Marcus and I managed to get all of the guests to their rooms. Since they were decidedly drunk, we told them it was all part of the Hemlock Cove experience and not to worry. I'd taken the opportunity – when no one was looking, of course – to chant a small spell outside each bedroom to ensure sweet dreams. All of the guests were asleep once their heads hit the pillows.

I did the same for Sam. Even though he was aware of the existence of ghosts, he'd been terrified by the show. I had no idea how much of that was real, and how much of it was due to Aunt Tillie's wine. I'd piled him into bed, wished him restful slumber, and left him in the bedroom alone.

There was a fire to put out on the main floor – and I was worried Aunt Tillie would be the one burned. Imagine my surprise when the only people left in the dining room were the Dragonfly's proprietors.

"I'm not sure what happened, Dad," I said.

"What was that?" Teddy asked.

I saw no sense in lying. "It was a ghost. I think. It's a little more ... scattered than the other ghosts I've seen, so I can't be a hundred-percent sure."

"Did you create it like you did last night?"

I sucked in a breath. It was time for some truth. "Technically, a real ghost appeared last night, too."

"What?" Dad was incensed.

"Bay and Thistle created the initial light show," I admitted. "Bay made the table dance a little, too. Somehow, though, we drew another ghost here. A real ghost."

"And when were you going to tell us?"

I shrugged. "We were hoping to get rid of it before you knew," I said. "We didn't want you to freak out."

"So, you lied?"

"We didn't lie," I said. "We just didn't volunteer the truth."

"Oh, well, that's convenient," Dad said. "Did your Aunt Tillie teach you that? Where is she, by the way? I have a feeling she had something to do with this."

I bristled under the statement. "She didn't have anything to do with the ghost," I said. "We think … and I stress the word 'think' … that the ghost was already here. Bay and Landon have been doing some research." I told them the story of Marian Lecter and her untimely passing. "The ghost was just attracted to the magic during the séance. It was an accident."

"And we're supposed to believe that this just happened at the same time Tillie showed up?"

I blew out a frustrated sigh. "She was here for a different reason."

"And what reason is that?" Jack asked.

"I … she just wanted to check up on us." Aunt Tillie wasn't wrong when she said I was loyal. I wouldn't throw her under the bus. No matter what.

"You're lying," Teddy said. "You always were the worst liar of the lot. I don't know what you're lying about, but you're definitely lying now."

"Hey, don't talk to her that way," Dad snapped.

Teddy took an involuntary step back. "I didn't mean that. I don't know why I said it."

I did. "Why don't you guys go up to bed," I suggested. "I think everyone drank too much – and fought too much – tonight. We're all on edge. We'll talk about this in the morning."

"What are you going to do?" Dad asked.

"I'm going to make sure everything is cleaned up," I said, rolling up my sleeves.

"By yourself?"

"It's fine," I said. "It won't take me very long. Everyone else is in bed, and you guys should join them."

Dad looked unsure. "I don't think … ."

"Just go," I said, rubbing my forehead wearily. "Trust me. I could use the time alone to … decompress."

I WORKED STEADILY, cleaning the dining room first and carrying all the dishes into the kitchen so I could wash them. I stacked everything in neat piles – just like my mother taught me – and then attacked a pile at a time.

After several minutes, I realized I wasn't alone.

Dad had changed his clothes, and he was now dressed in flannel sleep pants and a T-shirt. He joined me wordlessly at the counter and started drying.

I broke the uncomfortable silence first. "I told you to go to bed."

"I'm not tired," Dad said.

"You should be. You drank enough wine to knock out three men twice your size."

Dad chuckled. "There's something about being accosted by a ghost to sober you up."

"I guess." I was so used to it, it didn't even register anymore.

"I'm sorry about what Teddy said. He didn't mean it. He's not himself tonight. None of us were ourselves tonight."

"I know."

"I'm sorry about … everything."

"I know."

Dad stilled his hands, focusing on me. "Do you want to talk about it?"

"I don't know what there is to talk about."

"I think there's a lot to talk about, Clove," he said. "Do you want to start with why you're so mad?"

"I'm not mad."

"You're mad," he said, his voice gentle. "You have a right to be mad. We shouldn't have left."

"No, you shouldn't have."

"There are two sides to every story. You know that, right?"

"Of course there are," I said. "It's hard to listen to your side of the story when you're trying to tell it while saying horrible things about another member of my family."

Dad's eyebrows flew up. "Who? Aunt Tillie?"

I nodded, plunging my hands deeper into the scorching water to search for errant silverware.

"You and your cousins say horrible things about her all the time," Dad pointed out.

"That's because we can," I said. "She likes to mess with us. The truth is, we like to mess with her, too. She's always been there for us."

"I know."

"You know, when we were in middle school, there was this girl named Gracie who was torturing Bay," I said, my mind traveling back in time. "Bay can talk to ghosts. I don't know if you know that, but she can. When we were kids, people thought she was the weird girl always talking to herself. It's not like we could tell them the truth, so she just had to suck it up.

"Anyway, Gracie was ... horrible to Bay," I continued. "It didn't matter how many times we beat her up – and we did beat her up – she just kept coming. It was like she took Bay's very existence as some affront to nature.

"I think she knew, even then, that there was something different about Bay," I said. "She knew there was something different about all of us. Bay never liked to cry in front of our mothers and Aunt Tillie. They didn't like crying, and Bay always liked to pretend she was strong, even when she wasn't. Do you know who she cried to?"

Dad pursed his lips. "Chief Terry."

"He's the one who sat and listened to Bay cry," I said. "He listened to all of us, but Bay needed him more for some reason. He listened, and he hugged her, and he helped fix up a tree house so we had a place to hide and plot against Gracie."

"We should have been there," Dad said.

"Yes," I said. "You wouldn't have been able to fix the Gracie problem, though. Do you know who fixed it?"

"I have a feeling you're about to tell me that Aunt Tillie fixed it."

"She did," I said. "She started … messing … with Gracie. Every time Gracie tortured Bay, something bad happened to Gracie. When she stuck gum in Bay's hair, half of her hair fell out. When she told all the boys that Bay was a hermaphrodite, she grew a mustache."

Dad snickered, even though the moment was serious.

"And it wasn't just any mustache. It was like a full man's mustache. Every time Gracie said something nasty to Bay, it grew. She'd wax it, and shave it, but it just kept growing – even in the middle of the day. Finally, she put two-and-two together and realized that it was karma paying her back and she finally stop terrorizing Bay."

"Tillie has always been … difficult," Dad said. "I have never once doubted that she loves you all, though. You should know, I didn't leave because of you. I left because I loved you, and I loved your mother, but we just couldn't all live together anymore. I thought I was making it easier for everyone, and I think Teddy and Jack felt the same way. The only ones we were making it easier on were ourselves. By the time we all realized that … it was too late."

I lifted my eyes – finally – and met his tortured gaze. "It's never too late. Everything in life takes work, though. You have to put in the work."

Dad nodded. "I hope I'm up for the task."

"Me, too."

Dad walked me back to my bedroom, both of us pulling up short when we reached the top of the staircase and found Marcus leaning against the wall in the hallway.

"What's going on?"

He pointed to the room. "Look."

I wasn't sure I wanted to, but I was feeling brave this evening for some reason. When I pushed open the door, the sight that greeted me was … adorable. Thistle was spread eagle on the bed, her arm raised over her head as she snored heavily. The spot next to her – Marcus' spot – wasn't empty. Aunt Tillie, curled on her side, was noisily slumbering next to Thistle.

"She must be exhausted," I said, smiling.

"Where am I supposed to sleep?"

Dad smirked, never taking his eyes off Thistle and Aunt Tillie. "Crawl in there with them."

"That's like the worst threesome ever," Marcus complained.

"There's room on the other side of Thistle," I said. "They won't wake up until morning. I think you'll be safe."

Marcus sighed, resigned. "It's a good thing I love her. If I didn't, this is where I would draw the line." He glanced at me. "If you ever tell anyone about this, I'll never forgive you."

"Your secret is safe with me." Hey, it turned out I wasn't such a bad liar after all – and I even took a few photographs with my cell phone as proof.

NINE

"Good morning."

Sam's face was happy when he rolled over and faced me the next morning. Despite the events of the previous evening, I felt as if a weight had been lifted from my shoulders. I felt … good. "Good morning."

Sam wrapped his arms around my waist and pulled me closer, brushing a light kiss against my forehead as he let consciousness wash over him. After a few moments, he bolted upright. "Holy crap!"

"It's okay," I soothed.

"What happened to the ghost?"

"Aunt Tillie sent it away."

"For good?"

I shrugged. "I don't know. I don't think so."

"I … everything is so fuzzy."

I cocked my head, sympathy rolling over me. "That's because Aunt Tillie cursed the wine."

Sam stilled. "She did? Is that why everyone was acting so funny?"

"Yeah," I said. "That's also the reason she was here. When she found out we were all staying here, she was going to steal the wine back."

"But ... you were okay," Sam said. "I don't remember a lot, but you were totally in control."

"I didn't drink the red wine."

"Ah." Sam ran his hand through his hair. "Did I do anything really embarrassing?"

I kissed his cheek. "You were fine. I think Thistle and Landon are going to be the only ones feeling the burn from last night this morning. Well, and maybe Uncle Jack. I was worried he and Landon were going to come to blows."

"I kind of remember that," Sam said.

"Well, the good news is, if you're fuzzy – and you know what our lives are like – that should mean the guests will just figure they got really hammered and had a good time," I said.

Sam smiled. "You're always such an optimist." He leaned in and gave me a sweet kiss.

"I should probably check on Thistle and Bay," I said. "Oh, and Aunt Tillie."

"Aunt Tillie? She stayed here last night?"

I smiled broadly and grabbed my phone off the nightstand. "Oh, yeah."

Sam was grinning within seconds as he studied the photographs. "Can I get one of these framed?"

"Absolutely."

"**HE WAS** TRYING TO COP A FEEL."

"He was not."

"He was, too."

"He was not."

"Are you calling me a liar?"

I found Thistle and Aunt Tillie arguing in the hallway. "What's going on?"

Thistle's hair was a blue mess. It was standing on end, and the previous day's eye makeup was smeared halfway down her cheeks. "Aunt Tillie ... slept with us last night."

"I know."

"How do you know?"

"We found you up here sleeping together when we were done cleaning up," I said. "I have pictures."

"I'm going to beat you," Thistle warned.

"I think you were both exhausted," I said. "It's not like it's a big deal."

"Aunt Tillie claims Marcus was trying to feel her up while we were sleeping," Thistle said.

"He was," Aunt Tillie said, her hands on her hips as she regarded Thistle with thinly-veiled ire. "I'm a hot piece of woman. You should take notes."

"He was on the other side of me," Thistle argued.

For his part, Marcus looked horrified. "I swear I wasn't trying to feel you up. I was just snuggling with Thistle. I was half asleep. My hand slipped."

"And did you like what you felt?" Aunt Tillie asked.

"Of course not," Marcus said, oblivious. "I knew right away that it wasn't Thistle. It was too … low."

Aunt Tillie narrowed her eyes. "Is that supposed to make me feel better?"

Marcus was lost. "I'm so confused."

"You're fine," Thistle said, patting his arm. "She's just messing with you. Accidentally grabbing her boob was the most action she's seen in decades."

"You're back on my list, girl."

"When was I off your list?" Thistle challenged.

"You said I was a genius last night," Aunt Tillie said.

"Oh, well, now I know you're lying," Thistle said, looking to me for support.

I tried to wipe the rueful look off my face – and failed. "You did say it."

"Well, that's just … ."

"The wine was cursed," I said, putting Thistle out of her misery.

"What?" Thistle pondered my statement for a second and then swiveled her shoulders. "You."

The door to Bay and Landon's room swung open.

"Why is everyone yelling?"

Bay didn't look any better than Thistle.

"Marcus grabbed my boob in bed this morning," Aunt Tillie announced.

"It was an accident!" Marcus' face was so red I was worried he was going to pass out.

Landon appeared in the doorway behind Bay. "My head feels like it's going to explode."

"It's because you had too much wine," I said. "It was cursed."

"It was cursed?" Bay's face reflected a myriad of emotions, last night's events slowly falling into place. "Aunt Tillie."

"She was trying to steal the wine back," I said. "That's what she was doing here."

"I'm going to kill you," Thistle warned.

"Don't say things like that to me," Aunt Tillie warned. "I'll make you sorry."

"I'm already sorry," Thistle said. "I slept in a bed with my boyfriend and you last night. How can my life get any worse?"

"Well, we still have a ghost to deal with," I said.

Bay rubbed the side of her face. "Oh, right. I forgot about that. I was hoping it was a dream."

"Nope."

Landon rested his chin on Bay's shoulder, his long hair tousled from a restless night. "Is it too much to hope that my fight with Jack was a dream?"

"That was real, too," I said. "That was because of the wine."

Landon scorched Aunt Tillie with a look. "Are you happy?"

"I'm not unhappy," Aunt Tillie said. "I had fun. I got a good night's sleep. Oh, and Marcus felt me up this morning. Thistle should be worried. It's going to be a good day."

She started moving toward the stairs.

"What do you think they're serving for breakfast?"

"**I'M GLAD** you slept so well, Tillie," Dad said, fixing her with a tight smile.

"The bed was very comfortable," Aunt Tillie said, digging into her eggs and hash browns with gusto. "Thistle snores like a sailor, but I barely noticed. Calvin snored, too. It was like going back in time."

"Thanks," Thistle said, shoveling a forkful of potatoes into her mouth.

"I even got felt up," Aunt Tillie said, her eyes sparkling.

Dad gulped and then turned to me. "How did you sleep?"

"Surprisingly well."

"I slept great," Clara said. "I can't believe how fun last night was."

Dad balked. "Fun?"

"You guys put on a great show," Chet said. "I'm going to be recommending this place to everyone I know. It's amazing."

"While I thought the theatrics were a bit much, I still think this is an outrageous experience," Jim said. "It's nice to have something different."

Dad relaxed, if only marginally. "Well ... we aim to please."

"We do," Teddy enthused.

Landon and Jack were busy staring at their plates, each refusing to make eye contact with the other.

"I think you should probably take red wine off the menu," Bay said pointedly, placing her hand over Landon's. "I think everyone might have imbibed a little too much."

"Yeah," Landon said, his voice hoarse. "I know I did."

Jack sighed. "You're not the only one."

I bit my lower lip to keep from laughing. They were both stubborn, but the immediate storm had passed. "So, what time is everyone leaving today?"

"Three," Dad said. "I thought we might come up with a fun activity for everyone to do before they leave. Any ideas?"

"Let's have another séance," Clara suggested.

"No." Most of the men in the room had answered at the same time.

"How about some horseback riding?" Marcus suggested. "I can organize a nice outing."

"Oh, that sounds fun," Clara said.

The other guests nodded.

"I haven't been on a horse in years," Chet said.

"There are a lot of different horses to choose from," Marcus said. "They're all very gentle, and they know the trails."

"Can we?" Clara asked, her eyes sparkling.

"Of course," Jack said. "We want this to be a great experience for everyone. Horseback riding it is."

"OKAY, all the guests left with Marcus," Dad said, fixing everyone who remained with a pointed look as his gaze bounced around the room. "What are we going to do about the ghost?"

"We need to eviscerate it," Teddy said. "It can't stay. A fake ghost is one thing. A real ghost is a mess."

"How do you suggest we eviscerate it?" Thistle asked. She'd showered after breakfast, and she looked like a human being again, but she was still crabby.

"I don't know," Teddy said. "Start it on fire or something."

"You can't start a ghost on fire," Bay said wearily. "We're in a tough spot here. This isn't a normal ghost."

"Can you expand on that?" Jack asked.

"A normal ghost is ... fully formed," Bay explained. "Most ghosts remain because their soul attaches to some sort of trauma. If it is Marian Lecter – and we have no reason to believe it's not – then there's something unsettled about her death."

"I ran down her kids," Landon said. "They're both alive. They both married, and as far as I can tell, they both had happy lives. They were never arrested for anything. They had children. They even have some grandchildren now."

"Maybe she's haunted because she thinks no one knows her husband killed her," Jack said.

"Ghosts usually know the circumstances behind their deaths," Bay replied. "It's the last thing they remember, even if they try to forget the memory."

"The little ghost from the boat didn't," Landon pointed out.

"Erika was a special case," Bay said. "She was a child. She couldn't grasp the concept of death. She knew she fell asleep, and a certain part of her knew she never woke up. She still didn't understand time ... or vengeance."

"Who is Erika?" Jack asked.

Bay told the story. When she was done, Jack turned to Landon, surprised. "And you saw her?"

Landon faltered. "I'm not sure."

"Bay said that the ghost appeared to you and told you she was in trouble," Jack said. "That's how you knew to go to her. I didn't know you could see ghosts."

"I can't," Landon said.

"But ... ."

"We don't know how Landon could see Erika," Bay said, rubbing the back of his neck thoughtfully. "We just know that, because he could, he saved our lives."

"I know," Jack said. "Erika was smart enough to go to the one person she knew who could save you all. She willed Landon to see her, for which I will be forever grateful."

Landon's cheeks flushed with color. "It wasn't a big deal."

"Saving their lives wasn't a big deal?" Jack challenged. "Saving my daughter's life wasn't a big deal? Saving all those children wasn't a big deal?"

"No," Aunt Tillie said. "I save their lives all the time. It's an everyday occurrence. No one wants to give me a medal."

Landon smirked, relieved by the interruption. "I did what had to be done," he said. "I don't question it. I've learned not to question a lot of things since I met Bay."

"I guess you have," Jack said, his expression thoughtful. "I'm still thankful."

"I ... it's nothing," Landon said. "It's not like I could leave them there."

"No," Jack said. "You're not the type who leaves."

"He left once," Aunt Tillie interjected.

Landon scowled. "Thank you for that."

Aunt Tillie shrugged. "We have to go with the assumption that the ghost is Marian Lecter. She's our best option."

"I still don't understand why she's not fully formed," Bay said. "I've never seen a ... wisp ... this powerful."

"What's a wisp?" Teddy asked.

"It's like a fragment of a ghost," Thistle said. "It's like Marian's soul was shattered when she died, and only a part of it remains."

"Maybe the fragment is looking for the rest of the soul to join with," Jack said.

"Maybe," Bay said. "I don't know how to fix that, though."

"Of course you do," Aunt Tillie scoffed. "You fix it the only way you know how."

Bay arched an eyebrow. "And how is that?"

"With knowledge."

We all sighed in unison. "You want to have another séance, don't you?" I asked.

"Do you see another option?" Aunt Tillie asked. "All we have to do is call the wisp and then reunite it with the rest of her soul."

"And how do we do that?" Jack asked.

"Magic," Landon said, pinching the bridge of his nose. "It always comes back to magic. I think I need another drink."

TEN

"Are we sure this is where her body was found?" Landon glanced around dubiously. "I don't know," he said. "From the description in the case file, this is my best guess."

"It doesn't matter," Aunt Tillie said. "Even if her body was found here, that doesn't mean this is where she died."

"She has a point," Landon said. "Forensics wasn't the same back then. Her body could have been dragged. For all we know, she could have been killed in the inn."

"That doesn't matter either," Aunt Tillie said. "Most of that inn has been refurbished, or just outright replaced. There's no anchor there. This is as good a place as any."

"Why are you so excited about this?" I asked.

"I like a good séance," Aunt Tillie replied. "They're a good way to clear the channels."

"What channels?" Dad asked.

Aunt Tillie flicked his forehead. "The ones in there, moron."

"You're always a joy to have around," Dad said, rubbing the spot between his eyebrows.

"I know."

"That wasn't a compliment," Dad said.

AMANDA M. LEE

"I guess that depends on where you're standing," Aunt Tillie said. "Light the candles."

We were all used to Aunt Tillie – and her enthusiasm – so we did as we were told, building a circle of candles and lighting them with a snap of our fingers.

"That was amazing," Dad said, breathing hard.

"We just lit some candles," I said.

"But ... you did it without matches, or a lighter."

I patted his arm. "We're known to take a few shortcuts from time to time."

"What should we expect?" Teddy asked. "Will the ghost ... or wisp ... try to kill us?"

"It's not interested in murder," I said. "It's just ... lost."

"Define lost," Jack said.

"Haven't you ever just felt like you belong somewhere?" Bay asked. "Haven't you ever had a moment where you knew you were found?"

Jack shrugged. "I'm not sure."

"Then you haven't had it," Bay said. "It can come from an unlikely place." She glanced at Landon. "The simple act of resting your head on someone's shoulder can make you feel it."

"Or running your fingers through someone's hair," Thistle said.

"Or when someone smiles at you," I said, glancing at Sam and basking in the grin he sent my way. "It just happens."

"And Marian needs to be found?" Dad asked.

"She needs to be restored," I corrected. "She's fragmented."

"So, what happens when you call her?" Teddy asked.

"Hopefully, she'll be able to communicate with either Bay or Aunt Tillie," I said. "The circle should bolster her power and make the wisp strong enough to give voice to its thoughts. Thistle and I can usually hear a ghost once Bay registers its presence. Sometimes we can even see them, although it's rare."

"And if it doesn't communicate?"

"Then we'll have to figure something else out," I said.

"If this doesn't work, I'm done," Aunt Tillie said. "I already missed Jimmy Fallon last night. I'm not missing *The Walking Dead* tonight."

I scowled. "Thank you for the encouragement."

Aunt Tillie was nonplussed. "Let's get this show on the road." She extended her hands, Bay and Thistle joining with her – and then me – and focused on the center of the circle. "We call upon the powers of the West. Let us help this spirit on her quest."

"We call upon the powers of the North," Thistle intoned. "Let us help this spirit go forth."

"We call upon the powers of the East," I said, ignoring the wind as it picked up. "Let us release the overpowering beast."

Bay pressed her eyes shut. "We call upon the powers of the South," she said. "Give form. Give solace. Give words to her mouth."

I arched an eyebrow in Bay's direction.

"What? I didn't have time to come up with a good rhyme," Bay complained. "It's harder than it sounds."

"You did fine, baby," Landon said, scanning the area as the leaves started to rustle. "Just concentrate. I've got your back."

"We all do," Jack said, moving to the spot next to Landon so they could protect Bay's vulnerable figure together. "We're right here."

It was almost summer, but the leaves on the ground from the previous fall were still present. They started to cycle, taking form in the middle of our circle. They whipped – and whipped – and whipped. The cyclone before us had enough power to toss our hair, but not weaken our resolve.

Bay spoke first. "Marian?"

I detected a hitch in the cyclone. It didn't last, but it was there. "You made contact."

Bay nodded. "Marian, we're not here to hurt you. We want to help. Please, let us help. Talk to us."

The cyclone continued spinning.

"We want to know how you died," Thistle said. "We want to put you to rest."

No change.

"Hey, some of us have television to watch tonight," Aunt Tillie said. "You're starting to bore me. Daryl needs me."

We all shot her angry looks.

"What? It's a big deal," Aunt Tillie said. "If Daryl dies, I'm going to start a riot."

I bit my tongue. She was helping with the spell, but her heart wasn't really in it. I decided to take a different tactic. "Do you want to know about your children, Marian?"

The cyclone decreased its pace.

"They grew up, you know?" I said, looking to Landon for help. "They were happy. They got married. They had children of their own."

Landon stepped forward, unsure. He could see the cyclone, but he obviously had no idea if he was helping. "Ava married a soldier," he said. "He was career military, and he retired last year. They live in Georgia. They had two children. A boy and a girl. Their names are Marian and Scott."

I nodded encouragingly.

"Raymond married a nurse," Landon continued. "They live in Florida. They had three children. Two girls and a boy. Dylan is going to college soon. Alice and Madison are both in high school. They're happy."

The cyclone stilled some more, and then it spoke. "What about Will?"

I looked to Landon.

"Will is gone," Landon said, uncertain. "He was convicted of your murder, and he spent thirty years in prison before he died of cancer."

The cyclone started howling.

Bay furrowed her brow, considering. "Did Will kill you?"

The cyclone wailed.

"We can't understand you," Bay said, her voice even. "If you want us to understand, you have to take form. We can help. I promise. Just … please … take form."

The leaves exploded, causing everyone to duck for cover. We never let go of each other's hands, and when the dust settled, there was an ethereal form where the cyclone used to be. She was blonde, at least I think she was blonde. The green tint to the mist made it hard to tell, but that was my best guess. Her bone structure was angular and defined, but her face was tortured. Her mouth worked, but no sound would come out.

We waited.

We finally heard noise. It was low, but it was clear. "It wasn't Will."

Landon moved closer to Bay. He didn't touch her, but he was interested. "What happened?"

"We were on vacation," Marian said.

"Witnesses said you had a nice dinner," Landon said. "They said you and Will seemed happy. They said there were no signs of unrest."

"We *were* happy," Marian said. "We were … content. We had forever in front of us, and happiness around us."

"What do you remember?" I asked.

"I had to go to the bathroom," Marian said. "Will was asleep. The bedrooms didn't have individual bathrooms then. That's different now. They were at the end of the hall. When I left the room, Will was asleep."

"Where were the children?" Landon asked, his hand resting against Bay's hip.

"They were in the adjacent room," Marian said. "They looked like angels in the moonlight. They were happy. There was a fair in town that day. They had a good time. I checked on them. They were just so … beautiful."

We all waited.

"That was the last time I ever saw them," Marian said. "My last memory of them is … wonderful."

Landon, ever the investigator, had to press. "What do you remember next?"

"I went down to the bathroom," Marian said. "Nothing strange happened there. I was on my way back to the room when I heard a noise. People were arguing downstairs. I shouldn't have gone. I know that now. I should have climbed back into bed with Will and ignored the fight, but it sounded like someone was crying.

"I went to the top of the stairs," Marian continued. "I followed the voices. It was Dick and Sue."

I wrinkled my forehead, searching my memory.

AMANDA M. LEE

"Dick and Sue Warner?" Landon pressed.

"They were the owners," Marian said. "They were so nice when we arrived. I know now that it was an act."

"What were they doing?" Landon asked.

"They were fighting," Marian said. "Sue was crying. She said Dick was a ... ."

"Dick?" Aunt Tillie supplied.

Marian nodded. "They fought for a long time. Sue said he was going to get caught, and she couldn't take it anymore. She said she wouldn't risk the inn for his ... compulsions."

"What compulsions?" Landon asked.

"He gambled."

Landon nodded.

"He was in debt," Marian said. "The inn was in danger."

"Then what happened?"

"I hid at the top of the stairwell," Marian said. "I didn't want them to hear me. He hit her. I covered my mouth so he wouldn't hear me, but I didn't walk away. I should have walked away."

"It's not your fault," I soothed. "You couldn't have known what would happen. You were on vacation."

"I made a noise," Marian said. "Sue ran from her husband. I was going to go back to my room, but it was like I was frozen. He found me on the top of the stairs. He followed the noise."

"He strangled you, didn't he?" Landon asked, trying to ease her story burden.

Marian nodded. "It didn't take long. I remember ... I remember trying to scream, but no noise would come out. My last thought was of Will. I wondered what he would think when he woke up and I wasn't there."

"Did Dick kill you in the inn?" Landon asked.

Marian nodded.

"Do you remember anything about this place?"

Marian shook her head. "Should I?"

"This was where your body was found," Landon said.

"And Will was convicted of my murder," Marian finished.

"What happened to Will wasn't fair," Landon said. "I can't make excuses. He's gone. He's moved on."

"You need to move on, too," Bay said.

"I can't," Marian said. "I need ... justice."

'There's no justice left to get," Landon said. "Dick and Sue died twenty years ago. They're not here."

"He got away with it," Marian said, her face pinched with concentration. "He murdered me, and he got away with it."

"He didn't get away with it," I interjected. "He may have, at the time, but karma caught up with him. It always does. If you do good in this world, it will come back to you. He died a hard death. He had cancer, too. He fought because he was desperate to survive, but all his efforts were in vain. Karma came for him."

Marian focused on me. "Then why am I still here?"

"Only part of you is," I said. "The other part of you has moved on. The other part of you is ... ."

"With Will," Bay finished. "He's waiting for you."

Marian looked hopeful. "Do you think he's really waiting for me?"

"I know he is," I said. "He loved you. He would never have hurt you. He's waiting for you."

Marian was conflicted. "Do you promise?"

I was unsure how to answer, so I went with my gut instinct. "When you love someone, they're always waiting for you. Love transcends everything – even death."

"I'm tired of being here," Marian admitted. "I'm tired of ... hating."

"So, don't hate," I said. "There's no one left here to hate. They've already been dealt with. You can't go back in time. It's impossible."

"You can go forward, though," Bay said. "There's nothing left for you here. Go to Will. Wait for your children. Find ... peace."

"How do I leave?"

Bay shrugged. "I don't know. You just have to ... ."

"Let go," I finished.

Marian smiled. "Do you really think it will be better ... over there?"

"I think he's just over that ridge," I said, pointing. "Find him. Love him. Revel in a reunion that's been decades in the making. Find happiness."

Marian nodded. "Thank you."

On either side of me, Thistle and Bay clasped my hands tightly.

"We call upon the power of the four winds," I said. "Go with honor. Go with peace. Go with the knowledge that we will never forget you, and your story will never be forgotten."

The leaves started churning again.

"Clove?" Sam was worried, and he was behind me, his hand on my back.

"She's leaving," I said.

"Are you sure?"

The leaves exploded, knocking everyone to the ground with the force of abandoned vengeance – and longing. "I'm sure."

"Holy crap," Dad said, laughing. "That was ... amazing."

It wasn't the best of all worlds, but it was the best of Marian's world. Life moves on. Ghosts find peace. And witches?

"I'm hungry," Aunt Tillie announced. "I need some food before *The Walking Dead*. Come on." She snapped her fingers. "Someone needs to give me some chocolate cake."

Well, witches find their own form of happiness. Hey, chocolate cake does sound good.

WICKED BREW

A WICKED WITCHES OF THE MIDWEST SHORT

ONE

"Have you seen what's going on outside?"

I glanced up, fixing my gaze on my cousin Bay as she shuffled into the front library of The Overlook excitedly. She always manages to find me – even when I'm trying to get some peace and quiet. If I didn't know better, I would think it was a special ability. Unfortunately, we're so codependent, she just knows me – and where to look when I'm trying to hide.

I dropped the book I was reading onto the window seat and peered outside, grinning despite myself when I realized what she was referring to. "What is she doing now?"

"She's mad," Bay said, lifting my legs and shifting them so she could settle next to me on the window seat. "Open the window so we can hear."

"Go outside if you want to hear," I protested. *Sheesh. A person wants five minutes of peace. Try finding it in this house. Why do you think I'm always grumpy?* "I'm reading."

"No way," Bay said, tucking a strand of blonde hair behind her ear. "If we listen inside, then we won't be targets when Aunt Tillie blows. If we go outside, she'll curse us just because we're there. Come on, Thistle. Stop being a pain."

She had a point. I sighed, but I shoved the window open. I always love it when my mom and aunts go after my great-aunt. I just hate it when they inevitably back down – and they always do.

"You can't tell me what to do," Aunt Tillie said, her hands impatiently gesturing as she faced off with her three nieces. "I am an adult."

"We're not trying to tell you what to do," Winnie said.

"You're trying to tell me what I can't do," Aunt Tillie said. "That's the same thing."

"Hey, we don't care if you want to sell your wine," Aunt Marnie said. "You just can't do it at a stand at the edge of the driveway. It's illegal."

"Technically, selling my wine is illegal no matter what," Aunt Tillie pointed out. "I don't have a license."

"Yes, but everyone looks the other way if you do it on the sly," my mom said, twisting her hands nervously. My mom is terrified of Aunt Tillie. Taking her on makes her nervous. It makes me laugh.

"They'll look the other way if I do it here, too, Twila," Aunt Tillie said. "Who in their right mind would report me? They know I'll do something terrible to them if they do."

"You can't go around threatening people with curses," Winnie said. "That's why people in this town are so suspicious of us."

"People in this town are suspicious of us because they're cowards," Aunt Tillie said. "They fear what they don't understand. It's not my fault I'm the only genius in a town full of idiots."

"So, wait, now you're a genius?" Marnie was incensed. "It doesn't take a genius to know that you can't sell wine at the side of the road."

"Don't ever tell me what I can't do," Aunt Tillie said. "I am still the boss of this family."

"No one is the boss of a family," Winnie countered. "And, technically, we own this land. We – the three of us – not you. Our mother – your sister – left it to us. You can't set up a wine stand on our property. I'm sorry. It's just not going to happen."

Aunt Tillie narrowed her eyes. "Do you really want to take me on over this?"

"We're not taking you on," Marnie said, stepping up so she was shoulder to shoulder with Winnie. I couldn't help but notice that my mom was cowering a few feet behind them. "We're just telling you how things are going to go. For once, you're going to listen."

"Well, we'll just see about that, won't we?"

WE FOUND our mothers in the kitchen a few minutes later. They were talking in hushed tones, and all three of them looked worried. When they caught sight of Bay and me, they plastered identical fake smiles on their faces.

"Hello, girls," Mom said. "This is a nice surprise. Are you here for dinner?"

"It's barely noon," Bay said, snatching a cookie off the cooling rack in front of Marnie.

"Oh, are you here for lunch then?" Winnie asked. "It should be on the table in a half hour or so."

Bay and I exchanged humorous looks.

"Where's Aunt Tillie at?" I asked, utilizing my best "innocent" voice in an attempt to irk them.

"How should we know?" Mom replied. "You know very well, Thistle, that we are not your great-aunt's keepers."

"She's probably down at her greenhouse," Marnie said. "The construction is just about finished. She's been excited to pick out items to plant."

"And it won't be pot, right?" Bay asked. Her boyfriend Landon was an FBI agent, and he was well aware of Aunt Tillie's "special" field. He didn't believe her glaucoma claims, but he chose to look the other way – mostly because Aunt Tillie's magical wards kept him from being able to find the field. I don't think he'd ever turn her in, but I can see him accidentally burning it down if he gets the chance.

"We've warned her about illegal crops," Winnie said. "She promises that the only thing of interest she'll be growing in the greenhouse is basil."

"Why is basil of interest?" I asked, slipping my hand beneath Bay's so I could grab the cookie she was aiming to steal. She shot me a look as I stuck the cookie into my mouth. She's easy to rile, and I enjoy doing it.

Marnie made a face. "It's a joke," she said. "That was supposed to be your name, after all."

I faltered. Being plagued with the name Thistle was one of the banes of my existence – well, that and a nasty Aunt Tillie when she's feeling feisty. I never understood why my mother picked it. Bay was an herb, but it was still a pretty name. The same with Clove, my other cousin. Thistle, though? That's what you take when you drink too much. "What are you talking about?"

"Right up until the day you were born, Twila was going to name you Basil," Winnie explained. "She took one look at you, though, and she decided that Thistle was a better name."

I shifted my gaze to Bay, unsure. "Did you know about this?"

"No," Bay said, grinning widely. "Although, I do like the name Basil."

"Basil is worse than Thistle," I argued.

"Oh, I don't know, I think it's kind of fun," Bay replied. She enjoys getting under my skin, too. It's a family trait – and it's obnoxious. "Basil Winchester, fastest herb in the Midwest." She dissolved into giggles. She was never going to let me live this down.

I turned back to our mothers. "So, where is Aunt Tillie?" They were purposely trying to derail the conversation because they didn't want us to know what our persnickety great-aunt was up to. We're all masters of this specific verbal art, but it doesn't work well on those who regularly utilize the tactic.

"We told you, she's down at her greenhouse," Winnie said evasively.

"Oh, so she's not setting up a stand at the edge of the road to sell wine?" I pressed.

Bay pursed her lips.

"If you already knew, then why did you ask?" Mom's face was pale and drawn.

"Yeah, it's almost as if you were trying to play a game," Marnie said. "You know I don't like games."

Since Marnie was the master of throwing a board game into the air if she thought she was going to lose, I was definitely aware of her aversion to games. Don't even ask what she does during a raucous game of cribbage. "I just wanted to know what you guys were going to say."

"Well, she's not going to do it," Marnie said. "We've laid down the law. She knows what is – and what is not – acceptable."

"You've laid down the law?" Bay asked, arching an eyebrow.

"We have," Winnie said. "Aunt Tillie may not like it, but we're in charge here."

Aunt Tillie definitely wasn't going to like it. She also wasn't going to respect it.

"How about you let us try and talk to her?" Bay suggested.

I couldn't stop my mouth from dropping open. "No way!"

"Oh, come on," Bay prodded. "Do you really want Aunt Tillie to sell wine at the end of the driveway? The people in town are going to have a fit."

"You were the one who wanted to listen by the window in the library so she wouldn't see us and curse us," I pointed out.

Winnie knit her eyebrows together. "Excuse me?"

"You have such a big mouth," Bay grumbled.

"Well, since you two think this is so funny, I've decided that you should be the ones to deal with it," Winnie said.

"No."

"Yes," she said, fixing me with a hard look. "She's your aunt. You're both a part of this family. We've taken a vote. You two are now in charge of making sure Aunt Tillie does not open a wine stand."

"You took a vote?" This family is unbelievable sometimes. "When?"

"It was a silent vote," Winnie said, glancing at her two sisters in turn. "Right?"

Mom and Marnie nodded enthusiastically.

"We think you're the best witches for the job," Marnie said.

"Yeah," Mom added. "We have complete and total faith in you."

I pressed my lips together and focused on Bay. "I blame you for this."

Bay shrugged. "You usually do."

"**SHE'S** NOT GOING to listen to us."

"Then why did you suggest we come down here and talk to her?" Bay baffles me sometimes. She shifts from one extreme to the other. One minute she's an optimist, and the next she's a pessimist. It's like she has constant PMS. Me? I'm set on one extreme – annoyance – and I rarely shift.

"I don't know," Bay said. "I just thought it might be fun."

"If she wants to set up a wine stand, she's going to set up a wine stand," I grumbled, running a hand through my cropped blue hair as we trudged down the driveway. Since summer was officially here, I'd been toying with the idea of changing the color. I only opted for blue because it drives my mother nuts. She's starting to get used to it now – even though she still hates it. There are plenty of other colors in the rainbow to torture her with. I'm thinking a nice lavender to match the big bushes that are starting to bloom along the edge of the property might be in order. I've always loved that color.

"I don't have any intention of trying to talk her out of the stand," Bay said.

"You don't?"

She shook her head. "Landon will be here this afternoon. I figure he'll do it."

Landon's work often takes him out of Hemlock Cove during the week. He's here as often as he can be midweek, but he always goes out of his way to spend weekends with Bay. They've been pretty happy lately, which makes me happy. For law enforcement, he's not half bad. As long as he makes Bay smile, though, I'm willing to put up with his overbearing attitude. "She won't listen to Landon either."

"She might," Bay said. "She likes him."

"That doesn't mean she's going to listen to him," I pointed out. "She likes Chief Terry, and she won't listen to him." Chief Terry may be the top law enforcement official in Hemlock Cove, but that wasn't enough to dissuade Aunt Tillie from any of her nefarious deeds – even though he's a frequent visitor at the inn.

"That's because she knows Chief Terry is terrified of her," Bay said. "He would never arrest her."

"That's because our mothers would never forgive him," I said. "He likes all of the attention."

Our mothers like to play a game – yes, even Marnie – and Chief Terry is the prize. I'm not sure if he really wants to be claimed, but he enjoys being the center of attention, especially when they ply him with food. "I don't see why they just don't let her do it," I said. "She'll lose interest after a couple of hours. She's not exactly known for her stellar work ethic."

Bay pointed to the end of the driveway. "She's already got it set up. She seems serious."

"That's only because she knows it irritates our moms," I said. "She's nothing if not predictable."

Once we got to the end of the driveway, Aunt Tillie barely lifted an eyebrow as she greeted us. "So, they sent out reinforcements to talk me out of this?"

"We're not here to talk you out of this," Bay said. "We're here to ... help."

"Help?"

"Help you with your business," Bay said.

Aunt Tillie glanced at me.

"I'm not here to help," I said. "I wanted to stay out of it. Bay's big mouth is what got us in this mess in the first place. I'm just going to pretend I don't see a thing."

"You're smarter than you look," Aunt Tillie said. She pointed to a box. "Open that up and get a few bottles of wine out. I need people to see what I'm selling."

I sighed, but I did as I was told. "You know this is illegal, right?"

"Everything fun in life is illegal."

"Not everything," Bay said.

"Fine," Aunt Tillie acquiesced. "Everything worth doing in life is illegal."

AMANDA M. LEE

Bay shook her head and scanned Aunt Tillie's supplies. "You need a sign."

"Wait, so now you're encouraging her?" I was surprised.

"I'm not encouraging her," Bay said. "I just like to see things done right."

That's one of the things I hate most about Bay. She's got an odd organizational streak. It rears its head at the oddest times. "Well, make her a sign then."

"I'm not the artistic one," Bay pointed out.

I scowled. Now I knew why she suggested a sign.

"That's right," Aunt Tillie said, her eyes sparkling. "Thistle is the artistic one."

"I'm not making you a sign," I said.

"I want a good one," Aunt Tillie said, ignoring my statement. "Put some flowers on it or something. Glitter might be fun, too. I want it to look good. Make sure cars can read it from the road."

"Did you hear me? I'm not making you a sign."

"Don't you even think about arguing with me," Aunt Tillie warned. "I'm not in the mood. Right now, you two aren't on my list. You don't want that to change."

I swallowed hard. I certainly didn't want that to change. I hate being on Aunt Tillie's list. It usually ends with my pants not fitting, or a big zit in the middle of my forehead, or a noxious bacon smell emanating from my armpits. The woman is evil. "Fine," I said. "When our mothers complain, though, you're going to tell them you made us help."

"Fine," Aunt Tillie said. "If you want to be a 'fraidy' cat, go ahead. Blame it on the old lady."

I rolled my eyes. "I thought you were in the prime of your life?"

"Don't push me," Aunt Tillie said. "I've had just about enough of your mouth for one day."

Funnily enough, I was just getting warmed up. When I opened my mouth to see just how far I could push things, something else caught my eye. I was on my feet within seconds, my gaze trained on a small girl as she stumbled down the middle of the road. She seemed dazed – and lost.

"What? You're suddenly speechless?" Aunt Tillie asked. When I didn't return my attention to her, she followed my gaze. "Holy tarantula spiders." Aunt Tillie was moving before I had a chance to regain my faculties.

Crap. There's never a dull moment at The Overlook.

TWO

I followed Aunt Tillie to the road, Bay close at my heels. We all slowed our pace as we approached her. She was small, about eight years old if I had to guess. Her hair was long and dark, her pale features streaked with dirt and blood, and her green eyes were vacant.

"Are you okay, honey?" Aunt Tillie was the first one to reach the girl.

She stilled when she caught sight of us, her eyes finally focusing. She looked terrified.

Bay reached out for the girl carefully, brushing her long brown hair out of her face so she could get a better look. "Are you hurt?"

The girl didn't answer.

Bay looked to me for help. I shrugged. I had no idea what to do in a situation like this. If you need someone ticked off, call me. If you need someone to feel better, call anyone else. I knelt down in front of the girl so I could meet her gaze on an even level. "Can you tell us your name?"

Still nothing.

Aunt Tillie snapped her fingers in front of the girl's face, causing her to jolt and take a step backwards.

"Stop that," I snapped, slapping Aunt Tillie's hand away from the girl's face. "You're scaring her."

"I was just trying to see if she was deaf," Aunt Tillie sniffed.

"She's not deaf," Bay said, studying the side of the girl's head seriously. "She's hurt."

"What do you see?"

"She's got a bump," Bay said. "There's a cut right here, too. I think that's where the blood came from." Bay focused on the girl. "Do you have any other injuries?"

The girl didn't make a move to respond. She didn't shake her head, or nod. She didn't even open her mouth. She just stood there.

"I think we need to get her inside the inn," Bay said, straightening. "She's unresponsive. We need to call an ambulance."

"And the police," I added, shooting a warm smile in the direction of the girl. "I'm sure someone is missing our little friend here."

The girl suddenly made a move, just not the one I was expecting. She reached out and grabbed a piece of my blue hair, running it through her fingers as she studied it.

"It's blue," I said. "Do you like the color?"

The movement was hesitant, but the girl nodded. Well, it was something. At least we knew she understood us. I held out my hand. "Will you come with us? We can get you some food, and something to drink."

"And hopefully find out where you belong," Bay said.

The girl tentatively reached her hand out and placed it in mine as she let us lead her back to The Overlook. It wasn't much, but it was a start.

"OH, YOU POOR THING," Winnie cooed as she moved toward the anxious girl.

We'd only been inside for three minutes when our mothers descended with cookies, juice and fresh hand towels.

The girl visibly shrank as she buried her head into my side. I held up my free hand to ward them off. "You're overwhelming her."

"She's hurt," Mom said, nonplussed. "She needs to be taken care of."

"Why don't you call Landon?" I suggested to Bay. "He might be able to help us here."

Bay nodded as she pulled her cellphone out of her pocket. "I'll do it in the other room. You know, little ears … ."

"I think we should take her to the hospital," Marnie said. "She's clearly been hurt."

"I think we should feed her," Winnie argued.

"I think I should give her a hug," Mom said, dropping to her knees and holding her arms out wide. Mom's first response whenever anyone is hurt – or annoyed – is always to hug, even if her Ronald McDonald hair is enough to terrify anyone with a healthy fear of clowns.

"We're trying not to traumatize her, Mom," I said.

Mom swished her mouth from side to side, offended. "I'm not trying to traumatize her. I'm trying to … love her."

"Someone needs to get you a cat," I grumbled. I glanced down at the child. "Do you want to sit at the table?"

She shook her head.

"Would you do it if you were sitting on my lap?"

The girl tilted her head to the side, considering. Finally, she nodded. I sighed as I sat down at the end of the table and patted my lap. She climbed up quickly, immediately reaching for the glass of orange juice Winnie had placed there to entice her. She slammed it so fast I thought she was going to choke herself.

"Slow down," I said. "You can have as much of it as you want."

"Why don't we get her some water," Marnie said after a minute. "I think she might be dehydrated."

"Which means she needs food," Winnie said.

"Fine, Winnie, she needs food," Marnie said, rolling her eyes. "The answer to everything is food. You just have to be right. Why don't you see if you can shove some food down her throat and really terrorize her?"

"Why don't you shut your mouth," Winnie snapped back.

"Why don't you both shut your mouths," I suggested. I glanced back at the little girl. "Do you want some food?"

She nodded, her green eyes big.

"What do you want?"

She didn't answer.

"Do you want a sandwich? How about some soup?"

Still nothing.

"How about some cookies?" Winnie suggested.

The girl nodded enthusiastically.

Winnie disappeared into the kitchen and returned two minutes later with a plate of fresh cookies and a glass of milk. The girl shoved two of them into her mouth at the same time and munched away happily.

"She needs something more substantial than cookies," Mom said.

"We're having roasted chicken, vegetables, potatoes and chocolate cake for dinner," Marnie said. "I'm sure she can find something there that she likes."

"Do you think she's still going to be here at dinner?" I asked.

The girl stilled on my lap and stared up at me, worried.

I realized my mistake almost immediately. "You can stay here as long as you want," I said. "This is an inn. There are a lot of bedrooms, and there are a lot of people staying here. You'll be safe."

The girl didn't look convinced.

"It's going to be okay," I said. "I promise."

The girl finally started working her jaw again as she devoured the cookies. She wasn't talking, but she was relaxing – if only a little. I'd take it, for now at least.

"**LOOK** who I found out by the road selling wine."

Landon, his hand on the nape of Aunt Tillie's neck as he dragged her with him, strode into the dining room with a dark look on his face.

"We wondered where she was," Bay said, giving Landon a quick kiss.

Landon grabbed her neck long enough to deepen the kiss and then turned to everyone else. "Were you aware she was selling wine at a stand like it was lemonade?"

"We knew she was going to do it," I said. "We got distracted by ... ." I lowered my eyes to the girl on my lap. She'd refused to move, and it had been more than an hour. I was going to have to figure out a way to extricate myself from her – and soon – because I really had to go to the bathroom.

"I can't believe she used the discovery of a hurt child to go behind our backs," Winnie said.

Landon cocked an eyebrow. "I share your outrage. It's completely unlike her to use a distraction to get what she wants." Landon let go of Aunt Tillie. "You stay right here," he warned. "I'm not done with you yet."

"What is that supposed to mean?" Aunt Tillie asked.

"It doesn't mean anything," Landon said. "It just means I can only focus on one thing at a time. A small child wandering down a country road is more of a concern for me than you illegally selling wine that could kill the liver of a healthy adult in five minutes flat. That doesn't mean I'm just letting that go."

Aunt Tillie wrinkled her nose. "You're on my list."

"Well, then it should be a fun weekend," Landon said, moving slowly in my direction. It was obvious he was trying to approach the girl in the easiest way possible. "Hey, sunshine," he said, smiling widely. "How are you?"

The girl glanced up at me for support.

"This is Landon," I said. "He's a FBI agent. He's one of the good guys. He can help you."

"Don't listen to her," Aunt Tillie said. "He's trying to put me in jail. He's a bad man."

Landon shot Aunt Tillie a look.

"A very bad man," Aunt Tillie said.

The girl buried her face in my chest, her shoulders shaking. I hugged her gently, exchanging an apologetic look with Landon. "I think something bad happened to her."

"I'm going to lock you up and throw away the key," Landon growled, scorching Aunt Tillie with a look. "You're going to be sorry you ever met me."

"**I GUESS** it's good you don't have any guests until the weekend," Chief Terry said as he settled in an open chair at the dining room table.

"Yes, we love not having guests at the inn that pays our bills," Aunt Tillie replied, moving her chicken around her plate distastefully. "I told you I wanted a pot roast tonight."

Everyone ignored her.

"Try to eat some chicken," I said, prodding the little girl. I'd finally managed to get her off my lap, and leave her long enough to go to the bathroom, but she'd attached herself to my hip the minute I returned to the room. I had a feeling, until we found out where she belonged, I was going to have to find a way to deal with my new shadow.

She speared a piece of chicken with her fork and shoved it in her mouth. I watched, internally sighing as she returned her fork to the plate for more. She acted like she was starving, which made me wonder if she'd been mistreated. Other thoughts were dancing through my mind – and they were dark. I could only hope something truly awful hadn't happened to her.

"Is it good?" I asked.

The girl nodded.

"You don't have to lie," Aunt Tillie said, leaning over so she could garner the girl's full attention. "They'll still give you cookies if you don't like the chicken. Next time, tell them that you want a pot roast. When you're really old, or really young, you get whatever you want by pitching a fit. That's why it's good to be us. I'll show you how to get your own way later."

I thought the girl would be upset with Aunt Tillie's suggestion, but instead she giggled. It was the first noise she'd made since we found her on the road. It was … heartwarming.

Landon pursed his lips. "I'll arrest you for corrupting a minor," he said, forking some chicken into his own mouth. "You're on *my* list."

"Oh, I'm shaking in my boots," Aunt Tillie said. She turned to Chief Terry. "So, what do we do to help our new friend?"

I was surprised she seemed so keen on helping. This was the woman, after all, who had taken advantage of a horrible situation to make a quick buck.

Chief Terry's smile was warm and amiable as he directed it at the girl. He was clearly trying to send a message, and that message was that he was a good guy. "Well, first, I'm going to run her fingerprints," he said. "I brought a portable scanner, and Landon says he can upload them into the system with his laptop.

"Then, I was thinking we might want to take her to Dr. Williams and have her checked out," he said. "He lives here in town, so it won't be too traumatic."

The girl shook her head from side to side violently.

"Or, we can have Dr. Williams come out here," Chief Terry said, unruffled. "I just want to have that bump on your head checked out, sweetheart," he said. "No one will hurt you."

"What then?" I asked.

"I don't know," Chief Terry said. "I guess I need to see if I can get a social worker to come out here and … ." He broke off, conflicted.

"Why can't she just stay here?" Mom asked.

"You're not licensed to take in foster children," Chief Terry pointed out.

"So, we've raised children," Marnie countered. "Some of them are even tolerable."

"She clearly just needs people to take care of her," Winnie added.

Sometimes I think they *all* need cats.

Chief Terry was being pressed on three different sides. He still had one card to play, though. "What if someone dangerous is looking for her?"

"Then that person will wish they'd never come into this house," Aunt Tillie said, studying the girl thoughtfully. "Since she won't speak, though, we have to give her a name."

"Do you have any ideas?" I asked.

"I'm going to call her Basil," Aunt Tillie said.

I wrinkled my nose. "Basil?"

"What? It's a great name," Aunt Tillie said.

I shook my head and focused on Chief Terry. If we called her Basil long enough, maybe she would finally own up and tell us her real name. I knew I would. "Landon will be here, and Aunt Tillie is right, anyone who tries to come into this inn is going to be in for a rude awakening. Why can't she just stay here?"

Basil leaned forward, keenly interested as she waited for Chief Terry's decision.

"Fine," he said, rubbing the side of his face. "I know when I'm outnumbered."

"Good," Aunt Tillie said. She turned to Basil. "Are you ready for cake?"

"You haven't eaten your dinner yet," Winnie protested. "Cake is for dessert. Don't teach her bad habits."

Basil's face fell.

"Oh, fine," Winnie said. "I can't say no to that face. Who else wants cake?"

"I'm going to really like having you around," Aunt Tillie said. "We're going to have a lot of fun."

That was ... terrifying.

THREE

I stumbled into the dining room the next morning, grumpy. Since Basil had fought me returning to the guesthouse to sleep, I'd reluctantly taken a room upstairs – and shared a bed with a child that didn't stop tossing and turning the entire night. I'd finally passed out around four, and when I woke up, Basil was gone.

Bay and Landon were sitting at the table when I entered.

"You look awesome," Bay said.

I looked them up and down. They appeared well rested. Bay's skin was glowing, and Landon's smile was lazy and relaxed. It bugged me. "Why are you two so happy? I'm guessing you had the guesthouse to yourself all night."

"Clove spent the night out at the Dandridge," Bay said. "It was like a mini vacation."

Winnie appeared from the kitchen with two plates in her hand. She slid them in front of Bay and Landon. For some reason, knowing they'd slept well really irritated me. "And what did you two do on your vacation?" I asked. I knew exactly what they'd done. I also knew Bay would die of embarrassment if her mother asked any pointed questions.

"What vacation?" Winnie asked. "Your mom is bringing you out some eggs and pancakes in a second, Thistle."

"Thistle is just being grumpy," Bay said, focusing on her plate.

"I wonder why?" I said, my morning snark hitting high gear. "I had to share a bed with a kid who kicked me so many times my shins are going to be one big bruise. You two spent the night fornicating like teenagers."

Winnie pursed her lips. "What did you just say?"

"They were on vacation," I replied. "That's what you do on vacation."

Bay's cheeks were flushed, but Landon didn't appear to be bothered in the least.

"Do you think that's funny?" Winnie asked.

"I don't," I said. "I'm appalled at the lack of morality that occurred under my roof last night. Appalled, I tell you."

Landon smirked. "The only thing you're upset about is that you had to spend the night away from Marcus so you couldn't do the same thing."

Winnie smacked the back of Landon's head. "That's enough of that, young man."

Landon rubbed the back of his head. "What did I do?"

"I think she's sitting next to you," I said.

"I'm going to put you on my list with Aunt Tillie," Landon warned.

"Go ahead. I'm more afraid of her list than yours."

"Well, that's disappointing," Landon said, glancing at Bay. "You're scared to be on my list, aren't you?"

Bay shook her head. "You're a big marshmallow," she said. "Aunt Tillie is the devil."

Landon sighed. "Marshmallow?"

"I happen to love marshmallows," Bay said.

Landon rolled his eyes. "Speaking of Aunt Tillie, where is she?"

That was a pretty good question.

"I think she took Basil out to see the greenhouse," Winnie said. "She's taken a shine to her, and Basil seems to like her right back."

"Well, at least we know she's safe with Aunt Tillie," I said. "I keep hoping that, as long as we call her Basil, she'll find the courage to start talking and tell us what her real name is."

"That would be helpful," Landon agreed, snagging a slice of bacon from Bay's plate. "Right now, we just have to wait for her to trust us. She's not ready to tell us what happened. When she is, we'll be here to listen. If we're lucky, her fingerprints will hit."

"What if they don't?" I asked.

"Then we'll have to try and get Basil to talk," Landon said. "Why did Aunt Tillie pick that name, by the way?"

"To bug me," I grumbled.

Landon waited.

"I just found out yesterday that I was apparently supposed to be named Basil," I explained. "I'm deeply traumatized by the whole thing."

Landon snorted. "Is Basil somehow worse than Thistle as a name?"

"They both suck," I said. "Basil is worse."

Landon looked to Bay for confirmation.

"Basil is awful," she said. "Thistle always wished they would have named her Sage."

"That's a cool name," I said.

"Thistle fits your personality better," Landon said, finishing off his breakfast and getting to his feet. "I think we should find Aunt Tillie and Basil. I'm not crazy about them running wild all over the property."

"Aunt Tillie would never hurt Basil," I said. "She likes her."

"Thistle is right," Bay said. "Aunt Tillie was the first one to go to her. Thistle and I kind of froze in place. It was pretty impressive. She can move when she wants to."

"I'm not worried about Aunt Tillie hurting her," Landon said. "I'm worried about Aunt Tillie taking her to the pot field."

Uh-oh. I hadn't even thought of that. I got to my feet. "Yeah, let's find them."

"**OKAY,** here's what I want you to do," Aunt Tillie said. "When you see a car, I want you to smile really wide, and then dance with this in your hand."

Basil's green eyes were saucers as she took the wine bottle from Aunt Tillie.

"Twirl around a lot," Aunt Tillie said. "People can't say no to a cute little girl. That's why I always used Bay and Clove to sell stuff when they were little."

"Hey, what about me?"

Aunt Tillie turned swiftly, fixing me with a hard look. We'd surprised her. She hadn't heard us approaching. She was slipping. "You weren't a cute child."

I scowled. "I was a very cute child."

"You looked like you were hit with the ugly stick a few too many times," Aunt Tillie said. "You made up for it with a snarky personality. Don't worry. You outgrew it."

Landon snatched the bottle of wine from Basil's hand, causing her to shrink away from him. "I'm sorry, sweetheart," he said. "I ... ."

"Oh, good job, agent," Aunt Tillie said. "You've terrified an already traumatized child. Way to protect and serve."

"That's cops," Landon growled.

"Well, you're not much of a cop," Aunt Tillie said, focusing on the road. "Oh, here comes someone." She handed Basil another bottle and pushed her forward. "Dance."

Basil glanced between Aunt Tillie and Landon, worried.

"Go ahead," I said. "What? It's not like anyone is going to stop."

Basil danced a small jig at the edge of the road. She had an odd rhythm, but it was interesting to watch. To my surprise, the truck stopped. The passenger, a woman I recognized as a teacher from the elementary school, handed Basil a twenty and then grabbed the wine before her husband continued driving down the road. My mouth dropped open in surprise. "What the ... ?"

Basil handed the money to Aunt Tillie, who patted her on the head. "I knew you were going to be my good luck charm."

I watched as Aunt Tillie shoved the twenty into a metal tin on a folding chair next to her small display table. Landon followed my gaze and strode over to take the tin from Aunt Tillie. She put up a fight, but Landon was stronger – and more determined. When it opened, his mouth dropped open. He pulled out a thick wad of bills. "How much is this?"

"That's mine," Aunt Tillie said, reaching for the bills.

Landon raised them higher. "How much is this?"

"It's a thousand dollars, give or take," Aunt Tillie said. "Not that it's any of your business."

"You've made a thousand dollars in less than twenty-four hours?" I was impressed.

"I'm a good saleswoman."

"This is still illegal," Landon said.

"Oh, well, then arrest me," Aunt Tillie said, holding her hands out in front of her. "Arrest a little old lady and prosecute her for trying to scratch out a living. Way to protect the public."

"You have an inn," Landon said. "You don't need the money from this. You're just doing it to annoy everyone."

"I'm an entrepreneur," Aunt Tillie replied. "You're just jealous."

Landon glanced at Bay for support. "Do you want to chime in here?"

"I'm just wondering if selling newspapers by the edge of the road would be worth it," Bay admitted.

Landon turned to me. I held up my hands. "I'm going to bring some of the new lotions and candles I made out here. I think she's on to something."

"You people are unbelievable," Landon said, tossing the money back at Aunt Tillie and stalking back toward the inn. "Un-freaking-believable."

"HOW MUCH DID you end up with?"

I was watching Aunt Tillie count her bounty from across the dining room table. After dragging another table out to the road, and putting bottles of lotion, herbs and candles on it, we'd taken turns letting Basil dance. By the time the day was over, I'd raked in five hundred bucks – and watched Basil laugh for an entire afternoon. The laughter was worth more than the money in my book.

"It's just under sixteen hundred," Aunt Tillie said. "I'm halfway to my goal."

"What are you going to use the money for?"

"I need a new plow," she said. "Mine is shot."

Aunt Tillie likes to plow things in the winter. She says it's because she enjoys helping out those in need. Personally? I think she just likes to ram into things with her truck. Technically, she doesn't have a driver's license, so she shouldn't be plowing. No one in town – except Landon – ever calls her on it.

Basil, her cheeks pink from a little too much sun, slid into the open chair between us. She had a cookie in her hand and a smile on her face.

"Did you have fun today?" I asked.

Basil nodded.

"Are you ready to talk yet?" I pressed.

Basil pretended she didn't hear me.

Aunt Tillie watched her thoughtfully for a moment. "Don't bug her," she said finally. "She'll talk when she wants to talk."

Basil nodded in agreement.

"You know, when Thistle was little, she went an entire week without talking," Aunt Tillie said.

"I did not."

"She did," Aunt Tillie said, ignoring me. "She was mad. She thought her cousin Clove had stolen her doll and beheaded it."

A memory tugged at the recesses of my mind.

"She said she wasn't going to talk until Clove admitted doing it," Aunt Tillie said. "When someone asked her what she wanted for dinner, do you know what she did? She barked like a dog."

I wanted to argue, but the story sounded vaguely familiar.

"When someone asked her if she wanted a new doll, she barked like a dog," Aunt Tillie continued. "It was pretty freaking annoying. Finally, I had to tell her the truth – and I hate telling people the truth. Clove wasn't the one who beheaded that doll."

"It was you," I interjected.

"It was creepy," Aunt Tillie said. "It was like it was watching me. I swear it was haunted."

Basil's eyes widened.

"It wasn't really haunted," I said. "She's just making that up. She just didn't like the doll."

"It wasn't haunted," Aunt Tillie corrected. "It just wanted to be."

I shook my head. "Don't tell her that," I said. "You're going to give her nightmares. The doll wasn't haunted. It was just ugly. That's why I liked it. I knew it bothered Aunt Tillie."

"I knew it," Aunt Tillie said. "You picked out that doll from the antique store because you knew I hated it, didn't you?"

"I didn't even like dolls," I said.

Basil giggled. I tickled her ribs briefly. "Why don't you go and get washed up? Dinner will be served in a few minutes. I'll bet you're hungry."

Basil nodded and disappeared from the room. Seconds later, Chief Terry let himself into the dining room from the main foyer. "Hello, ladies." He pulled up short when he saw all the money on the table. "What's that?"

"They illegally sold goods next to the road all day," Landon said, breezing in from the kitchen with Bay and Clove on his heels. "I stayed in the guesthouse so I didn't see it and wouldn't have to arrest them."

"Holy crap," Clove said, eyeing the money. "You made that much just from selling lotion and candles next to the road?"

"It was surprisingly easy," I admitted. "I think Aunt Tillie is on to something."

"That's the smartest thing you've said all ... well ... forever," Aunt Tillie said.

"You both make me tired," Landon said, turning his attention to Chief Terry. "Anything?"

"We got a hit on her fingerprints," Chief Terry said, settling at the table and running his hand through his graying hair. "Her name is Annie Martin."

"Does she live around here?" Bay asked.

Chief Terry shook his head. "She's from Minnesota."

"What was she doing here?" I asked.

"That's a very good question," Chief Terry said. "All we know right now is that Annie Martin and her mother Belinda left the state of Minnesota three weeks ago. We don't know when they got to Michigan, and we don't know why they came to Michigan. We executed a search warrant, and we should have some credit card information tomorrow.

"For now, though, we just don't know," he said.

"What about her father?" Landon asked.

"We're trying to track him down," Chief Terry said. "From what I can tell, the parents did not live together and were never married."

"What about grandparents?" I asked.

"Her maternal grandparents are dead," Chief Terry said. "We have managed to get in contact with her paternal grandparents. They seemed surprised to hear we'd found her, but they wouldn't say why. They'll be here the day after tomorrow to collect her."

"You're just going to give her to them?" Aunt Tillie asked. "For all we know, they're the ones who hurt her."

"For all we know, her mother is the one who hurt her," Chief Terry countered. "They have the right to take her. There's nothing I can do."

Somehow, that news didn't sit well with any of us. Unfortunately, we were in a tricky spot.

FOUR

After another restless night, I woke up late the next morning. Annie was already gone, and I found my mom and Clove in the dining room when I finally stumbled downstairs on a coffee hunt.

"Your hair looks amazing," Clove said, giggling.

Why is everyone always picking on my hair? It's so unfair.

I glanced at my reflection in the mirror on the wall and cringed. My hair often has a mind of its own. This morning, apparently, it was feeling batshit crazy. Instead of engaging in a fight, I sat down next to Clove and snatched a piece of toast off of her plate. "I've been thinking about changing the color."

"Oh, that's good," Mom said. "The blue is all wrong for your complexion."

I ignored her. "Since Annie only seemed to come around when she saw my hair, I'm going to hold off until she goes home with her grandparents."

Clove's face softened as she looked me up and down. "You're worried about sending her away with her grandparents, aren't you?"

I shrugged. I wasn't sure what was bothering me. I just knew something was. "I don't think sending Annie away with people who had no idea she was even missing is a good idea."

"Why not?" Clove asked.

"Because it doesn't seem right," I said. "We found Annie walking down the middle of the road. She was dehydrated, and she had a bump on her head. We don't know if someone hit her. We don't know if she was in a car accident. We have no idea what happened to her mother."

"Maybe her mother is the one who hurt her," Clove suggested. "Maybe she ran away from her mother and is scared she'll find her."

"Maybe," I said, accepting the mug of coffee my mom slid across the table in my direction. "Or maybe something happened to her mother, and that's why she's traumatized."

Clove stilled. "Do you think someone killed her mother and she saw it happen?"

"I have no idea," Thistle said. "I just know I don't feel good about letting her go until we know what happened to her."

Mom patted my hand. "You're much more sensitive than we give you credit for."

"I'm not sensitive," I countered. "I'm just as … insensitive as I ever was. I just don't like thinking of a little kid being hurt if we can help it."

"Don't worry," Clove said, tucking her long hair behind her ear and grinning. "We'll keep telling everyone you're ornery if you want. It will be our little secret that you're really just a pussy cat in lion's clothing."

I shot her a withering look. I wasn't going to let her bait me. It wouldn't do Annie any good if she saw us fighting. Once she was gone, though? Oh, yeah, the gloves were off – and Clove was eating a whole garden of dirt. "Where is Annie, by the way?"

"Aunt Tillie took her out to the greenhouse to look around," Mom said. "She seemed excited to pick out plants. Aunt Tillie is even letting her do some potting."

I narrowed my eyes. "Are they really in the greenhouse? Or does Aunt Tillie have Annie out dancing by the road again?"

"They're really out in the greenhouse," Mom said. "Landon hid Aunt Tillie's wine stash. She's threatening him with great bodily harm, by the way, if he doesn't return it. He doesn't appear to be too worried."

"That's because she's never cursed him," I said. "Still, that was a gutsy move on his part."

"Bay is beside herself," Mom said. "She's convinced Aunt Tillie is going to curse her instead."

"Aunt Tillie probably will do just that," I said. "She loves making Bay suffer."

"She loves making all of us suffer," Clove said.

"Landon says he doesn't care," Mom said. "He's openly campaigning for the bacon curse."

I couldn't help but smirk. What is it with men and the smell of bacon? "I'm sure it will be okay," I said. "Aunt Tillie isn't going to do anything while Annie is here. She wouldn't dare. She seems to really like her.

"I think I'm going to go down to the greenhouse and collect her, though," I continued. "We have some stuff to do at the shop today, and a few hours away from this place might do her some good."

"You don't have to come to the shop if you don't want to," Clove said. "I can do everything."

"There's a big tour hitting town on Wednesday," I reminded her. "The summer season is officially set to begin. We're not ready yet."

"I can do the work," Clove said. "Annie should be your priority."

"She's really taken a shine to you, too," Mom said, her eyes sparkling. "Since children are usually terrified of you, I'm taking it as a good sign that I'll get grandchildren one day."

I finished the rest of my coffee and got up from the table. "Don't get your hopes up. Annie is only attached to me because she latched on to my hair. Once she gets over being traumatized, she won't even remember I exist."

"**THIS** IS A MAGIC SHOP," I said as I ushered Annie into Hypnotic. Clove and I had opened the store a few years ago, figuring it was a great way to embrace Hemlock Cove's magical rebranding and make a living at the same time. It had worked out well so far. We were one of the most popular – and most frequent – stops for tourists when they came to town.

Annie's eyes were bright as she glanced around.

"Go ahead," I said. "You can't break anything here. You can look around."

Annie still seemed unsure. "We just have some inventory to do," I explained. "We have to put things out on the shelves, and Bay is coming by for lunch. Do you remember Bay?"

Annie nodded.

"She's going to bring some sandwiches and potato chips," I said.

Annie seemed comfortable with the situation, and she promptly shuffled over to the tarot table in the corner and started flipping through the cards. Technically, reading tarot cards is a pre-cognitive gift. While we have hints of it in our family, no one is great at it. That doesn't stop Clove from doing readings. Most people just want to hear good things about their future, and that's a service Clove is always eager to deliver. She's a people pleaser at heart.

Clove arrived a few minutes later with a bag of cookies in her hand. "I figured you might want a treat later," she said, smiling at Annie. She studied the girl for a second. "Do you want me to show you how to use those?"

Annie glanced at me for permission.

"Go ahead," I said. "I'm going to be in the back for a few minutes, but I'll still be here. Clove is fun."

Clove beamed.

"And, if she's not fun, just kick her in the shins until she starts entertaining you," I added.

Annie giggled.

"You get more and more like Aunt Tillie every day," Clove grumbled.

"I'm taking that as a compliment," I said.

I left Annie with Clove, smiling to myself as she absorbed every quaint magical tidbit Clove bestowed upon her and got to work. Two hours later, the backroom was organized and our new inventory was

AMANDA M. LEE

spread out on the shelves. Annie had taken to organizing like a pro, and we left her to her own devices. She seemed to have a gift for it, and when she was done, the shelves were all beautifully arranged.

Bay arrived with lunch at noon on the dot, and we all settled on the couch and chairs at the center of the store for a break.

"How are you doing?" Bay asked Annie.

Annie smiled brightly in reply.

"Did you have fun here with Clove and Thistle today?"

Annie nodded.

Annie took her sandwich and chips and returned to the tarot table, sitting in one of the chairs and thumbing through the book Clove had given her to explain how the cards worked as she munched on her sandwich. I didn't think she could read – at least not at a level that the book required – but she seemed to be having fun pretending all the same.

"What did you find out?" I asked Bay, keeping my voice low.

"There's not a lot so far," Bay said. "I know that Belinda Martin got pregnant with Annie when she was eighteen. She was still in high school, but she graduated before Annie was born.

"As far as I can tell, Belinda was a good mother," Bay continued. "Annie was enrolled in school and she attended regularly. In fact, she rarely missed a day. She tested into special classes for reading and science, and never had any behavioral problems."

"How did you find that out?" Clove asked.

"I called the school she was enrolled in," Bay replied.

"And they just told you that?"

"I explained the situation here," Bay said. "They seemed eager to help. They even got Annie's teacher on the telephone. She said that Annie was bright and engaging. Everyone was surprised when Belinda yanked her out of school a few weeks ago. She didn't give an explanation."

"And she can talk, right?" I asked.

"Yes." Bay glanced over her shoulder to make sure Annie wasn't listening. "The teacher said Belinda dropped Annie off every morning and picked her up like clockwork every afternoon. While they didn't have a lot of money, Annie was always dressed in decent clothes and she was always clean. Belinda also came to every school function. She didn't miss one."

"That doesn't sound like someone who would just abandon their kid," Clove said.

"No," I agreed. "What about Annie's father?"

"There is no father listed on the birth certificate," Bay said. "Later, Jonathan Denham appeared on Annie's school documents as her father. He was never cleared to pick her up from the school, though, and he apparently never attended any of her school functions. The birth certificate was amended when Annie was five."

"I can't believe the school told you all of that," I said, impressed.

"They told most of it to Landon," Bay admitted. "He told me. They did talk to me after he cleared it, though."

"So, do we know anything about this Jonathan Denham?" Clove asked.

Bay shifted her gaze to Annie again and then leaned forward. "He was Belinda's teacher."

I made a face. "You're saying that she got knocked up by her teacher?"

Bay nodded.

"Why wasn't he prosecuted?"

Bay shrugged. "I guess we'll have to ask Jonathan's parents when they come. Of course, Belinda was eighteen when she got pregnant. There might not have been much they could do."

"I don't like this," I said, leaning back in my chair. "How old was Denham when he knocked up Belinda?"

"He was in his thirties."

"So, we have a man who had sex with his student, got her pregnant, and then didn't take responsibility for the child?"

"He appears to have taken responsibility at some point," Bay cautioned. "Landon and Chief Terry are running his background now. They're over at the police department."

"Well, I'm not okay handing Annie over to his parents," I said.

"Even if they didn't know what he'd done until after the fact, they still knew he was a demented pervert."

"I don't think we have a lot of choice in the matter," Bay said. "Chief Terry says it's the law."

I got to my feet. "Yeah? Well, we have Aunt Tillie. I believe a lot more in her powers than any law. She's not going to let this happen."

"What do you suggest we do?" Clove asked, helpless.

"We have to find out what happened to Belinda," I said. "She's the key."

"And what if Jonathan Denham killed her?"

"Then Annie isn't leaving with his parents," I said. "I don't care what we have to do to stop them."

"What if we never find out what happened to Belinda?" Bay asked. She wasn't arguing with my attempt to keep Annie safe, more with the logic I was utilizing with my efforts.

"We have to find out what happened to Belinda," I said, focusing on Annie momentarily. "Annie needs to know, and we need to help her find out."

"Okay," Bay said, getting to her feet. "I'll keep digging."

"What do you want us to do?" Clove asked.

"Just keep Annie busy and safe," Bay said. "We're going to need her to tell us what happened, and she's not going to do that until she feels safe."

"Don't worry," I said. "Keeping her safe is my top priority. I dare anyone to try and come in here and get her."

Bay smiled. "That would be a neat trick, wouldn't it?"

FIVE

When we got back to The Overlook, it was a little before three. It was too early for dinner and too late to do much else before supper. Since the season wasn't in full swing yet, we opted to close early. In an effort to engage Annie, Clove and I sat down at the dining room table and entertained her with a rousing game of Go Fish. I was hoping it would force Annie to talk. Instead, she claimed the notepad from behind the registration desk and wrote down what she wanted to ask for. At least I knew her mind was working, even if her vocal chords were refusing to play the game.

Bay arrived during our second game.

"Do you want to play?" I asked.

Bay shook her head, biting down on her lower lip as she regarded Annie. "Actually, I was thinking we could leave Annie inside to enjoy a cooking lesson with our moms while we ran an errand."

I furrowed my brow. "What are we going to do?"

"I thought we could take a quick walk out to the bluff," Bay said. "With candles."

Crap. She wanted to do a spell. "What kind of candles?"

"The blue ones."

The blue candles, in addition to smelling like blueberries, are used in locator spells. Now that she brought it up, I didn't know why we hadn't thought of it before. "That's a good idea," I said, forcing a smile on my face for Annie's benefit. "Do you think we should do it now, though?"

"I think we should do it before Landon and Chief Terry get here for dinner," Bay said pointedly. Even though both men knew about our witchy secret, neither of them liked to engage – or witness – our activities unless they absolutely had to.

Annie's gaze bounced between us curiously.

"Let's do it," I said, getting to my feet. "Come on, Annie." I held out my hand. "I know three women who are going to shower you with frosting and cake while you cook. I promise it will be fun."

I had her at frosting. She jumped up and followed me into the kitchen.

"What's going on?" Winnie asked, shifting her gaze from the roast she was tending as we entered.

"We were hoping you guys would give Annie a cooking lesson," Bay said.

"And what are you going to do?" Marnie asked, suspicious.

"We're going to take the blue candles out to the bluff for a little bit," I said.

The three women soaked in my admission.

"We would love to teach Annie to cook," Mom said, collecting the small girl from me smoothly. "I'm betting you want to learn how to make some vanilla frosting for a red velvet cake, don't you?"

Annie nodded eagerly.

"Thanks," I said. "We won't be gone long." I sent a reassuring look in Annie's direction. "And we won't be far."

"I DON'T UNDERSTAND why we're doing this," Clove said, clasping her hands together as she looked around the bluff.

She's such a worrier. It's beyond annoying. When we were in high school, she was the one who would admit to misdeeds before we were even called into the principal's office.

The piece of property where The Overlook is located has been in our possession for generations. The Overlook wasn't always an inn. In fact, it's only been an inn for several years. Before expanding on the homestead, the family was known for selling homemade goods and food. That's how we made our living. Eventually, we turned the big house into a bed and breakfast and then expanded our brand a little every year. Since expansive construction on the inn, our family has flourished. Our moms have found a calling, and we're exceedingly popular. The one thing we all agreed on, though, was that the bluff would remain untouched. That's why none of the expansion on the property has ever encroached on its beauty.

"We're going to do a locator spell," Bay said.

"To find Belinda, I know," Clove said. "How do we even know it will work? We don't have anything of Belinda's to use for the spell."

"We have her daughter," I pointed out.

"Then why isn't she out here?"

"Because we don't want to traumatize her even more," Bay said, shooting Clove a disgusted look. "If you don't want to be here, then go. No one wants to make you do anything you don't want to do. I mean, we're just trying to help a small child find her mother. Of course, your needs should come first."

I snickered. Bay was pushing Clove's buttons on purpose. I usually did that, but Annie's arrival had knocked me off my game.

"I didn't say I didn't want to help," Clove grumbled.

"Then shut up and help," I snapped. I reached into the duffel bag at my feet and pulled out a few candles. We'd returned to the guesthouse long enough to gather supplies, and while I knew Annie was perfectly safe with our mothers, I didn't like the idea of leaving her alone with their ... nonsense ... for a second longer than I had to. I just knew they'd have her in an apron with ribbons in her hair by the time I got back. They hadn't been able to dress us up for years. The opportunity to do it with Annie would be too much for them to ignore.

"You don't have to be so mean," Clove said. "I want to help Annie. That's not what I was saying."

"Then what were you saying?"

"What if the spell leads us to a dead body?"

I'd considered the possibility. "Then at least we'll know."

"What if it leads us to a killer?" Clove pressed.

"Then we'll beat the crap out of him and run," I said.

"What if it leads us to Belinda and we find that she just doesn't want her daughter anymore?" Clove wasn't giving up.

"Then we'll beat her up, too," Bay said.

"Fine," Clove said. She grabbed two candles from me and stalked to the far side of the bluff. "I just want you to know, when this goes bad – and we all know it will – I told you first."

"What makes you think this is going to go bad?" I asked.

"When have we ever done a spell and had it turn out right?"

She had a point. Still … . "We're doing it," I said.

"I just want to know why," Clove said, squaring her shoulders primly.

"Because I said so."

"More and more like Aunt Tillie every day," Clove muttered.

"I heard that."

"I meant for you to hear it," Clove said, sinking to the ground in resignation. "Let's do this. That roast they were putting together back at the inn looked good. I don't want it to be all dried out by the time we're done."

I rolled my eyes. "When have our mothers ever served a dry roast?"

"When Bay ran away from home when she was eleven," Clove said. "They forgot about it while everyone was out looking for her."

"I didn't run away," Bay protested. "I was … taking a break."

"From what?"

"You people," Bay said, settling in the spot next to Clove. "I still need a break from you people. I just call it work now."

I snorted as I sat down with them. "I don't know why you would ever need a break from us. Clove is an absolute joy, and I am the queen of all things light and love."

Bay stuck out her tongue. "You're the queen of all things annoying. Clove is right, though. Let's do this."

We joined hands and closed our eyes, concentrating so the candles flared behind us. Bay started whispering first. It didn't matter what she was saying, just that she was laying down the first thread. Clove followed suit a moment later, leaving me as the last one to jump in.

The power started to build, three small currents nudging each other and joining. Our powers never become one straight line. It's more like a wall of small lines holding on to each other. When our mothers join forces, their power lines meld as one. We weren't adept enough for it. Aunt Tillie always says it's because we're dabblers. I think it's because we're all too stubborn to hand our power over to something that is bigger than us.

It didn't matter now. We all focused intently, pushing the power to lead us to a specific spot as the spell began to grow.

The sound of approaching feet broke us from our reverie. I scowled as I turned, focusing on my mother and Marnie as they climbed the hill.

"Why did you have to climb this high?" Marnie complained. "I feel like I'm going to have a heart attack."

"You should get more exercise," Mom chided her.

"I get tons of exercise," Marnie countered.

"Torturing me is not exercise."

"It is when you do it right," Marnie shot back.

"Why are you guys up here?" I asked. If I didn't interrupt them, this could go on for hours.

Mom bit the inside of her lip as she met my angry gaze. "We … um … we … ."

"We lost Annie," Marnie admitted.

I jumped to my feet. "What?"

"We didn't mean to," Mom said. "She was sitting on the stool licking a beater. She was happy. We just had to go to the basement to get a box of canned tomatoes. We were only gone for a minute."

"When we got back, she was gone," Marnie said.

"Did you search the inn?" Bay asked, moving to my side. "Maybe she's taking a nap up in her room?"

"She's not in the inn," Mom said. "We've checked everywhere."

"Winnie called Chief Terry, and we came up to get you."

"You called Chief Terry?" Bay made a face. "That means he and Landon will be up here any minute."

"We needed help," Marnie said. "What if someone took her?"

"It wouldn't have happened if you hadn't left her alone," I snapped. "Did it really take three of you to carry a box of canned tomatoes upstairs?"

"It takes two of us to carry it," Mom sniffed.

"And they needed me to supervise," Marnie said.

I scowled. "Well, where would she go? She still has to be on the property." Something occurred to me. "Where is Aunt Tillie? Has anyone checked out by the road?"

"She has nothing to sell," Marnie said. "Landon hid all of her wine."

Bay sucked in a breath. "What about the pot field?"

I rolled my neck, cracking it loudly. "I'm going to kill her!"

"We have to find her first," Bay said, already moving down the hill.

Everyone followed her, Marnie and Mom struggling to keep up as Clove purposely loitered behind. She knew I was angry. She also knew I was probably going to pick a fight with Aunt Tillie. She didn't want to be lumped in with me in case Aunt Tillie decided to unleash vengeance. She's a total pain sometimes.

Bay and I raced to the far end of the property. We knew every rock and crevice well enough to avoid tripping as we moved. We'd played here for years. We'd hidden from our mothers as teenagers as we snuck back into the house after our curfew expired. We were sure-footed – and determined.

We hit the field at a dead run, only stopping when three figures came into view. I inhaled shakily as the small one jumped between plant rows and pointed excitedly. "Annie."

Aunt Tillie glanced up when she saw us. "What are you all doing out here?"

"Looking for Annie," I said, striding forward. "Why did you take her from the inn and not tell anyone?"

Aunt Tillie, her garden hat riding low on her brow, placed her hands on her hips obstinately. "Since when do I have to tell someone when I do something in my own house?"

"Since we've been looking for Annie everywhere," Marnie said. "We were terrified. We thought someone took her."

"No one can go into that house and take her," Aunt Tillie said. "I made sure of that."

I had no idea what she was talking about, but I had a feeling it wasn't good. She'd obviously done a spell, but that was the least of my worries right now.

"You still should have told us," Marnie said. "You could have given us heart attacks."

Aunt Tillie rolled her eyes. "You left Basil in the kitchen by herself. You weren't being very good babysitters. She wanted to come with me."

I glanced to the middle of the field where Annie was listening raptly as my boyfriend Marcus explained something to her. I still had no idea how Aunt Tillie had managed to con Marcus into helping her, but he was her right-hand man in her little pot business these days. He did it without complaint – like he did most things – and without compromise. I'd tried to talk him out of helping, but he steadfastly refused to acquiesce. "Her name is Annie."

Annie giggled so loudly I could hear it from fifty feet away. Marcus swooped her up in his arms and twirled her around like she was an airplane, causing Annie to laugh even harder. It was a cute scene.

"I've decided I like Basil better," Aunt Tillie said. "I'm going to keep calling her Basil."

"That's not her name," I said.

"And when she decides she doesn't like it, she'll tell me," Aunt Tillie said.

"But ... ."

"I'm sorry I took her without telling anyone," Aunt Tillie said, her apology taking me by surprise. "I certainly didn't mean to panic everyone. The girl needs fresh air. It's a beautiful day."

"You have her cultivating pot," I pointed out.

"She doesn't know that," Aunt Tillie said. "And we're technically not cultivating. We're just tending to some plants as they grow."

"What did you tell her it was?"

Aunt Tillie shrugged. "Oregano."

"She's going to be so messed up when she's a teenager," I grumbled. "I can't wait until some idiot tries to sell her a bag of oregano."

SIX

"So, she was just wandering around unsupervised?" Landon glanced at the assembled faces in turn, not believing us for a second.

"We're horrible babysitters," Aunt Tillie said. "That's why these three turned out to be such sneaky adults." She was gesturing at Bay, Clove and me as she spoke, her face guileless.

I bit my lip to keep from exploding.

Landon knelt down in front of Annie. "Did something happen?"

Annie shook her head vehemently.

"Would you tell me if something did?"

Annie shook her head again.

Landon sighed and got back to his feet. "I know something … odd … happened here."

"Nothing happened," Mom said. "Why are you so suspicious?"

"Because I know you guys," Landon said. "Winnie called Chief Terry. She was panicked because Annie had gone missing. She said that Marnie and Twila were off to get the girls – which means the three of you." He focused on Bay. "Where were the three of you?"

Bay averted her gaze nervously. "We were outside."

"Doing what?"

"What does it matter?" I stepped between Bay and Landon.

"Because I want to know what you were doing," Landon said firmly.

I glanced down at Annie. "Do you want more frosting? I bet my mom would love to give you more frosting."

Mom took Annie's hand. "Of course I would."

"Don't lose her again," I warned.

Mom furrowed her brow angrily. "Don't take that tone with me, young lady."

Once they were gone, I swiveled so I could meet Landon's expectant gaze. "We were doing a spell."

"I know," Landon said. "I'm not stupid. What kind of spell were you doing?"

"We were doing a locator spell," Bay said. "We were trying to find Annie's mother."

Landon sighed as he ran his hand through his shoulder-length hair. I've never understood why the FBI lets him keep it so long. Landon says it's in case he needs to go undercover. He hasn't been undercover since we met him, though. I think he just likes it – mostly because Bay enjoys running her fingers through it. He knows it makes him look hot. "Did you find anything?"

"Wait, you're not going to yell?" I was surprised he was being so calm.

"It doesn't sound like you were doing anything dangerous," Landon said. "You were trying to help. I only yell when you do something dangerous."

"You like to yell regardless," I said. "It gets you going."

Marcus moved in behind me and put his hand on my neck to still me. "Do you want to piss him off?"

"I haven't decided yet," I admitted, leaning back into him. Spending two nights in a row sharing a bed with a restless child had taught me one thing: I missed him. He made me feel … relaxed.

Marcus kissed the back of my blue head. "I think it sounds like a good idea."

"Did you find anything?" Landon asked.

"We were interrupted when our mothers lost Annie," Bay said.

"And she was just wandering around?" Landon pressed.

Bay exchanged a worried look with me. We needed to come up with a better lie. Aunt Tillie didn't give us the chance.

"She was with me," she said. "I found her in the kitchen and thought she could use some fresh air."

Landon pursed his lips. "And where were you?"

"I was communing with nature."

Landon ran his tongue over his teeth, considering. "Were you doing something you weren't supposed to be doing in nature?"

"You'll have to be more specific," Aunt Tillie said obstinately.

"Were you working in your field?"

"I have no idea what field you're referring to," Aunt Tillie lied. "I was talking to Mother Nature, and thanking her for all her blessings. Don't try to entrap me, agent. You're out of your depth."

Landon scowled. "If I find out you took that girl to help you plant pot I'm going to be really ticked off."

"I'm already ticked off," Aunt Tillie countered. "You stole my wine. I want it back."

"I didn't steal it," Landon replied. "I confiscated it for law enforcement purposes."

"You just want to drink it."

"Yeah, I like a functioning liver, thanks," Landon deadpanned. He turned when he heard the front door of the inn open to allow Chief Terry entrance. "We found her."

"Yeah, I got your text," Chief Terry said. "I'm glad she's okay."

"She was never in any danger," Aunt Tillie said. "She was with me. That's the safest place in the world."

Landon rolled his eyes.

"Where did you take her?" Chief Terry asked, curious.

"We were just out for a walk," Aunt Tillie said.

Chief Terry glanced at Landon for confirmation.

"She took her to her field," Landon said.

Chief Terry groaned. "I don't want to hear anything about a field. There is no field."

"Pretending it's not there doesn't mean it's not there," Landon said, throwing himself into one of the dining room chairs wearily. He snagged Bay around the waist and pulled her down on his lap. "The women in this family are making me feel old. I feel like the pot police."

Bay swished her lips back and forth. "Aunt Tillie says she told her it was oregano, if that helps."

"You have a huge mouth," Aunt Tillie said.

"I'm sorry," Bay said, rubbing the crease between her eyebrows. "I just don't see the point in lying. He knows it's there."

"You're on my list," Aunt Tillie said, extending a finger in Bay's direction. "You were already there because of the wine, but now you're on top."

"I don't have the wine," Bay protested. "He won't tell me where he put it."

"That's because I know you'll give it back to her," Landon said. "You live in fear of whatever deranged thing she's going to do next. I don't have that problem."

"You could have if you're not careful," Aunt Tillie warned.

"Bring it on," Landon said, his fingers restlessly roaming through the ends of Bay's hair as he thought. "Did you find anything else out about Jonathan Denham?"

Chief Terry settled in the chair next to Landon. "I found out he lost his job at Dorchester High School in Minnesota about a year after Belinda Martin graduated," he said.

"Is that because he was sleeping with his students?" I asked.

"The official reason was cutbacks," Chief Terry said. "The cops out there admitted the school fired him after they found out about Belinda, though. She was legally an adult, so he didn't do anything criminal. The school can fire him for ethical breaches, though, and that's exactly what they did."

"So, what did he do?"

"He tried to find another job teaching, but he wasn't able to secure one," Chief Terry replied. "Even though nothing official was ever put in his file, apparently someone called all the schools in the state and made them aware of Denham's history."

"Good," I said.

"Do you think it was Belinda?" Bay asked.

"I don't know," Chief Terry said. "She had every reason to do it."

"And it might be a reason for someone to try and get revenge on her," Landon said.

My heart stuttered. "Are you guys just assuming Belinda is dead?"

"We're not assuming anything, Thistle," Chief Terry said. "We don't have a lot of facts. Technically, we don't even have a case here. We have an abandoned child who was found wandering around the countryside in a state she doesn't legally reside in."

"I think something else is going on," I said, crossing my arms over my chest.

"What?" Clove asked.

"I don't know," I said. "I just think Annie is struggling with something, and we have to give her the chance to tell us what it is. She needs time."

"She doesn't have time," Chief Terry said. "Her grandparents are going to be here for her tomorrow. She's going to be put into their custody."

"NO!"

We all jolted at the sound of the voice. Annie was standing in the archway between the kitchen and dining room, and her green eyes were wide and filled with terror as she stared at us.

I took a step toward her. "You talked."

Annie's face crumpled as she dissolved into tears.

"It's okay," I said, reaching for her so I could draw her in for a hug. "It's good to talk."

Annie shook her head. Her body was trembling. I turned to Marcus for help. He immediately swooped in and gathered her up in his arms. He sat down on one of the open chairs at the table and rocked her while she cried.

"It's okay," he said. "We won't let anyone hurt you."

"He's right," I said. "Everyone here wants to help you. We need you to speak if we're going to do it, though."

"That's right, Basil," Aunt Tillie said, touching the top of the girl's head as Marcus swayed with her in his arms. "Tell us what happened."

It's funny. I don't remember Aunt Tillie being particularly sweet when we were children. There were times, though, and it was usually when we'd done something wrong and were in trouble with our mothers. She was the one who swooped in with a hug – and usually a reward – to make us feel better. What can I say? The woman does like her mayhem. She was often the one who encouraged us to be naughty. Now? Now Aunt Tillie was bolstering Annie the best way she knew how, and I couldn't help but be thankful for it.

"So, Basil, tell us what you remember," Aunt Tillie prodded.

"I don't like the name Basil," Annie said.

"Well, if you want me to stop using it, you have to tell me what you remember," Aunt Tillie said. She was back to being herself, and I couldn't help but be thankful for that, too. If anyone could push Annie into talking, it was her.

"I don't know what I remember," Annie admitted, her lower lip trembling. "I … it's all fuzzy."

"Okay," I said, keeping my voice level. "Let's talk about home. Do you remember being home with your mother?"

Annie nodded.

"What's the last thing you remember about home?" I asked.

"I remember Mommy picking me up from school," Annie said. "She seemed sad. She said we were leaving. She said we were going to move to a new place. She had a bunch of my stuff in the car."

"That's good," I encouraged her.

Marcus rubbed her back. He was still rocking her, but the movements were deliberate and slight. He was lulling her into a feeling of safety.

"Did you drive straight here?" Landon asked.

"We drove a long time," Annie said. "We had a new house. It was by itself."

"By itself?"

"There were no other houses around like before," Annie said. "It was just our house."

"How big was the house?" Chief Terry asked.

Annie shrugged.

"Was it as big as this house?" I asked.

Annie shook her head.

"Was it a lot smaller?"

"There were only two bedrooms," Annie said. "One for me, and one for Mommy."

"How long were you in the house?" Bay asked.

"I don't know," Annie said.

"Did you spend a few nights there?" Bay tried again.

"Yes," Annie said. "I was scared because of the trees by the house. Mommy slept in my room with me."

"That sounds like a good mommy," I said.

"I want my mommy," Annie said, breaking off into another crying jag.

I licked my lips. We needed more information, but I wasn't sure how hard to press Annie. I didn't want her to forget how to talk again. "Did your mommy put you in school here?"

Annie shook her head. "I'm on summer vacation. She said I would go to a new school in the fall."

Crap. That made sense. Annie would have only missed a few weeks of school when Belinda decided to move. That must have been part of her plan.

"Do you think your house is close to here?" Bay asked.

Annie shrugged.

"We should check with everyone that has rental property," Chief Terry said. "If Belinda bought a house, we would have found that when we ran her financials. I think she was living off cash, but she couldn't buy a house with cash."

"That's a good idea," Landon said.

"Do you remember going somewhere with your mommy?" I asked.

Annie's face was anguished. "I don't remember."

"It's okay," I said.

"It is," Marcus said, increasing his rocking pace. "It's going to be okay."

"I want my mommy," Annie wailed. "I want my mommy!"

Well, that was one thing we could all agree on. We all wanted her to have her mommy. I could only hope we weren't too late.

SEVEN

"Well, at least she's talking," Landon said. He was standing in the archway between the dining room and lobby watching Mom and Winnie dote on Annie at the rectangular table.

Dinner had been tense. Everyone had gone out of their way to make Annie feel comfortable – even Aunt Tillie – and the girl had slowly come out of her shell. She was insistent on remaining close to Marcus and me, so we settled on either side of her and urged her to eat.

Finally, with the introduction of a red velvet cake, Annie agreed to let Mom, Marnie and Winnie take care of her. She looked exhausted, but she was fighting every attempt to get her to go upstairs and sleep.

"We need to find Belinda," Bay said. "She's the only one who can answer our questions."

"She was obviously scared of something," Landon said. "Why else would she pack up everything, pick up the kid from school, and then flee the state?" He turned to Chief Terry. "Has anyone checked her phone records?"

"On what authority?"

"The authority that her child was found wandering country roads alone," Landon said.

Chief Terry sighed. "No one has reported her missing."

"Annie has," I challenged.

"Annie can't remember what happened," Chief Terry countered. "For all you know, Belinda tossed Annie out of the car and drove away."

"Then she committed a crime," I pressed.

"I'm not arguing with you, Thistle," Chief Terry said. "I happen to agree with you. Everything we've found out about Belinda Martin seems to imply that she's a good mother. She doesn't sound like the type of mother who would just abandon her child. I still have to work within the confines of the law."

"He's right, Thistle," Landon said. "There's nothing he can do. We've circulated her photograph to other law enforcement agencies in the area. We've contacted Annie's next of kin. What more do you want?"

"Yeah, and did you see Annie's reaction when we mentioned her grandparents coming?"

Landon cracked his neck. "Yeah. That wasn't good."

"We need to find out what's wrong with the grandparents," I said.

"I'll find out about the grandparents," Aunt Tillie said, breezing into the room from the front door of the inn.

Landon shifted. "Where were you?"

"Outside," Aunt Tillie said. "I like to take a walk after I eat. It helps with the digestion process."

Landon narrowed his eyes. "Since when?"

"Why are you always such a pain in my posterior?" Aunt Tillie asked. "Last time I checked, I was an adult. That means I can wander around outside as much as I want."

"Yes, but I don't trust you," Landon said. "I know when you're lying."

"Because her lips are moving?" I have no idea why I don't just shut up sometimes.

"You just took Bay's spot on the top of the list," Aunt Tillie said.

I groaned. "I didn't mean it."

"Oh, you meant it."

"Oh, fine," I said, giving in. "Just don't mete out any revenge until everything is settled with Annie. We don't want to terrify her."

"I'm not stupid," Aunt Tillie said.

"You're not stupid," Landon agreed. "You are sneaky and vindictive, though."

Aunt Tillie stuck her tongue out at him.

"Why can't you put him on top of your list?" I whined.

"He's got his own list," Aunt Tillie replied.

Bay was getting sick of our arguing, so she interrupted. "How are you going to get Annie to tell you about her grandparents?"

"I'm going to ask her."

"Nicely," I stressed. "You're going to ask her nicely, right?"

"Of course I am," Aunt Tillie said. "I'm always nice." She turned on her heel and flounced out of the room.

"Does anyone else think it's a bad idea to let Aunt Tillie question Annie?" Clove asked.

"I love how you always wait until she leaves the room to trash talk her," I said.

"That's why I'm usually the one who escapes when you two get cursed," Clove retorted.

"Yes, everyone loves a coward."

Marcus grabbed my hand. "Now is not the time for this," he said.

I hate it when he's right.

"So, what should we be doing now?" I asked.

"We finish what we started this afternoon," Bay said. "Everything is still up on the bluff, right where we left it."

I nodded. "That seems to be our only option."

Landon shifted so he was facing us. "I'm going with you."

"Why?" I didn't want to perform like a monkey for his amusement.

"Because, if you find a trail, you're going to need someone to go with you when you follow it," he said. "You might need someone to …"

"What? Protect us?"

"Call for help," Landon corrected. "We don't know what you're going to find."

I sighed. He was making sense. "Okay. Let's do it."

"I'm coming, too," Marcus said, following us as we moved toward the front door of the inn.

"Why are you coming?" I asked.

"I just want to be there with you," Marcus said, his smile warm as he gave me a quick kiss. "We've been apart for days."

"Oh, you two are just so sweet," Bay teased.

Landon tugged on her arm. "You're going to be sweet to me when all of this is over and done with."

"I'm always sweet to you," Bay protested.

"You're going to be sweeter than that," Landon said. "I'm going to want outfits."

"OKAY, SO WHAT DO WE DO?" Marcus asked, looking around the bluff dubiously.

I snapped my fingers to ignite the candles. It was a calm night, and when they flickered to life, they showed no signs of going out. "You and Landon stand over there," I said. "We need to be able to concentrate."

"You have to be quiet," Bay cautioned. "This spell is tricky because we don't have anything of Belinda's to anchor it."

"What does that mean?" Landon asked. He was curious about our magic, especially since Bay had put on a little show for his benefit a few weeks before, but I could tell he was still leery.

"If we had something of Belinda's it would be easier," Bay replied. "The only thing we have of hers is Annie, and she can't see this."

"Is it going to be scary?" Marcus asked.

"From your perspective, it's just going to look like a small light show," I said.

"Like what happened at the Dragonfly during the fake séance last week?"

I nodded.

"Well, that wasn't so bad," Marcus said, relaxing.

"Until the real ghost showed up," Landon grumbled.

"We're not using the same kind of magic," Bay soothed.

"I said I was cool with this," Landon said. "I'm not backing out. I want to see. Don't worry."

Bay smiled. "I'll wear an outfit."

Landon's eyes lit up. "I want to pick it out."

"Fine," Bay said. "If I look like a strip of bacon when you're done, though, we're totally breaking up."

Landon broke into a grin. "Hey, now that you mention it … ." He gave her a quick kiss. "Get to work, woman. I don't want to put too much pressure on you, but we're running out of time."

"Right," Bay said, snapping out of her reverie. "Let's do this."

We returned to our spots from earlier this afternoon and settled back in our circle, knees touching knees as we crossed our legs, and joined hands. Bay started first again. Clove and I joined her moments later, our power jumping with excitement as we let it out to play.

"That is awesome," Marcus murmured.

Landon shushed him.

I pressed my eyes shut, forcing myself to concentrate even though having Landon and Marcus watch us felt strange. After a few minutes, the feeling drained away and I was lost to the flickering magic.

The spell was more powerful now. I had no idea if it was because we were more dedicated, or if the ticking bomb that accompanied Annie's grandparents and their arrival was propelling us. It didn't matter.

"I'm not sure we're strong enough," Bay murmured. "It's like the magic wants to be let out to play, but there are walls in the way."

"Of course there are walls in the way," Aunt Tillie said, climbing the hill with a huff and a glare. "Why did you have to come up here?"

"It's pretty," Clove said.

"Yes, but I don't like to climb the hill," Aunt Tillie said. She moved over to us and wedged herself between Bay and me. "Move over."

"What are you doing?" Bay asked, shifting.

"I'm fixing your circle," Aunt Tillie said. "It's not strong enough for what you're trying to do."

"It might work," I said.

"It won't," Aunt Tillie said. "It won't work until you three stop screwing around and really give in to what you are. You're not ready yet, and we don't have time for you to get ready."

Landon was leaning against a nearby tree as he watched the scene curiously. "Why aren't they ready?"

"Because they're scared," Aunt Tillie said.

"I thought they were strong?"

"Of course they're strong," Aunt Tillie said. "I raised them to be strong. They're not ready to give in and let the magic take over. It's because they're strong that they fight it. That's not a bad thing."

"But they need you for this?" Landon asked.

"I'm the mightiest witch in the land, boy," Aunt Tillie said. "Everyone needs me."

I fought the urge to giggle. She does have a way with people.

"Okay," Aunt Tillie said, joining hands and entering our circle. "Now I'm going to show you how to do a locator spell."

"We're all ears," I said.

"And eyes," Bay added.

Clove's stomach picked that second to growl. "What? I didn't get dessert."

"Focus," Aunt Tillie snapped, her gaze fixated on the swirling lights in front of us. "Annie says she doesn't even know her grandparents. That can't be a good thing. We need to do this, and we need to do this right. Envision what you want."

We were all quiet for a moment, everyone doing as they were instructed.

"Stop thinking about the cake, Clove," Aunt Tillie chided. "It will be there when we're done."

"I wasn't," Clove protested.

I shot her a look.

"Okay, I was," Clove admitted. "I'll do better."

Once Aunt Tillie infused her magic with ours, the tendrils of colorful light exploded into the air. At first, each tendril went in a different direction. The lights climbed into the night sky before arcing back inwards and colliding into a big ball of light with a spectacular splash.

The freshly joined light hovered above us. Unmoving.

Aunt Tillie got to her feet, seemingly nonchalant, and brushed the dirt from her pants. "Okay. Let's go."

Landon arched an eyebrow. "Where are we going?"

"Wherever the light takes us," Aunt Tillie said.

"And what if we have to walk miles to find our destination?" Landon asked. "Do you think you can walk that far?"

"Who said anything about walking?" Aunt Tillie rolled her eyes as she reached over and flicked Landon on the ear. "You're driving."

Landon sighed. "Let's go."

When we got to his Explorer, Landon piled everyone inside. It was a tight squeeze, but with Marcus in the front seat with Landon, the four of us managed to wedge ourselves into the back seat, Aunt Tillie sitting on half of my lap and half of Bay's. Landon paused as he was rounding his vehicle and peered into the rear hatchback. He swore under his breath as he jumped into the Explorer.

"I knew you were up to something," he said.

"I have no idea what you're insinuating," Aunt Tillie sniffed.

"I had your wine in the back," he said. "It's gone."

"Huh," Aunt Tillie mused. "That's just awful. You should probably report the theft. Stealing from law enforcement has to be the lowest of the low."

"We're going to talk about this later," Landon promised.

"I can't wait," Aunt Tillie said. "I love a good cockfight. All that preening and posturing is good for my skin."

"I just ... ." Landon shoved his key into the ignition. "You're definitely dressing up like bacon, Bay. I've earned it."

EIGHT

"How are we going to explain this if someone sees us?" Marcus asked, peering out the front window so he could keep his eye on our speeding ball of light.

"I plan on telling people I was seduced by evil," Landon said, sending a reassuring wink to Bay in the rearview mirror.

"Watch yourself, fresh mouth," Aunt Tillie said.

"Who says I was talking about Bay?" Landon teased. "I'm going to blame you."

"You're going to tell people I seduced you?" Aunt Tillie was nonplussed.

Landon scowled. "No."

"That's what seduced means, dim bulb."

"Just … focus on your ball of light," Landon instructed. "It's not going to do us any good if it dissipates before we get to our destination."

"Young man, my spells don't dissipate," Aunt Tillie said. "Turn right at the next road."

"Are you sure?"

"If you continue doubting me, I'm going to kick you out of this truck and drive it myself," Aunt Tillie warned.

"It's my truck."

"I don't care."

Landon growled. "You drive me crazy."

"Welcome to the family," Aunt Tillie shot back.

I saw a small smile playing at the corner of Landon's lips in the mirror as he focused on the road.

"Slow down," Aunt Tillie instructed.

We'd been driving for about twenty minutes, our ball of light leading us over at least six different roads as we traveled farther into the country surrounding Hemlock Cove.

"If Annie walked the entire way to the inn, she must have been at it for almost a day," Bay said. "Even if she cut across fields."

"She's lucky she found us at all," Thistle said. "There's nothing out here."

"There's the old Henderson place," Marcus said thoughtfully.

I shifted, Aunt Tillie's weight starting to make me uncomfortable despite her diminutive size as she rested on my lap. "What's the old Henderson place?"

"You're right," Aunt Tillie said, tapping her lower lip. "I forgot about Zeke's place."

"Who is Zeke?" Landon asked.

"Zeke Henderson."

Landon made a face. "Really? Zeke Henderson lived at the Henderson house? I'm shocked."

"Just keep digging yourself in," Aunt Tillie said.

"Zeke Henderson was kind of a hermit," Marcus supplied. "He lived out here in the middle of nowhere for years. His house was pretty run down, more of a shack than anything else. He didn't have any friends, and he terrorized most of the townspeople so much that they stayed away from him."

"Oh, he sounds perfect for Aunt Tillie," Landon said.

"Dig, dig, dig."

"Anyway, when he finally died a few years ago, people didn't even realize it until his taxes went unpaid," Marcus said. "Chief Terry finally went out to check on him and found he'd been dead for months."

"Does anyone own the house?" Landon asked.

"I think it was bought at auction," Marcus said, wracking his brain. "I just can't remember who bought it. If anyone did buy it, they're not living out there. I think you'd have to be desperate to rent it."

"It sounds to me like Belinda was desperate about something."

"We just have to figure out what," I said.

Aunt Tillie sat up straighter. "Stop here."

"Where?" Landon asked, looking around blankly.

"Here!"

Landon slammed on his brakes. He put the Explorer into park and then shifted so he was facing us in the back seat. "Is there a reason you felt the need to scream?"

"That seems to be the only time you listen," Aunt Tillie said. She pushed open the back door of the Explorer and hopped out.

"What are we doing here?" Landon asked, pocketing his keys and following her out onto the road. "What do you expect to find?"

"Whatever the spell wants to show us."

"Which is?"

Aunt Tillie held her finger to her lips.

Landon huffed and stalked to the side of the road. His eyes were busy as they traveled across the underbrush searching for clues.

"What are we supposed to be looking for?" I asked.

Aunt Tillie shrugged. "Whatever we're here to find."

"Are you purposely trying to be cryptic?"

"I ... ."

"Over here!"

Everyone's eyes snapped up as Bay jumped down from the embankment and moved under the small bridge about fifty feet away from Landon's Explorer.

"Bay!" Landon was following her. "Be careful, Bay. If you hurt yourself, I'm going to kill you."

I raced after them, stumbling as I slid down the steep embankment. Landon caught me before I could hit the ground.

"Let's all be careful, shall we?"

"Sorry," I said. "I was just excited. What did she find?"

"It's a car," Landon said. "It looks like it was driven off the road from the opposite direction. No one saw it because it was hidden down here."

"Is … is it empty?"

"I don't know," Landon said. He let go of my arms and bent down next to the driver's side window. "Stand back."

"Why? Someone could be hurt inside," I argued.

"And someone could be dead inside," Bay said, taking a step back.

"We won't know until we open the door," I said, refusing to give in to the fear washing over Bay's face.

"Stay there, Thistle," Landon warned. He used the edge of his shirt to cover the door handle, trying to preserve evidence I'm sure, and then gave it a tug. The door sprang open, and my gaze immediately traveled to the pale hand hanging next to the seat. It wasn't moving.

"Is she … ?"

Landon reached his hand inside and pressed it to the occupant's neck. I couldn't see if it was a man or a woman, but intuition told me we'd found Belinda. "She's alive," he said. "Her pulse is faint, but it's there. We need to get some help out here." He pulled his cellphone out of his pocket. "Tell Aunt Tillie to get rid of that light. I refuse to explain that to emergency personnel."

"SO, WHAT DO WE KNOW?"

Chief Terry had arrived at the hospital minutes after the ambulance carrying Belinda. We were twenty minutes behind, so we were hoping he had some sort of an update on her condition.

"She's in bad shape," Chief Terry said. "She's was trapped in that car for days. If we work backward, I'd have to guess the accident happened about three days ago. Maybe earlier. We have no idea how long Annie was wandering around out there."

"So, she got the bump on her head in the accident?"

"That would be my guess," Chief Terry said. "I called out to the inn. Your mothers are bringing Annie here now."

My heart flopped. "What? Why?"

"Because that's her mother," Chief Terry said.

"But … what if she doesn't survive?"

"Then Annie deserves a chance to say goodbye," he said.

"What if it traumatizes her?"

"I don't know, Thistle," Chief Terry said, aggravated. "If it was you, what would you want more, never to see your mother again or to say goodbye?"

I knew he was right. Still … . "You should have waited until you knew more."

"He's not sure how much time we have, Thistle," Landon said.

"But we found her," I protested. "She's got a shot to survive."

"She does have a shot," Chief Terry said. "She's got an even bigger shot at dying."

I didn't want to hear this. "Well, I'm glad you've got so much faith."

Marcus walked up behind me and wrapped his arms around my waist as he rested his chin on my forehead. "It's not his fault, Thistle."

"No," I agreed. "It's ours. We should have done the spell the day Annie showed up."

I could see the same guilt washing over Bay's face that was coursing through my veins. "She's right."

"Don't do that," Landon said, drawing Bay in for a hug. "We all did what we could."

"It should have occurred to us, though," I argued. "We should have been more proactive."

"We can't go back in time and change things," Aunt Tillie said. "We have to look forward."

"Are you a fortune cookie now?" I wasn't really angry with Aunt Tillie. I was just frustrated. She was an easy target because she fought back.

"You need to calm yourself," Aunt Tillie said. "We're not going to be able to help Basil if you don't."

"Her name is Annie!" The light bulb in the lamp at the nurse's station exploded, causing the receptionist to take cover, the same moment my temper did.

Landon flinched. "Did you do that?"

I bit my bottom lip. I wasn't sure.

"She's out of control," Aunt Tillie said. "She needs to cool off. Her emotions are taking over."

Landon's face was thoughtful. "That happened in Bay's bedroom the other day. Are you saying they can do that?"

Aunt Tillie scowled. "Thistle did it because she was enraged. I think Bay might have done it for another reason."

Landon's chest puffed out slightly.

"Yes, you're a stud," Aunt Tillie said, rolling her eyes as she patted his chest dismissively. "That's clearly the important thing here now."

Landon deflated. "We need to put our heads together," he said. "Annie's grandparents arrive tomorrow. We have no choice but to hand her over if Belinda doesn't wake up."

"We can't do that," I argued.

"That's why we have to come up with a plan."

"I could take her and run," Aunt Tillie offered.

"We have to come up with a plan that isn't illegal," Landon said.

"Legal shmegal," Aunt Tillie said. "We have to do what's right."

"Before anyone even thinks of running off with that child, we're going to put our heads together," Landon said. "I can't condone anyone running with her, and I can't look the other way. This is too big."

Aunt Tillie sighed. "Fine. I won't run away with her."

"I know you're just saying that to get me to lower my guard," Landon said. "It's not going to work."

Aunt Tillie opened her mouth to argue, but she snapped it shut when Mom, Winnie, and Marnie turned the corner and headed in our direction. They had Annie in tow, and the girl was tugging so forcefully on Winnie's hand she was having trouble keeping up.

"Did you find my mommy?" Annie's eyes were hopeful.

"We found her car on the side of the road," Landon said carefully. "She was inside."

"Where is she? I want to see her."

"The doctors are working on her right now," Landon said.

"But I want to see her," Annie said, jutting her lower lip out into a pronounced pout.

Landon was patient, but firm. "I know you do, honey, but the doctors need to fix her up first."

"But ... ."

Marcus swooped in and gathered Annie up in his arms. "How about we go and check out the vending machine situation?" he offered. "I'm betting some candy will make you feel better."

"Will I be able to see my mommy when we come back?"

"We'll see," Marcus said, leading Annie down the hallway. "We have to let the doctors do their work. They're very good at what they do."

"Okay."

I watched them go, my heart filling with thanks that I'd found someone as wonderful as Marcus. The feeling didn't last long.

"Where is she?" I tilted my head as an older woman and man rounded the corner, their gazes landing on me first. "Are you the woman who has our granddaughter?"

My heart started to hammer.

"Who are you?" Chief Terry asked, stepping forward.

"Officer," the woman said, nodding to greet him. "I'm Arlene Denham, and this is my husband Tom. We're here looking for our granddaughter."

"I'm the one you talked to on the phone, ma'am," Chief Terry said.

"Is my granddaughter okay? Why is she here?"

Chief Terry narrowed his eyes. "How did you know we were here?"

"We got into town early," Arlene said. "The man answering the phone at your office told me you were here."

Chief Terry nodded. "I see."

"Why are you here? Is Annie okay?"

"Annie is fine," Chief Terry said. "She's getting a treat with a friend."

"You just let her wander off with a stranger?" I didn't like Arlene on sight. "Well, great, let's send my grandchild off with a potential child molester."

"Hey," I snapped.

"He's not a stranger," Chief Terry said, raising a hand to still me. "He's been helping to take care of Annie."

"Why did she need someone to take care of her?" Arlene asked. "Is it because her irresponsible mother abandoned her?"

"Her mother is here, too," Chief Terry said.

Arlene jerked at the news. I couldn't tell if it was surprise because she thought Belinda was dead, or surprise because she really thought Belinda had abandoned Annie. "Belinda is here? If Belinda is here, why did you call us?"

"Belinda was hurt very badly in a car accident," Chief Terry explained. "We believe Annie was hurt in that accident as well, but she has no memory of it. We discovered Belinda's car this evening. She's in pretty bad shape, but the doctors are working on her right now."

Arlene straightened. "Well, I hope she'll be okay."

"We all do, ma'am," Chief Terry said. "It might be a little while until we know something, though."

"Well, I still think it's prudent that we take Annie," Arlene said. "She shouldn't be hanging around a hospital all night. We'll get a hotel room and take her with us."

I balked. "She wants to be near her mother."

"She's a child," Arlene said. "She doesn't know what she wants."

"Still, ma'am, I think it's best to wait until we have more information about Belinda's prognosis," Chief Terry said. "We still don't know what caused the accident, and Annie is already traumatized. I think she should remain here until we know more."

"Are you her parent?" Arlene challenged.

"No, ma'am. You're not either, though."

I didn't notice the man sidling up behind the Denhams until he was almost on top of them. "No, she's not Annie's parent," the man said. "I am, though, and I want my daughter."

I felt as if the floor was dropping out from beneath me. "Jonathan Denham."

NINE

"You're Jonathan Denham?"

The man was handsome – for a low-life pervert. His short brown hair was neat, with just a hint of gray at the temples. His brown eyes were dark and predatory, and his smile was pleasing – even though I wanted to kick his teeth in on sight. Actually, I wanted to kick his teeth in and then pour some lemon juice in there just for good measure. Oh, and then I wanted to glue his mouth shut – but only after I cut all of his fingers off and shoved them into his mouth so he'd have something to chew on. Yes, I know, I'm incredibly mean and vindictive. Maybe I am turning into Aunt Tillie? Oh, who am I kidding? I'm way meaner than Aunt Tillie ever dreamed of being.

"I see my reputation precedes me," Denham said, his dimple coming out to play as he smiled in my direction. "And who are you?"

"This is Thistle Winchester," Chief Terry said, stepping in smoothly. "She was one of the people who found Annie."

"Well then, I guess I owe you a world of thanks," Denham said. "If it weren't for you, she might have wandered around the countryside until she died of exposure."

Something told me he would have preferred that outcome. "Well, that's not what happened," I said, forcing my tone to remain even. "We found her, and we took care of her."

"Oh, are you foster parents?" Denham was playing a dangerous game, and I wanted him to lose.

"No."

"Then how did my daughter end up with you?"

"She was traumatized after the accident," Chief Terry explained. "She wouldn't speak. She seemed attached to Thistle … ."

"And me," Aunt Tillie chimed in.

"And Tillie," Chief Terry said, not missing a beat. "We didn't want to traumatize her even more than she already was. The Winchesters run an inn. They had plenty of room, and food, and people to watch Annie. She was spoiled rotten during her stay."

Denham glanced around the room, his face unreadable. "Well, then I guess I owe you all thanks."

"You're welcome," Aunt Tillie said.

Denham smiled down at her. I knew what he saw: A sweet old woman who he could charm and wrap around his finger. He was in for a surprise. "I'll just bet you gave my little girl all the love she could ever need."

Aunt Tillie remained silent, but I could see her mind working from here.

"I'm sure it wasn't easy," Denham continued. "It's hard to take care of a little girl who won't speak. It's too bad she can't talk. She might have been able to tell you what happened to her mother. That is a tragedy."

"Belinda is alive." I took perverse pleasure in telling him.

Denham remained still, but I could swear his eyes momentarily flashed. "If Belinda is alive, why did you call us?"

"We just found her tonight," Landon said. "Her car was wrecked and hidden under an old creek bridge. She was alive, though. The doctors are working on her now."

"And what did she … tell you?" Denham asked.

"She hasn't woken up yet," Chief Terry said.

Denham's shoulders relaxed. "Is she going to wake up?"

"We're not sure yet."

"She's going to wake up," I said. "She fought this long. She'll wake up. She has something to live for."

"Do you have a problem with me?" Denham asked, the question a challenge.

"No, she doesn't," Chief Terry said. "Everyone is just worked up this evening."

"I have a problem with you," Aunt Tillie announced. For once, I was on her side.

Denham raised his eyebrows, placating the sweet old lady he saw in his mind with a smile. "Because I didn't get here fast enough? I am sorry. It was a long drive."

"Because you're a sick pile of bat droppings that's sat out in the sun too long and petrified," Aunt Tillie replied, matching him evil grin for evil grin.

Denham was taken aback. "Excuse me?"

Aunt Tillie wasn't anywhere near being done. "What kind of a man seduces and has sex with a high school student?"

"A sick one," I supplied.

"A sick one," Aunt Tillie agreed. "A predator. I'm guessing you preyed on Belinda because she was young and she didn't have a lot of parental influence. You knew exactly what you were doing. The pregnancy probably took you by surprise, but I'm sure your parents either paid her off – or threatened her off – to keep your name off that birth certificate."

"Now you wait just a minute," Denham said, raising a hand in protest.

"I'm not done," Aunt Tillie said. "You're a very lucky man, because if you'd messed with one of my girls like you did with Belinda, I would have cursed your manhood until it fell off."

Out of the corner of my eye I could see Landon push his tongue into his cheek to quiet himself, but he didn't make a move to stop her from rambling.

"Now, I'm sure there's not much manhood there to curse, and my eyes aren't what they used to be, but I'm thinking I would have found a way around that," Aunt Tillie said. She glanced at me and winked. "In fact, I think Thistle has a magnifying glass. We could have just sat you out naked in the sun and burned your little twig off without cursing it. It also would have allowed us to find it, because I'm betting you have to go after high school girls because they don't know how big a real one is supposed to be."

"I don't have to take this abuse," Denham said.

"I agree," his mother said, moving to his side. "We're here to claim our property."

"Property?" I hate these people. "A child is not property."

"She is our blood," Arlene said. "You take care of your own blood."

"She's also Belinda's blood," I said.

"Well, Belinda doesn't appear to be able to take care of her," Arlene said.

"Belinda is in the other room fighting for her life," I argued. "When she wakes up, she's going to want her daughter."

"Well, if that happens, then I'm sure we can set up some sort of visitation," Arlene said.

"Visitation? That's her daughter."

"We have an appointment with a local attorney tomorrow morning," Arlene said. "Our son will be getting custody of his daughter in an emergency session if we have anything to say about it."

"You can't just do that," I said. I turned to Landon. "She can't do that, can she?"

Landon looked helpless. "I'm not up on custody issues, Thistle."

"You're with the FBI, though," I pressed. "You should be able to stop them."

Denham shifted his full attention to Landon. "Why is the FBI here?" He seemed nervous. From the look on his face, Landon noticed it, too.

"I'm friends with the family," he said. "I was here for the weekend when Annie was discovered, and I was one of the people who found Belinda's car tonight."

"Oh, well, thank you then," Denham said primly.

"I'll also be heading the investigation into her accident," Landon said, his eyes focused on Denham. He was testing him.

"What investigation?" Arlene asked. "Surely it was just an accident."

"Well, there were some interesting marks on the road," Landon said. "We have a crime scene team out there right now taking photographs and measurements. We're also having the car brought in and looked at by a licensed mechanic to make sure it wasn't tampered with. Because of the nature of the accident, a full investigation seems to be warranted."

He was making that up. He hadn't paid any attention to the road while we were out there. It was too dark. He was bluffing. Since his words were visibly shaking Denham, I was happy to play along with the gambit.

"And Annie will be a ward of the state while the investigation is ongoing, right?" I asked.

Chief Terry put his hand on my shoulder. "She will," he said.

"These women aren't state workers, though," Denham pointed out.

"No, but Audra Cutler is," Chief Terry said. "She's a licensed foster mother. Winnie, I don't suppose you could get her number from my office and give her a call and tell her we need her down here, could you?"

Winnie nodded. "Absolutely. That sounds like a great idea."

"You can't do that," Arlene said, incensed. "We're that girl's blood."

"I just did it," Chief Terry said. "Now, you all can go and meet with your lawyers, but you should be aware that our investigation is ongoing. You cannot take that child until I say you can."

"And you're going to let these … women … tell you when that is, aren't you?" Denham sneered.

"I'm going to let the law tell me when it's time, son," Chief Terry said. "You see, I have the law on my side."

THE DENHAMS DECIDED TO REGROUP. They didn't leave the hospital, but they did vacate our general vicinity. Once they were gone, Landon and Chief Terry snapped to action.

"All right, we don't have a lot of time," Chief Terry said. "Landon and I are going back out to the scene of the accident right now. I don't like the way that guy was acting."

"That's because he's a sick bastard," Aunt Tillie supplied.

Chief Terry ignored her and focused on Landon. "Can you get someone to run Denham's financials tonight?"

"Are you thinking he was in the area?" Landon asked.

"He clearly didn't come with his parents," Chief Terry said. "He came in after them. Did you see his father? He was surprised to see his son. He doesn't appear to have much love for him."

"How can you tell?" I asked. "He didn't talk."

"He's henpecked," Chief Terry said. "He clearly lets his wife call all the shots."

"There's nothing wrong with being henpecked," Aunt Tillie said. "Some might call it a virtue."

Chief Terry rolled his eyes. "You guys need to keep Annie here. When Audra gets here, tell her what's going on. She'll agree to take Annie on. Once she's here, the state is officially involved and the Denhams have no legal standing."

"Annie isn't going to want to go with anyone," I protested.

"Hopefully she won't have to," Chief Terry said. "If we're lucky, Belinda will wake up before we have to deal with whatever slick suit the Denhams hire. There aren't a lot of choices around here."

"Will it go in front of Judge Crawford?" Marnie asked.

"He's the only judge we have," Chief Terry replied.

"I think I'm going to bake him a pie."

"I think I'm going to help," Mom said.

Chief Terry stilled. "You're not going to do anything funny to the pie, are you?"

"Of course not," Marnie said. "No man can say no to my pie. It's magic all on its own. It doesn't need any actual magic."

My mind went someplace dirty, and I fought the urge to snicker. A quick look at Bay told me she was thinking the same thing.

Mom cuffed the back of my head. "Don't be filthy."

"I didn't say anything," I muttered.

"You were thinking it."

"What should we do?" Bay asked.

"Just stand watch," Landon said, giving her a quick kiss. "I'll be in touch as soon as I can."

"Don't let those people in Belinda's room," Chief Terry warned.

"Do you think they would kill her?"

"I don't like them," Chief Terry said. "I wouldn't put anything past that mother, or her piece-of-crap son, for that matter."

Once they were gone, it was just Clove, Bay, Aunt Tillie and me, and we were at a loss. That's when Dr. Garfield came out of Belinda's room. I rushed up to him. "Is she going to be okay?"

Dr. Garfield looked tired – but hopeful. "She's very dehydrated," he said. "She has some broken ribs, but since she couldn't move around, she didn't aggravate them. That's a good thing."

"What's the bad thing?"

"She hit her head, probably against the steering wheel," Dr. Garfield said. "I have no idea if she'll ever regain consciousness. That's our biggest cause for concern. We're pumping her full of fluids, and her kidneys aren't in danger of shutting down, and her heartbeat is strong, but it's a waiting game now."

Dr. Garfield took his leave, and when he was gone, I couldn't take the silence. "It's a waiting game, and we're almost out of time."

"Then we're going to have to rig the game," Aunt Tillie said, her face animated.

"And how do we do that?"

"We're witches, grumpy puss. There are many ways to rig the game. Clove, this is what I need you to do ... ."

When she was done outlining her plan, I realized why Aunt Tillie never lost a game: She plays to win. I could only hope her winning streak would hold.

TEN

"Are you sure this is going to work?"

The spell ingredients Aunt Tillie had instructed Clove to gather out at The Overlook were cause for alarm. This wasn't some bargain-basement spell that we could half-ass and pull off. This was a spell that called for precision – something my cousins and I weren't known for.

"It's going to work," Aunt Tillie said.

"Have you done it before?"

"No."

"Then how do you know it's going to work?" I pressed.

"Because I have faith," Aunt Tillie said.

We were inside of Belinda's hospital room, and we'd purposely waited until Dr. Garfield finished another check on the woman before we spread out our supplies. Dawn was starting to encroach, and the day shift would start in another hour. It was now or never.

"Okay, what do you want us to do?" I asked.

Aunt Tillie pressed her lips together as she regarded me. "I need you to go outside and wait with Marcus and Annie."

"What?" She had to be joking.

"You're too unfocused, Thistle," Aunt Tillie said. "This spell calls for three witches. You're not going to be in here."

"But … ."

"No," Aunt Tillie said firmly. "We need someone to keep everyone out of the room while we do the spell. It's going to take some time. I need Bay with me, and Clove isn't mean enough to handle the Denhams. That leaves you."

"Are you just saying that because you think I'm unfocused?"

"I'm saying that because we only have one shot at this," Aunt Tillie said. "We have to do an awakening spell in a busy hospital while bad people are in the hospital trying to steal a little girl. What's more important, your pride or Basil?"

"Her name is Annie," I grumbled.

"I like Basil better," Aunt Tillie said. "You know I'm right."

Unfortunately, I did know that. "How long will it take?"

"As long as it takes," Aunt Tillie said. "I don't care what you have to do, but you make sure the Denhams don't take Annie and no one comes in this room. I don't care if you have to start this hospital on fire, you protect your family, and you protect that little girl."

She was setting it up as a challenge. I knew exactly what she was doing. "You make sure you do your job," I said. "Your legend will diminish if you don't."

"My legend will never diminish, missy," she said, puffing out her chest. "This will only cement it. I am the wickedest witch of the Midwest."

You can always count on Aunt Tillie's ego to pull her through. "Good luck."

"You, too," Aunt Tillie said, narrowing her eyes. "Something tells me you might be in more trouble than we will be."

I FOUND Marcus sleeping in a chair in the waiting room. Annie was sitting on his lap, her head settled against his chest. I wasn't sure if she was asleep, but she was at least resting her eyes.

Audra had arrived a few hours before, and she was slumbering in another chair a few feet away. Once we'd explained the situation, she'd been more than happy to help. She'd introduced herself to Annie – without being scary – and she'd started to build a rapport with the girl fairly quickly.

I sat down in the chair next to Marcus and focused on the closed door that separated my family from discovery. I had no idea what was going on in there, but I knew Aunt Tillie wouldn't fail me. Not this time. Sure, when I was in high school and needed her to curse a boy because he'd dumped me for a friend, she'd told me to suck it up and do it myself – but this was different. Huh, now that my mind was wandering, I couldn't help but wonder if Kayla Dobbins ever did find a pair of underwear that fit again.

My body was weary, but I couldn't make myself relax. Something was about to happen – and not just in Belinda's room.

"There she is."

I jerked my head up when I heard the voice. I saw Jonathan Denham and his mother round the corner a few seconds later. They had another man with them, and Tom Denham was trailing behind the small group with a morose look on his face.

Marcus snapped awake, and he was cradling Annie protectively against his chest as he looked to me for answers. He wasn't sure what was going on, but he was readying himself for a fight.

"They can't get in that room, and they can't have Annie," I said, my voice low.

Marcus nodded.

"Whatever I say, just go along with it."

He nodded again.

"Oh, and if I try to kill them, just let me," I added.

"Yeah, we'll have to agree to disagree on that one," Marcus said. "I'm not sure monthly conjugal visits will be enough to keep me honest."

He has an odd sense of humor sometimes.

I got to my feet and cut Denham and Arlene off before they could get too close to Belinda's room. "What are you doing here?"

"We're here to claim our grandchild," Arlene said.

"Well, Chief Terry said you couldn't," I replied. "He's in charge. You'll have to take it up with him."

"This is our attorney, Donald Hollingsworth," Arlene said. "He says your Chief Terry has no jurisdiction over this child." She moved toward Marcus and held out her arms. "You can give her to me."

Marcus shook his head. "You can't have her."

Arlene narrowed her eyes. "What? Are you some kind of pervert?"

"No, that would be your son," I said.

"Stop saying that," Denham snapped. "I am not a pervert."

"You knocked up your student."

"That was ... she seduced me."

"Yeah, right," I said, rolling my eyes.

Hollingsworth stepped closer. I didn't recognize him, which meant the Denhams had gone outside of Hemlock Cove to retain legal counsel. That was probably a good idea on their part. "Ma'am, you have to hand that child over."

"I don't have to do anything," I said. "And I'm not doing that. I don't care what you say."

"You listen here," Arlene seethed, wagging her finger in my face. "You're not in control here. I am."

"And that's what matters to you, right? Control?"

Arlene was taken aback by my challenge.

"I get you," I continued. "I get what you are. You're a woman who henpecked her husband and raised a monster. You're a woman who wants a chance to mold another young mind. You're a woman who wants to control everything.

"I've known women like you," I said. "Well, that's not exactly true. I've known women who need control – one in particular – but the difference is, she still manages to know what's right and wrong.

"Sure, she straddles the line," I said. "She often crosses it." Goddess, does she cross it. "She still manages to do the right thing. I don't even think you know what the right thing is. That's how far gone you are."

"Oh, you're so full of yourself," Arlene said. "You think you know how to read people. Now, let me tell you about you. You were raised in a family of all women, and you never learned your place. You want to stand out, so you dye your hair odd colors. You want to be special, but everyone else around you has something more – something better – to offer.

"You're insecure, and you've latched onto my granddaughter to make yourself feel important," she continued. "You think, if you somehow beat me, then you'll have everyone in your family applauding you. You still won't be special."

I snorted. She was trying to throw me off my game. I'd grown up with the master, though. She couldn't shake me. Still, I needed to play the game to buy time, and I was more than willing to do it.

"Oh, you couldn't be more wrong," I said. "I've always stood out in my family, and it's not because of my hair. It's because I'm generally unpleasant and bitchy. That's just how I roll. I dye my hair because it drives my mother nuts – which is funny, because her hair is so red she gives random circus clowns nightmares.

"In my family, no one has a place," I said. "In fact, everyone is so scattered that we can't remember what our place is from the previous day. I don't need accolades and applause from my family because we work for a living, and we believe in earning something instead of taking it.

"Your problem is that the son you raised to be entitled turned out to also be a sociopath," I continued. "You expected him to elevate you by virtue of his name. Instead, all he's done is drag you down. I have no idea what transpired when you found out Belinda was pregnant with your grandchild, but I'm guessing it wasn't pretty. You didn't want anything to do with Annie until you realized that Jonathan here wasn't going to amount to anything."

"You take that back," Denham spat.

I ignored him. "I don't care what you want, lady," I said. "I care what's best for Annie, and that's clearly not the woman who raised this piece of trash."

"Well, you don't have a say in that," Hollingsworth said. "You're not the law."

"No, but I am," Chief Terry said, striding into the room with

AMANDA M. LEE

Landon on his heels. He shot me a questioning look before focusing on the Denhams. "Is there a problem here?"

"Yes, this ... woman ... won't let me have my granddaughter," Arlene said.

"Well, she was instructed not to," Chief Terry said. "I think that means she's doing her job."

I froze when I saw Annie start to move on Marcus' lap. He smoothed her hair down, trying to lull her back to sleep, but it was too late. She sat up straight and rubbed the sleep from her eyes, her gaze landing on me first. "What's going on? Is my mommy awake?"

"Not yet," I said.

Arlene pushed past Chief Terry so she could get closer to Annie. "Oh, there's my precious girl."

Annie pulled back when she saw her. "Who are you?"

Chief Terry and I exchanged a look.

"I'm your grandmother," Arlene said. "And this is your father."

Annie shifted her face so she could look Denham up and down. She didn't immediately say anything.

"If you're such a good grandmother, how come your granddaughter doesn't know you?" I asked. Aunt Tillie had said that Annie didn't know her grandparents. I didn't realize that meant she'd never met them.

"That's a pretty good question," Landon said.

"Belinda wouldn't allow us visitation," Arlene said, straightening. "She's a horrible person."

"My mommy isn't bad," Annie snapped.

"Of course she isn't," Marcus murmured, tightening his arms around her.

"Don't you say my mommy is bad," Annie said.

"Young lady, you're going to have to learn that you don't talk back to your elders," Arlene said. "I understand you haven't been raised with a firm hand, but all of that is about to change."

Annie was confused. "Aunt Tillie says that you only have to respect adults if they don't say anything stupid," she said. "You're saying something stupid."

I couldn't help but wonder what other pearls of wisdom Aunt Tillie had been bestowing upon Annie. That was a question for another time, though.

"Stupid isn't a nice word," Arlene replied.

"It's not," I agreed. "In this case, though, it's the right word."

"Thistle," Chief Terry warned. "Mrs. Denham, I think it would be a good idea if you and your son came down to the station for some questions."

"Excuse me?"

"You heard me," Chief Terry said. "We have a few questions for you and your son. You probably don't want to answer them here ... in front of your granddaughter."

"I have nothing to hide," Arlene sniffed, crossing her arms over her chest obstinately.

"Okay then," Chief Terry said, not backing down. "First off, Jonathan, when did you first arrive in Hemlock Cove?"

Denham balked at the question. "What does that matter?"

"It's just a question. I need you to answer it."

Denham looked at his mother for support. She nodded in his direction. "The first time I stepped foot in this ... town ... was a few hours ago."

"Hmm. I see. How did you find out about Annie's situation?"

"What do you mean?"

"We couldn't find you," Chief Terry said. "We had to call your parents. You had no working phone number of record. I'm just wondering when you found out that Annie had been discovered?"

"I ... it was the other day," Denham said, flustered. "I don't remember exactly what day it was."

"Do you remember where you were when you got the call?"

Denham straightened. "I was at the mall by my mother's house."

"That's pretty interesting," Landon said. "Because we ran your phone records this evening. Actually, we had to track back the numbers that called your mother's phone and go from there. After we found one from a burner phone that called on a regular basis, we tracked the sale to a store in Minnesota, and you were the man we saw on store security video. We tracked the GPS on that phone, and it was in Traverse City when the call was made about Annie's discovery."

Denham's mouth dropped open. "You can't track a burner phone."

Landon drew a piece of paper from his pocket and unfolded it. He handed it over to Denham. "That's you, right?"

Arlene made a face. "What did you do?"

"Nothing," Denham said. "They're framing me."

"There were two sets of tracks out at the accident scene," Chief Terry said. "It appears that someone drove directly at Belinda's vehicle and tried to force it off the road, even clipping the front bumper to force her off into the ravine."

"Well, my rental car is out in the parking lot," Denham said. "You can check it. There's no damage."

"We already checked it," Landon said.

Denham smiled triumphantly.

"The problem is, you secured that rental car yesterday afternoon," Landon said. "The car you rented six days ago in Traverse City is another story. We contacted the owner of that facility – and he wasn't thrilled to be woken up in the middle of the night, let me tell you – and he said the car you turned in two days ago had some front-end damage.

"The owner said you claimed someone backed into the car when it was parked and you had no idea who did it," Landon continued. "Can you explain that?"

"I … I have no idea what happened to that car," Denham said. "Someone hit it and ran."

"And, can you explain what you were doing in this area before then?" Landon asked, his face serious.

"I was here on vacation."

"Why did you tell us you were at the mall by your mother's house?" Chief Terry asked.

They were tag-teaming him, and it was a sight to behold.

"I … you're trying to frame me," Denham said.

"Did he hurt my mommy?" Annie asked, her lower lip trembling.

"Of course he didn't," Arlene said. "Your mommy is the bad one."

"Stop telling her that," I snapped.

"Even if you take my son into custody, that doesn't mean I'm guilty," Arlene said, straightening.

"Mom?" Denham was worried.

"I'm still this girl's only relative who is capable of taking care of her."

"I wouldn't say that," Aunt Tillie said, appearing in Belinda's doorway. She wasn't alone. The woman standing behind her, who only an hour ago looked like she was minutes from death, now appeared like she was ready for action. Well, kind of. She was still pale, and she looked confused.

"I'm capable of taking care of her," Belinda said, leaning against the doorway for support as she cradled her ribs.

"Mommy!" Annie jumped off of Marcus' lap and raced toward her mother.

Bay stilled her approach worriedly. "Your mommy is sore. Be gentle with her."

Annie nodded solemnly as she carefully gave Belinda a desperate hug.

"I was so worried about you," Belinda said, petting her daughter's head. "I woke up in the car and you were gone. I couldn't get out."

"She found us," I explained. "I'm sorry it took us so long to find you."

"Don't be sorry," Belinda said, her eyes swimming with tears. "You saved my baby." She glanced up, her gaze landing on Denham for the first time. "What is he doing here?"

"He's being taken into custody," Chief Terry said. "We're going to need to talk to you, too. I need to know what you remember about the accident."

"I don't know what I can tell you," Belinda said. "I just know that a black car was heading right at us and I tried to swerve to avoid it. I blacked out, and when I woke up, Annie was missing. I tried to get out of the car, but I kept passing out."

"Yes, well, it just so happens that Mr. Denham rented a black car when he arrived in the area almost a week ago," Chief Terry said. "He's being taken into custody on attempted murder charges. Do you know why he would try to kill you?"

"I was going after child support," Belinda said. "I left him off the birth certificate because I didn't want anything to do with him, but he kept showing up. I figured, if he was going to keep hounding us, I should get the money he owed us.

"When I filed the paperwork, he started threatening me," she continued. "I realized what I'd done, and I decided to run. He was being ... scary."

Chief Terry nodded. "Did he threaten you?"

"Yes. He kept saying he was going to kill me and take Annie."

"Did you know he was in the area?" Landon asked.

"No," Belinda said. "I thought we were safe. I had no idea he'd come here. I don't even know how he found me."

"That will be a question he has to answer down at the station," Chief Terry said, pulling his handcuffs from his belt.

"Mom!" Denham was panicked.

"You're such a stupid moron," Arlene grumbled. "I have no idea how I raised such an idiot."

"It must be karma," Aunt Tillie said.

Arlene wasn't done yet. "That woman is not fit enough to take care of a child," she said. "It's going to be weeks before she's recovered. How is she going to take care of Annie?"

"She won't be alone," Winnie said, appearing from the other side of the nurse's station. I hadn't even realized she was over there and listening to everything. "She'll be staying at The Overlook while she convalesces. That will allow her to rest, and have plenty of free childcare."

Annie looked excited at the prospect. "Does that mean I can help Aunt Tillie in her garden?"

"No," Landon said.

Annie frowned. "But I want to learn more about the oregano."

Landon wagged his finger in Annie's face. "No, you don't. You can help Thistle in the store, though."

"And you can come with me to the stables," Marcus said.

"Can I ride a horse?" Annie asked, excited.

"You can ride ten of them," Marcus said.

"But what about the oregano? It needs to be cut back so it won't be all seeds."

Landon scowled.

"Don't worry," Aunt Tillie said. "We still have our wine business."

"No, you don't," Landon said.

"You're starting to test the limits of my endurance," Aunt Tillie said.

"Wait a second. You can't just hand my granddaughter over to these people," Arlene said. "I brought a lawyer."

"Yeah, well we brought a judge," Marnie said as she joined the crowd. I couldn't help but notice that a tired looking Judge Crawford was with her. He still had pie crumbs on his face.

"I've been made aware of the situation," he said. "Since the mother is on her way to recovery, and the Winchesters have graciously opened up their home to her, I see no reason to remove this child from her mother's custody."

"Except that Belinda can't hold down a job," Arlene said.

Belinda's face colored under the accusation. "That's because you called every one of my employers and told them lies about me."

"Well, you don't have to worry about that," Winnie said. "We've been considering adding another person at the inn to help with the day-to-day operations. I think Belinda will fit right in." She smiled at Annie. "And that will give us the opportunity to see Annie as often as we want."

Annie clapped her hands together excitedly.

"You can't do this," Arlene said. "I ... this isn't what I want."

"Oh, honey, we don't give a flying fart what you want," Aunt Tillie said, holding her hand out to Annie. "Come on, Basil. I think some breakfast is in order."

Belinda furrowed her brow. "Basil?"

I sighed. "It's a long story."

"With a happy ending," Annie said, laughing delightedly. She held out her other hand to me. "Are you coming? You're going to need a big breakfast if you want to sell wine with me and Aunt Tillie this afternoon."

"That's right," Aunt Tillie said. "We need to teach her to dance, don't we?"

Annie giggled.

I took Annie's hand. "I'm not dancing."

"You have to," Annie said. "That's how you sell stuff. We need to get a new plow for Aunt Tillie, missy."

I gave in. "Fine."

"What new plow?" Landon asked.

Everyone ignored him.

"I'd better not come back out to that inn and find any selling going on," Landon barked at our backs.

No one listened.

"Sometimes I feel like I talk and everyone just pretends my lips aren't moving," he grumbled.

"That's because you're full of hot air," Annie said.

Landon narrowed his eyes. "Who told you that?"

"Oh, we all told her that," Aunt Tillie said, chortling as she dragged Annie and me down the hall. "We all told her that."

I couldn't help but laugh. It was a happy ending for everyone, after all. Well, except for Landon.

"Don't worry," Aunt Tillie said, reading my mind. "He'll be fine."

"How can you be sure?"

"I put a little something extra in the wine bottle I left in his truck," she said. "He's going to be thanking me for weeks after he drinks it."

"Why? Does it taste like bacon?"

Aunt Tillie's eyes were sparkling. "You'll have to wait to find out."

I wanted to question her further, but I let it go. I was too tired to put up a fight. It had been a long few days, and a job well done. I was going to leave Aunt Tillie to her fun.

"Oh, and don't think I've forgotten about you," Aunt Tillie said. "Your punishment starts tomorrow."

And, then again, the woman is evil incarnate. "Oh, come on!"

ON A WITCH AND A PRAYER

A WICKED WITCHES OF THE MIDWEST SHORT

ONE

"Michaels, I have something to give to you before you go."

I glanced up from my desk, internally sighing as my boss, Steve Newton, sidled up to me with a file clutched in his beefy hands. "I'm leaving for my weekend."

"I know, Landon," Newton said, his eyes narrowing as they regarded me. "I'm not asking you to put off your weekend."

"That's good," I said. "Nothing in the free world could stop me from putting this place in my rearview mirror in exactly five minutes."

"Let me guess, you're spending the weekend holed up in Hemlock Cove with a certain blonde?"

I shrugged, nonplussed. "Do you have a problem with that?"

"Of course not," Newton said, gesturing toward the framed photograph on my desk. The blonde in the photograph had a huge grin, sparkling blue eyes, and she leaned in close to me, as though I whispered something to her. I loved that photo, and if I remembered that day correctly, I had been whispering something dirty to her – and that was exactly why I was in such a hurry to get to Hemlock Cove. "If I could spend the weekend in bed with that, I would, too."

I scowled. "We do more than spend the weekend in bed."

AMANDA M. LEE

Newton waited.

"We eat, too."

Newton's guffaw was loud and hearty. "You know, when you first started working here, I thought you were a bachelor for life. From what the other guys said, you didn't have any inclination to spend more than one night with the same woman.

"Now you spend every night you can with the same woman," he continued. "People are starting to talk."

"People should keep their mouths shut," I said, irked. "Bay is not their concern. She's my concern."

"Are you concerned about her?"

"I'm always concerned about her," I grumbled. "She collects trouble like other women do shoes and handbags."

Newton smirked. "I've noticed. Her name pops up in more files than I'm comfortable with."

I shifted uncomfortably, the idea of my boss focusing on Bay causing my stomach to roll. "It's not her fault. She's a good person. She just has an uncanny ability to uncover ... ."

"Crime?"

Unfortunately, that was exactly right. "It's not always her," I said, shifting to a different tactic. "Her family stumbles across trouble more than she does." That wasn't a lie. Of course, Bay was usually in the thick of it with her family, but I decided to ignore that little tidbit.

"I've read about her family, too," Newton said. "I especially like that aunt of hers ... what's her name ... Tillie? I'd love to meet her someday. She sounds like a real piece of work."

"You don't want to meet her," I said, picturing Aunt Tillie's combat helmet. "Trust me."

"Why? Is she mean?"

"She's ... crotchety."

"What's wrong? Doesn't she like you? Did you finally find a woman who doesn't puddle at your feet and fall under your spell?"

Because Bay's family was witches ... yes, real witches ... mention of spells set my teeth on edge. "She likes me." Sometimes, I added silently. "She's ... set in her ways."

"I still want to meet her," Newton said. "She sounds like a real pip."

"She has her moments," I said, trying to get the conversation back on track. "Did you have something you wanted to give me?"

"Yeah," Newton said, nodding his head. "We've got a new mandate from the higher-ups. They want us to start going through some of the cold cases."

"Great," I groaned, my shoulders sagging. "That's not a waste of manpower."

"I agree," Newton said. "I don't make the decisions, though." He handed the file over to me. "I figured this one was right up your alley."

"And why is that?"

"Because the woman in question went missing from Hemlock Cove."

I stilled, unsure. "Seriously? How long ago?"

"It's been more than twenty years," Newton said. "I honestly don't know whether you're going to find anything. Odds are, you won't. Still, you have close ties with the community. I'm sure the chief there will be willing to give you what the town has, and maybe your girlfriend's family even knew the victim."

"And you want this solved this weekend?" Irritation bubbled up, and I fought the urge to snap. That wouldn't get me anywhere. I knew that. Still, the happy fantasies of starry walks and breakfast in bed were starting to diminish in the back of my mind. So much for a lazy weekend with Bay, where clothing was going to be optional and her smile was the only thing I wanted to see for the next three days.

"I don't know that you're going to be able to solve it," Newton said. "We have to give it due diligence. If you don't get anywhere, you don't get anywhere."

That didn't sound so bad. "Fine," I said, taking the file. "I'm still giving Bay most of my attention this weekend."

"Isn't that how you spend every weekend? In fact, don't you sneak off there to spend the night every chance you get during the week, too?" Newton's eyes shined as he regarded me, and his voice was teasing, but I couldn't help but wonder whether my boss was hinting at something specific.

"I'm never late for work," I replied. "I still have my place here in Traverse City. I'm not sure what you're getting at."

"I'm not getting at anything," Newton said, clapping his hand on my shoulder. "I only want to know if I'm going to win the pool."

"What pool?"

"There's a pool on when you're going to propose."

A year ago, a suggestion like that would have been preposterous. Now? I wasn't looking for rings and I have no intention of proposing anytime soon, but the idea wasn't as terrifying as it once was. It doesn't make me feel sick to my stomach, and I'm not looking for an exit door. In fact, when I finally uttered the L-word a few weeks ago, it felt natural and right. That's progress, right?

"I think you guys are going to be waiting for a little while yet," I said, shoving the file into my bag and getting to my feet. "I'm perfectly happy the way things are." Actually, I was more than happy. I was … content.

"Is she happy?"

I grinned. "She's always happy where I'm concerned."

Newton rolled his eyes. "Does she like that ego of yours?"

"I haven't heard any complaints."

"Don't forget the cold case," Newton said. "And, while we're at it, what does her mother look like? You said she's available, right?"

I brushed past him, internally laughing. "You're not in her league, Newton. You wouldn't have a shot with any of them."

"You don't know that," Newton protested. "I can be charming, too."

"They don't do charming," I said. "In fact, if you're not comfortable screaming through dinner, you're not even going to be a blip on their radar."

"Do you scream through dinner?"

"At least once a week," I replied. "Speaking of that, I need to get going. If I'm late for dinner they won't feed me, and I've been looking forward to homemade pot roast for three days. See you Monday."

"**YOU'RE** DEAD TO ME!"

I barely registered the raised voices as I let myself into the guesthouse an hour later. I scanned the living room briefly, noting that Thistle, hands on hips, stood in the middle of the kitchen while Bay was closer to her bedroom. That was good for what I had planned later in the evening, but the argument would have to be wrapped up first.

"Hey," I said, kissing Bay's cheek by way of greeting and then slipping behind her so I could drop my bag on her bedroom floor.

"This is not my fault," Bay said. "I can't believe you're blaming me for this."

"Who else should I blame?" Thistle asked, her pink head bopping up and down as she gathered steam. "You're the one who gave Aunt Tillie the computer. She's had, like, eight things delivered during the past week alone. What do you think is in those boxes?"

"I'm just hoping it's not alive," Bay said. "We still haven't found that scorpion she ordered. What was his name again?"

"Fred."

"Yeah. What do you think happened to Fred?"

"I think he made a run for it," Thistle said, rolling her eyes. "Even a scorpion is afraid of Aunt Tillie."

"What are you arguing about?" I asked, returning to the living room. I tossed my workbag on the small sofa table and shuffled into the kitchen to grab a cola from the refrigerator.

"We're in trouble," Thistle said.

"You're going to have to be more specific," I said. "Where you guys are concerned, that could mean anything. You didn't do anything illegal, did you?"

Bay shot me a look, and I couldn't help but smile at the way her eyes flashed. She's cute when she's annoyed, and where the Winchester witches are concerned, she's always annoyed.

"When was the last time we did anything illegal?" Thistle challenged.

"Doesn't Aunt Tillie still make her own wine and sell it without a permit?"

"That's her, not us."

"Doesn't she have a pot field?" I asked, internally cringing that I not only knew about its existence, but because I could do nothing about it. She'd magically cloaked the field. I'd been looking every chance I got. I had no idea how she did it, but it was starting to get frustrating. I would never turn her in, but I would burn it without a hint of regret.

"Again, that's her. We have nothing to do with that field." Thistle was irritated. Since that was her perpetual state, I wasn't fazed by the dark look on her face.

"Let's start over," I said. "What seems to be the problem?"

"Bay got us in trouble," Thistle said, crossing her arms over her chest.

I rolled my eyes until they landed on Bay, losing myself in the snug fit of her jeans for a moment before I realized we were in the middle of another crisis. "What did you do?"

"Aunt Tillie has been ordering things online with the computer I gave her," Bay said, choosing her words carefully. "She's been getting a lot of packages. When we try to see what they are, she hides them."

That couldn't be good. "Can't you just go online and see what she's been ordering?"

"She hid it."

I fought the mad urge to laugh. Aunt Tillie was more work than any ten kids could ever be and, while the woman drives me crazy, she's always entertaining. "She probably ordered more obnoxious clothing and another combat helmet or something. Why is this bothering you so much?

"Seriously, I'm the biggest worrier in the world where she's concerned," I continued. "It's probably harmless, though."

Now it was Thistle's turn to roll her eyes. "When has Aunt Tillie ever done anything harmless?"

That was a pretty good question. "She's been quiet for weeks," I pointed out. I realized, after I said it, that wasn't a proper argument. When Aunt Tillie is quiet, that's when things get out of hand. That meant she was mustering her energy for something big. "She could be buying something completely harmless."

Bay cocked an eyebrow.

"Fine," I said, rubbing the spot between my eyebrows wearily. "I'll ask her what she's been buying when we get up to the inn."

"She's not going to tell you," Thistle scoffed.

"You don't know that," I said. "She's told me things before."

"When?"

I made a face. "She'll tell me."

"Whatever," Thistle said. "We have to figure out what she's buying. If we don't, our mothers are going to be all over us until we do."

"I have trouble believing you can't handle your mothers," I said. "Sure, they're ... insistent sometimes. They live in the same house with Aunt Tillie, though. Shouldn't she be their responsibility?"

"It's a good thing you're handsome," Thistle said. "I don't think you'd make it through life if you weren't."

I glanced at Bay for support. "She's going to tell me what she's doing."

Doubt flooded Bay's eyes. "Do you want to rest up before we go to The Overlook?"

The question confused me. "What do you mean?"

Bay tilted her head to the side, gesturing toward her bedroom. "Do you want to rest up?"

I couldn't help but smile when I realized what she was really suggesting. "That's exactly what I had in mind."

***

"**WE** HAVE TO GET DRESSED," Bay said, poking my side to make sure I was awake an hour later. "We have fifteen minutes to get up there."

"Give me a minute," I murmured, trying to wring a few more precious moments of quiet from my day before chaos descended.

"We can't be late," Bay said. "We're already on their list."

"Blame me," I said. "Your mother can't stay angry when I'm here. She's putty in my hands."

"Oh, please," Bay said. "The bloom is off where you're concerned. You've started bossing her around and taking charge in areas she thinks she has domain over."

"For example?"

"You wouldn't let her hover when I was … hurt … by Nick a few weeks ago."

I shifted my gaze, finding Bay propped on her elbow with her teeth embedded in her lower lip. That incident was still a sore subject between us, even though I was trying to let it go. "You weren't hurt," I said. "You were shot."

"I remember. I was there."

"I wasn't going to spend the night away from you after you were shot," I said, my mind roaming back to the day in question. "Your mother must understand that."

"She's used to people doing what she wants."

"Well, where you're concerned, I'm going to do what I want," I said, tugging her lip away from her teeth. "Stop doing that. You don't have to be afraid that I'm going to fly off the handle. Nick is locked up. You're safe. Let's … just drop it."

"That sounds good," said Bay, rolling out of bed and searching the carpet for her clothes. "Come on. I'm starving."

My stomach chimed in with a loud rumble, reminding me I hadn't eaten since breakfast. "Fine," I said, giving in. "They're still making pot roast tonight, right?"

"If that's what my mother promised you, then that's what you're getting," Bay said, tugging a brush through her hair and studying her reflection in the mirror. "She's going to know what we were doing."

"Do you really care?"

"Of course not." The look on her face told me otherwise.

I pulled my jeans and shirt on and took the brush from her, running it through my own dark hair before handing it back. "Better?"

Bay smiled, causing me to lean forward and kiss her lightly. "Come on," I said. "Now that you've mentioned food, I can't think of anything else."

"If you find out what Aunt Tillie has going on, I'll reward you later," Bay offered.

"I think you should have tried to negotiate that outcome before … this," I replied, gesturing toward the rumpled bed.

"Who says I was going to reward you with that?"
I frowned. What else was there?

TWO

"You don't have to drag me," Bay complained, tugging on the hand snugly engulfed by mine. "We still have two minutes. Are you really that hungry?"

I slowed my pace enough to let Bay's shorter legs catch up. "I'm sorry," I said, "but I've been dreaming about pot roast for three nights."

"And here I thought you spent your nights dreaming about me while we were apart."

"I do," I replied, unruffled, "and in my dreams you're covered in pot roast … and sometimes bacon."

I followed Bay through the back door of the inn, glancing around the cozy living quarters Winnie, Marnie, Twila and Aunt Tillie shared. It was always immaculate. While Bay, Thistle and Clove weren't pigs, the guesthouse was rarely orderly. I didn't really mind the clutter. There was something comfortable about Thistle's crafts corner, even if wax and clay were spread all over the place. I liked seeing Bay's laptop on the coffee table, mostly because that meant whatever work she had to do for The Whistler she would be doing at home – where I had easy access to her. Still, a little cleanliness wouldn't hurt the younger set of Winchester witches.

"Do you smell that?"

Bay turned to me, her eyes quizzical. "What is it? Please don't tell me you smell pot. We're definitely going to be late if you search Aunt Tillie's room."

I grinned. "I was talking about the pot roast, goof," I said, flicking the end of her nose. "Still, searching Aunt Tillie's bedroom isn't a bad idea. If you really want to know what she's up to, that would be the place to start."

"Are you saying you want to see Aunt Tillie's bedroom?"

"I ... ." Hmm, how should I answer that?

"I didn't think so," Bay said. "If you see Aunt Tillie's room, you're going to have nightmares for weeks."

"Why? What's in there?"

"Oh, there's nothing in there that's overtly suspicious, at least as far as I know," Bay said. "I only said you'll have nightmares because she cursed her room to give people nightmares if they enter without permission."

Witches! I swear! I was still getting used to their peculiar ways. "I can't decide whether you're messing with me or not."

"I'm not messing with you," Bay said. "I went in there to get knitting needles for Twila two weeks ago and then I had a dream that I was a big slice of bacon for two nights in a row."

The image made me smile – for more than one reason. "That sounds like heaven to me."

"Not when you're frying on a giant griddle."

Great! Now I'm going to have nightmares. "Okay, we're done talking about that," I said. "Let's get out there. I'm ready for my pot roast."

"I have one question to ask first."

I fixed my eyes on Bay, impatient. "Make it fast."

"Say there's a fire," she said. "Are you going to save me or are you going to save the pot roast?"

"That's not really fair, baby," I teased. "The pot roast doesn't have legs. It can't save itself."

"That's what I thought."

The kitchen was empty when we entered, tonight's preparation pots and pans soaking in the sink. I scanned the counter for signs of carrots, potatoes and gravy, practically crowing when I found all three. I moved faster, pulling Bay excitedly.

Numerous expectant faces swiveled our way when we emerged from the kitchen. Besides Bay's family, it looked as if Chief Terry, Sam and Marcus were joining us for the meal, as well as five guests I didn't recognize. Before getting involved with Bay, the idea of eating dinner with strangers every night was an odd one. I was used to it now.

"Good evening, everyone."

"You're late," Winnie said, tilting her head to the side. She had Bay's coloring and eyes, but she didn't smile when saw me ... at least not tonight.

"It was my fault," I said, congenially. "I ... forgot something back at the guesthouse."

"What?" Winnie was clearly in a mood.

"I'm guessing it was his pants," Thistle said, sipping from her glass of wine and shooting me a salty look.

"Thank you, Thistle," Twila said, glaring in her daughter's direction. "No one needs you to add to the discussion."

"I was just trying to help."

"You can help a lot more if you're quiet," Twila said.

I moved to the far side of the table and settled into what had become my regular seat between Bay and Aunt Tillie. While everyone else turned their attention to the heaping platefuls of food and idle conversation, I focused mine on the elderly Winchester matriarch. "Hello, Aunt Tillie. How are you today?"

"Well, I'm not wearing a girdle and I'm still alive."

I wasn't sure how to take that. "So ... no complaints?"

"Did you just meet me? Of course I have complaints." Aunt Tillie turned so she could scorch Winnie with a narrow-eyed glare. "I have a whole heck of a lot to complain about."

Uh-oh. It looked as if whatever she was up to was about to come to a head. "Who ticked you off now?" I gestured toward my empty glass when Bay started pouring wine. If Aunt Tillie was about to launch into a tirade, being hammered couldn't possibly hurt.

"I have a list," Aunt Tillie sniffed, viciously stabbing her fork into a piece of meat.

She always had a list. Thistle was generally at the top of it, but Bay and Clove shared top billing at least once a week. "Oh, yeah? Who is on top of it today?"

"Don't worry," Aunt Tillie said. "Your girlfriend is safe. Her pants will fit tomorrow morning, and she won't smell like anything she's not supposed to smell like."

That was a little disheartening. I was still holding out hope the bacon smell – and taste – would return. Those were the best two days of my life, I swear. Some people need big cars, a lot of money and inground swimming pools. I needed my girlfriend to smell like bacon. I guess I'm easy. "If you wanted to … ."

"Don't finish that sentence," Bay warned, her eyes flashing. She'd obviously read my mind.

"I wasn't going to say anything," I said.

"Eat your pot roast. You've been talking about it for an hour."

Finally, something I wanted to do. I attacked my plate enthusiastically, keeping one ear on the conversation as I dunked a freshly baked slice of bread into the best gravy I'd ever eaten. I could never tell my mother that, but it was the truth. While the Winchesters were loud – and generally pains in my ass – they were also the best cooks I'd ever met. I would put up with ten screaming matches a night for this gravy.

"So, did you do anything exciting at work this week?" Marnie asked me, smiling pleasantly even though she was clearly watching Sam and Clove out of the corner of her eye. Since Sam had been officially cleared as a murderer and bank robber – and saved Bay's life – he was now welcomed at the dinner table with more than suspicion. I don't think Marnie liked wondering where Sam's hands were wandering under the table, though.

"Just a routine week," I said. "It was mostly paperwork. My boss did give me a cold case to work on while I was here, though."

"You have to work this weekend?" Bay asked, disappointed.

"I have to ask a few questions," I clarified. "The case is twenty years old."

"What is it?" Chief Terry asked.

I shrugged. "I haven't looked at it yet," I admitted. "He gave it to me right before I left, and by the time I got to the guesthouse Bay and Thistle were fighting, so I got distracted."

"We weren't fighting," Thistle said.

"You were yelling."

"That's not fighting. That's talking. Loudly."

"Ah." I turned back to my dinner. "Is anything going on around here this weekend?"

"It's just a normal weekend," Winnie said.

"No festivals?"

"We don't have a festival every week," Bay chided.

"Just every other week," I said. "I stand corrected."

Since she was already irritated, I took the opportunity to steal a slice of bread from her plate.

"Hey!"

"You weren't going to eat it," I said, plastering my best "I'm a good guy and you know you love me" smile on my face. "I thought you wanted to reward me."

"You haven't done anything to warrant being rewarded," Bay said.

She had a point. I glanced back at Aunt Tillie, debating how to proceed.

"What are you rewarding him for?" Winnie asked, suspicious.

"I'll bet I know," Thistle sang from the other end of the table.

"You don't know anything," Bay said. "He's going to take up that ... thing ... we were talking about earlier. He's going to fix it."

"Oh." Thistle's eyes were thoughtful. "That's a good idea. I'll reward him, too."

That was a frightening thought. "I only want Bay to reward me."

Thistle scowled. "I was going to make you a bacon-scented candle, moron. Not ... that. You're sick."

"I'll definitely take the candle," I said, opting to ignore the rest of her statement.

Chief Terry, clearly uncomfortable with the turn in the discussion, decided to redirect the conversation. "What's your cold case?"

"I only know it's a woman who went missing from Hemlock Cove about twenty years ago."

Chief Terry pursed his lips, considering. "I'll bet it's Peg Mulder."

"Who is Peg Mulder?" I asked.

"She was a local woman," Chief Terry said. "She was a couple years behind me in school."

"She was in my grade," Winnie said.

I listened, interested. Even if it wasn't the same woman, anything was better than continuing the "reward" talk. I hoped everyone would forget about that by the end of dinner.

"She was married to John Mulder for about ten years, and then the marriage went south," Chief Terry said.

"Do you remember why?"

"He knocked up the babysitter," Winnie said, wrinkling her nose. "It was quite the scandal at the time."

Small towns never cease to amaze me. Not only does everything overlap because everyone knows each other, but the gossip spreads like wildfire. "Was this Peg Mulder divorced at the time of her disappearance?"

Chief Terry shook his head. "No. The rumor is they were going through a divorce, and John was going to have to pay up something fierce, but it wasn't finalized before Peg disappeared."

"Do you remember anything about the investigation?"

"Just that Peg was last seen at her house … by John … and when he brought their son back before dinner, she was gone," Chief Terry said.

"That sounds suspicious," I said. "Was he a suspect?"

"Of course. The problem is, we never found a body. If he did anything to her, he managed to hide it well. I was on the force back then, and I remember going out on searches with cadaver dogs, but we never found anything."

"What happened to John Mulder?"

"He married the babysitter," Marnie said.

"If Peg was missing and you never found a body, how did he manage to have her declared dead?"

"He didn't," Chief Terry said. "Since the divorce proceedings were

AMANDA M. LEE

already winding through the court system, they simply progressed until their natural end. Since Peg wasn't there to sign the papers, the judge ultimately pushed them through."

"How long after the divorce was finalized did he marry the babysitter?"

The inn guests at the far end of the table were listening, rapt. Apparently they liked small town gossip, too.

"Two days."

"Nice," I said, leaning back in my chair and rubbing my hand against the back of Bay's neck thoughtfully. Her skin was warm and silky above her shirt, and my fingers were soft as they caressed her. "Did they stay in town?"

"For a few months," Chief Terry said. "The babysitter ended up cheating on John with the Mulhern boy. What was his name?"

"Trent," Clove supplied. "He was so hot."

"He was," Thistle agreed.

"Then they got married and moved into John's house," Chief Terry said. "He ended up leaving his kid with the babysitter when he bolted from town."

"Does anyone know where he ended up?"

"I heard he was down in the Pinconning area for a while," Marnie said. "That was like fifteen years ago. I have no idea where he is now."

"If Peg is the woman from my case – and I'm not sure she is – I'm going to want to look at the files you have down at the station," I said.

"That's fine," Chief Terry said, unruffled. "I'd actually like to get that one off the books. It never sat right with me. Peg wasn't the type of woman to run off. Even though John cheated on her, she loved Luke."

"Is Luke her son?"

Winnie nodded. "He's a teacher at the high school now," she said. "He grew into a lovely boy. In fact, before you started dating Bay, I was going to set her up with him."

I made a face. "Thanks for telling me that ... I guess."

Bay snorted. "You were not going to set him up with me."

"I was so."

"You were not."

"He's a very handsome boy," Winnie said.

"He's also gay," Bay said.

Winnie straightened in her chair. "How do you know that?"

"He's got a man living with him and they hold hands when they walk," Bay said.

I couldn't hide my smile. "See, you're lucky to have me," I said, tugging on a strand of her blonde hair. "If it wasn't for me, you'd be dating a gay man. You should thank your lucky stars I came into your life."

Bay rolled her eyes. "Don't you have something else you're supposed to be doing?"

Crap. I was hoping she'd forgotten that. I turned my attention back to Aunt Tillie. "What are you having delivered?"

Aunt Tillie balked. "That's none of your concern."

"Just tell me," I said. "If it's nothing bad, you won't have a problem telling me. If it is something bad, I'm going to find out anyway."

"You're cute," Aunt Tillie said. "You're not that cute, though. What I buy online is my own business. For all you know, I could be buying that underwear that goes up my butt crack."

Conversation at the table came to an abrupt halt.

"Aunt Tillie," Winnie hissed, scandalized. "I can't believe you said that."

"I saw those underwear in the store the other day," Aunt Tillie said. "I think they're perfect for me."

I desperately needed to put an end to this conversation. "Well, great. Enjoy your ... ."

"Thongs," Thistle supplied, grinning.

"I'm going to have more pot roast," I said, reaching for the serving platter. "This is a wonderful meal, ladies. I think it's the best pot roast you've ever made."

Now Bay was the one smiling. "That was pitiful."

I ignored her. "So, how is your greenhouse coming along?"

Aunt Tillie made a gagging sound in the back of her throat, and for a second I thought she was choking. "Are you okay?"

"That's the sound she makes when she wants attention," Twila said, forcing a smile onto her face for the guests' benefit. "She's just … being her."

"What's really going on?" I asked, shifting my gaze to Bay.

"Don't ask me," she replied. "Let Aunt Tillie tell you."

I was afraid Aunt Tillie was going to start talking about her underwear again, but I didn't have a lot of choice in the matter. "Okay. Why are you making that noise?"

"Because I have to look at … pottery … in my greenhouse now," Aunt Tillie said, clearly annoyed. "Do you have any idea what amateur pottery looks like? Big lumps of … crud."

I pursed my lips, considering. There's never a dull moment in this family, and the collective ADD throws me for a loop. Still, I was missing something here. "Can someone explain what she's talking about?"

"Mom took up pottery again," Thistle said, jumping in. "She wants to start giving classes for inn guests."

"Oh, I love that idea," one of the women at the table said. "I've always wanted to learn how to do pottery."

"I'm missing the problem," I said. "Isn't that a good thing?"

"We don't have any place to put the kiln other than Aunt Tillie's greenhouse," Winnie said. "We cleared out a corner, and it's barely in the way, but she's having … a problem … with it."

"Why do you care?" I asked, turning to Aunt Tillie. "It's just one corner. That greenhouse is huge. I'll bet Twila will even make some pots for you."

"I don't want her pots," Aunt Tillie said. "That greenhouse is mine. It's for my plants and other … stuff."

I narrowed my eyes, suspicious. "What other stuff?"

"Never you mind."

I gripped Bay's knee under the table, forcing her attention to me. "What other stuff?"

"I have no idea," Bay said, wriggling. "That hurts."

I released the pressure. Something was definitely going on here. "I don't understand why this is a big deal."

"Of course you don't," Aunt Tillie said, patting my hand. "Eat your dinner. This is above your pay grade."

I scowled. The woman knows exactly what buttons to push to give me heartburn. "Maybe I should go take a look at the greenhouse and see if I can think of a better way to organize it so everyone is happy?"

"That's a great idea," Twila enthused.

"That's a terrible idea," Aunt Tillie spat.

"Why?"

"You don't even know what a kiln does."

"It … bakes pottery or something." That's right, isn't it? I'm not up on crafts. If I can't use Elmer's glue to fix it, I'm just not interested.

"Lucky guess," Aunt Tillie grumbled.

"I'll check it out tomorrow," I said, turning back to my dinner. "I'm sure we can figure it all out."

"Thank you," Twila said, beaming.

"What time tomorrow?" Aunt Tillie asked.

"Does it matter?"

"I … just give me a ballpark."

She was definitely up to something. "Noon."

"Fine. I can work with that," Aunt Tillie said.

That was good, because now I was searching that greenhouse before breakfast. Whatever she was buying online was out there, and I had a feeling it wasn't gardening gloves and seeds.

THREE

I rolled to my side the next morning, taking a moment to bask in Bay's warmth before I forced my eyes open. She was still asleep, preferring to burrow under the covers as long as she could before greeting the day. Her blond hair was a mess, like it always is in the morning, and her face was serene in slumber. I would never admit this is my favorite part of the day to anyone but myself – I have to maintain my street cred, after all – but there's something relaxing about watching a woman sleep, especially if she's usually buzzing around and getting into trouble.

I didn't want to wake her, but my stomach growled, causing her to shift. "Are you up?" She asked the question without opening her eyes. I think she hoped I wouldn't answer. Part of me wanted to let her go back to sleep, but the other part of me needed nourishment.

"I'm awake," I said. "You don't have to be if you don't want to."

"I think your stomach has other ideas."

I grinned, running a hand through my hair and shoving it away from my face. "I can go have some cereal. It's not a big deal."

"Whatever," Bay muttered, wrenching her eyes open and focusing on me. "You know very well you don't want cereal."

"Does that mean you're going to cook for me?" While breakfasts at the inn are extravagant affairs, morning meals at the guesthouse are simpler. I was perfectly happy with eggs and toast, especially if it meant Bay stayed in her pajamas for a few more hours.

"I can cook for you," Bay said. "They're making waffles at the inn, though."

I stilled. Homemade waffles did sound good. "Eggs are fine."

Bay snorted. "Hurry up and get in the shower," she said. "I saw fresh strawberries in the refrigerator last night. I know you don't want eggs when you can have waffles and strawberries."

"Do you think they'll have bacon?"

"I don't know," Bay said. "They'll either have bacon or sausage."

"Sold." I slapped her rear end playfully. "Start moving, woman! My stomach needs some attention, and I want to look in that greenhouse before we go up to the inn."

"I thought you told Aunt Tillie you were stopping in at noon?"

"Like I would tell her the truth," I scoffed. "I'm not giving her time to clean out whatever she's got in that greenhouse."

"I'm pretty sure she did that last night," Bay said.

"She went straight up to bed last night," I reminded her.

"It's a good thing you're cute," Bay said, slipping out of bed. "When it comes to reading little old ladies, you're always going to be a step behind. You're going to need your looks to fall back on if this whole FBI thing fails."

I considered her words, confident I was right. That lasted for exactly twenty seconds. "She drives me crazy," I said, throwing the covers off and jumping out of bed. "She's going to put me in a mental institution before this is all said and done. I just know it."

"SO THAT'S what a kiln looks like, huh?" I studied the large oven for a moment. "It's big, but it's not as if it's taking over the place. She has plenty of room to do whatever it is she's doing out here."

"She's potting plants," Bay said, dryly. She'd changed into simple cargo pants and a T-shirt, and her hair was freshly washed and dried. She was dressed casually for the day, and yet there was something appealing about her. I'd noticed it the first time I saw her at the corn maze. Everyone else was excited and putting on a show, but Bay was lost in her own head. I could tell that from fifty feet away, so I watched her. I couldn't explain then why I was drawn to her. I know better now.

"There'd better not be anything illegal growing in here," I said, shifting so I could study the sprouts in the post on the shelf. "Do you know what all of this is?"

Bay joined me, glancing down. "It looks like herbs."

"Are you sure?"

She shrugged. "I'm not big on plants. She's not stupid enough to plant pot in here, though. She and Marcus have been toiling in the field for weeks anyway. Why would she plant pot here and then transplant it? That's just extra work."

I scowled. I hated knowing Aunt Tillie was planting and cultivating marijuana. Letting it go went against my better nature. "I guess. Look around. Does anything seem out of place?"

Bay was blasé as she scanned the greenhouse. "Landon, I don't know what you're looking for," she said finally. "It's all pots and plants. Whatever she was hiding out here, she moved it last night."

"Do you think she moved it into her bedroom?"

"Do you want to risk looking in there?"

It was a challenge, and I like challenges. "I'm not afraid of dreaming about bacon. In fact, I do that on my own all the time."

"She didn't curse the room so everyone dreams that they're bacon," Bay replied. "She cursed it to determine everyone's biggest fear."

"Your biggest fear is being bacon?" She never ceased to amaze me. "Is that because you think I love bacon more than you? You know that's not true, right? I love you just as much as I love bacon."

Bay rolled her eyes. "I'm not afraid of being bacon," she said. "I'm afraid of ... ."

When she broke off, I focused on her. Sometimes she's an open book, and it's one I love reading. Other times, like this, she clams up. "What are you afraid of?"

"It's stupid," Bay said, swiveling so she could look over the rest of the greenhouse.

"It's not stupid if it bothers you," I said. "What are you afraid of?"

"I've always been afraid of burning," Bay admitted. "I guess it's that whole burning-witches-at-the-stake thing."

That made sense. Kind of. "Bay, I would never let you burn. I won't go into Aunt Tillie's room. It's not a big deal. Whatever she's got going, we'll find out eventually. She's not good with subtlety. She'll tip her hand at some point."

"Probably," Bay agreed.

I moved to her side and grabbed her hand, pressing a quick kiss to her fingertips before tugging her toward the greenhouse door. "Come on," I said. "I'm hungry, and you're thinking about burning to death. I think a nice breakfast will fix both of those things."

"I'm not thinking about burning to death," Bay protested. "I ... ."

"I know you," I said. "It's written all over your face. You can't help yourself. Come on. We'll get breakfast and then ... ."

"What are you doing in here?"

I balked when I heard Aunt Tillie's voice, raising my chin and facing her with what I hoped was a bland look. "Good morning."

"I asked you a question," Aunt Tillie said, shuffling into the greenhouse. "What are you doing? I thought we had a noon lunch date? You don't have a warrant to be in here."

"I just thought I would stop by on our way to breakfast," I said, refusing to back down. Aunt Tillie is like an animal. When she feels fear, she pounces. If she thinks you're not afraid of her, she regroups and picks something else to try to terrify you with. I'm used to her tricks. Of course, there's always the possibility that one of these days she is just going to rip off my leg.

"Well, as you can see, there's nothing here that the fuzz would be interested in," Aunt Tillie said, crossing her arms over her chest. "I told you I was being unfairly persecuted."

"I've asked you repeatedly not to call me 'the fuzz,'" I said.

"If the fuzz fits," Aunt Tillie grumbled. "Shouldn't you be up at the inn for breakfast?"

"Shouldn't you?" I countered.

"I already ate," Aunt Tillie said.

I didn't believe her, but I was done playing in her sandbox for the time being. "We're going," I said, pushing Bay in front of me. "They have waffles, right?"

"And bacon," Aunt Tillie said.

"This is going to be a great day," I said. "Bacon, waffles, a pretty blonde ... what could go wrong?"

"I SHOULDN'T HAVE EATEN SO many waffles," I groaned, stretching out on the guesthouse couch an hour later. "Now all I want to do is take a nap." I gestured toward Bay, who sat at the kitchen table doing something on her laptop. "Do you want to nap with me?"

"Can't you see she's working," Thistle asked, moving out from behind the kitchen counter and heading in my direction, a mug of coffee in her hand. She was still in her pajamas, her pink hair standing on end, and she was grumpy. I used to think it was mornings that made her such a pain. Now I know it's her basic personality.

"You missed out on a great meal," I said, focusing on her. "I'm surprised Marcus would pass up waffles."

"He left before dawn," Thistle said. "He had a big tour group that wanted to go on a sunrise ride, so he had to be at the stable to get the horses ready."

Well, that explained that. I watched Thistle as she moved to the sofa table and pushed my bag to the side. "Are you looking for something?"

"My keys."

"You're always losing your keys," I said. "Maybe you should put them in the same place every day. That way you would always know where they are."

"I know where they are."

"Obviously not."

"I thought you were going to take a nap?"

I ignored her and turned back to Bay. "What are you looking at?"

"I might have to go into the office," Bay said, annoyed. "There's a problem with the server, and I can't get into my email. I'll probably have to go there to do it."

That was not how I envisioned spending the day. "What do you have that's so important?" Thistle took the opportunity to open my bag, causing me to shift my attention back to her. "Can I help you?"

"I'm just checking," Thistle said. "I ... ." She jumped back, her face blanching.

I was instantly on alert and rolled to my feet, my full stomach protesting. "What's wrong?"

Bay glanced up from her computer, concerned. She left the laptop open and closed the distance, resting her hand on Thistle's shoulder. "What is it?"

"I think I just saw ... something," Thistle said, gasping.

"It's not Fred, is it?" Bay wrinkled her nose and glanced down at her feet to make sure nothing was crawling on her. "I knew we hadn't seen the last of that scorpion."

"How would a scorpion that got loose at the inn find it's way into my workbag?" I asked, irritated.

Bay ignored me. "Where did it go?"

"It wasn't Fred," Thistle said, running her hand through her hair as she tried to collect herself. "That wasn't what I saw."

"What did you see?" I asked.

"Was it porn?" Bay shot me a look. "Does he have naughty pictures in that bag?"

"Yes, Bay, I walk around with nudie magazines in my workbag," I said, rolling my eyes. "What's in there?" I racked my brain. Besides my laptop and a few errant ink pens, the only thing that should be in there was the cold case file.

Bay rummaged around the bag, pulling out the file. "Is this what you saw?"

Thistle nodded, biting her lip. "I touched it and ... I had a flash."

I furrowed my brow, confused. "A flash of what? Like a hot flash?"

Thistle shot me a look. Well, at least she was returning to her usual self. "Not a hot flash," Thistle said. "I saw ... it was kind of a vision."

"I didn't know you could do that," I said.

"I can't," Thistle said. "It's happened a few times, but very rarely."

"Clove is the one who has visions," Bay explained. "She hasn't had a true vision in years. They happened a lot when we were teenagers, but Mom said it was hormones and that Clove would settle into a pattern when she got older.

"Instead, she stopped having them," she continued. "I can't remember the last one she had. Now she's more of a medium than anything else."

"She probably passed them on to me," Thistle grumbled. "Great. Now I'm going to get flashes whenever I touch something. My life is ruined."

"Calm down," Bay said. "What did you see?"

"I don't know," Thistle said. "It was a woman. I didn't recognize her. She had red hair and green eyes. I saw her crying."

I slipped between Bay and Thistle and took the file from Bay's hands. I hadn't opened it yet, and now seemed as good a time as any. I flipped it open, my gaze landing on the photograph clipped to the front of the file. The woman was smiling, a toddler on her lap, and she had red hair and green eyes. "Is this who you saw?"

Thistle nodded.

"Margaret Mulder," I said, reading from the file. "She was better known as Peg. This is the woman Chief Terry was talking about at dinner last night."

"And Thistle saw her," Bay said, rubbing the back of her cousin's neck. "That can't be good."

"Well, wait a second," I said, thinking. "If Thistle can see what happened to her, we might be able to solve this case in a matter of hours."

"I don't want to see what happened to her," Thistle said.

"Just try." I pushed the file toward her again, causing her to slip farther away.

"I said no."

"Leave her alone," Bay said. "Can't you see she's overwhelmed?"

She looked normal to me. Of course, I didn't know how all of this witchy stuff worked. I was used to Bay talking to ghosts, and I was even coming to grips with Aunt Tillie doling out curses whenever the mood struck, but visions were new territory. It was ... intriguing.

"Fine," I said, pulling the file from Thistle and pressing it to my chest. "I won't push her. But I want to remind you that this woman has been missing for twenty years. She deserves some closure."

Bay shot me a look, and it was one I didn't particularly like. "Thank you, agent."

Uh-oh, I recognized that tone. I was going to have to do some backtracking here. "I'm sorry," I said. "She's obviously upset. I'll leave it alone."

"Thanks," Thistle snapped, pulling away from Bay and stalking toward her bedroom. "I'm so glad you've agreed to let me do things my own way in my own house."

She slammed the door hard enough to rattle the framed photographs on the wall. I risked a look in Bay's direction, expecting a blow up, but her face was thoughtful. "What are you thinking?"

"I'm thinking that there might be a way for us to track Thistle's vision to a conclusion, rather than forcing her to try to receive another vision."

"How?"

"I'll talk to Clove," Bay said, shaking her head and shifting her blue eyes to me. "I think we can do a spell."

Oh, good, because that never goes wrong. "Okay." What? I'm not picking an argument now. I'm not a coward, but I know when I'm beat. "What are we going to do now?"

"I need to go into the office," Bay said. "Didn't you say you needed to look at Chief Terry's files?"

"You're in this now, aren't you?" I was resigned. Bay has never met a mystery she didn't want to solve. I admire that about her. It also gives me migraines.

"I just ... I want to know."

"Fine," I said, leaning forward so I could give her a quick kiss on the cheek. "We're both going to work. This is exactly how I saw us spending our weekend."

FOUR

"How long do you think you'll be?"

Bay sat in the passenger seat of my Explorer, her hand on the door handle, a weary expression on her face. I should have let her sleep longer. She looked as though she needed it.

"I shouldn't be too long," she said. "What are you going to do?"

"I'm going to talk to Chief Terry," I said. "Then I was thinking of stopping by the stables to see Marcus."

Bay's eyes widened in surprise. "Why?"

"I was hoping he would be able to take me out to the house where Peg Mulder used to live," I said. "I have to start somewhere, and that's the last place she was seen alive."

"You think she's dead, don't you?"

"I think that the file makes it sound as if she was a good mother," I said, choosing my words carefully. "A good mother doesn't take off and leave her young son with her ex-husband and the babysitter."

"What if she was more depressed than she let on?" Bay chose her words carefully, too.

"You think she might have killed herself." The thought had occurred to me.

"I think losing your husband to the babysitter has to be … difficult."

"I think losing someone you love is probably difficult regardless," I said. "I also think that if you have a child, you put them before yourself. Peg Mulder is described singularly as a good mother. That's what everyone in the file said about her.

"They said she was upset about the divorce, but her attention was on the kid," I continued. "That doesn't sound like someone who would commit suicide."

"You're leaning toward John Mulder as a murderer, aren't you?"

"In all cases where a wife goes missing, the husband is the first suspect," I said. "In this case, we have a guy who had an affair with a barely legal teenager and knocked her up. He then left his wife for the babysitter, and he was looking at long years of child support and a hefty payout in a divorce.

"When his relationship with the babysitter ended, he left town," I said. "Maybe he didn't want to live with the guilt of what he did … especially when he did it for a woman who ended up cheating on him."

"I see where you're going," Bay said. "I'm not disagreeing with you. I just … I'd like to believe that doing one bad thing doesn't mean you'd do the ultimate bad thing."

"I know," I said, "but I have to start somewhere. Do you want to go out to the house with me?"

"I'm going to go down to Hypnotic when I'm finished at the office," Bay said. "I want to talk to Clove about that spell. You can pick me up there when you're done."

"Okay," I said, leaning over and giving her a soft kiss. "Don't cast that spell until I'm there to … watch."

"You were going to say supervise, weren't you?"

I was. She didn't need to know that, though. "I like to watch," I teased. "I find it fascinating."

AFTER LEAVING Chief Terry's office with his files, I tossed them into the back seat of my Explorer and drove to the stables. I found Marcus cleaning out a stall, his back to me, seemingly lost in thought.

"Hey."

Marcus jolted at the sound of my voice, turning swiftly. "You scared me."

"What were you thinking about?" Marcus had been a part of the Winchester witches' world longer than I had, but not by much. I considered him a kindred spirit when navigating their troubled waters. And, on a personal level, I really like him. He is even-tempered, and he's the one person in the world who can calm Thistle when she's on a tear. That was definitely a benefit.

"I was just thinking," Marcus said. "I'm trying to decide whether I should hire someone to work here."

I arched an eyebrow, surprised. I knew Marcus did okay at the stable, but it never seemed to be bustling with activity. "Do you need someone to help? I can help you do something now if that's the case."

Marcus shook his head. "I ... I've been considering adding on to the business."

"Oh, yeah? What are you going to add?"

"Well, I want to add a petting zoo," Marcus said. "I also want to add a big vegetable garden on the other side of the stable. I own all of that property, and it's just sitting there. Then I want to set up a booth on the front lawn to sell the vegetables. I think it could be a big draw."

"Is that why you've been spending so much time gardening with Aunt Tillie?"

Marcus' face flushed. "She actually knows a lot about gardening."

"I'm sure she does."

"You know I don't smoke any of that stuff out there, don't you?"

"I'm not the pot police, Marcus," I said, hiding my smile. "I don't really care. As long as you're not hurting someone else, it's not my concern."

"Do you need something?" he asked, quickly changing the subject.

"I was hoping you might be able to take me out to the Mulder house," I said. "I need to take a look around. I figured you would know where it was."

"Sure," Marcus said. " Do you want to drive or ride?"

It would be quicker to drive, but something told me Marcus needed to talk with someone. "Let's ride."

"Cool. Let me saddle up two horses. It will only take a few minutes."

WE RODE IN AMIABLE SILENCE, the only noise coming from the hooves of the horses for a long time before I decided to break the silence. Generally, I like quiet. Marcus and his deep thoughts were starting to make me uncomfortable, though.

"Have you talked to Thistle about your idea?"

Marcus shifted in his saddle, smiling. "No. I know I should. It's just ... it's going to take up a lot of my time when I decide to do it."

"You don't think she'll understand? She runs her own business. She knows it takes work. It's not as though you guys won't see each other. The stable is only two blocks from the store."

"The truth is, I don't want to spend time away from her," Marcus said. "I ... what I'm about to tell you is a secret."

I nodded encouragingly.

"I want to spend this summer getting the business up and running to the level I want and then ... well ... I want to propose."

The admission should have been surprising, and yet it wasn't. "I think that's a good idea."

"Do you think she'll say 'yes?'"

"I think Thistle loves you," I said. "Are you worried she'll say 'no?'"

"I'm worried that she's going to want to live with Bay and Clove forever," Marcus said. "I'm worried that she'll say 'yes,' and then expect me to move into the guesthouse with everyone else.

"Don't get me wrong," he added hurriedly. "I love Bay and Clove. I like hanging out with them."

"You just don't want to live with them," I finished.

"What if she's not ready to live away from them?"

"Well ... ." I was at a loss. Truth be told, for the past few weeks I'd been considering asking Bay to move in with me. It was one of those ideas tucked away in a small corner of my mind, thoughts of an apartment between Hemlock Cove and Traverse City wreaking havoc on my fantasy world. I didn't think Bay and I were quite there yet, so I was leaving it alone. For now, at least. "I'm hoping to move in with Bay at some point, too."

"You're just as worried as I am, aren't you?" Marcus asked.

"I don't think I'm worried," I said. "I think it's a daunting thing. They're extremely close to one another. The thing is, I think Clove is probably going to move in with Sam before it's all said and done."

"You think she'll leave first?" Marcus was surprised. "She and Sam haven't been dating that long."

"I don't think Clove is moving in with Sam right away," I cautioned. "It's just … Clove seems like the type of person who wants to settle down."

"And Thistle doesn't," Marcus said, miserable.

"I don't think Thistle knows what she wants at any given point of any given day," I said. "I do think she loves you, and I think she's going to say 'yes' if you propose. When do you plan to ask her?"

"Not until after the snow flies," Marcus said. "I was going to do it around Valentine's Day, but then I thought she might find that schmaltzy."

"She probably will," I said. "I think you should do what you want to do, though. It's as much your decision as it is hers."

"I guess."

"Why don't you handle the business stuff first," I suggested. "That's going to take months to get in order. Are you going to be able to get a garden planted behind the stables this late in the season?"

"I don't plan to plant this season," Marcus replied. "I need to till the field, and that's going to take a long time. I want a big garden. I'm also going to need to hire someone at the stable because I can't be in two places at once."

"Do you have the money for all of this?"

"The stable does really well in the summer, and it's more than enough to live on during the winter," Marcus said. "I have the money.

I just … what if Thistle is upset because I spend so much time on the new business?"

"Thistle gets upset about a lot of things I don't understand," I said. "She flies off the handle, and she always seems angry, but this is one thing I think she'll completely understand. In fact, I'm betting she's going to want to help you."

"Really?" Marcus looked hopeful.

"Really," I said. "Thistle isn't afraid of hard work, and she has respect for people who work hard. Why don't you tell her what you have planned and go from there."

"That's probably the best way to go." Marcus ran a hand through his long, blond hair. "What happens if we start fighting because we're spending too much time together working?"

Now that was something I could see. "Then gag her."

Marcus barked out a harsh laugh. "That's an idea." He sobered. "Are you really going to ask Bay to move in with you?"

"Not right now," I said. "She's not ready. We're still … feeling each other out on some stuff. I'm hoping that Clove pulls the trigger first and moves in with Sam. That will make things easier for me.

"As the oldest, Bay feels she needs to take care of Clove and Thistle sometimes," I said. "She doesn't, for the record. I still think, because they were so close growing up, they're always going to be close."

"You know, if Clove moves in with Sam, and Thistle and I do get engaged, you two could have the guesthouse all to yourselves," Marcus said. "That might work out for both of you."

Well, that was an interesting thought, one I quickly pushed out of my head. "We're not there yet. I'm happy with the way things are."

"Bay seems happy, too," Marcus said. "She was sad a lot of the time when she was a kid, but she's happy now. I think a lot of that is due to you."

"I forget you knew Bay as a kid," I said. "You didn't grow up here, though, did you?"

"Kind of," Marcus said. "I was here in elementary and middle school, and then my mother moved us south. I came back to town

AMANDA M. LEE

because I wanted to buy the stable from my uncle when he retired, and Mom wanted to move back to town, too. It seemed a natural fit.

"Even when I was away from Hemlock Cove, though, I was still here over the summers," he continued. "I would see Bay, Clove and Thistle running around town. They were always up to something, and it always looked fun."

"Did you hang out with them?"

"Me? No way. I was too shy. Even then Thistle frightened me."

"You finally got the courage to ask her out, though," I pointed out.

"That was my bravest moment," Marcus agreed. "It was also the smartest thing I ever did."

"I think you have a good head on your shoulders," I said. "I believe you know exactly how to get what you want. Just … don't push things. I have faith that things happen when they're supposed to."

"Like meeting Bay?" Marcus teased.

"Exactly like meeting Bay," I said. "If I hadn't gone undercover when I did, I never would have met her. If she hadn't happened to be at the corn maze that day, she probably would have been only the odd woman I saw going into a corn maze in the middle of the night and didn't follow."

"I don't believe that," Marcus said. "I think some things are destiny. I think Thistle and I are destiny, and I think you and Bay are, too."

"Destiny? I'm not sure I believe in destiny."

"Really?" Marcus arched an eyebrow. "You're in love with a witch who talks to ghosts and who comes from a family of women who can make things happen out of thin air. If you don't believe in magic, what are you doing here?"

He had a point, and it was one I was reluctant to tackle. "I believe in magic," I said. "It's just … do you really believe there's only one person out there for everyone?"

"I don't know," Marcus said. "I do know I can't imagine being with anyone other than Thistle. Can you imagine being with anyone other than Bay?"

"No."

"Isn't that destiny?"

"I guess it is," I said, considering the question. "I've never thought of it that way. You're pretty smart sometimes."

"I know," Marcus said, winking. "Don't tell Thistle, though. I like her to think she's in charge."

"Oh, please," I said, laughing. "Thistle is definitely in charge."

"Or do I just let her think she is?"

Now I wasn't so sure. "You're starting to scare me, man."

"I'm starting to scare myself," Marcus admitted. "Come on. The house is this way. It's abandoned now, so we should be able to look around without anyone bothering us."

"Are you going to tell Thistle about your business plans?"

"I am," Marcus said. "I just need to decide how I'm going to do it."

"I suggest chocolate martinis and candles."

"They're already on my list."

I laughed. "And don't get on Aunt Tillie's list before you propose, and I think you're golden."

"You're not going to tell Bay, are you?"

"Of course not," I said. "I love Bay, but she's got a huge mouth. There's no way she wouldn't let it slip to Thistle. Your secret is safe with me."

"Thanks," Marcus said. "Your secret is safe with me, too."

"I don't have a secret," I said. "Not yet. I'm not asking Bay to move in until I think she's ready, and I know she's not ready yet. It will happen, but I'm content with the way things are. When it's time I'll know it."

"That's because it's destiny," Marcus said.

"Sometimes you talk like a woman," I said. "How close are we?"

"Close," Marcus said. "This way."

I watched him move ahead of me on the path, my mind busy. Who knew Marcus was a dreamer at heart?

FIVE

"You didn't find anything?"

I studied Peg Mulder's file, only half listening to Bay as she rummaged around the guesthouse kitchen with Thistle and Clove a few hours later. I muttered a reply. In my mind, I formed words. Apparently Bay didn't think so. She stepped in front of me, hands on hips, and flicked the file.

I ignored the first two times she did it. By the third, I was officially annoyed.

"What?" I didn't mean to snap at her, and the look on her face told me I'd surprised her with my harshness. "I'm sorry. What do you want?"

"I wanted to know whether you found anything," Bay said, her voice low.

"No. I already told you that." I waited for her to say something else. When she didn't, I turned back to the file. "Is that all?"

"I'm sorry to bother you," Bay said, glaring at me. "I'll leave you to … whatever is so very important to you."

Women drive me crazy. At work, there's only one woman in the office. All the men there make sense. They understand when you need quiet to read something. Women are another story. On weekends, women surround me – well, Sam and Marcus, too – and the things they think or say rarely make sense. "Give me five minutes."

"Fine."

I recognized the tone. Sighing, I reluctantly closed the file and fixed Bay with my full attention. "Sweetie, do you need something?"

"Why would I possibly need anything?"

Great, now she was going to play petulant. "Because you seem to think I'm not paying attention to you."

"How can you possibly know that's what I was thinking?" Bay asked.

That was a trick question. "Because … I think I've been wrapped up in the file for too long when I clearly should be listening to what you're saying." That sounded like a safe answer.

"Smooth," Sam said, glancing up from the magazine he was reading. "Good answer."

"It was inspired," Marcus agreed.

Sam and Marcus may be men, but they know which specific woman they don't want to upset: the one they're dating. Marcus constantly lives on the edge with Thistle, and Sam has it easy with Clove. I'm somewhere in the middle – which makes Bay the really dangerous one. There was only one way to handle this. I needed to distract her. I reached up and snagged her around the waist, tumbled her into my lap and tickled her ribs until she giggled. "What were you saying, my queen?"

"What do you want for dinner?"

"Aren't we going up to the inn?"

Bay and Thistle exchanged a look.

"What am I missing?" I asked, pinching the bridge of my nose.

"You're not missing anything," Bay said. "It's just … Aunt Tillie is really on the warpath about the kiln."

"So? Aunt Tillie is always on the warpath."

"We don't want to be in her line of fire," Thistle said. "If she's going to curse someone, we feel it's only fair to sacrifice our mothers. They're the ones who refuse to have her committed."

I rested my cheek against Bay's forehead for a moment, considering. "We could go out to one of the diners in town."

"We thought we would just order pizza and have chocolate martinis," Clove said. "That's what we were talking about when you were ignoring Bay."

Did I say Clove was the easy one? In some ways she's the most manipulative. At least when you're dealing with Thistle she puts it right out there. Clove sneaks in with her guerilla verbal attacks. "I was not ignoring Bay," I replied. "I was going over the file again. I could never ignore Bay. She's too cute."

Bay rolled her eyes at the compliment. "You're such a charmer."

"I have my moments," I agreed. "Pizza and martinis sound fine."

"Are you sure?"

"I'm sure."

"I'll order," Thistle said, reaching for her phone. "I'm starving."

Bay moved to climb from my lap but I stilled her by tightening my arm around her waist. "Where are you going?"

"To the kitchen."

"Oh, no," I said. "You demanded my attention. Now you have it. You have to entertain me until the food arrives."

"What do you want me to do?" Bay's blue eyes were quizzical.

"I want you to tell me about séances."

"What? Why?" Now Bay was outright confused.

"If Peg Mulder was murdered, wouldn't it make sense she's a ghost?" I asked. "Isn't that how it usually works?"

"Most people don't come back as ghosts," Bay said. "The percentage is actually pretty tiny. Hemlock Cove is small. If Peg was a ghost, I think I would have seen her over the years."

"And you're sure you haven't?"

"I'm pretty sure," Bay said. "This case is really getting to you, isn't it? When you first got here you didn't care. Now, twenty-four hours later, it's all you can think about."

"Don't worry, I'm thinking about you, too," I said, tweaking her nose, "but the more I learn about this story, the more frustrated I get."

"Because her husband was a rampant jackass?"

"Partially," I conceded. "It's hard to imagine someone being there one second and gone the next. Someone has to know where she is."

"Maybe John killed her and dumped her," Bay suggested. "We would have to track him down and get him to confess, which seems unlikely unless he's feeling really guilty."

"I put in a call to the main office and asked them to start a search for John Mulder," I said. "I'm not sure when it's going to come through, but it shouldn't take too long."

"Are you going to leave when you get the information?"

"I'm not leaving here until Monday morning," I said. "Don't worry about that. It's just that … going out to that house this afternoon was sobering."

"Isn't it abandoned?" Thistle asked.

"It is," I replied. "It's extremely run down. You can tell someone took care of it way back when, though. It didn't look like a place someone would abandon."

"You're really stuck on it being a murder, aren't you?" Sam asked.

"I should say 'no,'" I said. "We have no proof that it's murder. Still … there's something off."

"That's why you want to conduct a séance," Bay said. "You want to talk to Peg's ghost and figure out whether you're right."

"It's not about me being right."

"Oh, look who you're talking to," Thistle scoffed. "We're the queens of having to be right."

"If Peg Mulder isn't a ghost, it's only a waste of time, isn't it?"

"Not necessarily," Bay hedged. "We have managed to communicate with a few spirits on the other side, but only if they were willing to cross back over."

"Who?"

Bay and Thistle exchanged another look. "We haven't done it in a long time," Bay said.

"The last time was in high school," Thistle said.

"I've seen you guys conduct séances," I argued.

"You saw us conduct séances to call ghosts who were stuck here," Bay clarified. "Those are easy."

"We still always screw them up," Clove said.

I smirked. She hated séances. Bay and Thistle had to drag her kicking and screaming when it was time to conduct one. "Can we at least try?"

"We can," Bay said.

"I would rather not," Clove said.

"You'll be fine," Thistle said. "We'll be there, and the guys will watch your back. Nothing bad will happen."

"That's what you said when we conjured Patricia Norton's ghost in high school," Clove said, crossing her arms over her chest. "No one wants that to happen again. I smelled like dirty water for a week."

Bay shuddered in my lap.

"Who is Patricia Norton?" I asked.

"She was this old woman who had a reputation for being really mean to kids when we were little," Thistle said. "She died when we were in high school, so we got drunk and thought it would be a good idea to call her back over after she died."

"I'm guessing it wasn't a good idea," I said. "By the way, who was serving you guys under age?"

"Are you honestly saying that you didn't drink in high school?" Bay asked.

"I'm saying we did it the normal way, by stealing from the refrigerators of our parents and paying a local bum to buy us liquor," I said. "Something tells me you three didn't have that problem."

"We stole from Aunt Tillie," Thistle said.

Clove glanced over her shoulder, as if making sure Aunt Tillie hadn't managed to sneak in and eavesdrop. "We didn't steal. We … borrowed."

"Oh, whatever," Thistle said. "We totally stole from her. She caught us so many times I lost count."

"What did she do to you?" Marcus asked, intrigued.

"Usually she just cursed us with the basics," Bay said. "Our pants wouldn't fit. We got tongue-tied when talking to boys. We'd blurt out strange things in the middle of conversations."

"Once she cursed us so that we had theme music whenever we

entered a room," Thistle interjected. "It took me forever to get the *Facts of Life* theme out of my head."

"That's a better song than the *Little House on the Prairie* theme," Clove grumbled. "At least your song had lyrics."

"Why the *Little House on the Prairie* theme?" Sam asked.

"Aunt Tillie always thought Clove was a goody-goody," Thistle said, smirking.

"What was your theme?" I asked, poking Bay in the side.

"The theme from *Dallas*." Bay made a face. "It didn't even have a dance beat."

"I don't get it."

"Aunt Tillie always thought Bay was a drama queen," Thistle said.

I couldn't stop myself from laughing. That made sense. "Why did you get the *Facts of Life*?" I asked.

"Because she knew I hated that song," Thistle said. "The best part was that she gave our mothers and herself theme songs for the week, too."

"Oh, I can't wait to hear this," Sam said, giddy.

I couldn't help but agree. "What were they?"

"Marnie's was *The Addams Family* theme," Bay said, smiling at the memory.

"She was really angry," Clove said.

"Twila's was *The Golden Girls*. She actually liked her song," Bay said.

"Aunt Winnie's was *Charlie's Angels*," Thistle supplied.

"Why?"

"She was going through a weird hair-feathering phase," Bay said. "Aunt Tillie hated her hair, and it was meant to make fun of it from afar. It worked, too. Mom cut her hair three days later."

"What was Aunt Tillie's theme?" I asked, readying myself for the ultimate punch line.

"*The Greatest American Hero*," Thistle said. "She even took to wearing a cape."

And there it was. Stories like this are exactly why I love this family. I just can't help myself.

"**Did** we really need the blanket?" I asked, spreading an old comforter on the ground and watching as Marcus and Sam deposited copious amounts of liquor, glasses and an ice bucket on the corners. "Are we planning on staying out here long enough to drink all of that?"

"It's a nice night," Bay said. "We might as well enjoy it."

She had a point. Still .... "Can't we just drink in the guesthouse?"

"Are you afraid of the woods?" Thistle teased, placing candles in a circle on top of the bluff.

The land surrounding The Overlook is extensive, but when it comes to conducting magical rites the Winchesters always pick the same clearing. It's mostly bare, except for some distinctive rock formations cut into the hillside. I've thought about asking why they insist on going to the same spot, but part of me is perfectly fine being left in the dark. I want to know some things. Knowing too much is dangerous, though. "I'm not afraid of the woods. I just know when to give the woods a healthy ... respect."

Bay helped Thistle distribute candles, but she stilled long enough to send me a searching look. "Are you afraid of the woods?"

"I'm not afraid of the woods!" This conversation was starting to get away from me.

"Don't worry," Bay said, smiling. "I'll protect you."

Marcus and Sam snickered, causing me to bristle. "I'm not afraid of the woods!"

"Of course you're not," Clove said, sympathetic. "If you were, though, I would totally understand."

"That's because you're afraid of the woods," Thistle said, rolling her eyes.

"I'm not afraid of the woods," Clove said.

I thought about stepping in and helping her for a moment, but since everyone had shifted their attention to her I didn't want to give them a reason to come after me again. She's used to it. She'll live.

"You're afraid of Bigfoot," Thistle said.

"That's because Bigfoot is scary," Clove said.

"I'll protect you from Bigfoot," Sam said, winking at Clove. "He won't get near you."

"Bigfoot isn't real," I said.

"Are you sure?" Bay asked.

"I'm sure."

"A year ago you thought witches weren't real either," Bay reminded me.

That was a good point. Still … . "Are you saying you believe in Bigfoot?"

Bay's face was serious -- for exactly three seconds. Then she couldn't fight the spreading grin. "No. I just like messing with you."

I arched an eyebrow. "I'm going to make you pay for that later."

"I'm looking forward to your torture expertise." Bay gave me a quick kiss and then moved to the circle. "Okay, let's get this show on the road."

"One dead woman coming up," Thistle said, extending her hands and linking fingers with Bay and Clove. "This is where the fun begins."

THERE'S NO REASON TO POUT," I said, topping off Bay's chocolate martini with one hand and rubbing her neck with the other. "It was a good try."

"Nothing happened."

"It was still a good try."

After forty minutes of watching Bay, Thistle and Clove chant at the moon – frustration becoming evident when Thistle's chants turned to dirty limericks – the trio gave up. I was happy. The first five minutes watching them was exhilarating. After that, though? The real problem with the woods is that you can't watch *Sports Center* when you're bored.

The six of us gave up on the séance and started mainlining chocolate martinis. We'd been at it for about a half hour, and none of us were particularly interested in packing up and returning to the guesthouse. It seemed Bay and her cousins knew what they were doing when they thought ahead and brought the comforter and alcohol.

I relaxed on the blanket, propping myself up on one elbow as I sipped my martini. "You did your best. Don't let it get you down."

"We should have asked Aunt Tillie for help," Clove said.

"Did you take a stupid pill when I wasn't looking?" Thistle asked, cuffing Clove's head. "We can't ask Aunt Tillie. If we put her in a position to add alcohol and magic to her already bad mood she'll curse us to within an inch of our lives."

"I think you guys give her too much power," I said. "She only curses you because she knows she can get away with it."

"She curses us because she likes it," Thistle said. "Being mean is what keeps her alive."

"Sometimes I think you're bitter," I said.

"Sometimes I think you're right," Thistle replied, leaning her head against Marcus' shoulder.

"Well, it's not a total loss," I said. "We have a beautiful night and a full jug of martinis."

"I thought you were afraid of the woods," Bay prodded.

"I thought you were here to protect me," I said, grinning. "You're going to have to stay close if you want to do that."

"I'll do my best."

"The only thing that could make this better is a BLT," I said, pouring another martini for myself. "And a few pillows."

SIX

"Well, isn't this just a kick in the pants."

It took me a second to get my bearings, and when I did, I immediately wished I could go back to sleep. Bay was asleep beside me, her head tucked in next to my shoulder. The comforter from the night before was cluttered with four other bodies, too. Apparently the chocolate martinis claimed another night from us. I really should ban them. They're the Devil's drink.

I shifted my attention to the figure standing at the edge of the blanket and sucked in a breath as the early morning light bombarded my eyes. If I was dreaming, this was surely the nightmare portion of the big event.

Aunt Tillie, dressed in camouflage pants and a combat helmet, crossed her arms over her chest as she met my gaze. "This is undignified," she said.

"I've seen you get hammered and dance naked in this very spot," I said. "At least we're all dressed."

"What's going on?" Bay murmured, shifting. "Oh, man, my back is killing me."

"Join the club," I said, helping us both struggle to a sitting position.

"I don't know when it happened, but I'm officially too old to sleep on the ground."

"What's going on here?" Aunt Tillie asked.

"We conducted a séance," Thistle said, pushing herself to a sitting position on the far end of the comforter. "It didn't work, so we decided to get drunk. My head feels like it's going to explode, by the way."

Aunt Tillie narrowed her eyes. "Why were you conducting a séance?"

"We were trying to contact Peg Mulder," Clove replied. "It didn't work."

"Why do you want to talk to Peg Mulder?" Aunt Tillie asked. "What makes you even think she's dead?"

I froze, something in her question nudging the far corners of my muddled mind. "Oh … of course."

"Of course what?" Bay asked.

"You guys couldn't get the spell to work last night."

"I was there," Bay said. "There's no reason to rub it in."

"Maybe you couldn't get it to work because Peg Mulder isn't dead," I said. "You were trying to talk to a ghost that doesn't exist."

"Spirit," Bay corrected.

"Is there a difference?" Mornings aren't my favorite part of the day. Bay is usually grumpy when we first wake up, and I like to blame our morning quiet on her, but I'm as bad as she is.

Thistle made a sound like a cat in heat.

I shot her a look. "Don't push me this morning. I'm in pain." I rubbed my lower back, pulling my hands away when I felt Bay's fingers knead into the tender spot. "Oh, man, that feels good. I'll buy you a car if you keep doing that for an hour."

Aunt Tillie rolled her eyes. "I'm not saying Peg Mulder is alive," she said. "I'm saying we don't know for sure she's dead."

"What do you think?" I asked.

"I think she's dead," Aunt Tillie said. "That doesn't mean you can call her spirit over if you don't know what you're doing."

"We know what we're doing," Thistle said. "We've done it before."

"Oh, you mean that time you called Patricia Norton back over?" Thistle nodded.

"I did that," Aunt Tillie said. "I saw you stealing my wine and wanted to punish you. If I remember that night correctly, you got exactly what you deserved for stealing from me."

"That was you?" Clove jumped to her feet, cringing when her sore muscles fought the motion. "Do you know what happened to me that night?"

"You thought a ghost was trying to kiss you," Aunt Tillie replied, nonplussed. "In your haste to escape, you ran right into a bog. A particularly smelly bog, if memory serves.

"Your cousins then spent a week telling you that if a female ghost was attracted to you that meant you were a lesbian and you didn't know it yet," she continued. "Every time a woman touched you for the next month you thought she was hitting on you."

"I forgot about that," Thistle said, chuckling throatily. "We paid Lydia Simpson twenty bucks to tell you that your hair looked particularly nice one day. You were convinced she was going to ask you to the prom. Oh, man, that was so funny."

"It was not funny," Clove said. "I was a mess for ... well ... forever."

Thistle arched a challenging eyebrow. "Forever? Do you still think you have latent lesbian tendencies? Should Sam be worried?"

"I'm fine if she thinks she's a lesbian," Sam replied, still flat on his back and staring at the sky. "As long as I can watch, I'm good."

"You're a sick man," Aunt Tillie said.

"Whatever." Sam didn't appear to be a morning person either.

"What are you doing out here so early?" I asked, shifting my attention back to Aunt Tillie. "It's barely dawn."

"I'm ... taking a walk," Aunt Tillie said.

The pause was brief, but it was enough to tip me that she was lying. "Really?"

"Really."

Did I have the energy to push her on this? My back, even with Bay's magic fingers working out the kinks, screamed "no." Aunt Tillie must have sensed that, because she started shuffling toward the edge of the clearing. "If you're up to something, knock it off," I said. "If you're not ... then ... just keep doing what you're doing."

"I'm never up to anything," Aunt Tillie sniffed. "You keep maligning me in your mind."

"I'm sure," I said.

"You should all probably get going," Aunt Tillie said. "Breakfast should be on the table up at the inn in about ten minutes, and after missing dinner last night, you're all in trouble."

"What about you?" Thistle asked. "Aren't you eating breakfast?"

"I already ate," Aunt Tillie said. "Now I'm walking it off. I'm getting into shape. I'm going to run a marathon."

I didn't know a lot of eighty-year-olds running marathons, but I let it slide. "That sounds good to me," I said. "I need some bacon."

"I need some coffee," Thistle said, getting to her feet.

"I need someone to help me get up," Sam said. "I think my neck is frozen."

"I'm never sleeping on the ground again," Bay said, rubbing her sore bottom ruefully. "I think we're both officially old."

I gave her a quick kiss. "At least we still have our looks."

"I SMELL BACON." I pushed through the back living quarters and pointed myself toward the kitchen. "I'm going to eat a pound of it."

"You have a nose like a bloodhound when there's bacon around," Bay said. "I bought a new perfume last week and you still haven't commented on it."

"Bay, when is the one and only time I commented on your scent?"

"When I smelled like bacon," Bay said, her smile rueful. "Is that a hint? Should I roll around in bacon all day?"

That sounded messy. "Just take photos," I said.

Marnie, Winnie and Twila were working as I strode into the kitchen. They all looked up, bright smiles on their faces, until they saw our clothing.

"Isn't that what you were wearing yesterday?" Winnie asked,

furrowing her brow. "Why are you all dressed in the same clothes from yesterday?"

"They probably had an orgy," Twila said. That was always her go-to answer for everything. I had a feeling her history was littered with a few more naughty secrets than her sisters' – or maybe she was just worse at hiding it.

"We didn't have an orgy," Thistle snapped, heading straight for the coffee pot. "We were trying to have a séance and we fell asleep in the clearing."

"Why were you trying to have a séance?" Winnie asked.

"Peg Mulder," Bay replied. "We were hoping we could call her and she could tell us what happened to her. It would be so much easier than trying to track down John Mulder – or even her – now."

"Her?" Winnie pursed her lips as she shook the pieces of paper towel the bacon was drying on. "Do you think she's alive?"

"I think it's a possibility," I said. "We don't know for sure that she's dead."

"We don't know anything for sure," Winnie said. "I would like to believe that she's alive."

"That would mean she abandoned her son," Twila pointed out.

"She would still be alive," Winnie said. "Maybe someone kidnapped her and she's been held captive for twenty years."

"I think that would be worse than dying," Thistle said. "If someone kidnaps me, they'd better be ready to kill me. I'm not built for long confinement."

"Don't worry," I said. "If someone kidnapped you they could only put up with your mouth for an hour ... tops."

"Thanks."

"You're welcome."

Winnie waved a spatula in my face. "Don't poke Thistle when she's just waking up," she said. "You know very well she's crabby in the morning."

"Maybe I'm crabby in the morning," I said, snatching a piece of bacon and biting into it before Winnie could stop me.

"We're all crabby this morning," Bay said, reaching for my slice of

AMANDA M. LEE

bacon. Without thinking, I pulled it away from her, earning a harsh look.

"I'm sorry," I said. "This is my bacon, though. You can have your own slice ."

Winnie frowned and handed her daughter two slices of bacon to spite me. "What happened to you?" she asked. "You used to be such a nice boy."

"I'm still a nice boy," I said, debating whether I could snag one of Bay's slices without her pitching a fit. "I'm sore from sleeping on the ground all night and I have a monster headache."

"The coffee pot is over there," Winnie said, gesturing to the far side of the kitchen. "You're not getting any more bacon until you're seated in the dining room."

Bay studied my face for a moment and then handed me her second slice of bacon. "You owe me."

"I'll buy you a car," I said, kissing her cheek.

"I don't want a car."

"What do you want?" I was pretty much willing to give her the moon at this point. I only needed to figure out a way to catch it for her.

"I want to spend the week in Traverse City with you."

I choked on the bacon, surprised. I glanced at Marcus, worried for a moment that he'd told her what I'd been considering, but he looked as surprised as I was. "You want to spend the week with me in Traverse City?" I was stalling for time, unsure how to answer.

"Is that a problem?" Bay arched an eyebrow, but other than that, her face was unreadable.

"No," I said. "I just … you're going to have to drive back here every day. Is that something you want to do?"

"I don't have to drive back here every day," she said. "I only have to drive back on Wednesday and Friday."

"And I'll be coming back on Friday," I said. "You really want to stay in that small apartment with me?"

Everyone watched our conversation with a mixture of amusement and consternation. The consternation came mostly from Winnie, who wasn't a big fan of shacking up. She'd been trying to rein in her discomfort about our living situation for the past few months, though, so she was keeping her mouth shut. For now.

Bay opened her mouth to answer and then snapped it shut. Her eyes clouded briefly, and I could see her mind working. Unfortunately, I couldn't figure out what she was thinking.

"I don't need to come to Traverse City," Bay said. "That was a stupid idea."

"It wasn't a stupid idea," I said. "I'm just worried that being cooped up in that small apartment while I'm at work ... no cousins to amuse you when you get bored ... is going to drive you crazy."

"Are you sure that's the reason?"

What other reason would there be? "I'm sure. If you want to come to Traverse City for the week I'd be happy to have you with me."

"She can't go," Winnie said, squaring her shoulders.

"Why not?" I asked.

"Because she has work," Winnie said, averting her gaze.

"You just heard her say that she can do most of that work from my place," I said. "Traverse City is only an hour away. If she needs to come back, she can come back."

"What if her cousins need her?" Winnie wasn't giving up. Not yet, at least.

"She has her phone," I said, keeping my voice calm. Winnie getting used to Bay spending more time away from the inn could only help my future plans. I decided to dig my heels in. "If Thistle and Clove need something, they have Marcus and Sam to help. They have all of you ... and Aunt Tillie."

"Aunt Tillie won't help us," Thistle said.

"She'll just point and laugh," Clove agreed.

I pressed my lips together and shot Thistle a dark look. "Really?"

"We'll be fine," Thistle said, giving in. "It might be nice to have one less body in the guesthouse this week. It's starting to feel claustrophobic."

That was an understatement. I turned back to Winnie. "Is there another reason Bay can't stay at my place this week? She is an adult, after all."

"Wait, you really want me to stay with you?" Bay's eyebrows shot up. "I thought maybe you were just saying that and you didn't want me in your space."

"I have no problem sharing my space," I said. "I was surprised you suggested it. I would love to have you in Traverse City for the week. We can go out to the movies, and maybe go for a walk on the beach. It will be nice spending time together."

"You're spending the whole week together," Winnie said, wringing her hands. "What if she gets lonely?"

I tilted my head to the side as I regarded Winnie. She looked as if I'd suggested Bay throw herself into a volcano instead of staying an hour away for five days. "What if we come back for dinner Wednesday night?"

"That's not necessary," Bay said. "I'm old enough to spend a week away from home. I spent years away from home, in case you've forgotten."

I held up my hand to quiet her, realization washing over me. Winnie lost Bay once before when her daughter moved away to find herself. When she returned, the family was made whole again. Winnie worried I would steal Bay away. "It's only an hour away," I said. "Instead of us coming here for dinner on Wednesday, why don't you come to Traverse City for dinner on Tuesday. Tuesday is a quiet night for the inn, right?" I looked to Marnie and Twila for confirmation. They both nodded, but their eyes were fixed on Winnie. "It's really going to be okay," I said. "You'll see."

Winnie finally nodded. "Fine. I get to pick the restaurant, though."

"I can live with that," I said.

Sensing the crisis had passed, Marnie and Twila returned to their breakfast preparations. After a few moments, Twila left the kitchen and moved into the back of the house. When she returned a few minutes later, she had a puzzled look on her face. "Aunt Tillie isn't in her room."

"She's in the woods," Thistle said. "She's the one who woke us up."

"But what about breakfast?" Marnie asked.

"She said she already ate," Clove said.

Twila didn't look convinced.

"What's wrong?" I asked her.

"I guess nothing," Twila said. "I was worried she was missing because of the ghost on the back porch."

SEVEN

"What ghost?" I asked, instantly alert.

"There's a ghost on the back porch," Twila said.

"Who?" Bay asked. "Did you recognize her?"

"The sun is so bright back there," Twila said, shifting from one foot to the other uncomfortably. "I didn't get a good look."

"She means she was afraid to look," Thistle said, pushing away from the counter and heading for the door. "She's afraid of ghosts."

"I am not afraid of ghosts," Twila said. "I just think they're … freaky. I'm glad I only see them on rare occasions."

"That's the same as being afraid," Thistle said. "Come on. I'll bet it's Peg Mulder."

I followed the line of excited witches – and a mostly "meh" Marcus and Sam – until we stood by the big bay windows at the back of the living quarters. The porch looked empty to me. Of course, I'd seen only one ghost in my life – and that was because Bay's life had been in danger. I wasn't really expecting to see another one now. "What's going on?"

"There's a ghost out there," Bay said. "It looks like the photo of Peg Mulder, but Twila is right about her being … blurry."

"Blurry?" That didn't sound good.

"Blurry isn't the right word," Bay said, her face thoughtful as she stared out the window. "She's ... brighter ... than a normal ghost."

"That must be because we pulled her over from the other side," Thistle said. "That could explain why she looks different."

"Does that mean she's an angel?" Marcus asked, awed.

I wanted to laugh at the question, but given the surreal nature of the conversation, that didn't seem wise. Besides ... . "Is that a possibility?"

"Are you asking me to comment on the nature of life and death?" Bay asked. "If you are, I don't have any answers for you. I don't know what happens when you cross over."

"I'll bet the woman on the porch does," I suggested.

Bay worried her bottom lip with her teeth, conflicted. "We called her here to ask how she died," she said. "We now know she really is dead. I don't feel comfortable asking about ... other things."

Sometimes I forget how sensitive she is. I brushed Bay's hair, smoothing it. "You don't have to ask her anything you're not comfortable with," I said. "Just ask her whether she knows how she died and ... well ... where her body is."

Bay nodded, her face lightening considerably. "Okay."

"Screw that," Thistle said, pushing between us. "I want to know what's on the other side. Let's go."

"YOU DON'T HAVE TO HIDE," Bay said, peering around the tree on the corner of the lot worriedly. "We're not here to hurt you."

It turns out Peg Mulder hadn't been waiting for us on the back porch. In fact, when we all slipped outside of the inn, she'd run. Wait, do ghosts run? She probably floated. That sounds more likely.

After ten minutes, Winnie, Marnie and Twila excused themselves to serve breakfast to the inn guests. I knew they were eating all my bacon.

"Why don't you guys go inside and have breakfast," Bay suggested. "This might take a little time."

My stomach agreed with her. My heart put up a fantastic fight. "No," I said. "I'm staying with you. The rest of you can go inside."

Bay's face was conflicted. "You're starving. What about your bacon?"

"I'd rather have you than the bacon," I replied. "I'm not leaving you alone with an unknown entity – even if I can't see it."

"She's not Floyd," Bay said, referring to a nasty poltergeist from a few months before. "She won't hurt me."

"She won't," I agreed. "I'm still staying here."

"Make sure you ask her about the other side," Thistle instructed, letting Marcus drag her toward the door. "I need to know what's out there."

"I wouldn't worry about that," I said. "You're going to go to the bad place."

"That's a horrible thing to say," Thistle snapped.

"Don't worry, you'll have Aunt Tillie for company." I shot her a cheeky smile. "Save me some bacon."

"I'm eating it all now because you made that little comment," Thistle replied. "Every last slice."

"Enjoy your major coronary," I said.

Thistle extended her tongue and blew an inelegant raspberry before disappearing with Marcus, Sam and Clove. When they were gone, I turned back to Bay. "We're going to have to go to town for breakfast. I feel cheated."

"Go eat," Bay said. "It's right inside. There's no reason to suffer."

"Come with me," I said, knowing what her answer would be.

"I can't just leave her," Bay said. "We're the reason she's here. We're the reason she's so unsettled. We're the reason she's so ... traumatized."

My heart rolled. She was so earnest sometimes. "Then we're staying here together," I said. "I can wait until we go into town. I'm not going to die of starvation." My stomach growled a complaint, but I was far enough from Bay she didn't hear it. "Maybe we should sit still and let her come to us. Isn't that what you do when you find a stray animal?"

"She's not a dog," Bay said.

"I didn't say she was," I replied, grabbing a lawn chair and turning it so it faced the tree. I did the same with another and then settled into the first one. "I think you following her around the tree like you're playing a really creepy game of tag isn't the way to go."

Bay made a face but she reluctantly left Peg to ... whatever it was she was doing ... and joined me. I reached over and grabbed her hand, rubbing my thumb over her knuckles as she studied something only she could see.

I often wondered what it was like to be her. I'm not interested in the petty cousin business, or the co-dependent family spats, or even the highs and lows of running a weekly newspaper. Seeing ghosts, though, that was something I couldn't wrap my mind around. Sure, I'd seen one myself, but I'd been so worried about Bay at the time I couldn't think about it. Now, when I look back, it was one of those fuzzy memories wrapped around a traumatic event. The traumatic event – almost losing Bay – got top billing.

"What are you thinking?" I finally broke the silence, mostly because Bay's expression tugged at my heart. She looked worried.

"What if we can't get her back?"

"What?"

"What if we can't get her back?" Bay turned to me. "What if we ripped her out of a happy place? What if ... ?"

"It's okay, sweetie," I said, gripping her hand tighter. "We'll get her back."

"How do you know that?"

"Because you don't fail," I said simply. "We'll figure it out. Don't tie yourself into knots about something that we haven't even tried yet. You're going to give yourself an ulcer."

"I'm not tying myself into knots."

I smirked. "You're a worrier," I said. "It's in your nature. I think it's because you're the oldest."

"I'm an only child," Bay reminded me.

"You may have been born an only child, but you grew up to be the

AMANDA M. LEE

big sister," I said. "You're as close – closer maybe – to Thistle and Clove as any siblings. Don't deny it."

"I love them," Bay said. "I would never deny it."

"But?"

"But sometimes I want to gag them both and lock them in their rooms."

I brought her hand up to my mouth and brushed a light kiss against her palm. "That's also part of being the big sister."

"Do you feel that way about your brothers?"

"I love my brothers," I said. "I also think it's best we only spend a limited amount of time together. If we spend too much time together, I want to wrestle them down and give them wedgies. That's probably why you, Clove and Thistle are always arguing."

"I thought you said that was estrogen?"

I was still debating that point. "Maybe it's both."

Bay's face split with a wide grin, and even with her morning-tousled hair, she was utterly charming to look at. "Thistle was right. You can't be wrong."

Her charm comes and goes. "It's not that I can't be wrong," I said. "I'm rarely wrong."

"I stand corrected."

I leaned forward and brushed her hair out of her face with my free hand. "Are you excited to come and stay with me this week?"

"I honestly didn't think you would agree when I suggested it," she said. "You surprised me."

"Why?"

"Because you always come here," Bay said, shrugging. "I thought you liked your own personal space."

"You've been to my apartment before," I reminded her. "You've spent the night."

"Yeah, but … ."

I waited.

"Aren't you worried that I'm going to infringe on your bachelor pad?"

I swear, it's never what you think it is when you're dealing with women. "My bachelor pad? Sweetie, that place is just an apartment to me. It's not a home. It's two bedrooms and some particleboard furniture. I don't even have matching plates."

"Is that why you always want to spend the weekends here?"

"This place is a home, Bay," I said. "The guesthouse is small and loud, but it's comfortable. The inn is big and homey. You guys fight, but you love, too. This place is more fun."

"I don't have to go with you," Bay said. "I … if you'd rather come back here next weekend, I'm fine with that."

"We're coming back here for the weekend," I replied, matter-of-fact. "We're still spending the week together at my apartment. We'll just have to go out to dinner every night, because neither one of us can cook."

"I told you I can cook," Bay said, pouting.

"I'll take your word for it," I said. "There are some nice restaurants on the water. I'll take you to a few of those … plus whatever restaurant your mother wants to go to. Besides that, my boss has been making noise about meeting you. This will be a good way to get it over with."

"Your boss wants to meet me?" Bay looked surprised. "How does he even know about me?"

"He knows I come here every weekend," I said. "There's also a photo of us on my desk."

Bay's cheeks colored. "There is?"

"Good grief, woman," I said. "You're like an insecure teenager sometimes. Of course there's a photo of us on my desk. I like to look at you. You have a photo of us on your desk, too. I've seen it."

"That's different," Bay said, ever pragmatic. "I'm a girl. That's what girls do."

"I guess I'm a girl then," I said, nonplussed. "Let it go."

Bay pursed her lips, shooting a look in my direction out of the corner of her eye. I could feel her internally mocking me.

"I know what you're doing," I said. "You're being all … girly."

"I am not," Bay said, squaring her shoulders. "I'm just … ."

The sound of gunfire cut off the rest of her sentence and shattered the morning serenity. I jumped to my feet, scanning the woods for a sense of direction. Another shot exploded, and I instinctively reached for Bay so I could shelter her with my body. She fought my attempts.

"No one is shooting at us," she said, slapping my hand away. "The shots are too far away."

"Can you tell where they're coming from?"

Bay tilted her head to the side, listening. When another shot rang out, she pointed. "It's the bluff."

"Are you sure?"

She nodded.

"Stay here," I ordered. "If I don't come back in twenty minutes, call Chief Terry and have him bring some armed deputies."

"You're not armed," Bay said, irritated. "You can't follow the sound of gunfire without a weapon of your own. I won't stand for it."

"I'll be fine," I said. "I promise. I have to go and see what that is. You know that."

"Then I'm coming with you."

"You are not," I said, emphatically shaking my head. "You were just shot a few weeks ago. You're staying right here."

Bay was hearing none of it. "If you're going, I'm going."

I didn't have time to argue with her. I grabbed her hand and growled. "You stay right with me."

She nodded.

"If I say duck, you duck."

She nodded again.

"If you get shot again I'm going to kill you," I said, leaning in and giving her a quick kiss. "You do exactly as I say."

"If you get shot I'll never forgive you," Bay said, her blue eyes wide.

"Then I guess we both need to keep from getting shot." I tightened my hand around Bay's, and then we bolted into the woods, running to the sound of gunfire. That's never a good idea, just for the record.

EIGHT

"Where?" I asked, closing my eyes and listening. I couldn't hear anything but the normal sounds of morning. This is why I hate the woods – although I'm not keen on all nature, if I'm telling the truth.

Bay pointed to my right. "It's just beyond those trees."

"I don't suppose you'd wait here for me?" I had to try one more time. Pulling her into danger was foreign to me. I couldn't wrap my mind around it.

Bay shook her head. "I'm going with you," she said. "Besides, I don't think we're going to find what you think we're going to find."

"What does that mean?" I was confused … and conflicted. I didn't know which one was worse.

"Where do you think Aunt Tillie was going so early in the morning?"

I stilled. That was a very interesting question. "You think it's her? Where would she get a gun?"

"She used to have a handgun and a rifle until my mom deemed them contraband and took them from her," Bay said. "She was looking for money a few weeks ago. She has access to a computer."

"You have to show identification to get a gun," I said.

"Not if you magically rig the game."

I considered the suggestion. Would Aunt Tillie actually order a gun over the Internet? Could she be that stupid? Oh, who am I kidding? That woman does what she wants when she wants. She's like a magical little Nazi with no rules and no parental guidance. "You still stay behind me," I said. "If she accidentally shoots someone, I want it to be me."

"What if it's not her? I could be wrong."

"I don't think you're wrong," I said. "I still want you behind me. If it's someone else ... if I say run, you run."

Bay wrinkled her nose. "We'll see what's going on and make our decisions then," she said. "I'm not leaving you."

"You drive me crazy."

"It runs in the family."

She wasn't wrong. "Let's go." I tugged on her hand and led her through the trees, slowing my pace so I could approach quietly. When the gun fired again, I cringed. We were definitely closer. The sound of the gun going off was followed by a series of whoops and excited uttering. It sounded like ... teenage girls.

I shifted my eyes to Bay, confused. She merely shrugged. Obviously she had no idea what was going on either. We were about to find out. I led her through the final line of trees and pulled up short so I could study the people assembled on the bluff.

Aunt Tillie was definitely here, and she wasn't alone. There were seven teenage girls with her, all dressed in yoga pants and hoodies, and Aunt Tillie was instructing them on the finer points of rifle utilization.

Bay moved up beside me, silent, and watched as Aunt Tillie pointed to a spot over the bluff. The elderly Winchester matriarch then bent over and lifted a pot from the ground and tossed it in front of the girl – as far out as she could.

The girl with the gun pulled the trigger, shattering the pot into shards, and causing the other teenage girls to break out into enthusiastic applause.

"That was great, Shiloh," one of the girls said.

"Thanks, Madison. It's much easier once you get used to the gun's kick," Shiloh said.

"It seems heavy to me," one of the other girls said.

"You have to get used to it, Cinnamon," Aunt Tillie said.

"My name isn't Cinnamon," the girl said. "It's Cherise. I've told you that like a thousand times."

"You have red hair," Aunt Tillie said. "Cherise is a stupid name. You're either Cinnamon or you can go."

Cherise looked conflicted. "Fine. You can call me Cinnamon. You really are a mean lady, though. You know that, right?"

"I've worked hard to earn and maintain my reputation," a blasé Aunt Tillie replied. "I see my legacy is safe."

I knew what I saw, and yet it didn't make sense. If Bay and her cousins were to be believed, the townspeople lived in fear of Aunt Tillie. Why would some of the town's youngest and most easily influenced denizens be hanging out with a crazy old woman who cursed people?

I cleared my throat. "Does anyone want to tell me what's going on here?"

The teenage girls had the good grace to look embarrassed ... and frightened. Aunt Tillie didn't even turn in our direction. "Shouldn't you be eating breakfast?"

In the course of my career, I've found the most interesting criminals to be those who think they haven't done anything wrong. In some cases, like protecting a child, their instincts are understandable. In others, like when dealing with a true sociopath, you don't agree with what they've done but you understand they don't care they've hurt others.

Aunt Tillie is her own little bastion of crazy.

"Something came up," I said. "We were outside when we heard the gunfire. We thought something bad might be happening."

"Nothing bad is happening," Aunt Tillie said, placing her hand on Shiloh's shoulder. "Ignore him. Get ready for another."

Shiloh didn't look convinced. "But ... ."

"Ignore him," Aunt Tillie instructed. "We're not doing anything wrong."

I strode forward, angry and incredulous. "You're not doing anything wrong? You're out here shooting a gun with a bunch of girls who don't look legal to me."

"So what?" Aunt Tillie didn't look bothered in the least. "It's not as if I'm touching them inappropriately. I'm showing them how to use a gun."

I looked to Bay for help. "Why?" she asked. "Are you all going hunting or something?"

The girls snickered, and Aunt Tillie rolled her eyes. "Yes, I'm starting a hunting club. We're going to call ourselves Witch Commander. We're going to sell venison on the side of the road and get rich. These girls are going to retire before they're twenty."

I tamped down the urge to strangle her – especially with so many witnesses present.

"Wait, can we really get rich selling venison?" Cherise looked intrigued by the idea. "I think I could shoot a deer … just not a little one."

"No one is shooting anything," I said, grabbing the rifle from Shiloh's hands. I looked it over, scowling when I realized I was looking at a new weapon and not some relic Aunt Tillie managed to scrounge up on the property. "Where did this come from?"

"The gun fairy," Aunt Tillie replied, not missing a beat. "I left my dentures under my pillow and I woke up to find a rifle. It's just what I always wanted."

Instead of fixating on her aunt, Bay was more interested in studying the teenagers. "Why are you guys really out here?"

The girls shifted uncomfortably, keeping their eyes cast toward the ground.

"We're starting a hunting club," one of them said.

"Yeah, a hunting club," another echoed.

"Do you guys know that I'm an FBI agent?" I asked. "That means you have to tell me the truth or I'll put you in jail."

Audible gulps filled the air, and someone whispered "No way."

"He's lying," Aunt Tillie said. "He's not with the FBI. He's a janitor at the tampon factory over in Pinconning."

"There's no tampon factory in Pinconning," I said, annoyed. "Stop telling them lies."

The girls' gazes bounced between Aunt Tillie and me, unsure. They obviously didn't want to land on the wrong side of law enforcement, but the terror of Aunt Tillie had them rooted to their spots.

"If he's with the FBI, where is his badge?" Aunt Tillie asked.

That seemed to bolster some of the girls.

"Yeah," Madison said, hands on hips. "Where's your badge?"

I knew exactly where my badge was: on Bay's nightstand. "I don't have it with me," I said. "It's very close, though."

"I think he's lying," Aunt Tillie said. "I saw a story on *Dateline* where men pretend to be law enforcement officials, and then they kidnap and rape women. Some of them keep the women as slaves and make them clean toilets all day. I'll bet he would do something like that."

"I'm going to throttle you," I warned, extending a finger in Aunt Tillie's direction. "You're in so much trouble you're going to need a tractor to dig yourself out."

Aunt Tillie tapped her chin, thoughtful. "I could really use a tractor," she said. "I like to dig for things. How much do you think a tractor costs?"

"More money than you have," I snapped.

"I'll have you know I'm an entrepreneur," Aunt Tillie replied. "I'm going to be rich by the time I retire."

"You're already technically retired," Bay said.

"How do you figure?"

"What work do you do?"

"You take that back," Aunt Tillie said. "I work very hard. I own an inn, in case you haven't noticed."

"You don't work at it, though," Bay said. "Mom, Marnie and Twila do all the work."

"You're dead to me," Aunt Tillie said, narrowing her eyes. "You're officially out of the will."

I love the Winchesters. I really do. Times like this, though … . I sucked in a calming breath. "Girls, I need to know what you're doing here," I said, keeping my voice purposely light. "I am with the FBI. If you don't believe me, ask Bay. You all know her, right?"

They nodded.

"Ask her," I prodded.

"She doesn't tell the truth, though," Shiloh said. "Ms. Tillie told us that all her family is afflicted with Lyingitis."

I pinched the bridge of my nose to keep from exploding. "I'm sorry. What is Lyingitis?"

"It's when you can't tell the truth," Madison supplied helpfully. "Ms. Tillie told us she was saved from the disease because of her superior intellect. I said that correctly, didn't I?"

Aunt Tillie patted her head fondly. "Perfectly."

"I see," I said, grinding my molars together. "If I'm understanding this correctly, you believe that … Ms. Tillie … is the only one in the family who tells the truth. Is that right?"

More nods.

"Don't you think it's far more likely that she's the liar and you're somehow … I don't know … falling under her spell?"

Aunt Tillie balked at the word "spell," fluttering her hands angrily. "Just what are you insinuating?"

I couldn't believe I was missing out on the world's best bacon and eggs for this. I tried to remain calm, and failed miserably. "I've had it," I said. "I want to know what's going on out here, and I want to know right now!"

The teenagers took an involuntary step back while Aunt Tillie held her ground.

"Aunt Tillie, you need to tell him," Bay said. "We've had a development since we saw you this morning. We don't have time for this. You're going to give him an aneurism if you don't tell him. Please."

Aunt Tillie scowled. "Fine." She crossed her arms over her chest. "These girls want to learn the fine art of shooting because they want to protect their virtue."

"Their virtue?"

"Teenage boys are horny beasts," Aunt Tillie said. "These girls have the right and the might to protect their virtue."

"So mote it be!" All the teenage girls raised their fists into the air in unison.

I rolled my eyes until they landed on Bay. "I'm going to have to kill her. You know that, right?"

Bay held up her hand to still me. "I don't understand," she said. "Can't you just tell the teenage boys you're not interested?"

"They don't know how to stop themselves," Shiloh said. "Words aren't enough."

"That's why we need guns," Cherise said.

"Their hormones are like angry invaders," Madison added. "They're like the aliens in the *Alien* movie, although I've never seen that so I don't know what that means. I don't watch black-and-white movies. Ms. Tillie told us, though."

Well, now I was really ticked off. "First, *Alien* is not a black-and-white movie," I said. "It's in color, and it's a classic. You should watch it the second you get home."

"I'd rather watch *The Vampire Diaries*," Madison replied, unruffled. "I don't like old stuff."

"Then why are you hanging around with Aunt Tillie?" I asked.

"Hey! I am not old." Now Aunt Tillie was getting angry. That was good. That was exactly how I wanted her. She would be more likely to spill her intentions if she couldn't control her emotions. "You're at the top of my list, mister."

"Great," I said. "Now tell me what you're really doing out here."

"That is what we're really doing out here," Cherise said, whimpering. "We wanted to be able to protect ourselves from the horny beasts, and we thought Ms. Tillie was the best way to go. She decided to teach us how to shoot a gun."

Bay moved next to Aunt Tillie, studying the ground. "Are these Twila's pots?"

"I told her not to put that kiln in my greenhouse," Aunt Tillie said. "She deserves what she gets."

"She spent a lot of time on these," Bay protested. "She's really getting good."

"Those things are ugly," Aunt Tillie said. "They're also possessed. I think they're haunted with the souls of former horny beasts."

"Whatever," I said, checking the chamber of the rifle. "Girls, you need to go home. You're not to come back out here for shooting lessons. If you have problems with the ... horny beasts ... just kick them in the nuts."

"You can't tell them that," Bay hissed.

"Why not? Aunt Tillie has already filled their heads with nonsense."

Bay tilted her head to the side, considering my reply. Her tactic when she turned to the teenagers was much more reasonable. "Girls, teenage boys are horny beasts," she said. "That doesn't mean your virtue is in danger ... unless you want it to be."

"Who would want it to be?" Shiloh asked, confused.

Aunt Tillie pointed at Bay. "She and her cousins spread their virtue all over the town when they were your age," she said. "They're still spreading their virtue around. You don't want to end up like her. She's ... virtue-less."

I'd heard enough. "Girls, go home," I said. "Your shooting lessons are over. If I catch you out here again, I'm going to arrest you all."

"How can a janitor arrest us?" Madison asked.

"Go!"

"What about our money?" Shiloh asked.

My heart sank. "What money?"

"The money we paid for our shooting lessons," Cherise supplied. "We were supposed to get three of them. We barely got one. I want my money back."

"Me, too," another voice chimed in.

"I want my money back, too."

Aunt Tillie scowled. "I told you when you signed the contract," she said, "no refunds!"

"But ... ?"

"Everyone get out of here," I said, pointing toward The Overlook and gesturing emphatically. "Go now."

The girls grumbled, but left. When Aunt Tillie tried to slip by me, I snagged her by the back of her shirt and pulled her back. "You and I need to have a talk."

"Sure," Aunt Tillie said. "I need breakfast first, and I believe you have some bathroom stalls to clean. I'll meet up with you once your cleaning duties are done for the day."

Aunt Tillie tore her shirt from my grasp and headed toward the inn. "You're still on my list," she said by way of a parting shot.

Bay moved to my side. "I know you're angry," she said. "In the grand scheme of things, she wasn't doing anything really bad – except for ruining Twila's pottery. I can't wait until Twila finds out about that, by the way."

"I'm still going to have to kill her," I said, linking my fingers with Bay's and tugging her down the hill. "Do you think there's any bacon left?"

"If not, I'll take you into town and buy you breakfast."

"That's good," I said. "After that, I'd like to take another shot at making sure you're still without virtue."

"Only if you give me a massage later," she replied. "My back is killing me."

"Sold."

Bacon, eggs and missing virtue – what's not to love? This is the best way to spend a weekend.

NINE

"We saved you some bacon," Winnie said, pushing a warm plate in front of me as I slumped in my usual spot at the dining room table. The guests were gone, their meals ingested and digested. I was glad for that, because I was about to go nuclear on Aunt Tillie – as soon as I had some breakfast.

"Thank you," I said. "I'm starving." I glanced around the table. "Where did Bay go?"

"She's washing up in the bathroom," Winnie said, patting my shoulder. "Don't worry. She didn't go back outside. I checked. She said that Peg disappeared while you guys were dealing with Aunt Tillie."

"We need to find Peg," I said, glancing over my shoulder to make sure Bay wasn't loitering in the shadows. "She's going to be really upset if we don't make sure that Peg is returned to wherever she was."

Winnie seemed surprised. "What do you mean?"

"Bay is worried that we ripped Peg from … a good place … when we did the séance," I explained. "I don't want her feeling guilty about this."

"Because she did it for you," Winnie said.

Was that why? "Yes," I said. "I asked her to do it. I don't want her upset. I don't like it when she's trapped in her own head."

"That doesn't happen as often as it used to," Winnie said. "When she was a child, she was always trapped in her own head. It worried me."

"And now?"

"And now you and Thistle won't let her live her life that way. You're both good for her that way."

"Then why don't you want her to come back to Traverse City with me?" It was a pointed question, but I really wanted to know.

Winnie pursed her lips and pushed a strand of blonde hair behind her ear. "She's my daughter."

"And you think I'm going to hurt her?"

"I think you're going to make her happy," Winnie said. "I also think I don't want her moving away from Hemlock Cove. Not again."

That seemed reasonable, which was a foreign concept in this house. "She's going to be an hour away," I said. "She'll be back for the weekend."

"I know," Winnie said, "but ... Bay needs this family."

"I know Bay needs this family," I said. "If you want to know the truth, I need this family, too. I would never try to take her away."

Winnie sighed, her emotions weighing heavily on her face. "I'm very fond of you, Landon," she said. "You make Bay smile more than anyone ever has. What about your job, though?"

"What about it?"

"You're with the FBI," Winnie said. "What if you get transferred?"

I opened my mouth, ready to tell her that wouldn't happen. I was good at my job, and I liked my location. Most people were transferred for failing to accomplish their goals. That wasn't me. I couldn't guarantee that I wouldn't be transferred, though. I could put up a fight but, in the end, I might not have the final say. I decided to tell her the truth. "I would fight that."

"What if you couldn't stop it?"

I shrugged. "I honestly don't know."

"Would you take Bay with you?"

Would I take Bay away from her family? Could I? I knew I didn't want to be away from her, but I didn't think I had it in me to make her miserable. "I can't answer that question," I said. "I'm happy where I am. My boss is happy with my work. I can't worry about hypotheticals. I can only worry about what's in front of me.

"Right now, I'm staying here," I continued. "If a transfer comes up, I'll tackle it then."

"Will you let Bay make the decision with you?" Winnie wanted an answer, but she was also fearful about what it would be. Her conflicted face made that much obvious.

"I wouldn't make a decision like that without Bay," I said. "I love her."

"Are you going to marry her?"

That was an uncomfortable question ... and then some. "We're not there yet."

"Do you think you'll get there?"

Are all mothers like this? I pictured my mother, relaxing slightly when I realized they were. This wasn't only about Bay. It was a mother trying to get a handle on her daughter's future. "Probably."

Winnie seemed happy with my answer. "You're still a good boy, Landon," she said, patting my shoulder. "I'm going to make you bacon every day for a month."

I smiled. "You're definitely my favorite Winchester right now," I said.

"What about Bay?"

"She has her own level."

"You're a charmer," Winnie said, moving toward the kitchen. "You know you're golden when even Aunt Tillie likes you."

Speaking of Aunt Tillie .... "By the way, where is she?"

"I'M NOT TALKING ABOUT THIS," Aunt Tillie said, leaning forward so she could show Annie Martin how to plant a petunia correctly.

After eating breakfast and returning to the guesthouse long enough to shower, we were back at the inn – and I was ready to take on Aunt Tillie. I didn't give a fig about her list. "Oh, you're talking about it."

For her part, Annie seemed interested in the conversation. A few weeks before, an injured Annie stumbled upon Thistle, Bay and Aunt Tillie at the end of the driveway. She'd been in a car accident, and her mother Belinda was missing. Thanks to hard work, diligence, and a little witchy intervention, Belinda was found alive and saved. Now she worked at The Overlook full time, and Annie spent quite a few afternoons with Aunt Tillie so Belinda didn't have to hire a babysitter. I couldn't decide whether spending time with Aunt Tillie was good or bad for Annie. Aunt Tillie seemed to dote on the girl, but Annie was picking up a few bad habits.

"I didn't do anything wrong," Aunt Tillie said. "I was teaching those girls a valuable skill."

Annie nodded solemnly. "There are horny beasts around every corner."

That did it. "You can't tell her things like that," I said. "You're going to warp her."

"I'm not going to warp her," Aunt Tillie said. "Basil, am I warping you?"

Aunt Tillie likes to change people's names, and Annie was no exception. Even after finding out the girl's real moniker, Aunt Tillie continued with the one she'd christened her with when she wasn't talking in the initial hours after her discovery.

"She's not warping me," Annie said. "She's molding me in the image of the niece she always wanted."

Bay balked. "Hey! What about me?"

"You're as good as you're ever going to get," Annie said. "You're not bad, but you're not perfect. I'm perfect."

Bay's face softened and she patted her lap. "Annie, will you come here please?"

Annie acquiesced, climbing up on Bay's lap and fixing her expressive green eyes on her. "Did I do something wrong?"

Bay shot a look at Aunt Tillie. "You didn't do anything wrong," Bay said. "You should know that everything Aunt Tillie tells you isn't necessarily the truth."

I snorted, earning a glare from Aunt Tillie.

"I am not a liar," Aunt Tillie said.

"No, but you have a skewed perspective and you shouldn't be forcing Annie to think as you do," Bay said, keeping her voice even. "I know you love Annie, but do you really want her to grow up believing everything you say is the truth?"

"Everything I say is the truth," Aunt Tillie replied. "If you had listened to me when you were her age, how much better would your life have been?"

"I happen to like the life I have right now very much," Bay said, smiling at me. "You helped me a lot when I was a kid, but you also knew when to back off and let us figure out stuff on our own. You don't seem to be doing that with Annie."

"I'm her apprentice," Annie said. "I'm helping her with the planting ... and the oregano field."

The oregano field? Now I really wanted to throttle Aunt Tillie. "That's not oregano."

"What is it?" Annie's eyes were wide, and I realized I couldn't tell her the truth.

"It's ... ."

"Oregano," Aunt Tillie said, her tone clipped. "Don't you even think of telling her otherwise."

"It's oregano," I said. "You need to stop going out there with her, though."

"But that's my job," Annie said, her eyes filling with tears. "I like to help."

Great. How did I become the bad guy in all of this? "You can help her in the greenhouse," I said. "You can help her up by the inn. You just can't go to the oregano field." I fixed my attention on Aunt Tillie. "You need to work with me here. I can only put up with so much, and you know what you're doing out in that field is wrong for a little girl to be mixed up in."

Aunt Tillie sighed. "Fine. Basil, you can't go to the field. We'll spend more time in the greenhouse."

"But what about Marcus?" Annie asked. "He's never in the greenhouse. He's always in the field. How will I ever see him again?"

"I have a feeling you're going to be able to help Marcus with his own project in a few weeks," I said, realizing too late that I'd tipped my hand and was on the verge of revealing Marcus' secret.

"What project?" Bay asked, suspicious.

Crap. "I ... ."

Aunt Tillie smelled blood in the water and began to circle. "Is Marcus going to be cultivating his own ... oregano?" She didn't wait for me to answer. "I knew it! He's stealing my secret blend."

"He's not stealing your secret blend," I snapped, rubbing the back of my neck. It's too bad I can't travel back in time. I'd like to take the bulk of this conversation back. "I can't believe I opened my big mouth. I gossip like a woman. I swear." I turned on Bay. "You've totally corrupted me."

"Just tell us what's going on," Bay said, calmly. "If you don't, our minds will run wild and then we'll let something slip to Thistle and this whole thing will blow up."

I considered the offer for a moment. I knew she was right. The smart thing to do now was tell the truth. "You have to swear not to tell anyone." Isn't that how all true gossipers start a sentence? I've sunk so low.

"I swear," Bay said, pressing her hand to her heart. From her lap, Annie nodded with big eyes and mimed crossing her heart.

I turned to Aunt Tillie.

"I swear," she said. "Unless he's stealing my blend. Then I'm going to blow his ass ... I mean butt ... sky high." She glanced at Annie. "I didn't say the A-word."

Annie ran her fingers over her lips, imitating a zipper closing.

I sighed. "Marcus is going to expand his business at the stable," I said. "He's going to till the field behind it and sell the vegetables. No oregano, just vegetables. He's also going to open a petting zoo."

I cut off my story there. I would never betray his trust on the proposal, and there was no way Bay could keep that to herself. I could only hope they'd focus on the business expansion and not realize I was holding something back.

"That's a great idea," Bay said, excited. "Why isn't he telling anyone?"

"He wants to surprise Thistle," I said. "He's worried she'll be upset because it will take up a lot of his time."

"That's nonsense," Aunt Tillie said. "Thistle will be the first to volunteer to help. We all will. I agree with Bay. That's a great idea. He's clearly thinking. Now I know why he's been so fixated on asking me about root cuttings and irrigation systems. I'm proud of him."

The sentiment took me off guard. "You are?"

"He's a good boy," Aunt Tillie said. "He's good for Thistle. Don't worry, I won't tell anyone. He'll be surprised when he tells Thistle. She's going to be excited about it, and she's going to want to help. Heck, she could make a few sculptures for the petting zoo. I'll bet she'll enjoy that."

Every time I think Aunt Tillie can't throw me she proves me wrong. She's mean and nasty and cold when she wants to be. She's also loyal, loving and delightful when the mood strikes. She's a true enigma.

She's still a pain in the ass.

"Thank you for not telling anyone," I said. "It's important for Marcus to be able to tell Thistle himself."

"Is he going to have goats?" Annie asked.

"Where?"

"At the petting zoo," Annie said. "I love goats."

Bay smiled and smoothed Annie's flyaway hair. "I'm sure he will," she said. "We can ask him when he's ready."

"How about ducks?"

"Oh, ducks are a must," Bay said. "I'll bet he lets us feed them."

"What about unicorns?"

Bay pursed her lips, unsure. I decided to answer for her. "Unicorns are very rare," I said. "It's illegal to put them in petting zoos."

"That's a bummer," Annie said. "Maybe we can get a unicorn for the greenhouse?"

"No four-footed friends in the greenhouse," Aunt Tillie said. "They make a mess."

"Well, that sucks."

Bay frowned. "Who taught you to say that? Did Aunt Tillie teach you that?"

Annie shook her head. "I heard it from you."

"Oh." Bay faltered. "Well, I shouldn't say that. Don't say that again."

I couldn't help but laugh. Seeing Bay with Annie, even though the girl gravitated more toward Aunt Tillie and Thistle, made me smile. "None of us should say it again," I said. "In fact … ."

I broke off when I saw Bay's attention drift to the spot behind Aunt Tillie. I had a feeling I knew what she was looking at.

"Um, Annie, why don't we go inside and get some lemonade?" I offered, extending my hand to the girl.

"Why?" Annie asked.

"Aren't you thirsty?" I didn't want to frighten her, and the idea that a ghost was there – even if she couldn't see it – would do just that.

Annie shook her head.

"How about a cookie then?"

"Why are you trying to bribe her?" Aunt Tillie asked, risking a glance over her shoulder. She frowned when she focused on … something. I was guessing she could see Peg floating a few feet away. "Oh. Well, great. I guess this is the development you guys were talking about earlier. The spell worked after all."

I shot her a look. "We shouldn't be talking about that now," I said. "Come on, Annie. Let's get some cookies."

Annie scrunched up her face. "I don't want cookies," she said. "I want to see what the floating lady has to say."

And here I was thinking things couldn't get more complicated. I was obviously wrong. There's never a dull moment in Hemlock Cove – and this day had just tipped into overdrive.

TEN

"You can see a floating lady?" Bay asked carefully. "Where?"

Annie pointed to the spot behind Aunt Tillie. "She has red hair and she looks sad."

I grabbed Annie from Bay's lap and lifted her. "We're going inside."

"But I want to talk to the floating lady," Annie complained. "I don't want cookies."

"You'll live," I said, carrying Annie into the inn even though she wriggled wildly. "It's better this way."

I dropped Annie in the kitchen, putting her hand securely in Marnie's before turning to leave.

"What's going on?" Winnie asked.

"We have something to deal with on the back patio," I said.

"Oh." Winnie obviously understood.

"It's a floating lady," Annie said. "They don't want me to talk about her or see her, but I know she was there."

Winnie pursed her lips. "We'll talk about the floating lady," she said. "We can do it with cookies and lemonade."

"I want to see her," Annie said, jutting out her lower lip. "She was … sparkly."

I glanced at Winnie. "Can you handle this?"

Winnie smirked. "This isn't the first sparkly lady a child has told me about," she said. "Don't worry."

I couldn't help but smile. Of course she'd be the best person to deal with this situation. "You might want to talk to her mother, too."

"She's upstairs cleaning rooms right now," Winnie said. "I can handle that."

"Are you sure?"

"Go help Bay," Winnie said. "Find Peg's body. Bring her home."

I mock saluted, although part of the gesture was heartfelt. "We'll keep in touch."

"WHERE ARE WE?" I asked, wiping the sweat from my forehead.

"Do you see those trees?" Aunt Tillie asked, pointing.

I nodded.

"We're in the woods."

"Now I know why you drive Bay and Thistle batshit crazy," I said. "I think it's in your DNA."

"And just think," Aunt Tillie said, "Bay is going to end up just like me."

That was a sobering thought.

Bay patted my arm to reassure me. "I'll probably be more like my mother than Aunt Tillie."

I wasn't sure that was a better outcome. "It's fine," I said. "I just … are we sure we know where we're going?"

After twenty minutes of prodding, Bay finally managed to get Peg to talk. Her answers were vague, though, and she seemed tortured by her new reality. Finally, Bay told her she could cross back over as soon as she revealed the site of her body. If Bay's description was to be believed, Peg seemed happy with the offer.

So, after a brief drive to her old house, I followed an elderly woman in a ridiculous gardening hat and her reticent niece into the woods. They, in turn, followed a dead woman I couldn't see. I wanted to complain, but it was impossible. It wasn't as if this was the first time this had happened. How sad is that?

"I won't let you get lost," Bay said.

I knew she wasn't talking down to me, but it still felt like it. "Great."

"And I won't let Bigfoot get you," Aunt Tillie added.

"What?"

"I heard you're afraid of the woods," Aunt Tillie said. "Don't worry. I won't let Bigfoot get you."

"Bigfoot isn't real," I said.

"That's what people said about Santa Claus," Aunt Tillie said.

"He's not real either."

"That must be why you get so few presents at Christmas," Aunt Tillie mused.

I moved to the other side of Bay, putting her between Aunt Tillie and me in case my hands slipped and closed around her throat before I could stop myself. "You know I love you, right?"

Bay nodded, watching her footing as she navigated around a large rock. "I love you, too."

"I don't want you to take this the wrong way, but I'm going to kill Aunt Tillie," I said. "When it happens – and it will happen – I want you to know I still love you."

Bay smiled, not worried in the least. "It's going to be okay," she said. "We're finally getting somewhere. You'll be able to sleep tonight."

"I slept last night," I said. Of course, the chocolate martinis helped.

"When you get a case, you dream about it," Bay said. "You toss and turn. You didn't last night. Well, you might have. I was passed out so I didn't notice. You tossed and turned the night before, though."

I felt bad. "Did I keep you up?"

"I sleep like a rock. You know that. I just … feel … when you're restless."

Was that a witch thing? "You feel it?"

Bay nodded. "I feel your heart when you're sleeping," she said. "Most of the time it's peaceful. When something is bothering you, though, I feel that, too."

"Because you're a witch?"

"Because I love you."

Well, she was officially charming again. I shook off my melancholy, making a mental note to reward her with something truly great when we were done with this case. "Is Peg saying anything?"

"She's said a few things."

"And?"

"I ... I'm not sure you want to hear it."

Bay's face was red from the hike, but her eyes were misted with something else. I think it was regret. "I just want to know the truth."

"She wasn't murdered," Bay said. "She doesn't remember a lot about that time in her life. She says it's ... hard to focus. She remembers going for a walk, though. She also remembers falling and hurting her ankle. She slid down a ravine, and she couldn't get back up. After about forty-eight hours, she lost consciousness. She never woke up."

"Are you saying it was an accident?"

Bay nodded. "I'm sorry."

Was she really apologizing for solving my case? "Why are you sorry?"

"Because you were convinced she was murdered," Bay said, holding a branch back so I could move ahead of her. "You don't like to be wrong."

I barked out a coarse laugh. "You're right. I don't like to be wrong. Do you want to know the truth, though?"

"I always want to know the truth."

"I've been wrong so many times in my life I can't even count them," I said. "I was wrong when I said that Nickelback was a good band."

"We were all wrong about that," Bay said. "That first single misled us all."

I smiled. She was giving me an out. I wasn't going to take it, though. "I was wrong when I thought you were up to no good in the corn maze. I was wrong when I thought you were rude. I was wrong when I found out what you were and I left. That was the most wrong I've ever been."

Bay nodded, as though it was the most normal thing ever, but I could tell she was on the verge of tears.

"Do you want to know what I was right about?" I asked, not waiting for an answer. "I was right the first time I saw you and thought there was something … otherworldly about you. I knew when I saw you that you were going to amaze me.

"I was right when I had faith that you were a good person," I continued. "I was right when I followed my instincts and believed you, even though my head told me what I was seeing couldn't possibly be real. I was also right when I told you I loved you, although I should have told you sooner – and under better circumstances."

"You can't pick your life," Bay said. "You can only decide how you want to live it."

"I'm happy with the way I'm living mine," I said, grabbing her hand.

"Are you sure? I'm a lot of work … and my family is even more."

"You're worth the work, and your family is worth the work," I said. "You're fun and beautiful and you make me smile. I don't think there's anything more important than that."

"You make me laugh, too," Bay said.

"Don't forget to tell me how handsome I am," I said.

"You're very handsome."

"Oh, you two make me want to puke," Aunt Tillie said.

Despite her tone, I was happy she chimed in when she did. If Bay started crying now, we'd never find Peg's body. I was ready to put this case to rest and salvage a few hours alone with a blonde witch and her bright smile. "I make myself want to puke a little," I admitted.

"You're cute," Aunt Tillie said, her voice soft. "You remind me of … my Calvin."

Aunt Tillie often talked about her late husband, and always with reverence and respect. That was probably the best compliment she could ever give me. "Thank you."

"You're still a pain."

"So are you," I said.

Bay let go of my hand and rushed forward, peering over the edge of a ravine and scanning the area below. "We're here."

I followed her, studying the heavy underbrush dubiously. "Are you sure? That's going to take forever to search. We should have brought help, although I have no idea how I would have explained calling them in without finding the body first."

Bay pointed to a glint on the ground, and when I focused, I realized what she pointed at. It was a skeletal hand – the rest of the body hidden by a big bush – a wedding ring still on the third finger. We'd officially found Peg Mulder.

I leaned over and gave Bay a quick kiss on the cheek, not because she needed it but because I wanted to give it to her. We still had a long couple of hours ahead of us. I pulled my cell phone from my pocket. "I'll call Chief Terry. He should be able to get a retrieval team out here. We'll make sure she's put to rest."

"Thank you."

"No, sweetie," I said, giving her another soft kiss. "Thank you."

"**WELL,** this wasn't how I saw our weekend going," I said, digging into the thick steak on my plate with gusto. "This is a great way to end it, though. I love steak. I didn't even know you guys grilled."

"I grilled the steaks," Aunt Tillie said from her spot at the head of the table.

"They're still good," I said.

"Is that supposed to be funny?"

She makes me tired. "Eat your dinner."

After hours in the woods, Peg Mulder's remains were lifted from her makeshift resting place and Chief Terry promised he would make sure she found a final resting place. Since only bones were left, determining a cause of death would be difficult. I told Chief Terry what Peg relayed to Bay, and he said there wouldn't be enough evidence to go after John Mulder anyway. The man was probably living in a hell of his own torment. He didn't need any more. It wasn't the end I envisioned, but in a way it was better. Knowing Peg Mulder hadn't met a final betrayal at her husband's hands was something. I just didn't know what.

Bay offered to take Peg to her son so she could see him, but Peg only laughed. She told Bay she saw her son as often as she wanted, and even the cursory questions Bay asked about the other side went unanswered. Before her body was removed from the ravine, Peg's ghost dissipated – leaving Bay with only a warning about pulling people from places they didn't want to leave. Bay was chagrined, but relieved Peg was back where she belonged.

Because it was late Sunday, The Overlook's weekend guests were gone. It was only family – and that included Marcus, Sam and myself – at the dinner table. Chief Terry begged off, but only because he had to deal with Peg's remains. He was family, too. The Winchesters had a way of enlarging their family through loyalty and love – and that was only one of the reasons I loved spending weekends here.

"What time are you guys leaving tomorrow?" Winnie asked.

"Early," I said. "I want to make sure Bay is settled in the apartment before I go to work."

"And you'll call, right?" Winnie pressed, glancing at Bay. "You'll call if you get lonely."

"I won't get lonely, Mom," Bay said, laughing. "I can't get lonely."

"You'll be on your own all day," Winnie said. "Landon will be at work. You'll have your own work to do, but you'll still be alone. You're used to having lunch with Thistle and Clove every day."

"We're going to Skype," Thistle said.

"I don't know what that means," Winnie said, pursing her lips. "That's not something … dirty … is it?"

Thistle snorted. "It's a computer program. We're going to eat in front of our laptops and talk every day."

I didn't know why, but the knowledge Bay would still be eating lunch with Clove and Thistle made me happy. "That sounds fun."

"She's also going to take photos of everything in your underwear drawer and show them to us," Thistle said.

That sounded less fun. "I can't tell you how much I'm going to miss you, Thistle," I said.

"Oh, I'm going to Skype with you, too," Thistle said. "I can't go five days without a Landon fix. That's unthinkable."

Worry about Bay turning into Aunt Tillie eased as I gazed at Thistle. If any of them were going to turn into their curmudgeonly great-aunt, it would be the fiery pink-haired menace across the table. "I can't wait."

Winnie was the only one still fighting the inevitable, and as she focused on her daughter I felt a strange tug in my chest.

"What did you mean when you said you couldn't be lonely, Bay?" Winnie asked.

Bay smiled. "You're not only here in this house," she said. "You're here." She tapped her chest. "How could I possibly ever be lonely when you're always with me?"

Okay, she really is charming. "Someone pass me the wine," I said.

"Not too much," Bay warned. "We have to be up early."

"Just one glass," I said. "I have a feeling it's going to be a … peaceful night."

Bay's smile reinforced that feeling. I sipped the wine, internally toasting yet another level of Winchester delight.

It was going to be a good week.

It was going to be a good life.

"I'm going to start up my gun class again tomorrow," Aunt Tillie announced, ruining my good mood.

I growled, frustrated. "You're going to be the death of me," I said. "I just know it."

YOU ONLY WITCH ONCE

A WICKED WITCHES OF THE MIDWEST SHORT

ONE

"I'm not going!"

Sometimes children are quiet. Sometimes they're playful. Sometimes they're pleasant. Most of the time they're lovable – even when they're obnoxious. The one stomping her foot and swinging her blond hair around at my side was none of those things. Don't get me wrong, I love her. But glad she's an only child. If there was more than one of her I worry I'd turn into one of those mothers who lock their child in the basement to gain some peace and quiet.

I sucked in a breath to calm myself, turning my attention from the cooler of food I was packing, and fixed Bay with a serious look. "You're going."

Bay crossed her arms over her chest, causing her tank top to ride high on her narrow frame, and her blue eyes were murderous as she regarded me. "I don't want to go."

Raising a child is tedious business. Sure, there are love and kisses when they're little. There's cuddling and genuine affection. Once they hit those pre-teen years, though, the sweet child you raised turns into a melodramatic demon overnight. Bay was now fourteen, and I'd been dealing with the demon for two years. Her cousins, Clove and Thistle, had also been possessed in recent years. They were a fearsome threesome – and one of the main reasons I had a migraine prescription on standby at the pharmacy.

Instead of matching Bay pout for pout, I opted to try to reason with her. "Why don't you want to go? You were excited about summer camp the last time I checked. It's only four days. It's not as if you're going to be living there permanently."

"I was excited for summer camp when I thought I was getting away from you," Bay said, her barb pointed and sharp. "Now you're going. No one wants their mother there. It's embarrassing. How is that supposed to be fun for me?"

"It's not my fault," I said. "Donna Wilder was supposed to run the girls' camp with her sisters, but … well … she's gone missing. Either camp gets cancelled or your aunts and I run it ourselves. We thought we were doing you a favor."

"You're not," Bay said. "If you want to go to camp, I'm staying home."

So much for reasoning. "You're going," I said. "Clove and Thistle are going. Marnie and Twila are going. Heck, even your Aunt Tillie is going. We're all going, and we're all going to have a good time. So stop your screeching and … go pack or something."

Bay's eyes widened, this time in fear instead of anger. "Aunt Tillie's going?"

I nodded. I wasn't any happier about the situation than Bay, but leaving my aunt home without supervision is never a good idea. I figured she could help keep the kids in line, even if she terrorized them at the same time. Most of the kids in town were afraid of Aunt Tillie. Bay, Clove and Thistle knew exactly what she was capable of, though, so they were more likely to behave if they thought Aunt Tillie might curse them into submission.

My name is Winnie Winchester and I'm a kitchen witch. In fact, I come from a long line of witches. My mother was a witch, although her soul is now at rest. My aunt is a witch, even though she likes to embrace the darker arts to get her own way more than anything else. My sisters are also kitchen witches – and drama queens. As the oldest, it's been my sad lot to rein them in when they gallop off the rails. I worry Bay is going to have to play the older sister role for Clove and Thistle, too. I'm worried she's not bossy enough for the job. Thistle might inherit it out of sheer determination, if not age.

"Aunt Tillie can't go," Bay said. "She'll ruin everything."

"She won't ruin anything," I said. "She'll be a lot of fun." Sometimes you have to lie to your kids, because … well … if you tell them the truth they'll scream. I've had my fill of screaming for one day.

"She won't be fun," Bay whined. "She'll threaten everyone with curses."

"That could be fun."

"On what planet?"

"This one," I said, tugging Bay's long hair to pull her attention to me. "I promise you're going to have a good time. Everything is going to be fine. I'll go out of my way not to embarrass you."

"What about Aunt Tillie?"

That was a loaded question. "She'll be … on her best behavior." Of course, that wasn't saying much.

Bay quieted for a moment, and I thought I was finally getting somewhere with her.

"I'm not going, and you can't make me!"

"WHERE DID YOU PUT THE MEAT?" Marnie asked, tucking her dark hair behind her ear and surveying the picnic table dubiously. "We need to feed these little monsters before they turn on us."

As the middle sister, Marnie was supposed to be the calming force between sister storms. Instead, she was the tornado at the epicenter. As a mother, she had it easy. Even though Clove was a drama queen, she was the easiest to get along with. Clove was a thinker, and she often worked out the end scenario before Thistle and Bay even jumped on the idea. That made Marnie's life much easier than mine.

For my part, I was the mother of a dreamer, and Bay's head was often in the clouds. I had no idea what she was dreaming about, but whatever it was made her equal parts happy and sad depending on the day. She lost herself in deep thoughts – and regret – and contending with the swings was tiring. I had hope she would grow out of it, but I knew that time was still far off.

Of course, my job was easier than Twila's. My free-spirited sister was the least grounded of us all. She raised Thistle with a certain bohemian flair that lent itself to lax parenting. Thistle was loud and obnoxious, and she was also desperate for the attention Twila naturally absorbed. Despite her propensity for bullying, I never worried about Thistle. She was always ready to fight, and her fierce loyalty meant that she was ready to fight for anyone she deemed worthy. The list was short, but Thistle was a scrapper.

"It's in the blue cooler," I said, turning to Marnie. "I say we go simple tonight and just do hot dogs."

"Can we drug them with sleeping pills?" Marnie asked.

That was an interesting suggestion. "No," I said finally. "Keep them handy, though."

"I brought two bottles," Marnie said. "With thirty pre-teen girls to deal with, there's going to be a lot of drama. I'm so glad you volunteered us for this."

I rolled my eyes. Marnie likes to get in digs whenever she can. She knows exactly how to irk me. "It was either run the camp ourselves or cancel it. The girls were looking forward to it."

"They're not any longer," Marnie said. "They're embarrassed we're here."

"They're teenagers. They'll outgrow it eventually."

"Really? We're still embarrassed by the things Aunt Tillie does and I'm nearing thirty," Marnie said. "When am I going to outgrow that?"

She had a point. Still ... wait a second. "Nearing thirty? You're thirty-three."

"No, I'm not."

"Yes, you are."

"No, I'm not," Marnie said, crossing her arms over her chest. "I'm twenty-nine."

"Oh, so you had Clove when you were high school? I always knew that reputation the football players whispered about was well-earned," I said.

Marnie scowled. "I've decided I don't like being in my thirties," she said. "I'm now officially twenty-nine ... forever."

I wanted to laugh, but that seemed like a legitimate way to go. "You can't be twenty-nine forever," I said. "I'm a year older than you, and I don't want to be thirty either. I'm twenty-nine. You can be twenty-eight."

"Fine," Marnie said. "I want credit for this idea, though."

She always wants credit. It's a terrible trait. "You can't have credit," I said. "I was the one who made you a year younger. I should get the credit." Okay, I can admit it. The trait runs in the family.

"This is so much fun," Twila bubbled, appearing at the edge of the picnic table with a stack of paper plates. "Do you remember when we went to this camp as kids? We had so much fun."

"Yeah, and do you remember how much we hated the chaperones?" Marnie asked, raining on Twila's effusive parade. "We're now the chaperones."

"Oh, you don't have to be such a ... you know what," Twila said, lowering her voice. "We're not going to be like the chaperones we had. We're going to be cool chaperones. We're going to be hip chaperones. We're going to be ... chaper-fun."

That was Twila's problem in a nutshell. She has an inflated sense of ego, and she's more interested in being Thistle's friend than parenting. That's how Thistle got to be such a little bully.

"We're going to be chaperones," I said. "We're going to make sure they don't run with scissors. We're going to make sure they don't go swimming right after they eat. We're going to make sure they don't get lost in the woods. Oh, and we're going to make sure that they don't terrorize each other to tears. That's what we're going to do."

"That doesn't sound like any fun at all," Twila said, pouting.

"It's not," Marnie said. "We're not fun now. We're adults. We have children. They get to have fun. Our lives are over. We're almost thirty and our lives are over."

Twila furrowed her brow. "Almost thirty?"

"Oh, yeah, you're twenty-seven now," I said, brightening. "You can thank me later for thinking of it."

AMANDA M. LEE

"I thought of it," Marnie said. "You just leeched on to my idea."

"I took your pathetic little germ of an idea and made it better," I argued.

"Whatever," Marnie said. "Speaking of germs, does anyone know where Aunt Tillie got to?"

"I told her to make sure all the girls were settled in the cabins," I said. "There are thirty girls and three cabins, so there are ten to a cabin."

"That should go over well," Marnie said. "Did you make sure to tell Aunt Tillie to keep Lila Stevens far away from Bay?"

I nodded, my heart clenching. I know you're not supposed to hate children, but every rule has its exception, and Lila Stevens is the exception to that rule. She's a viper. You can see already that she's going to grow up to be a rotten adult – just like her mother. For some reason, she's fixated on Bay. She knows there's something different about my little witch – and there is – but Lila doesn't know what it is. She can't put a name to her fear. So, instead of trying to figure it out and be friends, she's mean and nasty. If Lila were to get lost in the woods I wouldn't shed a tear. Oh, I'd call for a search party ... after she'd been missing for a few hours. A little suffering won't hurt her, and it might straighten her up a bit. Of course, that might be wishful thinking.

"I told Aunt Tillie to put Lila in the cabin closest to the campsite and Bay, Thistle and Clove in the one closest to the woods," I said. "That way they only have to cross paths at meals."

"What about while swimming and kayaking?" Marnie asked.

"I figured we would take them in separate groups," I said. "Can we just please try to keep Lila away from Bay?"

"You know that you can't protect Bay forever, right?" Marnie asked, her dark eyes serious. "Sooner or later, she's going to have to stand up to Lila on her own."

"I know that," I said. "But Bay is so ... sensitive right now."

"It's the hormones," Twila said. "They're at that age where their bodies are blossoming into womanhood and they don't know what to do with the new feelings and emotions."

"Blossoming into womanhood?" Marnie arched an eyebrow. "Yeah. You're going to be chaper-fun. Keep saying things like that. We should start a pool to see when you go missing. I'll keep checking the shed to see whether they've locked you up in there."

"Whatever," Twila said. "I ... ." She broke off, her gaze trained on the parking lot over my shoulder.

I turned swiftly, following her line of sight, and swallowed hard when I saw two familiar figures heading in our direction. How could I have forgotten?

"Aunt Willa," Marnie said, rubbing her hands on her pants to clean them. "I ... forgot you were bringing Rosemary to camp this year."

Willa was our aunt by blood, the youngest sister behind Aunt Tillie and our mother. While Aunt Tillie took over maternal duties to make sure we were taken care of after our mother's death, Aunt Willa became nothing more than a semi-familiar face we saw only during family reunions and extended holidays. Her granddaughter, Rosemary, was her spitting image – in temperament and looks. What do I mean by that? Just wait.

"Marnie," Aunt Willa said, pursing her lips. "You look ... older."

And there you go.

Marnie scowled. "Thank you."

"Twila. Winnie." Aunt Willa nodded in turn to us, her shoulders stiff. "You look older as well."

"I guess that can be said about all of us," I said, forcing my face to remain placid. As tempestuous as Aunt Tillie is, she's much easier to be around than Aunt Willa. "I hate to say it, but I forgot Rosemary was coming this year."

"Well, I remember how much Nettie loved this camp when she was a girl," Willa said, referring to her daughter. "I thought Rosemary might like a couple of days in the great outdoors."

Despite growing up in Hemlock Cove, Aunt Willa opted to move south with her husband and family twenty years earlier. She landed in mid-Michigan, but she still drops in when she feels like it – which is usually right around the time we're feeling happy and content. She likes to ruin that for us.

At fourteen, Rosemary is tall and gangly for her age. Her long hair is blond, but reddish streaks are starting to infiltrate the flaxen masses. Her green eyes are set far apart, and instead of general mischief, they're tinged with overt disdain. She looks down on us and our children by association. All of that stems from Aunt Willa's hateful tongue.

She's only a child, I reminded myself. It's not her fault. She was raised to be suspicious of us. She's probably a good kid in a bad situation. I tell myself these things every time I see Rosemary, which – thankfully – isn't very often. There's still something off about her.

"Is your summer going well, Rosemary?" I asked.

"It was until I found out I had to come here," Rosemary said, making a face. "Now it sucks. Big time."

"Her nose is just a little out of joint," Aunt Willa explained. "She's not a big fan of nature."

"I guess that makes summer camp a great fit for her," Marnie snarked.

Aunt Willa ignored her. "I'll pick her up at the end of camp. She doesn't eat saturated fats and we try to go light on the carbs with her. She tends to carry weight in her thighs if we're not careful."

That sounded ... terrible.

"All we have are saturated fats and carbs," Marnie said. "We're not going shopping just for her."

"I thought you would say that," Aunt Willa said, lifting a cooler. "This is food specifically tailored to Rosemary's digestive needs. There's a note with instructions in her bag. I trust you'll follow my instructions to the letter."

Aunt Willa leaned over and mashed a cold kiss into Rosemary's cheek. "Have a good time."

Rosemary nodded obediently. "I will."

"Wait, don't you want to see Aunt Tillie before you go?" Twila asked. "She's here."

"I have no inclination to see my sister," Aunt Willa said. "I'm sure you can pass on my ... greeting."

"Sure," I said. "Have a nice couple of days, Aunt Willa."

"Oh, I intend to."

TWO

"Do you think we can trust these kids to grill their own hot dogs?" Marnie asked, glancing around the campsite worriedly. "I'm thinking that fire and hot metal sticks could be dangerous."

I hadn't thought of that. "We'll have to watch them," I said.

"Or we could grill the hot dogs ourselves," Marnie countered. "I'd rather do the work than try to dig a flaming stick out of Lila's eye if Thistle loses her temper."

I hate it when she's right. "Okay, we'll grill the hot dogs. Have you seen Aunt Tillie?"

"She's helping Bay, Clove and Thistle unpack," Twila said.

"Does she know about Rosemary yet?"

Twila shook her head, her bright red hair flashing against the green backdrop. "I thought you would want to tell her."

Marnie snorted. "You mean you were too scared to tell her," she said. "You know very well that Aunt Tillie is going to have a fit when she finds out Rosemary is here. She hates that kid."

"We all hate that kid," I muttered.

Marnie pursed her lips. "It's not Rosemary's fault that Nettie and Aunt Willa raised her to be so … cold."

"I know that," I said. "I'm constantly reminding myself of that every time I see that girl. But still, she's ... odd."

"Bay, Clove and Thistle are odd, too," Twila said. "I happen to like odd."

"Rosemary is evil odd, though," I said.

"You might want to keep thoughts like that to yourself," Marnie said. "Rosemary is going to report back on every little thing we do. You're only going to give Aunt Willa more ammunition if you're mean to her."

"I have no intention of being mean to her," I said. "Do you think I'm a monster?"

"You have your moments," Marnie said. "I don't think you'll be mean to her, though. I still think you might want to keep your distance."

"Does that mean you're going to take Rosemary in all your groups?"

"Of course not," Marnie said, making a face. "I can't stand that kid. She's going to have to be Twila's problem."

"I think you guys are overreacting," Twila said. "Rosemary is going to loosen up now that she's away from Nettie and Aunt Willa for a few days. Just wait and see."

Marnie flicked the end of Twila's nose, causing her sister to jump back. "What was that for?"

"I'm trying to see whether your rose-colored glasses are invisible," Marnie said. "It's nice that you have faith Rosemary is a good kid. I don't share that faith. Speaking of Rosemary, which cabin is she in?"

"I put her in the first cabin," Twila said.

"Uh-huh." Marnie glanced over her shoulder, making sure it was still only the three of us within hearing distance. "Did she talk to any of the girls when got in there?"

"Yeah," Twila said. "She was friendly. In fact, she seemed to make instant friends with a few of the girls."

"Which girls?"

"Hope Daniels and Lila Stevens." Twila realized what she said. "Oh, crap."

"Lila Stevens?" My voice sounded squeaky. "Are you telling me Lila and Rosemary are hanging out?"

"Well, that can't be good," Marnie said. "That means evil is joining with evil. Everyone should run for their lives now."

I shot her a look. "We're going to have to watch them," I said. "They're going to cause trouble. They were going to cause trouble apart, but now that they're together they're going to cause bigger trouble. We can adapt. We can deal with it."

"I have a better idea," Marnie said, turning and moving toward the cabins.

"What?" I asked, worried.

Marnie didn't answer. Instead, she opened her mouth and let loose a bellow that could be heard three counties away. "Aunt Tillie!"

"I CAN'T BELIEVE THAT LITTLE ... ."

"Don't call Rosemary names," Twila warned. "It's not fair. She's still just a child."

Aunt Tillie gripped her hands together, trying to remain calm. "Fine. I can't believe that little ray of sunshine is our problem for the next few days. I just ... why didn't you tell me?"

"I honestly forgot," I said. "I was going to tell you last week, and then Donna went missing. Everyone was so worried about her that everything else fell by the wayside. Then, when we decided to run the camp ourselves, it got lost in all the stuff we had to prepare."

"You should have sent her away," Aunt Tillie said.

"We couldn't do that," I said. "It's an open camp. We can't single out one child and ban her."

"I could have," Aunt Tillie said.

"We know," Marnie said. "That's why we've decided that you're the one who gets to ... deal ... with Rosemary and Lila if they get out of hand."

Aunt Tillie arched an eyebrow. "Lila?"

"Apparently Rosemary and Lila have hit it off," I said, choosing my words carefully. "It seems they may have found something they like about one another."

"I'm guessing it's bitchiness," Aunt Tillie muttered.

I tilted my head to the side, sending her a mental admonishment. I knew she couldn't read my mind, but I hoped she could read my expression. It didn't work.

"I'd be glad to take over the punishment of Lila and Rosemary," Aunt Tillie said. "Leave it to me."

I grabbed her arm. "We didn't say you could punish them," I said. "We want you to watch them, and if they get out of hand you can report back to us. We'll deal with it."

"Sure."

Aunt Tillie was never this easy. "Sure?"

"I'd be happy to watch over the little ... darlings. I can't tell you how happy this makes me. It gives an old woman purpose in the face of her dwindling years. Now I can go to my deathbed knowing that my true purpose in life was to act as babysitter and snitch at summer camp."

Sarcasm is a family trait, and the Winchester witches have it in surplus. Instead of calling Aunt Tillie on her dramatic retelling of the facts, though, I opted to ignore it. "I'm glad you understand. Thank you so very much."

Marnie snickered. "This is going to be a great couple of days," she said. "I can feel it in my bones."

"We should really get lunch moving," Twila said. "What time is Terry bringing the boys over?"

Crap! That was another thing I'd forgotten about.

Detective Terry Davenport was an old friend from high school. He was older than us by a few years, but he'd been an invaluable confidant as we traversed adulthood. He'd taken a position at the Hemlock Cove Police Department right after graduating from the police academy in Traverse City, and he'd been working his way up the ranks.

Because he was a good man, Terry donated his time with various children's groups. He was the one who initially reopened the campground from our childhood, bringing groups of boys from southern urban areas up for hiking, fishing and swimming weekends. He said city kids deserved a chance to enjoy the country, too.

Once Donna Wilder took over the girls' cabins, the two camps – separated by a small lake – ran in conjunction. While day-to-day activities were mostly separate, meals were served together to save on food bills and work hours.

"I can't believe I forgot Terry was bringing the boys over," I said. "He said he would be here around one. What time is it now?"

Marnie glanced at her watch. "He should be here in a half hour. That means we need to get the potato salad, buns and condiments ready. We should also round up the girls and get them out of the cabins. They've been in there since they arrived. What do you think they're doing?"

"Plotting the downfall of mankind," Aunt Tillie said, grabbing a radish from the vegetable tray Twila unwrapped.

"Oh, good," I deadpanned. "You'll fit right in. It's your job to get the girls out here. Count them. Make sure we don't lose any."

Aunt Tillie jumped to her feet and clicked her heels together, mock saluting as she sent me a saucy wink. "Yes, ma'am."

I bit my lip to keep my temper in check. Sometimes it feels as if there are four children in the house. "Thank you."

Once she was gone, I turned to Marnie. "She's going to drive me insane before this is all said and done."

"That's what she's trying to do," Marnie said. "She's good when she has a task she wants to fulfill."

"We need to find something to keep her busy over the next few days," I said. "I don't know what that is, but we need to put our heads together."

"Let's get through lunch first," Marnie suggested. "How many kids does Terry have at his camp this week?"

"Um ... twelve I think," I said.

"Oh, well, thirty girls and twelve boys," Marnie mused, "that seems like a great way to foster female togetherness."

"What do you mean?"

"It's those hormones Twila was talking about," Marnie said. "All the girls here are of an age when they're boy crazy. There won't be enough boys to go around. How do you think that's going to end?"

That was a problem I hadn't considered. "They're not even going to be around the boys all that long," I said. "It will be fine."

"Sure," Marnie said, moving her face closer to mine.

"What are you doing?" I asked, pulling my head away.

"I'm looking to see whether you borrowed Twila's rose-colored glasses."

I swear, sisters are both a blessing and a curse.

"LUNCH LOOKS WONDERFUL, LADIES," Terry said, beaming at me as he doused his hot dog with ketchup. "I can't thank you enough for letting us eat with you."

"Oh, you don't have to thank us," Marnie said, slipping a spoonful of potato salad on his plate as she sidled closer. "We love taking care of you."

"We do," Twila agreed, sliding a slice of pie onto his plate. "Feeding you is one of the great pleasures of our lives."

They make me want to puke sometimes. This isn't one of those times. Now I only want to poke them in the eyes and make them cry. "Will you two stop throwing yourselves at Terry?" I asked pointedly.

Twila had the grace to look abashed, but Marnie was beyond caring. She knew she was on my last nerve, but she didn't care.

"Where are your boys from, Terry?" I asked, trying to draw the conversation to a safer ground.

"They're from the Saginaw and Bay City area," Terry said.

"I take it they don't get to spend a lot of time in the woods," I said, as I scanned the boys. They all sat at their own picnic table, occasionally shooting mischievous looks in the girls' direction. "They look a little citified."

"They are," Terry said. "They're all excited to go swimming and kayaking, though. They're good kids. They just haven't had a lot of time to spend in nature. This is their chance."

I shifted my gaze to the girls, studying the table configurations. To my chagrin, Lila and Rosemary paired off at the far end of one of the tables. They whispered and laughed to each other, and every time one of them chuckled they shot dark looks to the adjacent table. Unfortunately, that happened to be the table where Bay, Clove and Thistle sat.

Terry followed my gaze with his steady eyes. "Why did you let Lila Stevens come? You could have banned her. You know that, right?"

"I can't ban a child simply because she doesn't like my child," I said. "That's not fair."

"Who cares about fair? Lila goes out of her way to make Bay miserable," Terry said. "The kid deserves a few days of peace."

"I think you're saying that because you spoil her rotten," I said, smiling. Terry doted on all three of the girls, but he shared a special bond with Bay.

"I don't spoil her," Terry said. "She's just a little angel."

"Well, my little angel acted like a dark devil when she found out we were running the camp this week," I said.

"Why?"

"She's embarrassed," I said. "She doesn't want her mother to be the one in charge."

"It's her age," Terry said, patting my shoulder. "No kid that age wants their mother around. This is when kids start asserting their independence. That's all she's doing."

"I hope so."

"All kids pull away," Terry said. "Most of them come back, though. Bay is one of the best kids in the world. She's always going to come back."

"If people like Lila Stevens don't make it too hard for her to come back," I added.

Terry sighed, running a hand through his dark hair. Hints of gray were starting to show at the temples, but he was still handsome. "Bay is a fighter," he said. "She'll find the strength to do what she has to do where Lila is concerned. I have faith. You should, too."

"I have faith that she's stronger than she realizes," I said, "but I need her to realize it."

"She will."

Bay picked that moment to get up from the table. She turned her head sharply when Lila and Rosemary dissolved into loud guffaws. I had no idea what they'd said, but it clearly bothered Bay. She was still trying to shake it off when she moved up beside me and tossed her plate into the garbage bag at my feet.

"How was your lunch?" I asked.

"It was good," Bay said. "You made the potato salad."

"How do you know that?"

"I can always tell the difference between your potato salad and Marnie's," she said, shrugging.

"Mine is better, right?" Marnie said, poking Bay in the side in an attempt to get her to smile.

"They're both good," Bay said, rolling her eyes. "In fact, they're both equally good."

"Oh, such a smart cookie," Marnie said, tweaking her nose.

Terry finished his lunch and tossed his plate in the garbage bag. After wiping his hands with a paper napkin, he opened his arms to give Bay a hug. She stepped into his wide embrace wordlessly. He rubbed her back for a moment. "How is my favorite girl?"

After a moment, Bay pulled away and fixed a tight smile on her face. "I'm good."

"Good," Terry said. "Make sure you stay away from those boys I brought. They're bad news."

"I thought you said they were good kids," I said.

"They are good kids," Terry said. "They're not good enough for my Bay, though."

"Don't worry about that," Bay said. "I'm not interested in those boys. They're all over there making barking noises whenever one of us walks by."

Terry frowned. "I'll talk to them."

"It doesn't matter," Bay said. She turned to me, weary eyes making me cringe internally. She was too young to look so tired. "Can I go by the lake for a few minutes?"

I nodded. "Do you want your cousins to go with you?"

"I just want to be alone."

"Don't go in the water," I warned.

"I don't want to go in the water," Bay said. "I only want to talk to the ghost."

I froze, glancing around worriedly. Had anyone heard her?

"What ghost?" Terry asked, not missing a beat. He was aware of Bay's abilities, and he didn't once question them or cast aspersions on her.

"It's some woman."

"Do you recognize her?" I asked.

Bay shook her head. "She's not fully formed. She's either new or hiding."

I was caught. People thought Bay was weird because she walked around all day talking to herself. In reality, she was talking to the ghosts that only she and Aunt Tillie could see. I didn't want to change who she was, but I also didn't want to give Lila and Rosemary any excuses to go after her. "I'm not sure … ."

"It's fine," Terry said, patting the top of her head. "We'll keep everyone away from you. Just keep it quiet."

Bay nodded at him, the smile she shot him so earnest it almost broke my heart. "Okay." She shuffled off.

When she was gone, I turned to Terry. "Do you really think that's a good idea?"

"I think she's a good person," he said. "You have to let her be who she is. This is who she is."

He was right, but letting her go off by herself still felt wrong.

THREE

"Maybe I should take her home."

I knew the words were a mistake as soon as I uttered them. Still, something in my heart warned me that Bay shouldn't be here.

"You can't take her home," Marnie said, keeping her voice low. "She's already here. If she leaves now, everyone will know that something happened. It will only draw more attention to her."

"Marnie is right," Twila said. "If Bay leaves now, Lila will think she drove her away and that will give her power."

"I don't really care about power," I said. "I care about Bay. Can't she have one weekend without a ghost showing up to ruin everything?"

"Nothing has been ruined," Marnie said. "Everyone is having a good time."

I looked toward the lake where Bay walked the shoreline, her head down so no one could see her lips moving. She was making a big show about studying the rocks on the ground, but I knew what she was doing. A quick glance in Clove and Thistle's direction told me they knew, too. They were heading in our direction.

"Where are you two going?" Marnie asked, snagging Thistle's arm when she tried to move around her.

AMANDA M. LEE

"We're going to hang out with Bay," Thistle said. "She shouldn't be over there alone."

"She's looking at the rocks."

"We all know that's not what she's doing," Thistle said, yanking her arm away.

"Just leave her alone," I said. "We don't want to draw attention to her."

"That's why we should be over there," Clove said. "People will think she's talking to us."

I gave in, mostly because what Clove said made sense. "Go ahead, but don't interrupt Bay."

"We're not two years old," Thistle said. "We know the drill."

"Thank you, Thistle," I said.

"You're welcome." Thistle and Clove scampered off, and I watched them take up position near Bay. They immediately launched into some conversation only they could hear. Bay barely acknowledged their presence.

"She's pretty intent on whatever she's doing," Twila said. "Who do you think she's talking with?"

That was a pretty good question. "I don't know. No one lives out here. Has anyone ever died out here?"

"I have no idea," Marnie said. "If the ghost is new, maybe we should be looking for a body."

"It's probably old," I said. "Who would have died out here recently?"

"Well, Donna Wilder is missing," Twila said.

My heart rolled and I shifted slightly so I could study Twila. When she's the one who comes up with the answer, you know you're in trouble. "You don't think it's Donna, do you?"

"She's been missing for more than a week now," Marnie said. "Maybe she came up here to get the camp in order and … I don't know … something happened to her."

"Usually people only come back as ghosts if something violent happened to them," I pointed out. "Are you saying you think she was murdered?"

"Calm down," Marnie chided. "We don't even know it's Donna. We'll talk to Bay later and see whether she knows who it is. We can't freak out before we know what we're dealing with."

"I'm not freaking out."

"You always freak out."

"I do not."

"You do, too."

"We all freak out," Twila said, stepping between us in an attempt to keep the peace. "We can't do this now. We have to focus on the camp. That's our main job for now."

"And what happens if there's really a dead body out here?" Marnie asked. "What do we do then?"

"I guess it's good we have a police detective right across the lake," I said, gesturing toward Terry. He sat at the table with the boys, and whatever story he was reenacting had them in stitches. "If there really is a body out here, he'll be able to deal with it."

"What if there's a murderer out here?" Twila asked.

"Then we'll deal with it," I said. "Any murderer who comes after us is going to realize he's bitten off a little more than he can chew."

"You've got that right," Marnie said. "Come on. Let's get the lunch stuff cleaned up. Terry wants to take the kids swimming, and then we'll have a big bonfire after dinner tonight."

"Terry is staying here all day?" I was surprised.

"He said he wants to stay close to Bay," Marnie said. "I think he's as worried about her as you are."

I didn't think that was possible. "Okay, let's get cleaned up. At least if the kids are in the water we don't have to worry about Thistle setting Lila on fire as retribution."

"No, we only have to worry about her drowning Lila," Marnie said.

I sighed. "Someone find Aunt Tillie. Make sure she keeps an eye on the girls in the water. If someone drowns, we're never going to be able to chaperone anything again."

"That sounds chaper-fun," Marnie said, grinning.

"OKAY, everyone get settled around the fire," I instructed.

The rest of the afternoon was mostly uneventful. When I questioned Bay about the ghost, she seemed more confused than anything else. She said the woman wouldn't talk, but kept pointing to the far side of the lake. I didn't know what it meant any more than Bay.

After a raucous dinner – an afternoon of swimming turning the boys into excited little monsters – it was time for a bonfire and ghost stories. Terry would have to take the boys back across the lake before it got too late, but for now everyone was having a good time.

"Who knows a ghost story?" I asked.

Lila's hand shot up. Of course.

"She didn't say skank stories," Thistle said. "No one wants to hear your stupid stories, Lila."

"Thistle," Twila snapped. "Don't speak that way. That's not how I raised you."

"Yeah, Thistle," Lila sang. "That's not how Ronald McDonald raised you."

Twila scowled. "Go nuts, Thistle."

I grabbed Twila's arm. "That is not good parenting."

"I don't care," Twila said. "I've always taught Thistle to fight against evil. I can't stop her from doing that now."

I started to move in Thistle's direction, worried she would take her mother's words to heart, but Terry cut me off and settled in the spot next to Twila's wild child.

"You know that killing her will only result in you going to jail, don't you?" Terry asked.

"I think I'm okay with that," Thistle said.

Terry smiled. "How about you tell the ghost story instead," he suggested. "I'll bet that busy mind of yours can come up with some good stuff."

That was an understatement. Thistle once told Clove that gnomes lived in our basement and they fed off the lint between our toes. Clove refused to walk barefoot in the house for a month because she was convinced the gnomes would crawl between her toes and chew her foot off.

"I don't want to tell a story," Thistle said. "I'm not in the mood."

"Oh, you're in a mood," Terry said, tousling Thistle's hair. "You're just not in a fun mood. Who else wants to tell a story? Boys, do you know any stories?"

"I once heard a story about a woman so ugly she turned men to stone," one of the boys said.

"Was her name Lila?" one of the other boys asked.

I bit my lip to keep from laughing out loud. In her efforts to entice the boys to her side earlier in the day, Lila had done the opposite. She'd insisted she couldn't get wet, and refused to put on a bathing suit. When you're dealing with fourteen-year-old boys, they want to have fun, not listen to a spoiled brat complain for two hours.

"Ho, ho, ho," Lila sneered. "That's so funny I forgot to laugh."

"And you're so ugly you could break mirrors," Thistle said.

I needed to stop this before it got out of hand. "No one knows a ghost story? Really?"

"I know someone who knows a ghost story," Thistle said, turning to me.

"Who?"

Thistle pointed to Aunt Tillie, who was watching the show from a lawn chair on the far side of the fire.

"Absolutely not," I said, emphatically shaking my head. "If she tells you a ghost story you'll be up all night thinking you see zombies in every shadow."

"Oh, whatever," Lila scoffed. "She's an old lady. How scary can her stories be?"

Aunt Tillie arched an eyebrow. I could tell she wasn't particularly happy about entertaining forty teenagers, but her hatred of Lila made the thought of scaring her a definite perk.

"I'll tell a story," Aunt Tillie said.

I pressed my eyes shut briefly. This wouldn't end well. Still, Lila Stevens needed to be taken down a peg or two … or ten. "Try to keep it clean," I said.

"Meaning?"

AMANDA M. LEE

"No weird stories about demons impregnating virgins and the fetuses eating their way out of the mothers from the inside," I said.

"I told that story once," Aunt Tillie said. "I wanted the girls to know what would happen if they didn't share their Halloween candy with me."

"Yes, well ... pick something clean."

"And scary," Thistle said, casting a dark look in Lila's direction.

"I think I know just the story," Aunt Tillie said, leaning forward in her chair. "Who here has ever had a china doll?"

Oh, no. I knew this story. This definitely wasn't going to end well.

"WELL, Terry left with the boys and all the girls are in their cabins," Marnie said, pulling the curtain back in our small cabin and surveying the quiet outdoors.

"I saw the boys leave in their canoes," Twila said, giggling. "They kept looking over their shoulders in case a china doll was waiting to scratch their eyes out."

"Making the doll look like Lila was a nice touch," Marnie said. "If the boys weren't suspicious of her before, they definitely are now."

"A lot of the girls are afraid of her, too," Twila said. "She's not the queen bee right now. That's probably going to ruin her week."

"Good," Marnie said.

"It's probably going to make her lash out," I said. "That makes her more dangerous."

"But she'll have fewer allies," Marnie said.

"Will she? Or will she make sure Bay becomes the bad guy in all of this?"

"Oh, Winnie, you have to stop doing this," Marnie said. "Bay is fourteen years old. She's almost grown. She's not some shrinking violet. When push comes to shove, Bay is going to shove back."

I wanted to believe that. "What if Lila shoves her so hard she tumbles over a cliff first?"

"Then she'll have to learn how to fly," Marnie said.

"You have to stop freaking out about Bay," Twila said. "You're clamped on to her so tightly the girl is going to struggle to breathe at a certain point."

"And when that happens, Bay is going to have no choice but to run away from Hemlock Cove," Marnie said. "The thing is, she won't only be running from the likes of Lila Stevens and her ilk, she'll be running from you, too.

"She might not realize it right away, and she might not ever understand it, but she'll need room to breathe if you want her to flourish," Marnie continued. "Give her room to breathe."

"I'm not trying to smother her," I said, frustrated. "I'm trying to ... protect her."

"You're trying to give her a soft pillow to land on every time she falls," Marnie countered. "That's not how life works. Give her some space."

"Fine," I said, not wanting to admit Marnie may have a point. "I'll promise to ... leave her alone over the next few days."

"Good."

"As long as Lila Stevens doesn't go too far," I added.

"If Lila goes too far, I don't think you have to worry about Bay having problems as much as you're going to have to worry about Lila going missing without a trace," Marnie said.

"Meaning?"

"Aunt Tillie has her eye on Lila," Twila said. "She's waiting for her to screw up."

"And when she does, Aunt Tillie will make Lila's life a lot worse than Lila can ever make Bay's," Marnie said. "Don't you remember when people messed with us in high school? How did that work out for them?"

"Not well," I conceded.

"Don't worry about Lila," Twila said. "Karma has a funny way of catching up with people when they most deserve it."

"And Lila is going to have a whole lot of karma chasing her," Marnie said.

I smiled, the first real smile I'd managed to muster in what felt like days. "You guys are right. I'm being ridiculous. Bay is going to be fine."

"They're all going to be fine," Marnie said.

"Speaking of Aunt Tillie, does anyone know where she is? I haven't seen her since she made the girls scream by dropping tree branches from the sky. That was risky, by the way. She shouldn't be using magic in front of witnesses."

"They thought it was the wind," Marnie said. "Still, you're right. Where is Aunt Tillie?"

"She didn't come back to the cabin with us," Twila said. "I think she's still out by the bonfire."

"That can't be good," I said, striding toward the door. "If she's still out there, that means she's planning something."

"Like what?"

I didn't get a chance to answer because multiple screams echoing throughout the dark drowned out my response. We bolted through the door, racing toward the cabins. In my head, I knew the girls were likely only reacting to Aunt Tillie's story. What if it was something else, though?

We pulled up short outside the first cabin. Lila stood in the doorway, her hand pressed to the side of her face and an angry expression clouding her eyes.

"What's wrong?" I asked, almost dreading the answer.

"Someone thought it would be funny to scratch at the window," Lila said. "These idiots thought it was a china doll and overreacted."

"How did they overreact?"

"They attacked me because the doll in the story looked exactly like me." Lila narrowed her eyes. "I know that was on purpose, by the way."

"Is anything else wrong?" I asked, ignoring Lila's jab.

"No."

"Then go to bed," I said. "No one is to attack anyone, and no one is to leave this cabin for any reason. Do you understand that?"

The girls nodded, solemn. We watched as everyone climbed back into bed and then switched off the lights and shut the door. We could hear them whispering even as we walked from the cabin.

A hint of movement caught my attention, and when I peered

closer I saw Aunt Tillie pacing us from about twenty feet away. She was trying to beat us back to our cabin so she would have plausible deniability.

"I see you," I said.

Aunt Tillie straightened. "Good. I was getting tired of sneaking around."

"Do you feel better now that you've scared them?"

"I'll feel better after a good night's sleep," Aunt Tillie said. "Tomorrow is a new day, and I'm going to need my rest if I plan on torturing Lila some more."

"Do you think that's really necessary?"

"I don't know whether it's necessary," Aunt Tillie said, reaching for the door handle to our cabin. "It is fun, though. I have to get my jollies somewhere this week."

She's incorrigible sometimes – well, all the time. "Try not to go overboard."

"I never go overboard," Aunt Tillie said. "It's not in my nature."

Whatever. "Just go to bed," I said.

"What do you think I was doing? Geez, you're so suspicious."

It was going to be a long couple of days.

FOUR

After four more ruckuses in various cabins, the girls finally settled down and called it a night. By the time morning hit, though, I was more tired than when I'd gone to bed.

The girls moaned and groaned when we roused them, and I hoped a full day of activities would mean a full night of sleep tonight. There was a moratorium on ghost stories from here on out. Aunt Tillie couldn't be trusted, and the girls were too anxious to trust their better judgment.

The only person who woke with any sort of energy was Aunt Tillie. After the first kerfuffle, she passed out and didn't so much as twitch the rest of the night. While the girls screamed and panicked, she snored. While Marnie, Twila and I convinced the girls they were imagining things, Aunt Tillie remained comfortably burrowed beneath her blanket.

I wanted to strangle her.

"Where are the eggs?" Aunt Tillie asked, popping up by my elbow. "I'm starving."

"Why? You weren't the one working up an appetite last night."

"What are you talking about?" said Aunt Tillie, pasting her best

"I'm your aunt and you have to love me" smile on her face. "Did you not sleep well?"

I narrowed my eyes. "You know very well that we were up half the night because the girls thought every noise in the woods meant a china doll was coming to scratch their eyes out."

"That was a great story to tell, by the way," Marnie said, flicking Aunt Tillie's ear as she moved past her with a pan of hash browns. "You're officially banned from telling ghost stories."

"Hey, they wanted it," Aunt Tillie said. "I gave them what they wanted. The truth is, I'm really a giver. That's my problem. I only want to give people what they desire. That's my whole goal in life."

"Yeah, that's your problem," I said dryly. "What are the girls doing now?"

"They're all sitting at the tables trying to wake up," Aunt Tillie said. "Lila and Rosemary are whispering about something, and I have a feeling it's nothing good."

"Lila is going to be worse now," I said. "I just know it."

"The only way she could be worse is if she sprouted fangs and wings and embraced her true nature as a creature of the night," Aunt Tillie said.

"Just ... give it a rest," I said, pinching the bridge of my nose. "If we're lucky, a full day of kayaking is going to exhaust these girls and make them want to go to bed early."

"Oh, you're cute," Aunt Tillie said. "You think just because that's what you want it's automatically going to happen. Trust me. They're going to get their second wind after breakfast."

I had a sneaking suspicion she was right. "Don't push any buttons today," I warned. "I can only take so much. I'm a woman on the edge."

"You always did need a full eight hours of sleep," Aunt Tillie said. "You're crabby if you don't get it."

"Since you did get your full nine hours of sleep, I don't think you have much room to talk."

"Whatever. How long until breakfast?"

"About five minutes," I replied.

"And we're going kayaking after that?"

I arched an eyebrow. Aunt Tillie generally hated the water. She was like the witch in the *Wizard of Oz*. She melted in anything stronger than the shower. "You're going kayaking?"

"I happen to love kayaking."

That was news to me. Still …. "Good," I said. "That will allow us to break the girls into smaller groups. I'll take Bay, Thistle and Clove with mine."

"You only want to keep an eye on Bay," Aunt Tillie said.

"You're right." I wasn't going to deny it.

"Fine," Aunt Tillie said. "I'll take Lila and Rosemary in my group."

I considered arguing, but allowing Aunt Tillie free rein over Lila seemed a good way to utilize my best weapon against my biggest problem. "Have fun."

"I'M STUCK IN THE TREES," Thistle sputtered, ducking her head lower as the overhanging branch clawed at her face. "I'm going to cut all of my hair off, I swear. It's too long and it just gets in the way."

"Then you'll look just like your mother," I said.

Thistle scowled. "That's the meanest thing you've ever said to me."

"You'll live," I said. "Use your paddle to push away from the tree. I don't understand how you keep running into the trees. Why can't you stay farther out from the shore?"

"It's not like I'm aiming for the trees," Thistle said. "They just keep … sucking me in. I think they're possessed."

Something here was possessed, but I didn't think it was the trees. "Just … stay calm and push yourself away from the trees."

"You stay calm," Thistle shot back.

"I am calm."

"Then work yourself up," Thistle said. "I could be trapped under this tree forever if you don't help me."

Every time I think the girls hit a new level of drama they manage to climb another rung on the teenage theater ladder. "Really? You think you're going to be trapped there forever?"

"You're starting to really bug me," Thistle growled.

"Join the club."

"You're dead to me!"

I couldn't help but smile. Marnie, Twila and I often said the same words to each other. The girls picked up the saying at a young age. It was actually a weird term of endearment. "You can free yourself, Thistle," I said, forcing myself to remain calm. "If I come over there I'm only going to make things worse."

"They can't get much worse."

Bay, always an expert kayaker, was at the end of her rope. "Oh, good grief," she said, floating forward. "You're being a pain."

"You're being a pain," Thistle said. "Get me out of here!"

"What do you think I'm trying to do?"

"Give me an ulcer."

Bay used her paddle to try to dislodge Thistle's kayak from beneath the branches. The sound of laughter behind us caught my attention, and I glanced over my shoulder to find Rosemary and Lila floating lazily a few feet away.

"Oh, nice," Lila said. "Good job, Thistle."

"Why are you guys over here?" I asked. "You're supposed to be with Aunt Tillie."

"I'm not staying with her," Lila said. "She's being mean to me."

"Mean to you?"

"She is," Rosemary said, her eyes wide. "She keeps muttering stuff under her breath and I swear she's planning to do something awful to Lila. My Grammy told me that Aunt Tillie is an evil person, and I believe her."

"Aunt Tillie is not evil," I said. "She's a very good woman. Your Grammy is … just trying to turn you against us." That was probably not the best thing to say given the circumstances. I couldn't help myself.

"My Grammy is a great woman," Rosemary insisted.

"I'm sure she is," I said. She was a lousy aunt. "I understand she's been very good to you. I hear she spends a lot of time with you."

"And you're jealous because your daughter doesn't have a grandmother to spend time with," Rosemary said. "My Grammy told me that, too."

Bay shifted her head in Rosemary's direction. "I have a grandmother," she said. "Aunt Tillie is my grandmother."

"I'm not old enough to be a grandmother," Aunt Tillie said, floating into view behind Lila and Rosemary. "Thank you for the sentiment, though." She flashed a bright smile in Bay's direction, something unspoken passing between them. "Just because I'm not your grandmother, though, that doesn't mean we don't have fun together."

"See, you don't have a grandmother," Rosemary said. "Your grandmother died before you were even born."

"Thanks for the update," Bay snapped.

"My Grammy says that you would be better people if your grandmother had lived." Rosemary refused to stop talking. "She says allowing Aunt Tillie to take over and finish raising your mothers made them evil."

"Your Grammy says a lot," I said. "In fact, I think your Grammy says too much."

"She always did," Aunt Tillie said.

"My Grammy only tells the truth," Rosemary said. "She says you're all evil."

"They are," Lila said. "They're evil and ... weird."

Something crackled in the air and the atmosphere warmed. Magic! I swiveled quickly, fixing Aunt Tillie with a hard stare. I had no idea what she was doing, but it couldn't be good. Instead of the wrinkled nose that usually accompanied Aunt Tillie's spells, though, her face was blank. She wasn't looking at Lila and Rosemary. She was focused on Bay.

I turned back around, involuntarily shuddering when I saw the look of abject hatred on my daughter's face. A burst of wind skimmed the top of the lake, and when it reached Lila it rolled her kayak and sent her face first into the water.

Bay's eyes widened as the spell dissipated. I wasn't sure whether she realized what she'd done. Lila surfaced, sputtering as she flailed her arms. "Omigod!"

"You're perfectly fine," Aunt Tillie said, regaining her composure. "The water isn't even above your head. Put your feet down and stop your bellyaching."

Lila did as instructed. Well, she put her feet down. The complaining was another story.

"Who did this to me?" she shrieked.

"You tipped over," I said. "No one did it to you. No one was even close to you."

"I didn't just tip over," Lila said. "I've been kayaking since I was eight. I'm an expert. Someone flipped me over!"

"Maybe it was the lake monster," Thistle suggested. "It probably smelled a horrible beast and knew you needed to take a bath."

"Kiss your tree, Thistle," Lila said. "No one is talking to you."

"Lila, no one tipped you," I said. "You must have shifted your balance. It's not the end of the world. Haul your kayak to the shore and change your clothes. It's almost time for lunch anyway."

"This isn't over," Lila said, glaring at Bay. "I know you did this. I'm going to make you pay."

"You're not going to do anything," Aunt Tillie said. "You're going to go back to your cabin and change your clothes. Don't even think about doing something you'd regret."

"What makes you think I'd regret it?" Lila challenged.

"Because if you do anything to Bay, I'm going to do something twice as bad to you," Aunt Tillie said. "Rosemary is right. I am evil. I'd like to show you how evil I can be."

"You can't threaten me," Lila said. "It's against the law."

"Tell Terry all about it when he comes over for dinner tonight," Aunt Tillie said. "For now, get out of the water and get away from my nieces."

"You're going to be sorry you threatened me," Lila said. "My father is a lawyer. He's going to sue you."

"Your father couldn't sue his way out of a paper bag," Aunt Tillie said. "Last time I checked, he used that paper bag to cover the bottle of whiskey he keeps in his car. Don't you even think about threatening me. You're not going to like what happens if you do."

"I already don't like what's happening."

"Then you should quit while you're ahead," Aunt Tillie said. "Trust me."

"TERRY DIDN'T COME for lunch today," Marnie said, cleaning the picnic tables and gathering the trash so it wouldn't attract scavengers. "Were we expecting him?"

"Not today," I said. "He took the boys on a hike and they were going to eat sandwiches on the trail. They'll be over for dinner."

"That's good," Marnie said. "Lila has been demanding to talk to him since she got dumped in the lake today. What happened with that, by the way? Did Aunt Tillie lose her temper?"

I shook my head. "Bay lost her temper."

Marnie's eyebrows flew up. "Bay did it?"

"I don't even know if she knew what she was doing," I said. "She just got this look on her face and … bam!"

"Well, at least she's standing up for herself."

"I'd rather she stand up for herself with words," I said. "She can't use magic to solve her problems. She could really hurt someone if she's not careful. We got lucky this time. Lila only got wet … and she was already unhappy, so there's no loss there."

"Well, you can't talk to her about it here," Marnie said. "It will have to wait until we're home. If someone overhears … ."

"Then things will only get worse," I finished. "I know. Just … help me keep an eye on Bay."

"I think we need to keep an eye on Thistle, too," Marnie said. "She's plotting something against Lila, and it's not going to be an accident when she does it. She's going to mean it."

I had the same worry. "Speaking of Bay and Thistle, where are they?"

"Thistle is with Clove over there," Marnie said, pointing. "I'm not sure where Bay is."

"I saw her head into the woods," Twila said.

Something pinged in the back of my brain. "When?"

"About five minutes ago," Twila said. "I thought she told you she was going for a walk."

I hadn't talked to Bay since the incident in the lake. I didn't know what to say to her, so I'd opted for denial. "Where?"

Twila pointed to the trailhead next to the cabins. "I'm sure she didn't go far."

"Watch the girls," I said, moving toward the trail. "I'll find Bay and bring her back."

"Do you want me to come with you?" Marnie asked.

"No. I'll be fine. We'll be right back."

Finding Bay wasn't as easy as I initially thought. After traipsing through the woods for ten minutes, stopping a few times to listen, I finally found her. She'd left the trail and was hidden by a stand of trees. I heard her before I saw her.

"You don't have to be afraid of me," Bay said. "I just want to talk to you."

I stilled my approach. Eavesdropping wasn't nice, but neither was sneaking into the woods without permission.

"I don't want to know your life story or anything," Bay said. "I just want to know what happened to you."

She obviously wasn't getting the answers she wanted.

"I saw you watching me by the lake earlier today," Bay said. "It looked like you wanted to talk to me. I couldn't talk then, but I can now. What do you want?"

I tilted my head to the left until I could see Bay. Her blond hair was pulled back in a ponytail, and her face was red from too much afternoon sun. She looked intent on her conversation and obviously hadn't noticed me.

"If you want me to help you pass over, you're going to have to talk to me," Bay said. "I can't help if I don't know what you need … and I want to help."

Bay was getting frustrated.

"Fine! Do what you want," Bay said. "I won't be here forever, though. You're running out of time for me to help you. I think you need help, so I'll wait for you to come to me. Just don't wait too long."

When Bay returned to the trail, she jumped as I moved in closer. "What are you doing here?" she asked, breathless.

"Looking for you," I said. "You shouldn't run off into the woods without telling anyone."

"I wasn't going far."

"I see that."

"I ... ." She looked uncomfortable, clearly unready to talk.

"Let's go back to camp," I said. "We both need something to eat after our busy morning."

"That's it? You're not going to yell at me?"

"No," I said, deciding to repeat her words back to her in an effort to help. "You don't need to be yelled at. When you're ready for help, you'll come to me."

I hoped that was the truth.

FIVE

"How was your day?" Terry asked, sidling up to me as I flipped burgers on the charcoal grill. I'd been lost in thought, so I hadn't even heard him approach.

"I'm fine."

"You don't look fine."

"Thanks."

"You know what I mean," Terry said, his smile rueful. "You always look fine. In fact, you look better than fine. You don't look as if you feel fine, though."

My cheeks burned under the compliment. "You're a sweet talker today, I see."

"I'm always a sweet talker," Terry said. "Why don't you stop pretending nothing is wrong and tell me what's bothering you. The faster you talk about it, the faster I can help with the problem."

"I don't know that there is a problem," I said. "I … well … things happened today."

"Such as?"

"Well, for starters, Bay lost her temper and flipped Lila's kayak," I said.

"Kid stuff," Terry shrugged. "Lila should have stayed away from her if she didn't want to get wet."

"Bay was twenty feet away from her."

Terry stilled. He was aware of our witchy heritage; the secrets of our upbringing and genetics trickling out over the years. He never asked questions, instead accepting everything we told him on faith. I had a feeling something else informed some of his knowledge base – something with Bay, in fact. He never talked about it, though, and Bay was known for keeping her cards close to her vest.

"How do you know it was Bay?" Terry asked, his eyes scanning the group of kids milling about next to the tables. "Couldn't it have been someone else?"

"I know you want to think Bay is perfect," I said. "I like to think that sometimes, too. But I'm certain it was her. I don't think she realized what she was doing until after it happened. And, if I know her, she's probably trying to rationalize what she did even now."

"She only dumped her in the water," Terry said. "It's not as though she hurt her."

"You always rush to her defense."

"That's because she's a good girl," Terry said. "She's sweet and kind. You've raised her well."

"She's still got a lot going on right now," I said. "She's at a bad age. All three of them are at bad ages. She's also got the … other thing … going on."

"You mean the ghosts," Terry said. "Has she seen the one by the lake again?"

"Yes." I told him about following Bay into the woods. When I was done, he swore under his breath.

"She can't wander off into the woods on her own," Terry said. "She could get lost … or hurt."

"She didn't go very far," I said. "That's not my biggest concern right now, though. Don't get me wrong, I don't like her wandering around on her own, but right now I'm more worried about the ghost."

"Do you know who it is?"

"No. I don't think Bay does either. The thing is ... ." I broke off, unsure how to proceed.

Terry waited.

"Do we have any idea what happened to Donna Wilder?"

Terry furrowed his brow. "You think she's talking to Donna?"

"I have no idea," I said. "Has anyone ever gone missing out here? Has anyone ever drowned in the lake? Have there been any mysterious deaths in this area?"

"I'm not familiar with every case, Winnie," Terry said. "I don't ever remember reading about anything, though."

"We all thought Donna going missing was out of character," I said. "She was known for being responsible. That's why we all trusted her with our kids."

"The truth is, we have no idea what happened to Donna," Terry said. "Her car was parked in front of her house. There were no signs of a break-in. There was just ... nothing."

"She lived close enough to walk here," I pointed out. "It would have been a long walk, but she liked to hike. What if she came out here to get the camp in order and something happened to her?"

Terry rubbed the back of his neck. "I think something happened to her," he said. "I just ... I'm not sure I think she died out here. That's a stretch. Why would she come out here alone?"

"Don't you go over to the boys' camp alone?"

"Yes, but ... ."

I arched an eyebrow. "But what? You're a big strong man and she was a frail woman?"

"You know very well that's not what I meant," Terry said. "It's just that I have no idea how to find Donna if something did happen to her out here. Her body could be in the water. It could be in the woods."

"It could be buried," I added.

"You think someone murdered her and buried her in the woods? Now you're really stretching things."

"Most people who die natural deaths don't come back as ghosts," I said. "It's very rare."

"You don't know it's Donna, though," Terry said.

"I don't."

"Well, until we know, there's nothing we can do," Terry said. "I think you should keep an eye on Bay. When this ghost is ready to talk, Bay will listen. Hopefully she'll come to us then. We can't force her to do something she has no control over."

"I know that," I said, "but I'm worried. Between Lila and Rosemary going after her and this ghost, this whole camping trip has been ruined for Bay."

"Nothing has been ruined for Bay," Terry said.

"How can you say that? She's miserable."

"Really? She doesn't look miserable to me." Terry pointed to a table where Clove, Thistle and Bay were laughing hysterically.

"Oh, sure, now she's happy," I grumbled. "She has to wait until the exact moment where I look like an alarmist to finally laugh."

"I'm sure she had it planned," Terry laughed. "She seems fine. Leave her be. When she's ready to talk, she'll talk. For now … let her have a good time."

"Fine."

"Great," Terry said. "So, how long until dinner's ready? I'm starving."

"**WHAT'S** GOING ON OVER HERE?" I asked, moving behind Bay, Clove and Thistle as they happily chattered away.

"We were examining the nature of life," Thistle replied evasively.

She always was a loquacious little minx. "I see," I said. "Well, let me but in for the mundane news that dinner is almost ready."

"We're very excited about tonight's menu," Thistle said. "I'm a big fan of burgers and macaroni salad."

"Me, too," Clove said, her brown eyes solemn. "I could eat it every night for a year and never get bored."

They were up to something. "I'm very happy to hear that," I said. "I would hate to bore your taste buds."

"No one wants that," Aunt Tillie said, muscling her way between

Thistle and Bay and forcing them to separate so she could sit between them. "I'm excited for the hamburgers, too."

"You don't even like hamburgers."

"You don't know what you're talking about," Aunt Tillie said. "I love a good hamburger."

She was up to something, too. "I'm happy when you're happy."

"Great," Aunt Tillie said.

I remained in my spot, studying the four of them suspiciously. When the conversation stalled, I searched for a way to restart it. "So ... ."

"Shouldn't you be grilling the hamburgers?" Aunt Tillie asked, cutting me off. "We don't like them when they're burned."

"Marnie is watching them."

"Marnie is hitting on Terry," Aunt Tillie said.

I glanced over my shoulder, frowning when I saw Marnie rubbing Terry's forearm as she offered him a slice of fresh watermelon. She was doing it to tweak me. I knew it and yet ... . "I should go and check on the hamburgers."

"You do that," Aunt Tillie said. "I'll sit here with the girls and make sure they don't get into any trouble."

I wasn't especially worried about the girls, at least not now. "Girls, why don't you make sure your Aunt Tillie doesn't get in any trouble, too?"

"That was our plan," Thistle said, making little shooing motions with her hands. "Now go and handle the burgers so we don't have nasty black things on them when we eat them. That would be gross."

I rejoined Marnie and Terry, my gaze bouncing between them and Aunt Tillie.

"What's going on?" Marnie asked. "Are they up to something bad?"

"I have no idea," I admitted. "They're clearly up to something, though."

"The girls or Aunt Tillie?"

"I thought it was just the girls," I replied. "Then Aunt Tillie sat down and the conversation completely died. She said she was going to watch over them so they don't get into any trouble."

"That's good, right?" Terry said. "You're worried about them retaliating against Lila and Rosemary. Aunt Tillie will stop that."

Marnie rolled her eyes. "Have you met Aunt Tillie? She's not going to stop them from going after Lila and Rosemary. She's going to help them."

"Even if that's true, what could she possibly do?" Terry asked. "Are they going to short sheet all the beds? Are they going to go on a mad poison ivy spree? They're stuck at a campsite. There's no way they can get into any serious trouble."

It's a good thing he's handsome, because he's beyond naïve sometimes. "Aunt Tillie can conjure trouble with her bare hands," I said.

"Literally," Marnie added.

"Would she really go out of her way to hurt two teenage girls?" Terry still wasn't convinced.

"If those teenage girls hurt the teenage girls in her family she would absolutely go after them," I said. "Aunt Tillie already dislikes Lila. Rosemary's friendship with her only makes matters worse."

"And what's the deal with this Rosemary kid? I don't think I've ever seen her before. Does she live in town?"

"She's ... family," Marnie said carefully. "Kind of."

"Family?"

"Aunt Tillie has another sister, other than our mother I mean," I said. "Her name is Willa and she's ... unique."

"Aunt Tillie is unique," Terry said. "Are you saying Willa is worse?"

"Definitely," Marnie said. "She's also very different. She's a ... cold ... woman. She thinks women have a certain place in the home, and that never sat right with Aunt Tillie. They've always fought like cats and dogs. Willa wants women to stay in their place."

"And that place is the kitchen," I said.

"You guys like to cook," Terry said. "How is that a bad thing?"

"It's not a bad thing," I said, "but Aunt Willa thinks the only thing a woman should do is cook."

"Ah. I see."

"She also doesn't think a woman over the age of eighteen should wear pants, and she certainly doesn't think a woman should hold a job outside of the house," Marnie said. "She has these antiquated beliefs, and we've never fit into the world as she'd like to see it."

"So why did she bring Rosemary here?"

"My guess is that she wanted a few days to herself," I said. "Rosemary's mother, our cousin Nettie, learned her mothering skills from Aunt Willa. She's cold, too, and when she doesn't feel like dealing with Rosemary she dumps her on Aunt Willa."

"That kind of makes me feel bad for the kid," Terry said. "It's hell when no one wants you."

"We've tried to be nice to Rosemary," I said.

Marnie rolled her eyes.

"We have," I said. "When she was younger, we went out of our way to engage her. We wanted her to be friends with Bay, Clove and Thistle. We were never close with Nettie. She was a horrible kid. We didn't want the same thing to happen to the next generation."

"That sounds good," Terry said. "Where's the problem?"

"Rosemary is the same kind of kid her mother was," I said. "She was mean to the girls when she was around them. She thought she was better than them. She pulled their hair. She made up stories. She went out of her way to get the girls in trouble."

"When we didn't believe her stories, Rosemary turned on us and Aunt Willa became even more distant," Marnie said. "She wanted us to spank the girls and punish them, all on the word of a child who is clearly a pathological liar and manipulator. When we refused, things sort of blew up."

"We barely see Aunt Willa these days," I said. "We've seen Rosemary only a few times in five years."

"And we haven't seen Nettie in more than five years," Marnie said. "Our branch of the family and their branch don't mingle well together."

"That still doesn't explain why Willa would dump her on you guys for a few days," Terry said. "If anything, she should want to keep the kid away from you."

"We're not sure what's going on there either," I said. "Maybe she wants Rosemary to spy on us."

"To what end?"

"I have no idea."

Terry shrugged. "I think you guys are making a mountain out of a molehill," he said. "I'm used to it, but this seems especially out there. As far as I can tell, Lila and Rosemary are at one table and your girls are at another table."

"With Aunt Tillie," I said.

"I'm glad she's with them," Terry said. "Lila and Rosemary will think twice about doing anything horrible with Aunt Tillie around."

"I can see you don't know a lot about teenage girls," I said. "At this age, they don't think about the ramifications. They only think about immediate victory over someone else."

Terry was nonplussed. "I'm not going to get worked up about this," he said. "We won't let Rosemary and Lila win. It's pretty simple in my book."

Oh, if he only knew how really wrong he was.

SIX

"I'm so glad your hamburgers didn't have burnt black stuff on them," Marnie teased, poking me in the side. "That would have been really nasty."

I shot her a look. I knew she was trying to lift my spirits, but my mind was too busy with witchy stuff to worry about the mundane. I often thought Bay spent too much time hiding in her own head. I was starting to wonder whether it was a trait she picked up from me.

That was a sobering thought. Crap. Who needs that? I decided a long time ago that I would take credit for all of Bay's good traits and disavow all of the bad ones. What? Isn't that how all parents survive?

"Everyone seemed to enjoy their dinner," I said. "The girls had a good time, and Aunt Tillie stuck close to them. Maybe they're not up to anything."

"Sometimes I think you're bi-polar," Marnie said. "One minute you think Aunt Tillie and Thistle are going to burn the whole campsite down to get to Lila and the next you think they're just sitting around flapping their angel wings."

"Which instinct do you think is right?" I was genuinely curious.

"I think the truth lies somewhere in the middle," Marnie said. "I think it's far more likely that Thistle and Aunt Tillie will set the camp on fire with their angel wings."

I involuntarily snorted, relief flooding through me. I can always count on my sisters to yank me out of a depressing reverie – even if I'm not particularly keen on making the trip. "They seem to be calm now," I said. "Let's just go with the flow. We'll have a bonfire, some s'mores, and then we'll send them to bed. There won't be any ghost stories, and if we're lucky, there will be a whole lot of sleep tonight."

"When was the last time we were lucky?"

"I like to think we've always been lucky," I said.

"I see you found your rose-colored glasses again," Marnie teased.

"You're really starting to bug me."

"That's why I'm here."

We returned to our cleanup, and I was surprised when Aunt Tillie joined us a few minutes later. Manual labor was usually on her not-to-do list, so any time she decided to help my trouble detector flipped into high gear. "What's going on?"

"Nothing," Aunt Tillie said. "I'm just making sure that everything gets put in the garbage. We don't want any little varmints running around in the middle of the night."

"Are you talking about animals or kids?"

"Both."

I smirked. "What were you talking about with the girls?"

Aunt Tillie pursed her lips, considering. "Minor stuff," she said. "I only wanted them to feel safe."

She never ceases to amaze me. Just when I think she's up to no good, she turns around and plays the dutiful aunt. "Thank you."

"To feel safe, they have to take Lila down."

I scowled. "Seriously? I was just giving myself a mental butt-kicking because I felt bad for thinking you were up to no good."

"Keep doing that," Aunt Tillie said. "Everything I do is good. When you fill your mind with bad thoughts, you sully our family bond."

"I'm going to sully you if you don't behave," I said. "Don't encourage those girls to do something bad. After this afternoon ... ."

"Bay knows what she did," Aunt Tillie said, her eyes serious. "She didn't at first, but it didn't take her long to figure it out."

"Did she tell you that?"

"Not in so many words," Aunt Tillie said. "I know that she's talked to Clove and Thistle about it, though."

"And what did they say?"

"Clove is worried Bay is going to go all Carrie-at-the-prom and Thistle is hoping she does," Aunt Tillie said.

That sounded about right. "What is Bay worried about?"

"Bay is worried about a lost soul in the woods," Aunt Tillie said.

That figured. Even though she's a dreamer, Bay takes a pragmatic approach to her problems. Lila isn't going anywhere. She's always going to be a problem. The ghost is another story. With limited time at camp, of course Bay is more worried about the ghost. "Does she know who it is?"

"No."

"I'm worried it's Donna Wilder," I admitted.

Aunt Tillie inhaled heavily, her mind working as she considered the possibility. "I guess that makes sense. She could have come up here to get the camp in order. Something could have happened to her."

"We know people who die accidentally don't usually return," I said. "If it is Donna, doesn't that mean something bad happened to her?"

"Just because it was bad, that doesn't mean it wasn't an accident," Aunt Tillie said.

"Have you seen any ghosts hanging around?"

"I haven't been looking," Aunt Tillie replied. "I've seen a few flashes, though. I've been more interested in watching Lila and Rosemary. I'm ... bothered ... about Rosemary's reasons for being here. She clearly doesn't want to be here. That means it was Willa's idea."

"Maybe it was Nettie's idea."

"Nettie has never had her own ideas," Aunt Tillie said. "That's the way Willa likes it. No, this was Willa's idea, but I can't figure out what she thinks it's going to get her."

"Maybe she only wants a few days away from Rosemary," I

suggested. "I've been around her twenty-four hours and I'm already at my limit."

"She is a particular little ... ."

I lifted a challenging eyebrow.

"... Ray of sunshine," Aunt Tillie finished through gritted teeth. "Willa would have to be desperate to dump Rosemary here, though. The kid is fourteen. If she needs a couple of hours alone, Rosemary can take care of herself."

"Unless she can't," I said. "It's not as though Aunt Willa raised Nettie to be self-sufficient. The same is probably true of Rosemary."

"Well, we can't do anything but watch the little ray of poopy sunshine," Aunt Tillie said. "Oh, don't give me that look. I held off for as long as I could."

"Just keep your eyes peeled for the ghost," I said. "And if you notice Lila and Rosemary plotting anything, I want to know right away. Don't handle it yourself."

"They're definitely plotting something," Aunt Tillie said. "I'm not sure what it is, but you shouldn't be worried. I'd put Thistle's devious brain up against both of theirs combined any day of the week."

Thankfully, so would I. "Just ... watch them. We have only two more nights and two more days here. I'm sure we can survive."

"Oh, everyone is going to survive," Aunt Tillie said. "I just can't promise what mental state a few of these little ... darlings ... are going to leave in."

"Be good."

"I always am."

OKAY GUYS, NO GHOST STORIES TONIGHT," I said, distributing marshmallows, graham crackers and chocolate to the assembled kids. "We're going to make some s'mores, have a few laughs and then we're going to bed."

"There will be no screaming and panicking tonight," Marnie warned.

Terry lifted an eyebrow in my direction as he took his chocolate bar. "Screaming?"

"It seems someone scratched on the window at the first cabin and the girls thought it was a china doll trying to scratch their eyes out last night," I said. "Since the doll from the story resembled a certain someone, she was attacked."

Terry fought the urge to smile. "I see. Who scratched the window?"

I shot a pointed look at Aunt Tillie, who steadfastly ignored me and directed Thistle to roast marshmallows for her. "We're not sure," I lied.

Terry chuckled. "I had a feeling that was going to happen," he said. "How many times were they up last night?"

"Five."

"I'm glad I have boys," Terry said. "Other than a nervous trip across the lake in canoes, my kids passed out right away."

"You only have twelve of them, too," I pointed out.

"Have you ever considered I'm just better at corralling the mayhem?"

He was trying to be cute. "No," I said.

"I don't get what we're supposed to be doing." One of the boys, a blue-eyed teenager with black hair and an impish grin, focused on me. "Are we building little marshmallow sandwiches here?"

"Haven't you ever had a s'more?"

"I'm from the city, lady," the boy said. "Our sandwiches have meat and mayonnaise on them – like they're supposed to."

Boys were a mystery to me. Our family had always been made up of girls. Sure, we dated and married men, but our offspring were always of the female persuasion. I was used to the highs – and lows – of raising a petulant girl. A mouthy boy was a whole other animal.

"Do you like chocolate?"

The boy nodded.

"Do you like marshmallows?"

Another nod.

"Do you like graham crackers?"

The boy rolled his eyes and sighed. "I see where you're going with this," he said. "You're saying if I like those three things separately, I should like them together."

"You're a smart kid," I said, smiling.

"Hold that thought," the boy said. "I also like tomato soup, bacon and cola. Those things aren't going to taste good together."

He had a point. Crap. "Eat your s'more."

"You don't have a lot of patience, do you?"

Terry's shoulders shook with silent laughter as he watched us interact.

"I happen to think I have a great deal of patience," I said. "It's just that smart-mouthed kids give me a headache."

"Then you must live in constant pain," the boy said. "You're surrounded by smart-mouthed people."

"Eat your s'more." I left Terry to his wards – and his silent laughter – and made my way to the other side of the bonfire, where I could watch all the kids without straining my neck.

A glance at Bay, Clove and Thistle told me they were enjoying themselves. They took turns putting s'mores together for Aunt Tillie, and even though they were isolated in their own little world, the four of them seemed to be having a great time.

I studied the other girls. They'd separated themselves into little groups, which is the way of teenage girls. Things would only get worse as they got older. The Winchester girls were always in their own little group, as was Lila.

Hey, speaking of Lila, where did she go?

I scanned the crowd again. She was gone. So was Rosemary. Well, that couldn't be good. I was about to alert Marnie when Bay turned sharply and stared at the dark spot over her shoulder.

Instead of asking Bay what she saw, I strode to the area to search it myself. If Lila and Rosemary were there plotting something, I was going to nip it in the bud. When I got to the spot in question, though, it was empty.

I checked a few of the bushes, even searched under the picnic tables to make sure no one was hiding there. Nothing.

I jumped when a hand come down on my shoulder. I knew it was Terry before turning around.

"What's wrong?" he asked.

"I'm not sure," I said. "I noticed Lila and Rosemary were missing, and then Bay shifted and I swear she was staring at something over here. I was making sure something bad wasn't about to happen."

Terry nodded, understanding washing over his face. "You think Rosemary and Lila are going to make a scene?"

"I think that teenage girls like drama," I said. "Evil teenage girls like evil drama."

"Well, let's find them," Terry said. "I'm not particularly worried about the evil, but I'm not thrilled with the idea of those two wandering around the woods on their own."

"Do you think something could've happened to them? Do you think they could've been kidnapped?" Marnie calls me an alarmist. I see it, but I can't stop myself from doing it.

"I think anyone who tried to kidnap them would throw them back within five minutes," Terry said. "I'm more worried that they might get lost in the woods. Those aren't the type of girls who can survive on their own."

"Are you worried wolves might eat them?"

"They're more likely to eat the wolves," Terry said. "I am worried one of them could rip their clothes and lose their mind, though."

He makes me laugh. I can't help it. He has a dry sense of humor, but he's always funny. "Well, maybe they went back to their cabin."

"In an ideal world, they'd be in bed," Terry said. "We don't live in an ideal world, though. Let's ... ."

He was cut short when a chorus of screams erupted around the bonfire. We both turned quickly, scanning the flailing and screaming kids for the source of their panic.

It didn't take me long to see the reason. Lila stood in the middle of the group, her face powder white and fake blood dripping down the side of her head. She'd made herself up to look like a deranged china doll. While most of the kids scattered to give her room to work, signifying they realized what was going on, Bay remained seated.

Lila jumped at her, extending her fingers and clawing at the side of Bay's face. In her haste to get away, Bay tipped her chair, her legs tangling with the plastic at the bottom of the chair and causing her to fall to the side.

The second Bay hit the ground, the rest of the girls – and most of the boys – erupted into hysterical laughter.

"Oh, man, did you see her face?" one of the boys asked.

Lila, clearly proud of herself, high-fived Rosemary. "I told you I would get you back," she said, glaring down at Bay.

Thistle and Clove were on either side of Bay, but they had trouble hoisting her to a standing position. Like a pack of wild hyenas, a bevy of the girls filled the space behind Lila, pointing in Bay's direction, laughing.

Bay's face was hard to read, but I could see the unshed tears glittering in her eyes. Before I could make a move to go to her, though, the dark-haired boy pushed the girls out of the way and knelt next to Bay.

"You guys are so stupid," he said. "That wasn't even scary. She didn't fall because she was scared. She fell because she got tangled in the chair. Stop being idiots."

My earlier ire with the smart-mouthed s'mores boy evaporated. He may be mouthy, but he was also brave. He didn't care what the other kids thought about him. He only cared about doing the right thing.

"What's his name?"

Terry shrugged. "I can never keep their names straight. I just call them all 'son' and hope I don't offend them. I see too many faces."

"He's a good kid," I said.

"That's probably why he decided to help the other good kids," Terry said. "Do you want to do something with Lila?"

"If I go after her, it's just going to reinforce her status at camp," I said. "It's better to ignore her."

"That's progressive thinking."

"It is," I said. I squeezed his hand briefly and then moved back toward the fire. Bay was back in her chair, her arms crossed over her chest, as Thistle leaned in and whispered in her ear. If they weren't plotting something before, they definitely were now.

Aunt Tillie shuffled up beside me. "This is my fault," she said.

"It's Lila's fault," I replied. "I'm trusting you to fix it."

Aunt Tillie's eyes widened. "Seriously?"

"Keep it quiet," I said. "Let Lila have her suspicions that it was the four of you, but don't let her be able to prove it."

"That shouldn't be a problem," Aunt Tillie said, rubbing her hands together gleefully. "Can I do whatever I want?"

"Go nuts," I said.

Aunt Tillie was already moving.

"Oh, Aunt Tillie?"

She paused long enough to give me a quick look over her shoulder. "I want them to cry."

"Consider it done."

What had I just done?

SEVEN

"Should we wake up the kids or let them sleep?" Marnie asked, casting a glance over her shoulder in the direction of the quiet cabins the next morning.

After an uneventful evening – other than Lila's prank at the bonfire – the boys left to go to their own camp and the girls retired to plot another day. I couldn't say I was sorry for the quiet, although I was worried about the events I'd set in motion the night before.

"Let them sleep," I said.

"What's bothering you?" Marnie asked. "Is it what Lila did to Bay? I honestly don't think Bay was scared. I think she was trying to put some distance between her and Lila. I think she was more embarrassed about tripping than anything else."

"I'm not happy about that," I said. "That's not what's bothering me, though."

"Do you want to tell me, or do you want me to guess?"

"I told Aunt Tillie to go after them last night," I said.

"Who?"

"Lila and Rosemary." I was mortified by my actions, embarrassed. What grown woman gives another adult free rein to terrorize children?

"Good," Marnie said.

Okay, what other grown woman? "You don't think I acted immaturely?"

"I think when you're dealing with teenagers constantly it's hard not to let the immaturity affect you," Marnie said. "I wouldn't worry about it. After last night, Aunt Tillie was going to go after them anyway. You didn't push her toward anything."

"I told her to make them cry."

Marnie snickered. "Well ... we'll keep that little tidbit to ourselves."

"What do you think she's going to do?" I was almost afraid to ask.

"She's not going to do anything that puts them in physical danger," Marnie said. "She's mean. She's not stupid."

"I still told her she could do it."

"You can't give Aunt Tillie permission to do anything, just like you can't forbid her to do anything," Marnie said. "She's going to do what she's going to do."

"What are we talking about?" Twila asked, setting a large bowl on the center of the table. "Where are the eggs, by the way?"

"They're in the refrigerator inside the cabin," Marnie said.

"No, they're not," Twila said. "I checked. They're all gone."

"We had like twelve dozen eggs," Marnie said. "Where could they all go?"

Uh-oh. I shifted my attention to the first cabin – the one Rosemary and Lila slumbered in. "They were there last night," I said. "I saw them when I put the leftover chocolate bars in before going to bed."

"They're not there now," Twila said. "Who would have taken all those eggs?"

Marnie was already joining my thought train. "Has anyone seen Aunt Tillie this morning?"

"I didn't see her last night, either," I said. "After I talked to her by the bonfire, she kind of ... disappeared."

"I'm sure it's nothing," Twila said. "I'm sure she's just ... ."

The morning quiet was shattered by the sound of screaming. I pressed my eyes shut briefly, hoping against hope I was still asleep and this was a dream. Marnie pinching my arm to bring me back to reality shattered that illusion.

"We have to go see what it is," Marnie said. "You know that."

"This is all my fault."

"This is Lila's fault," Marnie said. "Let's go see what karma delivered her."

WE WERE careful when we entered the cabin, making certain to look above our heads and below our feet before taking a step. Aunt Tillie is a master trapper, and I wasn't sure whether all of her "surprises" were already sprung.

Lila stood in the center of the room, cotton shorts and a tank top covering her thin body. That wasn't all that was on her, though. There was something else. A weird ... paste.

None of the girls in the first cabin were unscathed, although Lila and Rosemary clearly bore the brunt of the attack. The paste looked as though it had dropped from the sky, dispersing evenly. Something told me this little gift was delivered magically, although proof of that would be impossible to find.

Even though the paste was still fresh, it gave off a pungent odor. As I stared at Lila's face I realized it was also changing color. It was darkening and ... wow ... it's starting to smell like someone died in here.

"I'm guessing this is where all the eggs went," Marnie murmured.

"It smells awful," Twila said, pinching her nose. "It's like ... skunky."

"I think it smells like a dead body," I said.

"Really? I think it smells just like rotten eggs," Marnie said.

"Are you going to do something about this?" Lila asked, her hair swinging as she swiveled to face us. "All our stuff is covered in this ... crap. We smell."

I pursed my lips to keep from laughing. "Well, we didn't do it," I said. "What do you want us to do about it?"

"Someone did it to us," Lila said. "I'm betting it was your loser daughter and her loser cousins. She did it as payback for the china doll thing last night."

"Did anyone see Bay, Clove and Thistle in here last night?" I asked.

No one raised their hands, causing Lila to frown. "I saw them."

"Did you really?"

"I did," Lila said. "They came in here and they dumped all of this stuff on us. Then they snuck back out."

"If you saw them sneak in here, why didn't you tell me last night?" I asked.

"I ... ." Lila was having trouble coming up with a lie. Instead, she absent-mindedly started scratching her arm. "They must have drugged me," she said finally. "I saw what was happening, but there was nothing I could do about it."

"They drugged you? How did they manage that?"

"How should I know?" Lila started scratching harder. "They're evil witches. They have ways of doing things. They probably hypnotized me before they did it."

Lila was really digging her fingernails into her arm now. I moved toward her, being careful to step around the paste, and grabbed her hand away from her arm. "Why are you scratching like that?"

"I ... I don't know," Lila admitted. "I'm itchy."

Uh-oh. I think the paste was more than just ugly. I studied Lila's arm, being careful not to touch the red bumps that were lifting. "You have poison oak."

"What?" Lila screeched, ripping her arm away. "How did that happen?"

I had an idea. I glanced around the cabin. "Are all of you itchy?"

They nodded.

"Okay," I said. "Um ... I think you need to go down to the lake and rinse off. We can't take a good look at you until we can see what we're looking at."

"I want Bay punished for this," Lila said. "This is not funny."

"You have no proof Bay did this."

"I told you I saw her. Ow!" Lila's hand flew up to her face and she started furiously scratching at her cheek.

Every lie Lila told increased her discomfort. This had Aunt Tillie written all over it. She was known to build lessons into her curses. This one was almost inspired.

"Go down to the lake and rinse off, Lila," I said. "We'll try to find something to help with the itching."

"The only thing that's going to help with the itching is Bay being punished," Lila said. "I saw her and I want her punished. She's evil. Evil. Evil. Ow!"

Lila's hand drifted to the spot between her eyebrows, and even as she scratched I saw red bumps start to rise. The spell was ongoing. I wasn't sure washing off the paste would fix it.

"Go rinse off, Lila," I said. "We have to take this one step at a time."

"**DO** THEY ALL HAVE POISON OAK?" I kept my voice low as I grouped with Marnie and Twila near the picnic tables.

"Everyone in the first cabin has some form of it," Marnie said. "Conveniently, the girls who have had the least amount of contact with our girls have the smallest amount."

"And Lila has it the worst," I finished.

"Rosemary has it pretty bad, too," Twila said. "She hasn't said a lot, though. Lila's keeps getting worse every time she opens her mouth. Rosemary has been quiet."

"Maybe she's thinking evil thoughts," Marnie suggested. "That sounds like something Aunt Tillie would do."

"Where is Aunt Tillie?" I asked.

Marnie pointed. I glanced in the direction she indicated, shaking my head when I saw my elderly aunt standing under a tree with Bay, Clove and Thistle grouped around her. They were watching the show, and they seemed to be enjoying themselves.

"What do you think?" Twila asked. "Did they do it?"

"I'm narrowing down my field of suspects to the four over there who had access to the eggs," I said. "They needed the eggs to make that paste. I've never seen anything like that, by the way. Do you remember reading about that paste in any of our magic books?"

"I think that was something Aunt Tillie created all on her own," Marnie said. "You should know that the smell is hanging around even though they washed all the paste off and changed their clothes."

"What about the cabin?"

"It's still a mess."

I rubbed the heel of my hand against my forehead. "Well, I'm not cleaning that up ... and we know Aunt Tillie isn't going to clean it up."

"I suggest we make them clean it up," Marnie said.

"That's not going to go over well."

"I don't care," Marnie said. "It has to be done, and none of us are doing it. I'll tell them what's going on once you're out of here."

"Out of here? Where am I going?"

"You're taking Bay, Clove and Thistle for a hike," Marnie said. "Until this ... calms down ... Lila is going to be a wreck. I think our girls should be away from the camp for a few hours."

"What if it's still a mess tonight?"

"Then we'll deal with it then," Marnie said. "You take our girls – and Aunt Tillie, if you can convince her to go, although I don't think that's likely – and spend a few hours looking for Bay's ghost. It will give you something to do."

"What are you going to do?"

"I'm going to order the girls to clean up the cabin and then send the other girls out on the lake with Twila," Marnie said. "I have a feeling this spell is only going to get worse before it gets better ... especially for some people."

Her gaze was fixed on Rosemary and Lila, who had their heads bent together as they energetically scratched their arms, necks and faces. They were obviously plotting, and that was only making their affliction worse. They didn't realize the cause and effect.

"Okay," I said. "I won't go too far. But be careful. Lila is going to be out for blood."

"I can handle Lila," Marnie said. "It's Rosemary who really has me worried."

Me too. The odd child was getting odder by the minute – and that was a frightening thought.

"**WHAT** are we looking for?" Clove asked, taking the lead as our small expedition moved through the thick trees surrounding the lake. "Are you going to tie us to trees and leave us out here?"

"Why would I do that?"

Clove is the most nervous of the three girls. When they've done something wrong, she's always the one who breaks first. Thistle holds on out of spite, and Bay refuses to squeal out of loyalty. She doesn't care about getting punished herself, but she's not fond of getting her cousins into trouble.

"Because of what we did last night," Clove said.

Thistle reached over and pinched her. "Shut your mouth."

"I already know you guys are responsible for what happened last night," I said. "Don't worry about that. You're not in trouble." There was no way I could punish them for actions I set into motion.

"We didn't do anything," Thistle said. "Clove is talking nonsense … like she always does."

"You're dead to me," Clove spat, taking a swipe at Thistle's messy hair.

I stepped between them, pushing their antsy bodies away from one another. "Knock that off. I already told you that you're not in trouble."

"Yeah, but you could just be saying that," Thistle said. "You're the type who is smart enough to lie, and then when we own up to what you think we did, you'd punish us anyway."

That was a backhanded compliment. Kind of. "Why do you think I would punish you?"

"I think you like it."

I couldn't hide my smile. Despite her occasional obnoxiousness, Thistle has one of those personalities you can't help but love. She's has charisma. "I don't like punishing you," I said. "Besides, I can't punish you because I'm the one who told Aunt Tillie to do what she did."

Thistle narrowed her eyes. "You did?" She obviously didn't believe me.

"I didn't tell her to do that specifically," I said. "I told her to make them cry. She didn't do that."

"Give it time," Thistle muttered.

I stilled. "Time for what?"

"I have no idea what you're talking about," Thistle said, averting her gaze.

"I'll give you the leftover chocolate in the refrigerator when we get back to camp if you tell me," I offered.

Thistle rolled her eyes. "Are you really trying to bribe me?"

Of course not. Thistle can't be bribed. She'd rather go hungry for days than give in. "I was talking to Clove."

Clove's dark eyes widened. "Really?"

"I'll curse that chocolate so it tastes like flies if you turn on me," Thistle warned.

She's frightening sometimes. She's like a tiny mixture of Aunt Tillie, Marnie and her own mother. It's a terrifying combination. "Just tell me what the spell does."

"If you're a good person, it doesn't do anything," Clove said, shooting a worried look in Thistle's direction and cowering slightly at the scowl on her cousin's face. "The worse you are ... the more lies you tell ... the more bad thoughts you have ... the worse the spell gets."

I'd already started to figure that out on my own. "How long does it last?"

"That's up to the person infected," Clove said. "If they try to make amends, they'll get better. If they don't ... well ... it never ends."

I sighed, running a hand through my hair as I studied the two girls. "It can only last until they go home. You know that, right?"

Thistle shifted to me, her face unreadable. "You're fine with the spell going on?"

"I'm fine with karma working its own way out," I said. "I'll make sure Aunt Tillie ends the spell by the time everyone leaves tomorrow. The last thing we need is Lila's mother coming out to the house on a rampage."

"I think we should cast the spell on her, too," Thistle said.

"Maybe if you're really bored when school starts up," I said, grinning. I reached over and tweaked her nose. "Enjoy the spell while you can. For now, though, we need to get back to the camp. I've left my sisters to their own devices for far too long. Where is Bay?"

Thistle shrugged, and a quick scan of our surroundings caused my heart to drop. "Bay!"

She didn't answer.

"Bay!"

"Take a chill pill," Bay said, moving into my line of sight. She'd wandered into the trees and was picking flowers as she looked around. "I'm right here."

"Don't wander off," I said.

"I didn't wander off," Bay replied, irritated. "I'm right here."

"Come on," I said. "We need to go back to camp."

"We can't go back until I find the ghost," Bay argued. "She needs help."

"We can't make the ghost come to us, Bay. She'll have to come when she's ready. Are you even sure it's a woman?"

"It's a woman," Bay said, her nose wrinkling. "She's sad."

"I know she's sad, Bay. There's still nothing we can do until she's ready to be helped." That was true of the living as well as the dead. "When she wants help, she'll ask for it. Now, come on. You guys didn't get breakfast and I think we could all use some lunch."

"But … ." Bay wasn't ready to give in.

"Come on," Thistle said. "Don't you want to see how bad Lila looks? She probably looks like a giant zit that needs to be popped. I'm not missing that."

Bay brightened considerably. "Okay."

Funnily enough, Thistle is the one who always knows how to cheer Bay up. That was another part of her charm.

EIGHT

"Is anyone else glad this is our final night here?" Marnie asked, handing the hot dog platter to Twila and gathering the utensils so we could wash them back at the cabin. "In twenty-four hours, we're going to be back home with only three teenagers to deal with."

"Don't forget Aunt Tillie," Twila said.

"I could never forget Aunt Tillie."

"How are the infected girls?" I asked, lifting my head so I could study the crowded field where Terry was taking advantage of the limited light left in the day to play freeze tag with all of the kids. Well, to be fair, it wasn't all of the kids. Lila, Rosemary and a few of the others who were still struggling with poison oak symptoms were hanging around the bonfire pit.

After a few hours under the watchful eyes of Bay, Clove, Thistle and Aunt Tillie, most of the girls figured out pretty quickly that they felt better when they stopped casting verbal – and mental – stones. Only five girls were still sick, and Lila and Rosemary looked like rejects from an episode of *The X-Files*.

Their faces – which were hideously spotted – were enough to keep all of the boys (and most of the girls) away. Lila was spitting nails by the time Terry showed up for dinner, and she gave him an earful about wanting Bay arrested. After listening to her complaints – from a safe distance, mind you – and asking her a few questions, he informed her there was no evidence of Bay's guilt.

Lila didn't take it well. She'd spent the past hour conspiring with her limited group of cronies, and I had a feeling we weren't quite out of the woods yet. No pun intended.

"They're crabby," Marnie said. "Only three of the girls agreed to clean up the cabin. They were the ones who felt better first. Their faces cleared up before they were even done."

"Did the other girls notice?"

"The smart ones did," Marnie said. "I'm betting you can guess who the stupid ones are."

"Rosemary is the one who surprises me," I said. "She knows about magic. Aunt Willa isn't a practitioner, but Rosemary still knows … something. She should have figured it out first."

"Maybe she has. Maybe she just doesn't care how she looks."

"I don't think anyone could ignore those big pus balls on their faces," I said.

"Maybe Rosemary is more interested in revenge," Marnie suggested.

That thought occurred to me, too. "We have to watch them tonight," I said. "We just have to get through tonight."

"Maybe we should split up and sleep in the cabins with the girls," Twila said. "If one of us is in each cabin, they'll be forced to behave themselves."

That was an idea. Still …. "Who wants to sleep in Lila's cabin?"

Marnie and Twila immediately started shaking their heads.

"I think that should be your job," Marnie said. "You're the one who let Aunt Tillie off her leash."

"I'm not sleeping in that cabin."

"You could sleep in the hammock," Twila said. "It's right by the cabin."

"I'd rather do that," I said. "Let's just watch things. Maybe Lila and Rosemary will give up before things really get out of hand."

"You're giving them too much credit," Marnie said. "If they haven't figured out what's going on yet, they're not going to."

"I just keep hoping there's a decent person deep down in both of them," I said. "At this point, it would have to be really deep. Something has to be there, though. They can't be this ... empty."

"I think they're exactly this empty," Marnie said. "Keep your rose-colored glasses on, though. They look good on you. I'm going to take the dishes back to the cabin. Why don't you get the fire started? We only have to get through tonight and an afternoon of kayaking tomorrow. Keep telling yourself that. That's how we're going to survive."

I smiled. "Well, for now, Terry has them all busy playing tag."

"Have you noticed that the boy who came to Bay's defense last night keeps chasing her when it's his turn?" Twila asked.

Indeed, I had noticed that. "I think he might have a crush on her."

"Have they even talked, though?"

"Bay, Clove and Thistle haven't talked to anyone but themselves," I said. "I think that boy just likes blondes. I wouldn't worry about it. He'll have a broken heart for five minutes when he leaves tomorrow and then he'll move on to another blonde."

"Those rose-colored glasses might need an updated prescription," Marnie teased. "I'm not saying they're going to fall in love and spend the rest of their lives together. It's just kind of cute to see them discovering boys."

"I'm guessing we're all going to feel differently in two years."

Marnie shrugged. "Maybe. It's fun for now."

"I'll give you that," I conceded, smiling as the boy chased a squealing Bay. "It's definitely fun."

"CAN WE HEAR A GHOST STORY TONIGHT?"

"Sure," Aunt Tillie said, leaning forward.

"Absolutely not," I said, wagging my finger in her direction. "No ghost stories."

Aunt Tillie rolled her eyes. "You're such a downer."

"I can live with that."

"Even as a child you were a downer," Aunt Tillie said. "You were the one who told on me when I snuck you candy."

"That's because we weren't supposed to have more than one piece before dinner."

"See? Downer."

Aunt Tillie was playing to her audience, and she was having a good time doing it. Whispers spread throughout the campers that 'she was the one responsible for the "plague" earlier in the day. Since then, the girls couldn't stop themselves from sucking up to her. That's exactly how Aunt Tillie liked to live her life: with fans.

"We're going to make s'mores again," I said. "Then we're all going to go to bed early. It's been a really long couple of days."

"You're just getting old," Thistle teased. "You don't have enough energy to keep up with us."

"I think that every day of my life, Thistle," I said. "Three of you is bad enough. Forty of you is ... too much."

"Mom says I'm too much on my own," Thistle said.

"In your case I'd say that was true." I tousled her hair affectionately as I moved past her. "Just try to be good tonight."

"I'm always good."

"I hope you're grading yourself on a curve," I said. "Otherwise I might think your nose is growing."

Thistle scowled. "Are you calling me a liar?"

"Watch the fire, Thistle."

I joined Terry a few feet away. He was leaning against a tree, his arms crossed over his chest, and his face was thoughtful as he watched the kids.

"Are you going to be happy to send them on their way tomorrow?" I asked.

"They're a good group of boys," Terry said. "They haven't been any trouble."

"That must be a nice experience," I joked.

"Yeah, it looks like you had another eventful night," he said. "What's the deal with Lila's face?"

"She woke up with poison oak this morning."

"That's inconvenient," Terry said, nonplussed. "She just woke up with it? Out of the blue?"

"She must have accidentally rubbed against it while out in the woods yesterday," I said evasively.

Terry barked out a coarse laugh. "That girl hasn't set foot in those woods since she got here," he said. "I'm guessing she got the poison oak by other means."

"I have no idea what you're talking about."

"The kids have been talking," Terry said. "The rumor is that Bay, Clove and Thistle cursed the people in Lila's cabin. I notice most of the girls look fine, though. Just a handful of them are suffering. How does that work?"

I felt he was putting me on the spot. "Why are you asking me?"

"Because I saw the look on your face last night when Lila went after Bay," he said. "I have a feeling you know what happened."

"I didn't do anything."

"I didn't say you did anything," Terry said. "In fact, I'm guessing Aunt Tillie is the ringleader, and she dragged Bay, Clove and Thistle along for the ride."

"I guess anything is possible."

Terry smirked. "Are the ones still scratching the ones who refuse to apologize?"

"The ones still affected are the ones lying and plotting," I said. "If they stopped both of those things, they would go back to normal."

"That's an interesting punishment," Terry said, rubbing his stubbly chin. "It would teach most kids a lesson."

"Most," I agreed.

"Was that Aunt Tillie's idea?"

"I told her to do whatever she wanted," I admitted. "If you think I'm proud of my actions, I'm not."

"I'd be proud of it," he said. "It's kind of like the best of both worlds. You get to see the ugly within on the outside. If everything in life was like that, it would make my job a whole lot easier."

"They're still just kids," I said. "I kind of feel … guilty."

"Don't," Terry said. "A lesson learned is a valuable thing. A lesson ignored is also a valuable thing. Lila is going to learn something here this weekend. We don't know what it is, but I guarantee she learns something."

"I'm worried Bay, Clove and Thistle are going to learn something, too," I said. "I'm worried I'm teaching them that revenge is the way to go."

"Sometimes it is."

"Not always, though."

"No, not always," Terry agreed. "In this case, though, revenge is the only weapon they have. Let's just see how it all plays out."

"You're being awfully calm about this," I said. "Usually when we talk about ... this stuff ... you like to pretend you can't hear us."

"Did you say something?"

"I ... ." I rolled my eyes, realizing what he was doing. "You're a funny guy."

"I am," Terry agreed, pushing himself away from the tree. "Let's get this show on the road. I realize I'm starting to feel my age. Long days watching twelve boys who have boundless enthusiasm is making me feel old."

"I think we all feel that way," I said.

"DO WE HAVE ANY MORE CHOCOLATE?" Thistle asked, scanning the area around the campfire. "I want another s'more."

"You've had three," I said. "You don't need another one."

"I'm on vacation," Thistle said.

"You're at camp."

"That's still a vacation for kids," Thistle pressed.

"What are you getting at?"

"When you're on vacation, you get to eat whatever you want," she said. "I want chocolate."

She's such a pain. "If there's more chocolate, go nuts. You're still going to bed early, and if I catch you out of bed I'm going to make sure you don't see a bar of chocolate for two weeks once we get home."

"You really are a downer," Thistle muttered.

I turned to Twila. "She's your little bundle of joy," I said. "Can't you make her behave?"

"Not if history is any indication," Twila said. "She's her own person. I can't change it, and I don't want to."

"You don't have to change her," I said. "Can't you ... I don't know ... gag her or something?"

Twila smiled. "I think she's cute."

Of course she did. I turned my attention back to the campfire, counting heads. When I came up two short, I started over again. The outcome was the same. Two girls were missing, and I didn't even have to conduct a roll-call to figure out which ones.

"Where are Lila and Rosemary?"

Twila straightened and scanned the crowd, jerking her head every which way. She looked like a constipated chicken. "I have no idea."

"Sonova ... ."

"What now?" Marnie asked, appearing at my side. "I can tell by the look on your face that something has happened."

"Lila and Rosemary are gone," I said. "That can only mean one thing."

"They're plotting revenge," Marnie said. "Great. What should we do?"

"We're sending the boys across the lake and the rest of them to bed," I said. "I'm so tired of this. I don't remember camp being this exhausting when we were here."

"That's because we were kids and everyone else was doing the worrying," Marnie said. "Now we know how it feels when the shoe is on the other foot."

"Yeah, it doesn't fit and it hurts," I said. "Okay, gather the girls. I'm officially declaring the last night of camp over."

"This should go over well," Marnie muttered.

I clapped my hands together. "Okay, girls, it's time for bed."

"It's not even ten yet," Thistle complained.

"You'll live. Let's go."

Terry raised his eyebrows but didn't argue. "Let's go, boys. I'm

AMANDA M. LEE

tired, and we still have to get across the lake. You can start a bonfire over there if you want."

"That's good," the dark-haired boy said. "This place is freaky. They've got girls running around here who look like their faces are about to explode they're so bumpy."

"Thank you, son," Terry said.

"Speaking of, where did those ugly girls go?"

Terry shifted, and I could see his mind working as he looked over the grumbling girls. He glanced up at me. "Is that why you're sending them to bed?"

"Yup."

"Do you want me to help look for them?"

"I ... ." I broke off, biting my lip. Did I?

Terry sighed. "Stay here, boys. I'll just be a minute. We have to find the poxed twosome before we can go."

"Oh, great," the boy complained.

"It won't take long," Terry said. "Girls, stay around the fire for a minute. I need to ... what the hell?"

I couldn't see what happened, but the change in Terry's tone told me whatever it was couldn't be good. I scampered in his direction, my mind busy with horrible thoughts.

"I'm so sorry, Mr. Davenport." I recognized Lila's voice. "We didn't think you would be the one coming through here."

When I got close to Terry, I realized he was covered in something. Under the dim light, I couldn't tell what it was. He ran his fingers over his face, wiping the red liquid from his eyes and scowling. "What is this?"

"It's just water," Lila said, wringing her hands. Her face was even worse now than it had been an hour ago. I wanted to shove a mirror in her hand and force her to look, but I didn't think now was the time. "There was some food coloring in it and, well, we might have put some poop in it, too."

"I see," Terry growled. "And who was this little concoction meant for?"

"Bay," Lila admitted. "She deserves it after what she did to us. We didn't mean to do it to you. We heard someone coming and we thought it was her."

"Well, great," Terry said. "This is just great!"

Uh-oh. The man who always kept his temper in check was about to go nuclear.

"I can't tell you how much I've enjoyed this weekend," Terry said. "I've really loved all the sniping and backbiting and gossiping that accompanies teenage girls. Boys don't have this problem. They just tackle each other and swear at each other and get it out of their systems.

"Not girls, though. No. Girls have to plot and poke and screech like little banshees," he said. "Well, you've officially pushed me too far. I want every single one of you in your cabins right now!"

None of the girls moved, fear rooting them to their spots.

"Now!" Terry roared.

The girls started moving, giving Terry a wide berth as they raced toward their cabins. They didn't say a word, the only sounds coming from their shuffling feet.

Bay moved to Terry's side, her face conflicted.

"I'm really sorry," Lila said. "You should know this wasn't my fault. This is all Bay's fault."

"Go to bed, Lila," Terry snapped. He shifted his attention to me. "You were right. They're monsters. Every single one of them is a monster."

Terry moved back toward the fire, not bothering to cast even a small look in Bay's direction. I could see her lower lip quivering, but she didn't call after him. She didn't say a word.

"Boys! Get in those canoes and get moving. I can't stand to be here one more second. Let's get away from the monsters. Everyone run for their lives."

NINE

"Did any of them get up last night?" Marnie asked early the next morning, running in place and swinging her arms to get her circulation going. Her face was unnaturally pale, the shadows under her eyes pronounced. She looked as tired as I felt.

"I didn't hear a peep from them," I said, rubbing my lower back. Despite Terry's tirade, I opted to sleep in the hammock after all. I told myself I was doing it to make sure the unthinkable didn't become a reality. Part of me wanted to be close in case Bay needed me, though. Her face after Terry's outburst was enough to break my heart. He'd never ignored her before. She didn't come to me, though, and that made for a restless night. Because I was up with the sun, I made sure my sisters shared the privilege. They'd been less than thrilled when I shook them awake.

"Well, that's something at least," Marnie said. "Two more meals and we're out of here."

"I can't wait," I said. "Next time I volunteer us for something like this, hit me over the head and lock me in a closet until I regain my senses. This was one of my worst ideas ever."

Marnie smirked. "Do you think Terry is going to bring the boys over for lunch? He was supposed to, but after last night … ."

"I wouldn't count on it," I said.

"I've never seen him that way before," Twila said. "He never gets angry."

"He never gets filthy poop water thrown on him."

"Yeah, that was something," Twila said. "Do you think Lila learned her lesson?"

"I don't think Lila is ever going to learn her lesson," I said. "It's not in her nature. She's one of those people who will keep pushing people until she meets someone willing to push her back."

"The girls did push back," Marnie said. "Instead of knocking her down a peg or two, though, all it did was make her go to a really ... gross ... place."

"Yeah, who thinks of something like that?" Twila asked, wrinkling her nose.

"Rosemary."

Marnie and Twila turned to me, twin expressions of confusion etched on their faces. "Why do you think Rosemary thought of it?"

"I don't know," I said. "It's just a feeling. I think Lila would have been more ... generic ... with her revenge choices."

"Well, Aunt Willa should be coming for her this afternoon," Marnie said. "We'll be free of her."

"It will be the highlight of our day," I said. "Well, other than seeing Aunt Willa, that is. Maybe we can hide when we see her car. Why don't you guys go wake the girls. I'll finish getting breakfast ready."

"Are you sure you want to poke the sleeping beasts?"

"Don't you mean the monsters?"

Marnie sighed. "He didn't mean that about our monsters," she said. "He was just ... angry."

"I know he didn't mean it," I said. "Bay doesn't know that he didn't mean it, though. Did you see her face?"

"Once Terry has time to cool down they'll make up," Marnie said. "I'm sure he has no idea how much he upset her. He's going to feel awful when he realizes he hurt her feelings. He would never purposely do that."

"I'm sure he's already sorry." I shook my head, dislodging the morning melancholy. "Go get the girls up. The sooner we start this day the sooner we can end it."

"So mote it be," Marnie said.

"WHAT'S FOR BREAKFAST THIS MORNING?"

I jumped when I heard Lila's voice, shifting so I could study her out of the corner of my eye before fixing my full attention on her. Her face was the same as before, red bumps everywhere, and she'd clearly been scratching at the infected areas, which was only making things worse. "Pancakes."

"I don't like pancakes."

"Then don't eat," I said.

Lila narrowed her eyes. "You don't like me, do you?"

Well, this was a sticky situation. I'm not big on lying, but should I really tell the truth to a vindictive child? "No, Lila," I said. "I don't like you."

"Is it because you wish Bay was more like me? That's what my mother thinks."

"Your mother is an idiot," I said. "I would much rather have ten of Bay than one of you."

"You know there's something wrong with her, don't you?"

I forced myself to ignore her.

"Of course you know there's something wrong with her," Lila said. "There's something wrong with you, too. There's something wrong with your entire family. I know all about it. Rosemary told me."

Things shifted into place. That's why Rosemary was here. It wasn't just to spy, although that was surely part of it. It was to spread Aunt Willa's agenda. She did the same thing through Nettie when we were teenagers. I should have realized what she had planned.

"I'm sure Rosemary told you a lot of things," I said. "The problem is, Rosemary doesn't know any more truth than you do, Lila. You make things up in your head to explain what you don't understand. You purposely go after anyone who is different from you.

"The thing is, you think that makes you special," I continued. "But you're not special, Lila. You're never going to be special. You try to stomp out other people who are special. That's not greatness, Lila. It's jealousy. You'll learn that someday."

Lila shook her head, haughty. "I am not jealous."

"You don't even know what you are, Lila," I said. "Maybe you should go look in a mirror. Then you could see what you really are."

"Whatever," Lila said. "I don't want pancakes."

"Then don't eat."

"Winnie!"

I turned, dread washing over me when I saw Marnie and Twila racing toward me. Clove and Thistle were close on their heels, but there was no blonde head following them.

"Where's Bay?"

"She disappeared during the night," Marnie said, struggling to catch her breath. "We don't know when."

"Where did she go, Thistle?"

"I don't know," Thistle said, tears leaking from the corner of her eyes. "I didn't know she left. Honest. I would have gone with her if she told me. I wouldn't have let her go alone."

"Where would she go?" Twila asked.

I knew exactly where she was. "Feed the girls," I said.

"Where are you going?"

"After her."

TWO HOURS LATER, I was still wandering through the woods yelling Bay's name, although I was nowhere closer to finding her. I'd expected to come across her quickly. That's why I'd left Marnie and Twila behind. I didn't think magic would be necessary, but now I was starting to doubt that decision.

Either Bay couldn't hear me or she refused to acknowledge me. I didn't know which option scared me more.

The sound of heavy footsteps on the trail behind me caused me to whirl around, hope welling in my chest. It wasn't Bay's face that jumped into view, though. It was Terry's.

"Did you find her?" he asked, panting.

"Do you see her here?"

Terry took an involuntary step back, my anger surprising him. "I know you're upset," he said. "Just ... calm down."

"You know I'm upset? Really? Did you need your crack detective abilities to figure that out?" In my head I knew this wasn't his fault, but I kept picturing Bay's face when he ignored her the night before. I kept seeing the look in her eyes when he called them all monsters.

I was angry. I was angry with Lila. I was angry with Rosemary. Heck, I was even angry with myself. There was no one to take that anger out on but Terry, though, so that's what I did.

"We'll find her," Terry said. "She can't have gone far. These woods aren't that big. Even if she got lost, she wouldn't be able to wander very far without coming across a road ... or a house ... or a person."

"Or a ghost," I finished. "She's out here looking for the ghost."

"I figured that much out myself," Terry said. "I took the boys to the camp for breakfast – mostly because I didn't feel like cooking. Twila and Marnie told me what happened. I left the boys with them to look for the two of you. She'll probably go back to the camp when she's done doing ... whatever it is she's doing out here."

"I'm not leaving these woods without her."

"Neither am I," Terry said. "Now ... come on. Let's look for Bay."

I fell into step beside him, my heart pounding and my mind revving. "She's upset."

"Because of what Lila was planning to do to her last night?"

"Because of you," I said, immediately regretting my words when Terry snapped his head in my direction.

"What do you mean?"

"You were furious last night," I explained. "We all understand why. I should have just let you go. That wouldn't have happened if I hadn't ... hesitated. It's my fault. You should have taken it out on me."

"I shouldn't have taken it out on anyone," Terry said. "Well, I should have taken it out on Lila and Rosemary, but they're the only ones. I didn't mean to yell and scare all the girls."

"It wasn't the yelling that upset Bay," I said. "She lives in a house with my family. She's used to yelling."

"Then what upset her?"

"She went to you ... after," I said. "I don't know what she was going to say to you, but you brushed right past her and ignored her. Then you called them all monsters and stormed off. That's what she's upset about."

"I didn't mean that she was a monster," Terry said. "I meant ... crap!"

"It's not your fault," I said. "This whole weekend was a bad idea. When Bay pitched that fit before we left, I should have listened to her. I thought she was being dramatic. She must have known how this was all going to go. This is all on me."

"Let's put blame where it's due, shall we? This is Lila's fault. We can't focus on that now, though. We have to find Bay."

"I don't know how," I said.

"You do," Terry countered. "She's your daughter. You know where she is. Just listen to your heart."

"I ... ." I closed my eyes, sucking in a breath and focusing on the beating of my heart. Was he right? Did I know where she was? Could I feel her? Could I find her in a sea of trees?

I snapped my eyes open and pointed. "She's there." I don't know how I knew, only that I knew.

"Then that's where we're going."

I HEARD BAY before I saw her. Her voice was small and plaintive, but I almost cried out in relief when I heard her talking.

Terry pressed a finger to his lips to quiet me. His message was clear: Listen.

"I'm sorry this happened to you," Bay said. She kneeled on the ground. I couldn't see who she talked to or what she looked at. "It's a terrible thing. You can't stay here, though. You're not meant to stay here."

She cocked her head to the side, as though listening.

"I'll make sure you're taken back to Hemlock Cove," Bay said. "They'll have a nice funeral for you. Your sisters won't be left wondering what happened to you. I'll make sure they understand that you didn't run away. It's going to be okay."

More silence. I shifted my attention to Terry's face, although whatever he was thinking was beyond my comprehension.

"I know you don't want to go," Bay said. "This isn't where you belong now, though. There's another place. I don't know where it is, and I don't know what happens there, but I do know you're supposed be there. You're not supposed to be here."

Terry cleared his throat and Bay jumped.

"I ... ."

"We know what you're doing, Bay," Terry said. "We know why you came out here."

"It's Mrs. Wilder," Bay said. "She's dead."

I moved around Terry so I could see what Bay kneeled next to. The body, ravaged by days in the woods, was the stuff of horror movies. I instinctively moved to pull Bay away, but Terry stilled me with a hand on my arm.

"Tell me what happened, Bay."

"She came out to the camp to set up," Bay said. "This was going to be her last season running the camp, so she wanted to spend some time out here alone. She loved the camp, and it made her sad to think this was the last time she would see it."

"What do you mean by that?"

"There was something wrong with her heart," Bay said. "The doctors told her she shouldn't be running the camp this year, but she wasn't ready to say goodbye. She walked out here, even though she knew it was dangerous. Her heart started beating really fast and she fell down. That's the last thing she remembers. She shouldn't have come out here alone."

"She wanted to see it one last time," Terry said. "I get that. It's a beautiful place. It's a place that's given a lot of kids great memories throughout the years. Donna always loved this camp, and she loved being a counselor."

"That's why she doesn't want to leave."

"You can't be responsible for her decisions," Terry said. "You found her. We're going to make sure her body gets back to her sisters. We're going to put her to rest."

"She has to put herself to rest," Bay said. "We can't do that for her."

"We can't," Terry said. "It's sad. It really is. You're not responsible for everything in this world, though. You're not responsible for everyone who lives, and you're certainly not responsible for everyone who dies."

"I had to find her."

"I know you did," Terry said. He held his hand out to her. "Now you need to come back to camp and have some breakfast. I'll call and have a team come out here. Donna will be home before it gets dark. I promise."

Bay studied his hand for a moment, unsure.

Terry looked as though he wanted to say something, perhaps apologize. Instead, he shook his hand again to get her attention. "I can help you get Donna's body home if you help me and come back to camp."

Bay took his hand, her smaller fingers wrapping around his larger digits and gripping tightly. "Okay."

Terry smiled. "Come on. We have a long walk back to camp. They were making pancakes last time I checked."

"I'm not really hungry," Bay said.

Terry glanced at the body. "I guess you probably aren't. Don't worry. By the time we get to camp you'll get your appetite back."

"How can you know that?"

"Because I know you," Terry said, leading Bay back down the path toward camp. "You're always hungry."

I followed them, silent. It seemed the one Bay needed help from this weekend wasn't me after all. You learn something new every day.

TEN

"Are you okay?" Marnie asked, studying my face as I leaned against the picnic table. I was only half listening. Most of my attention was focused on the log next to the lake. Bay sat on one end of it and Terry sat on the other. They were talking, although I had no idea what the conversation entailed.

"I'm fine," I said.

"I can't believe Bay found Donna's body," Twila said. "She must have been terrified."

"She was more worked up because Donna didn't want to cross over," I said. "She was barely fazed by the body."

"Kids are resilient," Marnie said. "Bay is resilient. I take it Terry apologized."

"He didn't," I said. "I thought he was going to, but instead he just held out his hand and made her come to him."

"Why do you think he did that?"

"He said he was willing to help her, but she had to help him first," I said. "She thought about it for a second, and then she … did it. It was like a miracle."

"I'm not sure it was a miracle," Marnie said, chuckling. "I think it's far more likely that Bay was ready for some help. She's a lot like you.

It takes her forever to admit when she needs someone to help her. She'd rather do it on her own. She gets that from you. You know that, right?"

"I don't think she'd like to hear that."

"Probably not," Marnie said. "Still, she's got a lot of you in her. Of course, she's got a lot of Aunt Tillie in her, too. I even see a little bit of Mom in her. They're all mixtures. None of them are exactly like us."

"That's probably for the best," I said. "I'm not sure I like myself some of the time."

"I like myself most of the time," Marnie said. "I love Clove all of the time. I love Bay and Thistle all of the time, too."

I arched an eyebrow. "All of the time?"

"Oh, don't get me wrong, I want to strangle them sometimes. I still love them."

I snorted. "Can you finish cleaning up? I want to ... ."

"Go and eavesdrop on Terry and Bay?" Marnie asked.

"Yes."

"Go. We've got this."

I approached Bay and Terry quietly, not wanting to disturb them. The magic of their relationship was in the simplicity, and when they thought someone was watching they clammed up.

"I shouldn't have yelled at you," Terry said. "It wasn't fair, and it wasn't nice."

"It's fine."

"It's not fine," Terry said. "You're not a monster. None of you are monsters."

"What about Lila?"

"Lila is a small monster," Terry conceded. "She's going to grow up to be a big monster. You're not going to, though. You're going to grow up to be an angel."

"You always say that," Bay said, giggling. "I'm not an angel."

"You are to me," Terry said. "Sometimes I can even see your halo. It almost never needs to be shined."

"You're only saying that because you feel bad about me taking off into the woods," Bay said. "I didn't do that because of you."

"Why did you do it?"

"Because Donna came to me in the cabin," Bay said. "She needed me to find her, and she knew she was running out of time."

"Why didn't you tell your mom?"

"I don't know."

"You don't know?"

"She has trouble with the ghosts," Bay said. "She doesn't like it that I see them. I can see that when I talk about them. She's embarrassed."

"Like you were embarrassed to have her run the camp this weekend?"

Bay nodded.

"Your mom isn't embarrassed by you seeing the ghosts," Terry said. "She thinks everything you do is magic. Well, most things. That sneaking around stuff you and your cousins like to do isn't fun, but most kids do that so I think she'll probably let it slide.

"She's proud you want to help the ghosts, Bay," he continued. "She's proud of you. She's also afraid that if anyone else finds out what you can do, things will become … difficult. She doesn't care whether things are difficult for her, but she wants your life to be great."

"I think she's embarrassed."

"I think you want to think that," Terry said. "I think, in your heart, you know that's not the case."

"If I promise to tell her next time, will you stop with the deep talk?"

Terry grinned. "No. We're not done yet."

"I knew you were going to say that," Bay grumbled.

"You can't wander off in the woods by yourself, Bay," Terry said. "You could get lost. You could fall. Something could happen to you. You have to promise me that you're not going to do that again."

"I promise."

"Don't just say the words," Terry said. "Mean them."

"I can't promise I'll always go and get my mom," Bay said. "I promise to at least take Clove and Thistle with me next time, though."

Terry sighed. "I guess that's better than nothing."

"Can I ask you something?"

Terry nodded.

"Why did you come back over to our camp this morning? I would have thought you'd stay away ... at least until lunch ... because of what happened."

"I honestly don't know why I came here," Terry said. "I only know that I had a feeling I needed to be here. I had a feeling you needed me to be here."

"What do you feel now?"

"I feel we should probably take a kayak ride and enjoy the lake one last time before we go," Terry said. "I think Donna would like that."

"You do?"

"I do."

Bay jumped to her feet and leaned over, giving him a quick hug. Her bright smile was back. "Can I tip you over?"

"No."

"Please?"

Terry sighed. "I don't even know why you're asking," he said. "You know I can't say 'no' to you."

"I know. I'll get Clove and Thistle."

Bay skipped off in her cousins' direction, and when Terry's eyes landed on me he couldn't do anything but shrug. "I may spoil her a little," he said.

That was okay. Sometimes she needed it.

"WHAT HAPPENED TO HER FACE?" Aunt Willa was beside herself when she caught sight of Rosemary.

"I think it's called karma," I said, placing my hands on my hips as I regarded her. "You and I need to have a talk."

"I'm not talking about anything with you until you tell me what happened to my granddaughter's face," Aunt Willa said, gripping Rosemary's chin and tilting it in my direction.

"You know exactly what happened to her face. It's poison oak."

"This is beyond poison oak," Aunt Willa hissed. "This is ... something else. Something wicked."

"Something witchy, you mean," I said. "Rosemary, why don't you tell your grandmother what happened to your face."

"I have no idea," Rosemary said, her eyes widening with faux innocence. "I woke up this way. I think someone wanted to hurt me, Grammy."

"What's going on?" Marnie asked, moving around the picnic table warily. "Do I need to get a rope to tie anyone up?"

"Aunt Willa and I were just about to have a ... discussion," I said.

"About what?"

"About why she really sent Rosemary to camp in Hemlock Cove," I said.

"I thought she could embrace her roots," Aunt Willa said. "Apparently that was a mistake. It seems her roots cast a curse on her."

"The curse was for everyone in the cabin." I was surprised by Aunt Tillie's sudden appearance. She's sneaky when she wants to be.

"How do you know that?" Aunt Willa asked.

"I'm the one who cast it."

"Why?"

"The curse was meant to teach some nasty little girls a lesson," Aunt Tillie said, shooting a pointed look in Rosemary's direction. "If the afflicted girl admitted what she did and wanted to make amends, the symptoms faded. If she lied or plotted or did something mean ... well ... then the symptoms got worse.

"There were ten girls in that cabin," she continued. "Three of them were cured right away when they cleaned up the mess. Two more were better by lunch because they're not bad kids, they were just hanging out with bad kids.

"That leaves five girls who showed continued symptoms," Aunt Tillie said. "Three of those girls figured out what was going on and adjusted their attitudes. Only two girls are still showing symptoms. And, go figure, those are the nastiest girls at the camp. Coincidence? I think not."

"I want this child's face back the way it's supposed to be right now," Aunt Willa commanded. "I'm not messing around."

"When Rosemary adjusts her attitude, her face will return to normal," Aunt Tillie said. "I'm not lifting the curse. I don't care what you want."

"I'll sue you," Aunt Willa warned.

"For what? Casting a curse? Do you really think you'll find a judge who won't throw that case out of court?" Aunt Tillie asked.

"This is ... outrageous," Aunt Willa thundered. "I sent this child here for a few days of fun. Look what you've done to her."

"She did it to herself," I said. "And you didn't send her here for fun. You sent her here to see what we were doing, and to whisper in a few little ears so you could try to cause trouble for our children."

"I did no such thing."

"Don't bother lying," Marnie said. "It took us a little while to figure it out, but you did the same thing when we were in high school. You sent Nettie here to undermine us. That's what you were doing with Rosemary. Isn't that true, Rosemary?"

"No," Rosemary said, shaking her head.

The lie caused another red boil to appear on the end of her nose.

I arched an eyebrow as I faced off with Aunt Willa. "You might want to tell her to stop lying," I said. "You also might want to pack her up and get out of our town."

"Excuse me?" Aunt Willa was livid. "I grew up in this town. This is my home. You can't kick me out of town. You don't have the right, and you don't have the power."

"You can make an argument about whether or not we have the right," Aunt Tillie said. "Don't doubt for a second that we have the power, though."

Aunt Willa involuntarily shivered, a hint of Aunt Tillie's power licking her skin with the wind. "You are not my boss!"

"As far as this town is concerned, we are," I said. "We want you gone. We want Nettie and Rosemary gone, too. Don't you dare come back to this town until you've had an attitude adjustment."

"Keep Nettie away from us," Marnie said. "Keep Rosemary away from our children. They're good girls. They don't need the likes of Rosemary around them."

"And you keep away from me," Aunt Tillie said. "We may be sisters, but we're not family. My family is these girls ... and their girls. They're my family. You're nothing but a ... disappointment."

"I don't have to stand here and take this," Aunt Willa said. "You can't threaten me. You can't get away with it. I won't stand for it!"

"Then go."

"Oh, I'm going," Aunt Willa said. "You just remember, though, this is going to come back to haunt you one day. I can promise you that!"

"We've dealt with our fair share of hauntings," I said. "We prefer the friendly ghosts. I wasn't joking. Don't you dare come back here unless you're ready to apologize for everything you've done."

"We're never going to apologize," Rosemary said. "We're the ones who are right."

"Go," I said, pointing toward the parking lot. "Take that ... thing ... with you."

"Come on, Rosemary," Aunt Willa said. "We're leaving."

"You're not leaving," Aunt Tillie said. "We're kicking you out."

"What about my face, though?" Rosemary looked worried. "It won't still look like this when school starts, will it?"

"Of course not," Aunt Willa said.

"What if it does?"

"Then we'll buy some good makeup. Come on. I can't wait to get away from this place. It's always been a cesspool. It's always going to be a cesspool as long as they're here."

"Can we stop at Burger King on the way home? I'm hungry."

"Burger King? Have you been eating saturated fats?" Aunt Willa was furious. "I can't believe this! I just can't believe it!"

AN HOUR LATER, the camp was mostly packed. Our girls were the only ones left, and they were running around the beach with Terry and the boys while we closed things down.

After showing the body retrieval team where to find Donna, Terry returned to camp. His boys would be gone within the hour, and he seemed to be having a good time playing with the kids.

"Are you all packed up?"

I jumped when I heard the voice, turning to find the dark-haired boy watching me from a few feet away. "I am. What are you doing? Why aren't you playing with the others?"

The boy shrugged. "I don't know. I was just curious about what you were doing."

"Are you excited to go home?"

"Not really," the boy said. "It's boring in the city. I like the country better."

"Well, maybe you'll move to the country one day," I said.

"I'm going to move here."

"Really? What makes you say that?"

"I like it here," he said. "It's quiet. It's fun. I like the girls."

I rolled my eyes. I knew exactly what girl he liked. "I'm sure you do."

"What's her name? The blond girl, I mean. What's her name?"

I thought about telling him, but in the end it didn't seem a good idea. It's not as though we were ever going to see him again. "I think you should get going," I said, pointing. "Terry is herding you guys into the canoes. I think he's ready to get you guys home."

"You're going to see me again," the boy said. "I know you think you're not, but you are."

"How do you know that?"

The boy shrugged. "I just know. Sometimes you get a feeling about things."

I couldn't argue with that.

Another boy, one with the same coloring as the first, raced up the embankment. "Come on. We have to go."

"I'm going," the first boy said, watching the second race back toward the beach. He turned to me one more time. "You really are going to see me again. Maybe we'll be neighbors."

"That would be nice," I said, smiling at him.

"Come on, Landon!" The second boy stood on the shore, gesturing wildly. "Stop screwing around. We're going to be late. Mom is going to be mad if we're late."

I watched the boys scamper off together, internally thanking the goddess for our girls. They may be dramatic, and they may be obnoxious at times, but at least they are easy to understand.

I glanced around the camp one more time, relieved to be saying goodbye.

"We should go," Bay said, stepping up beside me. "I want to go home."

"I do, too," I said. "Are you feeling okay?"

"I'm great," Bay said. "Can we stop for ice cream?"

I sighed. Terry wasn't the only one who couldn't tell her 'no.' "Sure. Get your cousins and Aunt Tillie in the car. It will be nice to go back to our boring lives."

"Oh, our lives are never going to be boring," Bay said. "They can't. It's in our genes."

I thought about arguing, but it seemed pointless. She was right. "It is definitely in our genes. Now get your butt in the car. I can't wait to get out of this place."

"It's not so bad," Bay said. "It's kind of pretty."

"Oh, now it's pretty?"

"It was always pretty," Bay said. "It's people who bring the ugliness."

That was pretty wise for a fourteen-year-old. "Are you worried about Donna not passing on?"

Bay shook her head, her ponytail swinging. "She'll go when she's ready. We all have to do things in our own time."

"That's not what you thought earlier."

"It's what I know now," Bay said, her eyes twinkling. "That's all that matters."

She was absolutely right. "Come on, kid," I said. "Let's leave the pretty place and wreak havoc at our own home. I think we'll all be happy then."

THE CHRISTMAS WITCH

A WICKED WITCHES OF THE MIDWEST SHORT

ONE

I've decided Christmas is the worst time of year. No, you heard that right. Good cheer? Only if it comes in a bottle (or three). Frosted sugar cookies? I prefer chocolate chip, especially if they're fresh out of the oven. Wrapped presents under the tree? No way. I ... actually, well, I'm fine with that. If you want to give me a gift you're more than welcome to do it. Make sure it's expensive, though. I deserve the best money can buy.

I know witches aren't supposed to have a materialistic streak. It goes against the tenets of our faith. I'm not a normal witch, though, and I'm fine with that. I think I'm going to buy a gift for myself this year. I've had my eye on a snowplow for as long as I can remember, and this is the year I'm finally getting it. Just you wait.

Tillie Winchester is not just a witch. No, I'm a wicked witch. I'm fine with the label.

What am I saying?

Well, I'm not one of those evolved Wicca-loving hippies who think nature is the greatest thing in the world. I like nature, don't get me wrong. I just don't feel the need to worship trees or whisper sweet nothings to flowers. They can't hear you, people. You make yourself look like idiots when you do it.

I don't get the froufrou robes and sparkly, dangle earrings. In my day witches didn't have a problem being evil – and were proud of it. We certainly didn't try to hide our nature behind crystal balls and pastel tarot cards. No, witches in my day were tough and terrifying. That's how I helped raise my three nieces (despite my sister's insistence that they were good girls). Those poor girls got mixed messages their whole lives. My teachings didn't technically work where Winnie, Marnie and Twila are concerned – but I have a whole new generation to impart my wisdom to.

Speaking of little witches, I need to find the terrible trio and get them moving. You know when three girls under the age of ten are quiet that means they're generally up to something. When the three devils – I mean darlings – who live under this roof go quiet, though, the mischief can literally blow up in our faces.

Now, where should I look? The house is far too quiet. That means they snuck out … again. They are really starting to get minds of their own.

It didn't take me long to find them. The sound of Clove's incessant whining drew my attention to the far side of the house. I watched them for a few minutes without giving away my presence. It's always better to know what your enemy is up to before they ambush you.

What? They're kids, but they're smart kids. I worry that one day they'll be able to outsmart me. By that point I'll probably be suffering from dementia instead of foot-in-mouth disease, so I won't know they're beating me. That's something to look forward to.

"We have to do it this way," Thistle said, tucking her shoulder-length dirty blond hair behind her ear. She sat cross-legged on the cold ground, her cousins Bay and Clove mimicking her as the trio formed a circle. I have no idea how they weren't frozen to their cores. "It's not going to work unless we're sneaky about it."

I sometimes think Thistle has too much of me in her. Twila, her mother, is the sweetest of her sisters. She's also the daffiest. Thistle has her mother's kooky sense of style but my penchant for evil, and she may be smarter than the lot of us rolled into one.

Wow! That's a terrifying thought.

"I think we should tell them the truth," Clove chimed in, her black hair glossy under the winter sun. She's always the Pollyanna of the group. Don't get me wrong, she'll lie if she has to. It's never the first thing that comes to her mind, though. Her first suggestion is always sweet and innocent. She balances Thistle's malevolence. Well ... some of the time.

"We can't tell them the truth," Thistle scoffed, making a face. "If we tell them the truth we have nowhere to go when they tell us no."

"How do you know they'll tell us no?"

"Have you even met our mothers?" Bay asked, her fingers working the ends of her blond hair. She has an insecure streak that manifests in weird ways. Talking to ghosts doesn't help. Oh, yes, she can talk to ghosts. I can, too. It's a difficult gift and Bay struggles to get a grip on it. "They're not going to give us what we want unless we trick them into giving it to us. Thistle is right."

Thistle puffed out her chest. "I told you. I'm always right."

"You're not always right," Bay snorted, letting go of her hair. As the oldest of the trio, she and Thistle grapple for the title of bossiest. What Thistle doesn't realize is that Bay often lets her win because that gives her a better position when they delve into the next fight. Thistle might be ridiculously smart, but Bay often outthinks her.

"When am I not right?" Thistle challenged.

"Last Christmas you told us that if we had bigger stockings Santa Claus would have no choice but to leave us more presents," Bay reminded her. "Did we get more presents?"

Thistle scowled and crossed her arms over her chest. "No."

"Did the longer stockings start a fire that almost burned the house down?" Bay pressed.

"I hate you sometimes," Thistle muttered.

Bay rolled her eyes and ignored her fiery cousin. "I think we need to trick them into getting us what we want, but we need to do it in a way that's not as ... horrible ... as what Thistle thinks we should do."

Well, this is getting interesting. Whatever they want, it's something big. I wasn't particularly perturbed by that realization. They're kids. Christmas is for dreaming big when you're young. These three had

AMANDA M. LEE

been morose for months, so I'm almost willing to bet their mothers give in and get them whatever they want if it assured of smiles Christmas morning.

Things had been rough for all three of them ever since their fathers left. They didn't do it as a unit. Jack, Bay's father, was the first to go. His relationship with Winnie deteriorated quickly and before either of them realized what was happening the relationship was officially over. He said he couldn't take my meddling. I told him to stuff it. Life goes on. Winnie can do better.

Warren, Clove's father, went next. There was no surprise that his marriage to Marnie imploded. They were too different when they married. Those differences only grew in scope as the marriage progressed. Frankly, I was surprised they made it as long as they did. They're both too bossy for their own good. I hate that in a person. Bossy only works for me. All others pale in comparison.

Finally, Teddy walked away from Twila after a particularly obnoxious argument. That one surprised me. Teddy and Twila are both bohemian spirits. Teddy thought Twila's scattered nature was adorable when they met – and even when they married. It grated over time, though, and Thistle's attitude didn't help. Teddy wanted to take a firmer hand in raising their daughter and Twila was a "live and let live" mother. Still, I thought the marriage would last a little longer than it did.

Ever since their fathers left Ashton Lake, though, these three rugrats have been more pouty and petulant than sweet and cute. Personally, I never thought they were that sweet – and that cuteness factor comes and goes depending on what they're plotting.

Seriously, though, what are they plotting? It can't be good. It never is.

"I just want a puppy," Clove complained. "I think if we ask they'll get it for us. Why do we have to lie?"

A puppy? We already have seven people living under one roof. Sure, it's a relatively big roof and we're down from the previous ten we had under it a year before, but come on. I had to put a stop to this, and I had to do it right now.

"You can't have a puppy," I announced, flouncing around the corner and resting my hands on my hips as I regarded the three tyrants in training.

Clove appeared shocked at my appearance, while Bay looked mildly concerned. Thistle merely narrowed her eyes.

"I knew you were eavesdropping," Thistle muttered.

"I'm an adult. It's not called eavesdropping when you're an adult."

"It is so," Thistle charged.

"It is not."

"It is so."

"It is not." I swear, these kids bring out the worst in me – and that's saying something.

"Whenever you listen to people who don't know you're there and you're not part of the talking, that means you're eavesdropping," Thistle snapped, jumping to her feet. "Tell her that's true, Bay."

Bay was slower to climb to a standing position. At just less than five feet, I'm tiny. Clove is going to be diminutive like me. The other two are already almost as tall as I am. It's frustrating. How can I yell at people who are taller than me? Oh, what am I saying? I always find a way to do it. My late husband was almost a foot and a half taller than me and I yelled at him all the time – and that man was a saint. Three hellions should be no problem.

"I don't think it matters," Bay said, knitting her eyebrows. She has a pragmatic streak that irks me. I wish she would let loose and go crazy sometimes. She doesn't have to be wild like Thistle, but if she yelled and screamed a few times she might be heard above the constant Winchester din. "She knows what we're doing and she's going to work against us."

It was my turn to narrow my eyes. "Why do you think I'm going to work against you?"

"Because you always work against us," Thistle interjected, crossing her arms over her chest.

"Why do you think that is?" Getting a feel for these girls is like swimming in quicksand. Whenever I think I'm getting somewhere the bottom falls out. Something told me that was about to happen again.

"I think Aunt Tillie is looking out for us," Clove sniffed, pushing herself up to stand, but still partially hidden by her bolder cousins. "She loves us."

Goddess help me, I do love the little rascals. I also hate them sometimes. I can also tell when they're trying to manipulate me with kindness, and that's Clove's best talent.

Thistle snorted. "She doesn't love us," she said. "She wishes we'd never been born."

"You take that back," I snapped, wagging a finger in Thistle's face. "That is not true."

"She doesn't hate us," Bay said, grabbing the back of Thistle's coat and hauling her away from me. I think she worried I would curse her or something. "She likes to mess with us. There's a difference."

"Not in my world," Thistle said.

Seriously, there are times I want to grab that little imp's lips and pull and pull until … .

"Don't you think a puppy would be a nice Christmas gift for us?" Clove asked, changing the topic to something safer. "We would take care of it. We would walk it and feed it."

"We would name it Tillie and whack it with a rolled-up newspaper," Thistle suggested.

"I'm going to make sure you don't get anything but a lump of coal in your stocking if you don't shut your mouth right now, Thistle," I warned, glaring at her.

Thistle is never one to back down. "And how are you going to do that?"

"I'm going to tell Santa to put you on his naughty list," I answered, not missing a beat.

"Santa isn't real."

I stilled, surprised by Thistle's declaration. I knew the girls didn't believe in Santa Claus anymore. Well, for the most part. They were at delicate ages. At nine, Bay definitely didn't believe. She was sensitive enough not to ruin it for her cousins, though. Clove was less sure. She was afraid of the possibility of ticking off the big guy, though, and she hedged her bets. Despite her age, Thistle is the worldliest and calls things like she sees them. Still, Santa is the best thing about Christmas. Well, him and the food.

"What makes you think Santa isn't real?" I asked.

"Because we all know Santa Claus is something parents make up so they can bully kids into being good all year," Thistle replied. "He's like the Boogeyman."

"I'll have you know that Santa Claus is real," I countered. "I met him."

"Oh, whatever," Thistle said, rolling her eyes.

Clove looked intrigued. "How did you meet him?"

"She's lying, Clove," Thistle said.

"Shut your mouth, Thistle," I said, shooting her a warning look before turning my full attention to Clove. "I was up late one Christmas Eve and I happened to run into him when he was putting gifts under the tree for your mothers when they were younger."

Clove's eyes widened. "Did you talk to him?"

"I did."

"What did he say?"

"He said that when girls are good they get a lot of gifts and your mothers were very good that year. They had so many presents I lost count," I said. "He also said when girls are bad they get ... ."

"Lumps of coal in their stockings, right?" Thistle interjected, cutting me off.

"I was going to say boots in their rears," I said, wrinkling my nose. "Why are you in such a mood, little missy?"

"I'm not in a mood."

"We're all sad," Bay admitted, putting her hand on Thistle's shoulder by way of comfort. Thistle wasn't big on displays of affection, but when Bay offered solace Thistle almost always took it. They had an interesting relationship.

"Why are you sad?" I pressed. "Is this about ... ?" Should I bring up their fathers? That was a sure way to get Clove to burst into tears and Thistle to hit someone.

"We want a puppy for Christmas," Bay answered. "We also want snow."

"Snow?"

"There's no Christmas without snow," Clove whined.

I hated to admit it, but they had a point. Even though it was cold and snow should have descended at least once on northern Lower Michigan during the month of December, we hadn't a flake to contend with and Christmas was only a few days away. The girls weren't the only ones missing a visit from Jack Frost. If it didn't snow I would have nothing to plow – and no one wanted that.

"You can't have a puppy," I said, gearing myself up for the onslaught of whining. "We don't have room for one. I'm sorry, but that's the way it is."

"You suck," Thistle muttered.

I pretended I didn't hear the snarky retort. "As for Santa Claus and snow, you guys should have a little faith. It's not Christmas yet."

"The weather people on the television say there's no snow coming," Bay argued. "I saw it this morning."

"Those weather people are idiots and don't know it's raining until their feet are already wet," I said. "It will snow. Trust me."

"How can you be sure?"

"Because if snow is what it's going to take for the three of you to be happy this Christmas, then that's what you'll get," I replied. "Try not to dwell on the negative."

"That's what I do best," Thistle said.

She wasn't wrong, and she wasn't alone in that particular personality defect either. "You three need to get moving inside," I ordered. "You need dinner and then you have that big school Christmas pageant tonight. Aren't you excited about that?"

"I would rather eat Santa's underwear than sing in public," Thistle said.

I don't blame her. I'm not looking forward to watching it. "I'll see if I can arrange that," I said. "Now, move."

Bay and Thistle hopped to it, quickly scampering in front of me and running in the direction of the back door. Clove loitered behind, causing me to focus on her. "What do you want?"

"Did you really meet Santa?"

"I'm not a liar and I said I met him, so what does that tell you?"

"I ... do you think he'll really come visit us this year?" Clove asked, her brown eyes wide. "Do you think he'll come even though we've been naughty?"

"I think he'll come," I replied. "You need to stop worrying about stuff like this. You're going to give yourself an ulcer."

"What's that?"

"You know that big spot Lila Stevens' mother has on her lip?"

Clove nodded.

"That's a lip ulcer," I said. "If you're not careful, you'll get one of those in your stomach."

"How did Mrs. Stevens get that?"

"She kissed a lot of frogs ... and mailmen ... and bums on the corner."

"I don't do that," Clove pointed out.

"Then you'll be safe from getting an ulcer," I said. "Come on. You need dinner and then you're going to sing ... and I'm going to wish I was deaf."

"Okay," Clove said, falling into step next to me. "I still think we need a puppy."

"I think you're going to have a marvelous Christmas even if you don't get a puppy," I said.

"I don't believe that."

"Well then, I guess I'll just have to prove it to you," I said.

"I guess so," Clove agreed, slipping her small hand into mine and letting me lead her the rest of the way to the house.

Huh. Now how was I going to do that?

TWO

&

"I love this time of year," Winnie enthused, smiling at the huge Christmas tree in Ashton Lake's downtown square. "Isn't that beautiful?"

I glanced at the tree in question, the tacky lights and garish ornaments momentarily causing me to see double. "It's a pine tree."

"I noticed," Winnie said. "Don't you think the lights and ornaments make it beautiful?"

"I think they make it look cluttered," I replied. "Also, what is the deal with that ghost on top of the tree? What does that have to do with Christmas?"

Winnie tucked her blond hair behind her ear and fixed me with a hard look. Of all my nieces, she looks the most like her mother. I can't help but like that about her. That look she gives me reminds me of her mother, too. I can't help but hate that about her.

"That's an angel," Winnie replied, nonplussed.

"It doesn't look like an angel."

"Well, it is."

I wrinkled my nose. I loath being told I'm wrong. I'm never wrong, just for the record. Sometimes the truth takes longer to catch up to me than it should. It's pretty simple. "Isn't an angel technically just a fancy ghost?"

One of the things I love most in life is watching my nieces try to handle me. When they were teenagers and their mother died, I stepped in to take care of them because their father was long gone. He took the path of Jack, Warren, and Teddy, and never looked back.

I spent three years getting them through the rest of their adolescence and then set them free on the world ... kind of. We were all still under the same roof. Granted, it was one I had to expand when I took them in, but it was still essentially the home my husband Calvin and I built together. The homestead on the family property has gone through many changes throughout the years and now it stands as a tall Victorian home.

I've heard whispers – my nieces don't know this, but I have – and there's talk of trying to turn it into a bed and breakfast. That's never going to happen on my watch. Never. I don't like people, and I certainly don't want them staying in the same house with me. Strangers ask questions. I don't like answering questions.

Roles have reversed over the years, and now my nieces are in charge – or at least I let them think they are. I encourage that. The more they try to handle me, the more I get away with. One of the greatest perks in my life is shirking any and all adult responsibility.

It's fun to be the crazy old lady in the paisley crop pants and flip flops in the middle of winter. You should try it when you get a chance. People live in fear when they think you're living in La-La Land.

"You know darned well that angels are different than ghosts," Winnie hissed, scorching me with her best impersonation of her mother. "Don't go telling people that angels are the same as ghosts. People won't like that – especially around Christmas."

I shrugged. I don't particularly care what people like and dislike. I figure the fewer people who like me, the fewer times I'll get stopped for inane chatter in the checkout line. "You can't tell me what to do," I sniffed, crossing my arms over my chest. "I'm an adult."

"Then act like it," Winnie said, her tone snippy. "We're having a hard enough time getting through Christmas this year without you adding your particular brand of mayhem to the mix."

Was that an insult? I can never tell. Whenever my nieces insult me they do it in sweet voices. I have a short attention span, so most of the time when they're done talking I honestly have no idea what they just said.

"Merry Christmas to you, too," I said, figuring that was a safe response.

Winnie shook her head. "Did you even listen to what I just said to you?"

Of course not. "Yes. Are you insinuating that I can't hear?"

"No."

"Are you trying to say I'm going senile and can't keep up with a conversation?" When someone accuses you of something, always turn it around on them right away. They'll be so flustered that they give up.

"That's not what I said and you know it," Winnie said. "You're not going to distract me on this one so ... stop right now."

Unfortunately, when you've run the same game on people who have known you for all of their lives the gambit can work against you sometimes. "I'm bored. Let's go home."

"We've been here exactly three minutes," Winnie warned. "You have hours of this ahead of you so ... get used to Christmas cheer and stay away from Abigail Hobbes' special holiday punch."

I'd forgotten about Abigail's special punch. The woman makes a shrew look cuddly, but her cocktail-mixing talents are second to none. "And where is the special punch going to be located this evening – just so I can avoid it, I mean?"

"Don't even think about it," Winnie said, wagging her finger in my face. "This night is about the girls. Don't you want to hear them sing?"

I've heard them sing plenty of times. Not one of them has a lick of musical talent. They make dying cats sound musical. "Not particularly."

"Don't you even think about embarrassing those girls."

"If I can't embarrass them, why did you have them?" I asked.

"Um ... because we love them."

"If that's your story ... ." I scanned the crowd, frowning when I realized just how many of Ashton Lake's finest were out and about. "Don't these people know that we're all going to wish we were deaf in about a half hour? Why would they possibly be here if someone didn't force them to be – like you did me?"

Winnie made a face. "Go find something to do."

"Okay."

Winnie grabbed my arm before I could move too far away. "No purposely picking fights. No dosing the coffee. No telling the kids that Santa is really a blood-sucking zombie. I know you told Lila Stevens that last week. Her mother called."

"She'll survive," I said. I hate Poppy Stevens. That woman gives new meaning to the word annoying.

"No giving the girls candy either," Winnie stressed. "We've got a special dessert for them at home."

"I never give them candy."

"You bribe them with candy whenever they catch you doing something you're not supposed to be doing," Winnie argued. "Don't lie to me. You forget that we share the same roof. I know all of your secrets."

She didn't know even half of my secrets, and the ones she did know were spoon-fed to her because I wanted her to think she knew them. She'd lock me up if she knew all of my secrets. Heck, I can't even remember all of my secrets. "Where are the girls?"

"They're around," Winnie said. "If you're bored you can go and find them. Just don't upset them. They have it rough enough right now."

"I never upset them."

"I ... go someplace else," Winnie ordered. "I've taken about all I can for right now."

"Yes, ma'am." I kicked my heels together and mock saluted, ignoring the scowl on Winnie's face as I moved toward the crowd. I fought the urge to scream "fire" in an effort to get breathing room and scanned familiar faces until I found the ones I wanted.

Bay, Clove and Thistle stood next to the hot chocolate stand, and whatever was going on had all of them staring down a dark-haired

AMANDA M. LEE

girl with an unfortunate nose as if they were about to set her ablaze. Lila Stevens. I don't believe in the Devil, but if I did I would think Lila was the offspring of the Devil and Adolf Hitler. Yes, she's that unpleasant.

I took a roundabout route to get to them, listening as I approached.

"You guys aren't going to get Christmas presents from Santa because everyone knows Santa hates witches," Lila said, bobbing her head up and down like one of those unfortunate dolls men affix to their dashboards. "It's a fact."

"The only thing that's a fact is that your nose looks like a candy cane," Thistle shot back, her hands on her hips. "Why are you even over here bugging us?"

"I'm not over here because of you," Lila replied, wrinkling her nose. "I'm here to make sure that you guys don't ruin Christmas for anyone else."

"I guess that makes you the Christmas police, huh?" Bay said, her hands clasped around a Styrofoam cup of hot chocolate. "Do they give you a badge for that?"

"I'm guessing they give her a stick to shove up her behind," Thistle said.

That was a good one! Wait. Crud on crackers. That's what I said about Fredericka Lassiter last week when I found out she was trying to join our euchre club down at the senior center. They probably heard that from me.

"Why would I have a stick up my behind?" Lila asked. The kid was a snot, but she wasn't worldly, like the Winchester witches.

"Because that's what happens when you have a bad attitude and someone has to reload you of it," Clove supplied.

"Relieve," Bay corrected. "Someone has to be relieved of a bad attitude."

Clove furrowed her brow. "I don't get it."

That was probably good. If Winnie, Marnie and Twila figured out exactly how much lingo the wee ones picked up from me we were all going to be in trouble. I still don't understand how my nieces ended up in charge of me.

"I don't get it either," Bay admitted.

That was good.

"I get it," Thistle said. "It means Lila is like a balloon and we need a stick so we can pop her."

That was as good an explanation as any. I cleared my throat to let the girls know they were being watched. Clove had the grace to look abashed but Bay and Thistle were too angry to pay attention to me.

Lila pasted a bright smile on her face as she regarded me. "Hello, Mrs. Winchester. You look particularly lovely this evening. I just love … flip flops."

"Hello, Laura."

Lila frowned. I always pretended I couldn't remember the monster's name just to mess with her. What? I have to get my thrills somehow and I can't do what I really want to do and make a voodoo doll of the little terror and let Thistle and Bay poke it with pins whenever the mood strikes.

"My name is Lila."

"I'm sure it is," I said, narrowing my eyes as I regarded her. You can just tell when someone is going to grow up to be obnoxious. Yes, I know I'm purposely obnoxious. I'm an acquired taste. The problem with Lila is that she thinks she's charming even though every kid in the school wants to lock her in the janitor's closet and forget her there every summer break. I know people hate me. I encourage it.

"It is," Lila sneered.

"Whatever you say, Lilac," I replied, focusing on the Bay, Clove and Thistle. "What are you guys doing?"

"Having hot chocolate," Clove said. "We're not doing anything bad."

That usually means they are doing something bad. Given that they were dealing with Lila, though, I didn't think they were doing anything bad enough. I would have to give them some pointers later.

"What are you doing over here, Lucifer?" I fixed Lila with a dark look. "Shouldn't you be stepping on puppy tails or starting some poor, unsuspecting kid's hair on fire?"

"That's not a very nice thing to say," Lila shot back.

"Really? I always thought the truth was welcome."

Lila narrowed her eyes, looking me up and down as she decided how to respond. She was afraid of me – and that's the way I like it. If she was a little older I'd show her exactly how to handle a bully. I would probably be arrested for that if I tried it now.

"I'm going to tell my mother you're being mean to me," Lila announced, as if that was somehow a threat that would bring me to my knees.

"You do that," I suggested. "While you're at it, tell her that if you don't stop harassing my nieces I'm going to give you a good dose of herpes on your lip to match hers. How does that sound?"

Lila balked. "I ... my mother does not have herpes. That's a beauty mark."

"Huh. I heard through the gossip vine that she got that beauty mark from the mailman," I said. "I heard she had to buy ointment at the pharmacy for it."

"That's a lie!"

"I don't lie," I countered, lowering my voice. "Here's a little tip, Locust. If you keep messing with my girls you're going to run into a big brick wall – and it's going to look a lot like me. When that brick wall falls, you're going to be crushed and we're going to laugh until we can't laugh any longer."

"You can't threaten me," Lila hissed. "I'll tell my mother."

"I can do whatever I want," I said. "You go and tell your mother that I'm waiting for her if she wants to talk. I think we'll have a really nice chat about you ... and your future ... and that herpes on her lip and how it will probably spread if you don't start behaving yourself."

"I ... you're a witch," Lila said. "Everyone knows it!"

"I am a witch," I agreed. "That means I can cast spells on you. I've been limited because you're a child. That won't last forever.

"Let me tell you a little bit about karma, Listerine. You've earned a big ball of it, and when it finally comes your way you're not going to like what happens one little bit," I continued. "I would start trying to make up for all the rotten things you've done if I were you."

"Well, that shows what you know," Lila said, tossing her greasy hair over her shoulder. "I don't believe in karma. I'm a princess."

"What you just said doesn't make any sense."

"Says you," Lila snapped. "My mother says I can be anything I want to be."

"Oh, I believe that," I said. "You're just the type of person who is going to do it with herpes on your lip and pit stains on your blouse."

Lila's lower lip began trembling, but I recognize an act when I see one. "I'm telling my mom!"

"Good," I said, unruffled. "I'd rather mess with her anyway. I can do truly awful things to her and not get in trouble. Go get her."

Lila scampered off and I could hear her screaming for Poppy as she disappeared into the crowd. I really was in a foul mood. The idea of taking it out on someone was just the thing I needed to get me into the holiday spirit.

"That was a stupid thing to do," Bay said, her blue eyes cloudy as they landed on me.

"Why is that?"

"She's going to make us pay for what you said to her."

"Not if I teach you how to get her back," I said.

Bay stilled and I could practically see her mind working. "Will you teach us how to curse her?"

"Will you tell your mothers if I do?"

Three heads solemnly shook in unison.

"Then I'll teach you how to curse her," I said. What? The kid has it coming, and if my kids do it there's no way I can get in trouble for it. "It's going to be our secret, though, and you can never tell your mothers."

"Deal," Thistle said, extending her hand for me to shake. She knows I won't go back on a promise once I shake someone's hand.

I clasped her hand tightly. "You're going to make some man really miserable some day."

Thistle's eyes sparkled. "I can't wait!"

THREE

"This is the worst thing that's ever happened in the history of the entire world!"

I followed Clove into the house a few hours later, spurring her on with my foot whenever her mother wasn't looking. She was overly dramatic on a daily basis. She is going to be a beast as a teenager.

"It's not the end of the world, Clove," Marnie chided, dropping her gloves on the table next to the door.

"Santa Claus is missing!"

I cringed. Clove's voice bordered on shrill on good days. Now that she thought reindeer were going to start falling from the sky she was practically panicked.

"Santa Claus is not missing," Marnie said, pulling Clove's coat from her shoulders and hanging it in the hall closet. "He was just … detained."

After the pageant ended – and the ringing in my ears ceased – the school Christmas spectacular was supposed to end with a visit from Santa Claus. When he didn't show, the kids started wailing. They didn't stop – not even for a five-second breather. I had a feeling some of them were still wailing.

"He was probably detained by a bottle of whiskey and whatever hot-to-trot waitress was staffing the bar at Hannigan's," I said, laughing at my own joke. Ashton Lake's resident Santa Claus was Bernard Hill. The man wasn't good with kids and he has wandering hands when it comes to the ladies, but he also has white hair and fits the suit. He got the job by default.

"That will be enough of that," Winnie warned, moving Bay so she could help her take her coat off.

"Do you think Santa Claus is dead?" Clove asked, her brown eyes widening. "Does that mean we're not going to get our Christmas presents?"

"Santa Claus isn't dead," Twila said. "He probably forgot to write down tonight's event in his day planner. There's no reason to get worked up."

"We're never going to get that puppy now," Clove yelled, burying her face in her hands as she burst into tears.

If I didn't want to be deaf during the Christmas pageant, I definitely wanted to be inflicted with selective hearing loss now.

"I think you're just tired, Clove," Marnie said, gently tugging on her hair in an attempt to get her to perk up. "You'll see in the morning that things aren't so bad."

"Santa Claus isn't even real," Thistle pointed out.

"Knock that off, fresh mouth," I said, cuffing her on the back of the head. "Santa Claus is real. I already told you that."

"I don't believe you." Thistle widened her eyes to comical proportions. "I think you're full of it."

"That's enough of that," Twila said, swooping in and gathering Thistle in her arms before I could retaliate. "I think you need some sleep. I think all of you need some sleep."

"I think that's a good idea," Marnie said, hoisting Clove up into her arms instead of cajoling her further. "Everyone needs some sleep. Things will be better in the morning."

"Does that mean we're getting a puppy?" Clove asked, tears streaming down her cheeks as her lower lip quivered. "We really want one."

Marnie looked caught. "I ... ."

"You're not getting a puppy," I said. "I already told you that, so stop asking. That doesn't mean you're not going to have a great Christmas … so stop all that whining. You're giving me a headache."

"Nice," Winnie said, flicking my ear as she moved past me. "We don't know where Santa is, but we've definitely found the Grinch."

I watched as Marnie and Twila wrangled Thistle and Clove up the stairs, finally settling my gaze on Bay. She was quiet for long stretches of time and that often led to her being overlooked.

"What are you thinking?" I asked.

"I know that isn't Santa Claus," she said, her tone serious. "Don't bother arguing. I know that's Mr. Hill."

"How do you know that?"

"I'm not stupid."

I smirked. No one could ever accuse Bay of being stupid. "No, that's not Santa Claus," I said. "He's a man pretending to be Santa Claus. The real Santa could never go to all the holiday parties around the world. You know that."

"I'm not getting into an argument with you about Santa," Bay said. "I just … if Mr. Hill is really missing, what does that mean for Christmas?"

"What do you mean?"

"The best part of Christmas is always the town party, and he's always the Santa there, too," Bay explained. "If he's missing, what happens to the town party?"

I've never understood Bay's love of Ashton Lake's Christmas party, but she's infatuated with it. "Santa will be at the party, Bay," I said.

"How can you be sure?"

"Because I'll make sure of it."

That seemed to do the trick, because Bay brightened considerably. "Do you think we'll get our puppy?"

"No."

"I think you're going to make sure we get our puppy," Bay said, her eyes twinkling. "You act like you don't like us, but I know you do."

"That's not an act, kid."

Bay rolled her eyes. "We want a big dog," she said. "We don't want any little runt dogs that yap and run around. We want something big so we can make it attack Lila if she shows her face out here."

"Is that why you want the dog?"

"We want the dog because we want something to love," Bay answered. "Biting Lila is just a bonus."

"I'll take it under consideration," I said, glancing around to make sure no one was watching before I slipped her a Hershey's Kiss. "Don't tell your mother."

Bay smiled as she took the candy. "I need one for Thistle and Clove, too."

I sighed but handed over the chocolate goodies. "Don't worry, Bay," I said. "I'll make sure your Christmas party is what it should be. You can count on me."

"Thank you, Aunt Tillie," Bay said, rolling up on the balls of her feet so she could give me a kiss on the cheek. "Make sure you pick out a good puppy for us when it's time."

"You are not getting a puppy!"

THE GIRLS WERE in better moods the next morning. Well, mostly. There was still a little pouting and trepidation, but they seemed less likely to melt down than the previous evening.

I'm not going to lie, when puberty hits this house I'm seriously considering hitting the road. I remember the terrible teen years with Winnie, Marnie and Twila, and the three of them had nothing on these three. I'm considering starting my own band. Anything has to be better than watching Bay, Clove and Thistle fight over boys, clothes and makeup.

On the flip side, I get a giddy satisfaction knowing that my three nieces are going to get a great big heaping of crap when their little darlings start hitting fun ages like thirteen … and fourteen … and seventeen. They seem to forget what horrors they were at those ages. That will be a stark reminder of what they put me through – and I look forward to watching them struggle with three wild teenagers of their own.

"We have two whole weeks without school, and I'm really happy about it," Thistle said, grabbing a slice of bacon and shoving it into her mouth. She chews like a horse sometimes, I swear. "We won't have to see Lila Stevens more than once, and that's pretty much the best Christmas gift anyone could ever give me."

"Don't talk with your mouth full of food," Twila ordered, patting Thistle on the head as she sat down next to her and started in on her own plate. "That's tacky and rude."

"Aunt Tillie does it," Thistle said, causing me to narrow my eyes in her direction.

"Aunt Tillie does a lot of things you shouldn't do," Winnie interjected.

"Like what?"

"Yeah, like what?" I asked, echoing Thistle.

"Like making wine in the basement," Clove teased, grinning as she poured syrup on her pancakes.

"And dancing naked under the full moon when she thinks no one is watching," Bay chimed in.

"That's gross, by the way," Thistle said. "They make horror movies about stuff like that."

Winnie leaned back so she could give Thistle her best "you've gone too far, little lady" look. "And what is that supposed to mean?"

"You're too old to be running around naked," Thistle said. "It's … scary."

"I didn't know things were supposed to hang that low until I saw Aunt Tillie try to dance like Michael Jackson on Halloween," Clove said. "I thought those were zombies of a different kind."

"Hey!"

"She was bad," Thistle said, laughing at her own joke.

"All right, that will be enough of that," I said, reaching over to Thistle's plate and stealing a slice of bacon. "I'll have you know that I'm in prime shape and people would be lucky to see me naked."

Someone near the kitchen door cleared a throat, drawing my attention from my great-nieces. Ashton Lake's lone full-time police officer, Terry Davenport, stood in the doorway next to Marnie and he looked as if he wished he could go back in time to miss my last statement. Hmm. He should be so lucky as to get a gander at my gams when the moon is full.

"Hi, Terry," Winnie said, her voice unnaturally bright. "What a nice surprise. Would you like some breakfast?"

Terry didn't get a chance to respond, because Marnie moved in on him and cut off Winnie's path off in the process.

"Of course he wants breakfast," Marnie said. "He loves it when I cook him breakfast."

"He loves it when I cook him breakfast," Winnie corrected.

I tried to tamp down my irritation as I watched the spectacle unfold. Terry was a good man, a great man even. My nieces act like dogs in heat whenever he's around, though. It was undignified ... and annoying. I have no idea what they would do if one of them ever actually caught the man.

"Breakfast sounds great," Terry said, shooting me a small smile as he settled next to Bay. "How is my favorite girl?"

Bay glanced at him, her face unreadable. Ever since her father left Bay has been drawn to Terry. I have no idea why. Whatever it is, Terry is good for her. He encourages her and shows an interest in her life. I think that's what Bay needs right now, even if she doesn't realize it.

"I'm worried," Bay admitted.

Terry lifted an eyebrow. "What are you worried about?"

"Santa Claus is missing," Clove supplied, her round cheeks quivering as she grimaced. "We're all very worried he's not going to come back in time to give us our puppy."

"What puppy?" Terry looked confused.

"There is no puppy," I said. "You're not getting a puppy. Stop whining about the puppy. We don't have room for a puppy."

"If we have room for you, we have room for a puppy," Thistle countered.

Terry pursed his lips to keep from laughing and turned back to Bay. "Are you worried about Santa Claus being missing?"

"I know that Mr. Hill isn't really Santa Claus," Bay replied. "I don't believe in Santa Claus."

"Don't start that again," I warned.

Bay rolled her eyes and ignored me. "The Christmas party needs a Santa Claus. Mr. Hill always plays Santa Claus. If he's really missing … well … Christmas will be ruined."

Something about Bay's expression tugged at my heart. It was an odd feeling. "I already told you that Christmas won't be ruined," I reminded her. "Mr. Hill was probably drunk and forgot where he was supposed to be. We'll all make sure he doesn't make that mistake again."

"Well … ." Terry forced a smile for Bay's benefit and then turned in my direction. "I'm not sure that's true."

"What do you mean?" Winnie asked.

"After Bernard didn't show last night … should I talk about this in front of the K-I-D-S?" Terry's face reflected concern.

"Probably not if you think we're so dumb that we can't spell kids," Thistle replied, nonplussed.

Terry frowned. "You're going to be a handful, young lady."

"I keep hoping that's true," Thistle replied. "We know that Mr. Hill isn't really Santa. There's no reason to get all … weird and whiny about it. We can take it."

That girl makes me laugh sometimes.

"Bernard hasn't been seen in a few days," Terry said, pointing at Thistle and mock shooting her with his finger. "When he didn't show up last night I went on a hunt for him. As far as I can tell, he's been gone for more than a week and no one has any idea where he is."

"Oh, no," Twila said, her hand flying to her mouth. "You don't think he's D-E-A-D, do you?"

Terry shrugged.

"He probably choked on the mistletoe when he tried to wash it down with his whiskey," Thistle said. "His body is probably rotting somewhere right now."

"You have a wonderful imagination, young lady," Terry said, frowning. "Where do you even come up with stuff like that?"

"We have HBO," Thistle replied, not missing a beat. "I've seen tons of movies."

"And now you're grounded from the television for a week," Twila said.

Thistle narrowed her eyes. "If I can't watch television then I'm going to have nothing better to do than watch you."

Twila faltered. "Oh. I ... um ... ."

"Yeah, you didn't think that one through, did you?" I asked, making a face. "Are you sure Bernard is missing? Maybe he moved or something."

"All of his stuff is still at his house, and the mail has been piling up," Terry replied.

"Maybe he's dead," Marnie suggested. "Where else could he be?"

That was a very good question. Thankfully, I had no interest in answering it. "Is there more bacon?"

"I told you Christmas was going to be ruined," Bay said, pointing an accusatory face in my direction. "You never listen to me."

"I promised you that I wouldn't let Christmas be ruined," I shot back. "Stop being such a ... kvetch."

"I don't know what that is, but I'm pretty sure I'm not whatever that ... thing ... is," Bay argued.

"Bay, I promised you the Christmas you want," I reminded her. "Do I break my promises?"

Bay nodded.

"When have I ever broken a promise?"

"You promised us that you would make Mrs. Stevens dance naked in the middle of town so everyone would think she was drunk," Thistle said. "That hasn't happened."

These kids remember everything. It's annoying. "It hasn't happened yet," I said. "*Yet* being the operative word."

"That had better never happen," Winnie said.

I ignored her and kept my focus on Bay. "You have to have faith," I said. "I'll make sure you have a great Christmas. I won't let you down."

Bay didn't look convinced. "You'd better make sure we get that puppy, too."

"Yeah," Thistle chimed in. "We don't want a rat dog either. We want a big one. Don't forget."

"You're not getting a puppy, so stop asking for a puppy," I said. "I will handle Santa Claus, but that doesn't mean you're getting a puppy."

"We want snow, too," Bay added.

Good grief. "Fine. I'll find Santa Claus and make it snow. Is there anything else besides a puppy that you want for Christmas?"

Bay considered the question. "World peace."

"I'll get right on that."

There's a reason I never had kids of my own. They suck. Yeah, I said it. How did I end up being the one who has to save Christmas?

FOUR

"I don't think we're supposed to be doing this," Clove said, her tone ominous as she watched me peer into Bernard Hill's bedroom window. "This is against the law."

Clove was never going to be a rule breaker. It was a bit disappointing. "I was wrong when I said Bay was the kvetch this morning," I said. "You're the kvetch, Clove."

"It's not an insult if we don't know what it means," Thistle pointed out.

"It means she's whiny and complains about things that are unimportant," I explained. "What I'm about to do is not important and it's definitely not something to whine about."

"Are you sure?" Clove looked dubious.

"I'm sure."

After watching my three great-nieces worry and pout through what should have been a perfectly nice breakfast – my three nieces throwing themselves at the same man notwithstanding – I knew I had to find Bernard to save Christmas. How I became the hero of Christmas was beyond me, but if I pulled it off I was buying a cape to wear around town.

"This place is a dump," Thistle said, glancing around and wrinkling her nose. "Who would live here?"

"Maybe Mr. Hill is poor," Clove suggested.

"Mr. Hill has a nice pension from when he served as custodian of the school," I said. "He could have a better house, but he prefers whiskey to home ownership."

"It sounds like whiskey is bad for you," Clove said.

"It depends on how you drink it," I shot back. "Okay, we need to get inside. Who wants me to boost them through this window?"

"Why can't you just use your magic and open the back door?" Bay asked.

"Because the back door is visible from the street and I don't want anyone to see us."

"Because we're doing something illegal," Clove said. "I knew it!"

She was starting to get on my nerves. When Winnie suggested I spend the afternoon with the girls so their mothers could get their Christmas baking out of the way without greedy fingers slipping in the frosting bowl I didn't exactly jump for joy. When I thought better of it, though, I realized they made the perfect alibi. No one would break into someone's home with children in tow.

See, this is why I'm a genius.

"I already told you we're not doing anything illegal," I countered. "We're doing something good."

"What?"

"We're trying to find Santa Claus," Thistle supplied, hitting Clove on the back of the head. "Duh!"

"I hate you," Clove hissed.

I snagged the back of her coat and dragged her from Thistle before the conversation dissolved into screams and punches. That would draw too much attention. Clove and Thistle are like oil and vinegar sometimes.

"You need to stop fighting right now," I ordered.

"Because you're afraid the cops will hear us and come arrest us," Thistle said. "Admit it."

"Because I'm embarrassed to be seen with you two right now," I clarified. "I have a reputation to uphold, and you are ruining it."

"I'll go in through the window," Bay offered, sighing dramatically as she edged Thistle out of the way with her hip. "There's no reason for everyone to fight."

I glanced at her a moment, taking in her solid thighs and hips, and then shook my head. She's not a big girl, but compared to the other two she looks downright huge sometimes. "It has to be Clove."

"What? Why?" Clove gnawed on her fingernails as the suggestion sank in.

"You're the smallest," I replied, hoping I sounded reasonable even though I wanted to throttle her. "Bay is too heavy for me to lift."

Bay scorched me with a murderous look. "Are you saying I'm fat?"

"Of course not," I snapped. "I'm saying you're bigger than the other two because you're older. Clove is easiest for me to lift. She's the smallest. I'm not as young as I used to be and I don't work out."

"I think you should use your magic," Clove said.

"I already told you I can't do that."

"But ... I don't want to be in there alone."

"Yes, but you'll be the hero when we tell this story later," I said, changing tactics. "When we find Santa and save Christmas, you'll get all the applause."

Clove preened under the suggestion. "Really? Do you think people will clap?"

"Absolutely. You'll probably get more gifts, too."

Clove moved in front of me, resigned. "Okay, but this has to be quick. If I go to jail for this, I'm going to be really mad."

"Duly noted," I said, sliding the window open with a little magical help. I laced my fingers together and inclined my chin toward them. "Put your foot in there."

Clove did as instructed, and even though she was tiny, it took all of my strength to hoist her over my head. Bay and Thistle had to step in and help. The added muscle propelled Clove through the open window and we heard her crash into something as she landed on the other side.

"Are you okay, Clove?"

No answer.

"Clove?"

I couldn't hear a thing inside of the house.

"Clove, this isn't funny," I said. "If you're hurt, you need to give me a sign."

"How is that going to work if she's knocked out?" Bay asked.

I shot her a quelling look. "She's not knocked out. She's … ." Oh, Goddess, please tell me she's not knocked out! If I have to call an ambulance and explain this, not only am I not going to save Christmas, I'll probably be forced to eat whatever the jail calls turkey for Christmas dinner. No one wants that.

"She probably has a big cut in her head and she's bleeding all over the place," Thistle said.

"She's probably dying," Bay chimed in.

I seriously hate kids! "Clove, if you don't answer me right now, I'm going to … ." What? What was I going to do? I couldn't threaten a hurt child, could I?

Clove picked that moment to pop into view, and although she had a disgusted look on her face she appeared none the worse for wear.

"Why didn't you answer me?" I asked.

"Because I was trying to figure out where my head was because it almost hit the dresser in here," Clove replied. "And I landed on a pair of underwear. Do you know how gross that is?"

I did. Bernard had a tendency to sleep with the dregs of society. There is no way I would tell her that, though. "They were probably clean."

"They aren't clean," Clove said, wrinkling her nose. "There are things on them."

"Gross," Thistle and Bay said in unison.

"I'll buy some of those clean wipes when we get out of here," I said. "It will kill all of the germs."

"I want candy, too," Clove said.

I narrowed my eyes. I was being shaken down by a child. It was insulting. "Maybe I'll just leave you in there and let you explain to the cops why you're breaking into someone else's house."

Clove's eyes widened. "I knew we were breaking the law!"

"Go open the back door," I ordered. "We're coming around. Be quick about it."

By the time Clove let us into Bernard's house she was practically beside herself. I pushed Thistle and Bay inside, shutting the door behind me to lock out prying eyes, and focused on Clove. "What's your problem now?"

"There are bugs flying around in the kitchen," Clove replied, horrified. "Big ones."

That didn't sound good. "They're not the type of bugs that go with dead bodies, are they?"

"What kind of bugs are those?"

"What kind of bugs are you seeing?"

"The kind that pop up on food when you don't finish eating it and leave it on the counter for days at a time," Clove replied. "It's gross. I can never eat again. I hope you're happy. I'm going to starve to death and die."

"If you don't stop complaining I'm going to make you eat that food and then you'll really have something to complain about," I threatened.

Clove snapped her mouth shut, disgusted.

"You're a horrible babysitter," Thistle said.

"Maybe that's because you three are horrible babies."

"Whatever." Thistle rolled her eyes. "Where should we start looking for clues?"

That was a good question. "I don't know," I said, glancing around. Clove wasn't exaggerating about the house being filthy. "Let's start in the bedroom."

"There's not going to be creepy stuff in there, is there?" Bay asked.

I had no idea. "What do you consider creepy?"

"Dirty underwear."

"Well, I think we all know there will be dirty underwear in there," I said. "Clove announced it to the entire street."

"I did not." Clove realized she talked when it was too late to drag the words back into her mouth. Instead of acknowledging her mistake, she clapped both hands over her lips, determined to make sure I didn't try to make her eat rotten food.

"I'm not going to make you eat that food," I said, giving into my sympathetic urges. What? They're rare, but they do happen. "I was joking."

Clove didn't look convinced.

"If I punish you it'll be with something a lot worse than rotten food," I tried again.

"She's right," Thistle said. "She's not going to make you eat gross stuff. She'll just make it so your pants don't fit if you eat good stuff. You know that."

Clove marginally relaxed, although she didn't drop her hands. I decided to let her be. "Let's search the bedroom."

"I don't want to see dirty underwear," Bay said.

"Do you want to find Mr. Hill?"

"Yes."

"Do you want to save the Christmas party?"

"Yes."

"Then shut up and follow me," I ordered, striding in the direction of the dark hallway. "Just don't ... touch anything. I don't want to have to explain how you guys inadvertently got crabs ... or tetanus ... or fleas from this place. No one wants that."

"What are we going to tell our mothers when we get back home?" Thistle asked. "They're not going to be happy that your idea of babysitting was teaching us how to break into a house."

"We didn't break into a house," I said.

"You just pushed Clove through a window and onto dirty underwear," Thistle challenged.

"That's not what happened."

"We all saw it," Thistle protested.

"No. We were walking down the road and saw the door open and decided to check on Bernard because we wanted to make sure he was safe. We're good Samaritans."

"That's a lie," Clove said. "We're not supposed to lie."

"Well, I'm telling you to lie and you're also supposed to listen to your elders." Let's see them get out of that one.

"Mom said we're only supposed to listen to our elders when it's the right thing to do," Bay said. "I'm not sure this is the right thing to do."

She was back to being a kvetch again. "If you don't shut up, you're all going on my list."

"Whatever," Thistle said, peering into the bedroom. "This place really is gross. Now I know why Mom makes me clean up my room every day. Don't tell her I said that, though."

Given the state of the room, it was hard to argue with her. The bed was unmade – and I had a feeling it had been that way for months. If those sheets had ever been 1 laundered they showed no sign of it. Clothes were strewn about the floor – and Clove wasn't lying about the dirty underwear. The top drawer of the dresser was open and clothing hung over the edges.

"Don't touch anything," I reminded them. "Look around and if you see something … out of place … call me over."

"Are you going to touch it?" Bay asked.

"I'm going to make you touch it under my watchful eye," I shot back.

After searching the bedroom and coming up empty, I led the girls back into the living room. Unlike the family room at our house, this one was devoid of everything but a couch and television – and about three layers of filth.

"There's nothing here," Thistle said, kicking a magazine and glancing underneath it. "If Mr. Hill is still living here, he hasn't been here in a long time."

"If he moved, though, he left everything behind," I said. "Most people take their belongings with them when they move."

"Would you take any of this stuff with you?"

"Probably not," I conceded. "I'm not Bernard, though. Maybe something came up at the last minute. Maybe he had a family emergency."

"Maybe he's dead in a ditch somewhere and Christmas is officially ruined," Bay interjected.

"Stop being such a defeatist, young lady," I ordered. "I didn't raise you to give up before we even get to the hard part."

"It's going to get harder than this?" Bay was incredulous. "Clove landed on dirty underwear and there are bugs flying around and getting in our hair. It can't possibly get worse than this."

"Guess again."

I froze when I heard the voice, swiveling quickly to find Terry standing in the doorframe that separated the kitchen and living room. When did he get here?

"We're being framed, officer," Thistle announced. I had to admire her chutzpah.

"We were walking by and the door was open and we had to check and make sure Mr. Hill was okay," Bay offered. She had the best memory and thrived under pressure. She would be the one to remember the lie.

Clove mournfully held out her hands. "Take us to jail. We broke the law. Now we're never going to get that puppy." I don't even know what to say about her.

Terry's gaze bounced between the three worried faces and then settled on me. "Do you want to tell me what you're doing here?"

"I'm saving Christmas. What does it look like I'm doing here?"

What? There's no reason to lie. The man isn't stupid – no matter how his face looks sometimes.

FIVE

"You're saving Christmas?"

I couldn't tell whether Terry wanted to laugh or strangle me, but this was no time to change my story. "That's what I said."

"I see." Terry licked his lips and glanced at my three partners in crime. "How did you guys get in here?"

I opened my mouth to answer for them, but Terry waved a finger in my face to silence me.

"I'm talking to the girls," he said, giving me a dark look. "The girls are the ones I want to hear from."

Well, this is going to bite the big one.

Terry focused on Bay first. "How did you get in here?"

Bay glanced at me, indecision flitting over her features. Lying to Terry isn't something she wanted to do, but neither did she relish betraying me. "I ... we were walking and we saw the door was open," she said, opting to continue with the lie. "We wanted to make sure Mr. Hill was okay. We weren't doing anything wrong."

"Aunt Tillie is completely innocent," Thistle chimed in. "We were doing our ... civil duty. That's all."

"Civic duty," Bay corrected, causing Thistle to scowl. Bay's vocabulary was large for a child her age and Thistle always scrambled to keep up. It drove her nuts that Bay appeared smarter than her when speaking with adults.

"I see," Terry said. He turned his attention to Clove and leaned over so he could look her in the eye. "Do you want to tell me how you got in here?"

Clove was the weakest link. We all knew it. We were going down. My great-nieces were going to be arrested before they hit puberty. That had to be some sort of record.

"I have no idea how we got inside," Clove said. "I forget things. I'm little. I can't help it."

I stilled, surprised by Clove's manipulation. She used that "I'm little" bit whenever she wants to get out of trouble. Because she was so petite, people fell for it. If you put a halo on her head she could double as an angel every day of the week – well, until the angel started whining, and then the gig would be up.

"Are you telling me you forgot how you got into this house?" Terry pressed. "I find that hard to believe."

Clove jutted out her lower lip into the cutest pout known to man. She knows what that lip is capable of, and Terry was about to be putty in her tiny hands. "I'm sorry I don't remember. I … please don't hate me. I couldn't take it if you hated me." Clove dissolved into tears.

Clove's performance was enough to make Terry distraught. "Oh, sweetie, I could never hate you," he said. He pulled her in for a quick hug. "I didn't mean to upset you. Don't cry, Clove. I don't like it when you cry."

"I can't help myself," Clove wailed. "I'm so sad!"

Terry hugged her again, casting a hateful look my way over her shoulder as he tried to soothe her. I had to give it to the kid; when she wanted to lay it on thick she was downright amazing.

After Clove's sobs subsided, Terry released her and fixed his attention on me. "I know they're lying," he said, his voice low. "The problem is, I can't upset them because then I'll be upset.

"I want you to know, though, that the neighbors called in a tip and they say you hoisted one of the girls through the side window," he continued. "I know darned well you broke into this house, and you should be ashamed of yourself for forcing these girls to lie."

I fought the urge to roll my eyes. "I have no idea what you're talking about. I would never force these sweet angels to lie. That's a horrible thing to say to an old lady."

"Horrible," Thistle echoed. "Now Aunt Tillie wants to cry."

I scorched Thistle with an angry look. "I'm not going to cry."

"Oh, you want to," Thistle said. "I can see it in the way your face is all pinched up."

"Yeah," Bay said, grinning evilly. "I think Officer Terry would like it if you cried. Then he'd believe you."

Five minutes ago those two were my favorites. Now I want to lock them in the closet with the dirty underwear and never let them out. "I'm crying on the inside," I said.

Terry made a face. "You really should be ashamed of yourself."

"Yeah, well, I'm not," I said, clapping my hands to get everyone's attention. "Girls, Terry is here to handle Mr. Hill's house and take care of all of that for us. We don't have to worry."

"He's still missing," Bay pointed out. "Christmas is still ruined."

I was about to go off on a Christmas rant when Terry stepped in front of me, cutting me off from a doozy of a meltdown, and knelt in front of Bay.

"Christmas won't be ruined," Terry said. "Even if Mr. Hill can't play Santa Claus, I promise that Christmas won't be ruined for you. It's going to be okay. You don't have to worry so much. You'll give yourself an ulcer."

"Like Mrs. Stevens has on her lip?" Clove asked.

Terry furrowed his brow. "I thought that was a cold sore."

"Aunt Tillie says it's herpes and an ulcer of the lip," Thistle supplied. "She says we never want one and the mailman gives them to you."

Terry scowled. "Nice."

"They asked," I said. "Come on, girls. I'll take you down to the bakery for some hot chocolate and doughnuts to brighten your day."

"I want chocolate and sprinkles," Thistle said.

"I don't care what you get on it," I shot back. "Go get in the car."

"I want chocolate and sprinkles, too," Clove said, falling into line behind Thistle. "It will make me feel better after my terrible day."

"I'm going to give you something to cry about if you don't get in that car now," I hissed in her ear.

Terry remained crouched in front of Bay, reaching up to brush her flyaway hair from her face. "I promise you're going to have the best Christmas ever," he said. "Try not to worry about this."

"Will you make Aunt Tillie get us a puppy?" Bay asked.

"You're not getting a puppy," I snapped.

Terry ignored me. "I'll do you one better," he said. "I'll talk to your mom and aunts about the puppy. They're probably going to be more open than your Aunt Tillie."

"Do you think they'll get us one?"

"I … ." Terry isn't the type of man to make empty promises to a child. I like that about him. "I don't know," he answered truthfully. "I do know that no matter what, you're going to have a great Christmas."

"I hope so," Bay said, dropping a quick kiss on Terry's cheek. "The rest of this year has sucked."

I watched her walk out of the house in search of her cousins, cringing as Terry moved up behind me.

"Don't bring them with you when you break and enter again," he warned. "If this place belonged to someone other than the town drunk you'd be in a world of hurt. This is the type of stuff that makes the newspaper."

I snorted. "The Whistler is a weekly newspaper and you know darned well William wouldn't dare print a story about this."

"That's neither here nor there," Terry said. "I know you're trying to help in your own way. I know you're just as desperate to give them a good Christmas as everyone else. This is not the way to do it, though."

"Oh, they're getting the Christmas of their dreams – except for the puppy," I replied.

"And how are you going to do that? Bernard is missing. I don't think we'll find him before the town party. How are you going to fix Christmas?"

I patted Terry's cheek, and then pinched it for good measure just because I could. "I'm Tillie Winchester. I can do whatever I want."

WHAT DO you guys want to eat and drink?" I asked, scanning the menu at Gunderson's Bakery twenty minutes later. "Hot chocolate and chocolate doughnuts?"

"With sprinkles," Thistle said.

"I didn't forget the sprinkles, Thistle," I snapped. "Do I look like the type of person who forgets the sprinkles?"

"Hey, we just lied to a cop for you so be nice to us," Clove said.

"Your performance was wonderful," I said, grinning. "That lip thing you do isn't going to last forever, but it's a great weapon right now."

"I have no idea what you're talking about," Clove said primly, placing her hands on top of the round dinette table the girls perched around. "I forgot what happened. I'm little. I can't remember everything."

"Well, at least you've learned a few of the lessons I've tried to teach you," I said. "I thought for sure you'd be the one to crumble."

"Since I didn't, can I have two doughnuts?"

"If she gets two doughnuts, I want two doughnuts," Thistle said.

"You're both getting one doughnut," I countered. "You'll be up all night from the sugar high if I get you two."

"You really are the worst babysitter ever," Thistle groused.

Bay was silent in her chair, her expression distant. I snapped my fingers close to her ear to get her attention.

"What?"

"Do you want a chocolate doughnut with sprinkles, too?"

"I don't need a doughnut," Bay replied, sighing dramatically and lowering her chin to her forearms on top of the table. "Who can think about doughnuts when Christmas is going to be ruined?"

Sometimes I think these kids are missing their calling. They should all be actors ... or circus folk.

"Have you decided?" Ginny Gunderson stepped out of the back of the bakery, fixing me with a tight smile. We have a long history. It wasn't always a happy history, but we put on a good show in front of others so they won't be suspicious.

"Yeah," I said, matching her uncomfortable smile with one of my own. "I need four hot chocolates and four cake doughnuts with chocolate frosting and sprinkles."

Ginny smiled, her gaze moving beyond me and landing on the girls. She'd never had children of her own. Unlike me, I think she was saddened by that outcome. Even though Winnie, Marnie and Twila aren't my daughters, they feel like it. And even though Bay, Clove and Thistle aren't my granddaughters, they are close enough. I didn't always feel lucky in that respect, but there are times I thank the stars above because I have them to focus on – and torment.

"I'll bring the hot chocolate and doughnuts over in just a minute," Ginny said. "I'll warm the doughnuts up in the microwave for a few seconds so they're extra-special gooey and good."

"Yay!" Clove clapped her hands.

"They're so cute," Ginny said, smiling fondly at them.

"Try living with them," I shot back.

Ginny brought the steaming hot chocolate and doughnuts to us a few minutes later. I watched her chat up each of the girls in turn, making sure to give everyone equal attention, and when she moved to walk away I stopped her with a hand on her arm.

Ginny arched an eyebrow, surprised at the contact. We don't spend much time together these days, and it's rare for me to visit the bakery. "Is something wrong, Tillie?"

"I don't know," I admitted. "Have you heard anything about Bernard Hill?"

"What do you mean?"

"He didn't show up at the school pageant last night, and Terry doesn't think he's been home in at least a week," I answered.

"And his house is gross and there are bugs inside of it," Thistle said.

"And he has dirty underwear on his bedroom floor," Clove added.

"And how do you guys know that?" Ginny asked.

"Aunt Tillie pushed me through the bedroom window so I could open the door and we could search his house," Clove said. "I landed on the underwear. I'm going to have nightmares."

Ginny pursed her lips and glanced at me. "Is that true? Did you force those children to break into Bernard's house? Tillie, what were you thinking?"

"I didn't force them to do anything," I corrected. "They're all up in arms about Santa not being at the town party. I was trying to make Christmas better for them. I was doing a good thing."

"She made us lie to Officer Terry," Bay said. "We had to tell him we saw the door open from the street."

"You lied to Officer Terry?" Ginny was scandalized. "Do you really think that's a good idea, Tillie? How did you know they'd lie and back your play?"

"I've worked really hard on the lying lessons," I said. "Bay and Thistle are naturals. Clove still needs some work. She pretended to have amnesia and cried. I found that to be more effective than the lying. It was a good lesson to learn."

Ginny scowled. "That is horrible."

"Oh, please," I scoffed. "Terry knew they were lying. He told me as much. What does it matter? It's not as though we tried to steal anything."

"Trust us. We don't want what he had," Thistle said, happily munching away on her doughnut.

"Don't talk with your mouth full," I ordered. "It's gross."

"You do it."

"It's cute when I do it," I said. "You guys all shut up for a second. I need to talk to Ginny and it'll be a lot easier if you guys aren't chattering at the same time."

"Seriously, you're the worst babysitter ever," Thistle said.

"I'm going to have that put on a sweatshirt and wear it when I drop you three off at school wearing nothing else but a bathrobe and flip flops if you're not careful," I warned.

"You don't take us to school."

"I'll start just so I can wear that outfit."

"Whatever," Thistle said. "You're crazy sometimes. Has anyone ever told you that?"

"Only seventy-five percent of the people I meet," I replied. "Eat your doughnut." I focused back on Ginny. "Have you heard any rumors about Bernard?"

"I know he was having a rough time of it," Ginny replied. "He's been depressed, but I didn't think it was bad enough to off himself or run away. I don't know what to tell you on that front. The holidays are hard for people when they're alone."

My heart went out to her. She'd been alone for a long time, ever since her jerkoff husband disappeared without a trace years earlier. When I lost my husband, I thought I'd never get over it. I still love him, but having six girls to focus on – even if they're complete and total pains sometimes – lessens that burden.

"You're always invited out to our house for Christmas dinner if you want," I offered.

"Thank you, but ... I'm not sure I'm up for that," Ginny said.

"You won't want to come to our house anyway," Bay said. "Christmas is going to suck this year because there won't be a Santa and there won't be any snow."

"Didn't I tell you I was going to fix both of those problems?" I challenged.

"You're going to make it snow?" Ginny looked dubious. "Since when can you control the weather?"

"I've always been able to control the weather."

"The weather forecasters say there's not a chance of snow between now and Christmas," Ginny pointed out. "I don't think you can bully the weather into doing what you want."

"Well, we'll just see about that, won't we?"

SIX

"Well, you all look happy," Marnie said, running her finger across the corner of Clove's mouth as I ushered everyone back into the house after our doughnut extravaganza. "Chocolate?"

"We had doughnuts and hot chocolate," Clove said.

"With sprinkles," Thistle added.

"Well, great," Marnie said, making a face. "I love hearing that an hour before dinner." She shot a pointed look in my direction. "Were you purposely trying to spoil their appetites?"

I considered telling her I was rewarding them for lying to the police, but I figured that would be pushing my luck. "They were good and they deserved a treat. You put me in charge of them and I decided they needed doughnuts. If you don't like it, don't ask me to watch them again."

Marnie scowled. "Why can't you be like all the other grandmothers in town and knit them scarves?"

"Knit," Thistle said, dissolving into giggles. "She doesn't knit."

"I could knit," I challenged.

"We don't want her to knit," Bay said. "That would be horrible for everyone."

"How so?"

"Then we'd have to wear what she knitted for us," Bay pointed out. "Do you want to wear hats and scarves that Aunt Tillie made? Think about it."

"Listen, mouth, if I want to knit I'll knit," I said. "And if I do make you hats and scarves, you'll love them."

The look Bay shot me was reminiscent of her mother – and not in a good way. "Whatever," she said. "Can we watch cartoons until dinner?"

Marnie nodded, pushing Bay's hair from her face a moment so she could study her. While all my nieces favor their own daughter, they also love their nieces beyond reason. With Winnie off doing ... whatever it is she was doing ... Marnie obviously decided Bay needed attention.

"Why do you look so sad?" Marnie asked.

"I guess I'm just tired."

Marnie arched a challenging eyebrow. "Really? You should be hopped up on sugar and fighting with your cousins like you usually do this time of day. What's really wrong?"

"Nothing," Bay replied, pulling her head away from Marnie. "We're going to watch television."

"We made roast beef," Marnie offered, knowing that's one of Bay's favorite meals. "We have mashed potatoes, corn, and chocolate cake, too."

Bay forced a smile for Marnie's benefit, although I could tell my niece didn't believe it any more than I did. "That sounds great."

Marnie watched the girls disappear into the bowels of the house and then turned to me. "Why is Bay so upset?"

"I think she was born that way," I said, my tone more blithe than I meant it to be.

"Why really?"

"Why do you think?" I asked. "She's convinced that she's going to have a miserable Christmas and she's made the other two believe it, too. This whole Bernard-going-missing thing only adds to the bad attitude she's been carrying around for months."

"What do you want us to do?" Marnie asked, her voice plaintive. "We cannot give them back what they lost. You know that as well as I do."

"What did they lose?"

"Their ... families."

I sighed. This was a subject we kept tiptoeing around. "They didn't lose their family," I corrected. "They lost their fathers. And they didn't technically lose them. They still exist. It's just a different family configuration."

"They're too young to see that now," Marnie said. "You can't make them understand something they're not equipped to understand. When they're older, they'll see this was the best decision for everyone because otherwise no one was going to be happy. There was too much fighting going on."

"I'm not arguing the point with you," I said. "I think they're going to be better off in the long run. The problem you have is the immediate future. They only know Christmas one way, and that's the way they want to celebrate this year."

"We can't fix that."

"I didn't say you could," I said, tugging on my limited patience so I didn't blow up at Marnie. I knew she hurt, too. "We can't give them the Christmas they want, but we can give them the Christmas they deserve."

"And what's that going to include?" Marnie pressed. "They want a puppy. You're adamant they can't have a puppy. They want snow. We can't make it snow. They want their fathers. We definitely can't give them that.

"Now Santa Claus has gone missing," she continued. "For them, it's like the world is stacking brick walls up and they're waiting for those walls to fall in on them. No matter how safe we try to make them feel, this is their new reality, and we can't chase all of their demons away.

"They're growing up," Marnie said. "As much as I would like to wrap them in cotton to protect them from the world, we all know that isn't possible."

It was a nice speech. It made me want to smack her. "Who raised you to think like that?"

Marnie was taken aback. "How should I think?"

"We're witches," I reminded her. "We can make the impossible possible."

"I don't know what that means and I'm not sure I want to know what you're up to," Marnie said. "I know you want to give them a great Christmas. We all want that. We can't give them everything they want, though. Sooner or later, they'll have to get used to disappointment."

Over my dead body. "That's not going to happen this year," I vowed. "This year they're going to get the Christmas they deserve."

"And how will that happen?" Marnie challenged. "Are you going to call to the four corners and make it snow? You're powerful, but I don't think you're that powerful. Are you going to track down Bernard and make him appear as Santa? What if he's dead? What if he doesn't want to come back?

"I love you," she continued. "You've been the best mother to us that we could ever hope for. You stepped in when we needed you and I will be forever thankful. Despite your ... quirks ... you've also been a wonderful grandmother to our girls. You're the only grandmother they've ever known. You can't do everything, though. We can only do the best that we can."

"I guess you need a little lesson in magic, too," I said, irritation bubbling up. "I can do whatever I want, and right now I want those girls to have a merry Christmas."

"I hope you can do everything you want to do," Marnie said. "You'll understand if I temper my enthusiasm and the girls' expectations, though. There's nothing worse than expecting to get the moon but getting only a star."

"We'll just see about that," I challenged.

DINNER WAS morose and the more Bay sank into her self-made depression, the more I wanted to smack her. Winnie, Marnie and

Twila split dish duty after the meal, and the girls wandered back into the living room to watch television.

That's when I made my move.

I gathered all the magical supplies I needed from my bedroom and made my way outside. I don't care what anyone says, I am strong enough to control the weather. If this were a Batman movie, I'd be the best super villain ever – and just wait until you see my cape.

It took me almost an hour to complete my task, and when I finished, even I was impressed. I threw open the back door of the house and yelled inside.

"Get your scrawny butts out here right now!"

Winnie was the first through the door. I think she expected to find me in the middle of mayhem. In a way I was. It was the best mayhem ever, though.

"What did you do?" Winnie asked, her eyes wide as she stepped into the accumulating snow and lifted her head to the heavens. "It's ... beautiful."

"I know." Smugness only works on some people. Actually, it doesn't work on most people. I'm the rare exception. "It's pretty cool, huh?"

"You made it snow," Winnie said, flabbergasted. "How did you do it?"

"I'm the most powerful witch in the Midwest," I shot back. "I can't believe you ever doubted me."

"It's not that I doubted you," Winnie said. "It's just ... thank you!"

"You're welcome," I said, grudgingly accepting her hug. "You did doubt me, though."

"Let's not get into that," Winnie said. She turned back toward the house. "Come out here, girls! You're never going to guess what your Aunt Tillie did for you."

Thistle was the first through the door, excitement positively rolling through her as she slid in the snow. She wore slippers and hadn't bothered to put on a coat, but she was sneaky and evaded Twila's hands as they tried to corral her.

"Snow! It's snowing!"

I may be their curmudgeonly great-aunt, but even I couldn't hide my smile at Thistle's enthusiasm.

"Young lady, you need your coat, hat and gloves," Twila warned. "You'll get pneumonia and die. Is that what you want right before Christmas?"

Thistle responded by tossing a loosely packed snowball and hitting her mother in the face.

"Holy crap!" Clove appeared in the doorway, her brown eyes wide as saucers. "I can't believe this. It's … snowing!"

"Your Aunt Tillie did this," Marnie said, choking up as she shot me a grateful smile. "This is your first Christmas present. Do you like it?"

"It's the best thing ever," Clove said sincerely. "Thank you."

"Don't thank me," I said, my cheeks burning. "I … come out and play in it. That's why I conjured it."

"I have to get my coat and gloves first," Clove replied. "I don't want to get sick."

Thistle hammered Clove with a snowball as Twila chased her around. "Thistle!"

"I'm going to make you eat snow," Clove warned, darting back inside. I had no doubt she'd return looking like the ghost of snowmen past and present.

Bay was the last to appear in the doorway, and the marvel on her face was something I won't soon forget. "It's snowing." The words were barely a whisper. "The people on the television said there was no chance it would snow. How did this happen?"

"Your Aunt Tillie did it," Winnie said, staring intently at her daughter. "She wanted you to have the best Christmas ever. Do you like it?"

Bay turned her attention to me, and I swear she looked as if she would burst into tears. "I … ."

"Don't you even think about crying, little missy," I warned, wagging a finger in her face. "Christmas isn't for crying. Santa isn't going to bring you any presents if you cry. You know that, right?"

Bay collected herself. "I still don't believe in Santa," she said. "You can't make me. I know the truth."

"Well, I guess you're not getting anything good this year then," I said, crossing my arms over my chest.

"I said I didn't believe in Santa," Bay said. "I do believe in you, though."

For some odd reason a lump formed in my throat. "I believe in you, too," I said. "You're going to get your Christmas, Bay. This is only the first step. I'm going to find Bernard, and Santa will be at the town party. Everything will be okay."

"You can't promise her you're going to find Bernard," Winnie whispered. "You don't know that."

"Did I make it snow?"

"Yes, but ... ."

"Am I all powerful?"

"Not last time I checked," Winnie shot back. "If you were all powerful, you wouldn't have to threaten the neighbor's dog every time you go out to collect the mail."

"Just you wait, niece," I said. "This is only the beginning."

Clove reappeared in the doorway, covered in so many layers of outdoor clothes I could barely see her. "Prepare to die, Thistle!"

"Oh, I'm so scared," Thistle scoffed. "I ... ."

I don't know what convinced me to throw the snowball. She's a child and I should take that into consideration whenever her antics get out of control. The look on her face when the snowball exploded against her cheek was priceless, though.

"That was so mean!" Thistle screeched, wiping the leftover chunks from her face.

"I think you had it coming," I said, my grin wide.

"I'm going to make you eat snow," Thistle warned.

"Not until you have a coat, gloves and hat on," Twila said, snagging Thistle around the neck. "Inside right now, young lady! You're not allowed out until you're dressed for the weather."

Thistle put up a fight but ultimately gave in. I happily watched properly dressed Clove and Bay cavort until my attention was drawn to a figure moving up the sidewalk.

Terry's face was filled with as much wonder as Bay's when she first saw the descending flakes.

"Does someone want to explain this to me?" Terry asked.

"It's snowing," Clove replied.

"I know it's snowing, Clove," Terry said. "It's snowing all over town. Do you want to know the interesting thing, though? It's only snowing here in our town. The other towns around us are still dry. What do you make of that?"

Clove shot Terry an impish grin and shrugged. "It's a Christmas miracle."

"I'll bet," Terry said, turning his attention to me. "Is this part of saving Christmas?"

"It's a step in the right direction," I replied, refusing to let his stern face dampen my fun.

"You can't just ... make it snow," Terry said. He was aware of our witchy gifts, even though he pretended to be in the dark. He couldn't explain them so he opted to ignore them. "People are going to talk. This could make national headlines, Mrs. Winchester."

"So what?"

"So ... what will people say?"

"If you're worried they're going to scream 'witch' and try to burn me at the stake, don't," I said. "No one can prove anything."

"You did do this, though, didn't you?"

I shrugged. "Like Clove said, it's a Christmas miracle."

"It's the best miracle ever," Bay said, beaming as she appeared at Terry's side. "Now all we need is a puppy."

"You're not getting a puppy."

Bay ignored my pronouncement, instead dumping a handful of snow down the front of Terry's coat. For a moment I worried he was too flummoxed by the snow to handle a little girl's happiness. I should never underestimate him.

"You'd better start running now," Terry warned. "Your mothers and I are going to challenge you little ones and Aunt Tillie to a snowball fight. You'd better start building your fort now or I'm going to crush you."

Bay giggled. "What do we get if we win?"

"What do you want?"

"A second serving of chocolate cake."

Winnie sighed. "Fine. If you guys win, we'll finish off the cake. We can bake another one tomorrow."

Bay squealed, delighted. "I think Christmas is going to be saved after all."

"I've been telling you that for two days! When will anyone in this family start believing me?"

"I'll believe you if we win the snowball fight," Bay said.

"Of course we're going to win the snowball fight," I replied. "If you think I'm letting someone else eat my cake, you're crazy. Come on, girls. It's time to prepare for war." I stopped in front of Terry before joining the girls on the side of the house. "May the Goddess have mercy on your poor soul."

"Bring it on," Terry said, smiling despite himself. "Christmas is coming early and you're going down for a change."

"We'll see about that."

SEVEN

"How did you get stuck with us two days in a row?" Thistle asked, watching as I mixed herbs in a bowl the next afternoon. "I thought you would be everyone's favorite person after the snow thing."

Funny. I thought so, too. "Maybe I volunteered to take you," I suggested. "Did you ever think of that?"

"Nope."

That kid is too smart for her own good. "Your mothers have a few things to do," I said. "Tomorrow is Christmas Eve. They're running out of time."

"Are they off getting our puppy?" Bay asked.

"I'm going to cast a spell and make you allergic to dogs if I hear about that puppy one more time," I threatened. "How does that sound?"

"Can't you just make us allergic to you?" Thistle asked. "I think we'd all be happy then."

I stopped mixing long enough to stare her down. "Thistle, in a few years you're going to be one of the all-time greatest snot-nosed teenagers to ever walk the face of the Earth," I said. "When that happens, I'm going to laugh at your mother because she earned all the trouble you're going to bestow upon her, and then I'm going to move to another house. Does that make you happy?"

"Geez, I was just joking," Thistle said, rolling her eyes. "There's no need to blow a basket."

"Gasket," Bay automatically corrected as she came into the kitchen.

Thistle made a face. "What's a gasket? How do you blow one?"

That was a pretty good question.

"How do you blow a basket?" Bay shot back.

That was an even better question. "You two need to stop squabbling," I ordered. "Santa doesn't like fresh-mouthed little girls."

"You like us, though, and you're better than Santa," Clove said, her eyes sparkling.

I leaned down so we were eye to eye. "I think you're even more manipulative than your two cousins put together," I said. "At least they're upfront about what they do. You sneak in behind them and wreak havoc when you think no one is looking."

Clove blanched. "I do not."

"I didn't say it was a bad thing," I pointed out. "The three of you all have special gifts. You're all different, but when you work together the sky is the limit on what you can accomplish. I can't wait until you're teenagers and you decide to work as a unit against your mothers."

"Why?" Bay asked.

"Because when your mothers were teenagers they made my hair go gray," I replied, pointing to my mostly ashy hair. It was once dark and lush like Marnie and Clove's, but time caught up with it years ago and I don't have the energy to dye it. "My hair used to look just like Clove's. Your mothers turned it this way."

"How did they do that?"

"By doing the things you guys are going to do in a few years," I said, measuring some hemlock and dumping it into the bowl.

"I can't wait to be a teenager," Thistle said. "That means we'll get to stay out as late as we want."

"And no naps," Bay added.

"And we'll get to date boys," Clove said, giggling.

I fixed her with a dubious look. "You're going to be boy crazy. I can already tell."

"Is that a bad thing?"

"Your mother was boy crazy, too," I answered. "In fact, all of your mothers were boy crazy when they were younger."

"Now they're just crazy about one boy," Bay said. "Officer Terry makes them all go bonkers."

I studied her for a moment, worried she was building up some great romance in her head. For a girl who wants a father, Terry is an awfully appealing figure. "Your mothers like to compete for Terry's affection because they always want to win," I explained. "I taught them that. What they do when Terry is around is more about them than him. You understand that, right?"

"I'm not sure," Bay admitted. "Are you telling me that I shouldn't like Officer Terry?"

"No," I replied, shaking my head. "In fact, the more you like him, the better. If you're ever in trouble, Bay, don't hesitate to go to him. He'll move heaven and earth to keep you safe and protected."

"So … what are you saying?"

"Terry is not your father," I said, opting for bluntness. "You have a father. You all have fathers. Terry is not going to swoop in and fill that hole in your hearts. I don't want you to think he is, because that's not a reasonable assumption."

"I know he's not my dad," Bay said. "I … he's fun, though. He always makes me laugh."

"I have a feeling Terry will always be there for you, Bay," I said. "Don't worry about that."

"That's good," Thistle said. "As long as he's in charge of the police we know we'll never be arrested. We can make him do what we want if we cry."

I pursed my lips to keep from laughing. Seriously, it's like looking in a mirror sometimes when I watch that kid. "I'm all for manipulating people to get what you want," I said. "What you need to remember is that if you do it too often, it will come back to bite you."

"What will?"

"Karma."

"That's what you were talking to Lila about," Bay said. "When is karma going to get her?"

"Soon."

"How soon?"

"As soon as I can free up some time in my schedule," I said, mixing the rest of the herbs together and sealing the concoction into a large baggie. "Okay, we're ready. Everyone, get your coats, and don't forget your hats and mittens. I do not want any of you getting sick."

"Because it will ruin Christmas for us?" Clove asked.

"Because I'll get yelled at by your mothers," I shot back. "Everyone, move your butts and head for the car. We've got a Christmas to finish saving."

"I DON'T UNDERSTAND what you're doing," Bay said, watching as I sprinkled my spell ingredients on Bernard's front porch. "Are you trying to make him come back here or are we going to go to him?"

Sometimes the way Bay's mind works is astonishing. I never considered trying to make Bernard come to us. That would've have been much easier to do. "If this doesn't work, we'll try to make him come to us," I replied. "Right now, we're trying to find out where he is."

"What if he's dead in a ditch?" Thistle asked.

"Why does your mind always go there? Is there a reason you're so morbid?"

"HBO."

I should have seen that coming. "Well, I'm going to make sure you don't watch HBO again," I threatened. "Not everyone who wanders away ends up dead in a ditch."

"Do some of them?" Clove asked.

"Only flaming asshats," I replied. "Okay, step back."

The girls did as instructed, keenly watching me. Magic is the one realm in which they opt for safety and never put up a fight when I order them to do something.

I pressed my hands together, muttered a short incantation – mostly because I didn't want prying ears to pick it up and repeat it in front of their mothers – and smiled as the ingredients flared to life and formed a magical blue line.

The line led away from Bernard's house.

"Are we going to follow the line?" Thistle asked.

I nodded.

"Will it lead us to Mr. Hill?"

"It should," I said. I didn't add that I hoped the line would lead us to Bernard still living and breathing. If it led us to a body, Christmas was officially going to be ruined – in more ways than one.

"Should we walk the line or drive?" Bay asked, her mind always hopping to the next task that needed to be solved. I've never been organized enough to think like that. She is going to make an interesting adult.

"We're going to drive," I said. "There's snow on the sidewalks and that will make walking hard."

"Thanks to you," Thistle said, grinning.

I returned the smile. "Also, I don't feel like walking," I said. "If Bernard isn't nearby we're going to have to walk back and get the car and … well … nobody wants that."

"Then let's get moving," Bay said, racing toward my car. "The faster we find Mr. Hill, the faster we save Christmas."

"And get our puppy," Clove said.

I flicked her ear, causing her to grab it and yelp. "How many times do I have to tell you that you're not getting a puppy?"

"Just because you don't like dogs doesn't mean we don't like dogs."

"I never said I didn't like dogs," I argued. "I said our house already has too many people and you guys are too young to care for a dog."

"You don't know that," Thistle protested. "We would be excellent pet owners."

"You'll never know unless you let us prove ourselves to you," Clove added.

She had a point. Still, I didn't want a dog. "You're going to have to get used to the fact that you are not getting a dog for Christmas."

"Bah humbug," Thistle muttered.

"And don't you forget it."

WELL, he came downtown after he left his house," I said, wrinkling my nose as I studied the path. Luckily for us, only witches could see the magical line. Downtown bustled with activity, and explaining a glowing trail that popped up out of nowhere wasn't something I looked forward to tackling.

"What was he doing?" Clove asked.

"Do I look omnipotent?"

"I have no idea what that means, but some people think you look like a hobbit," Clove replied, not missing a beat.

I scowled. "You really are turning into a pain like your cousins."

"Thank you."

After parking my car behind the library, I led the girls downtown so I could study the spell. People waved as they passed, ridiculous smiles on their faces as they wished me "merry Christmas" and "happy holidays." It would be easier if they bought a clue and didn't' talk to me.

"The trail leads out of town," Bay said. "That means he ran away and isn't dead in a ditch somewhere, right?"

"Probably," I conceded. "We don't technically know that he ran away, though. Maybe he had a family emergency or something."

"Just because he ran away out of town, that doesn't mean he's not dead in a ditch somewhere," Thistle said.

"Stop with the ditch!"

The face Thistle made was comical enough to make me smirk. The girl has star quality sometimes.

"Wherever Bernard is, he's not here," I said.

"Are we going to go after him?" Bay asked.

I knew what she was really asking. She wanted to know if laziness would stop me from keeping my promise. "We're going to follow the trail for as long as we can," I hedged. "If it goes too far, though ... ."

"We have to turn around because our moms will have a fit and you'll be in big trouble," Bay finished. "I get it."

"Bay, I'm doing the best I can," I said. "I ... ."

"Uh-oh." Clove's singsong warning drew my attention to the other side of the town square, where Poppy Stevens – Lila's hand clasped tightly in hers as she dragged her along – was heading in my direction. She appeared to have something on her mind. The closer she got, I realized she appeared to still have something on her lip, too – and it was growing.

"Well, girls, today is your lucky day," I said, straightening. "I think you're going to get another Christmas present."

"Are you going to make her strip naked and dance in the town square?" Thistle asked. "That's what you promised."

It was an interesting suggestion. Unfortunately, there were too many people hanging around for me to pull it off and slink away without anyone noticing. "We're saving that one for the summer, when it's warmer," I replied. "We want to make her pay, but we don't want to kill her with frostbite. That's an important distinction."

"Hurting bad," Thistle said, her tone mocking.

"Revenge pretty," Bay finished, giggling.

I was starting to like them more and more as their evil inclinations got a foothold. By the time Poppy stopped in front of me, her chest heaving as she fought to catch her breath, I was ready for just about anything.

"Mrs. Winchester, it has come to my attention that you threatened my daughter the other day," Poppy said, her face murderous. "I'm here to tell you that things like that won't be tolerated."

Lila was smug as she crossed her arms over her chest. It wasn't nearly as adorable on her as it was on me.

"Really? What are you going to do to me if I threaten little Licorice again?"

"Her name is Lila," Poppy snapped. "If you threaten her again I'll report you to the police. How do you like that?"

"My word against a ten-year-old terror who has been suspended from school three different times for sticking gum in other kids' hair? I'm fine with that."

My response must have thrown Poppy, because it took her a few moments to collect herself. "Mrs. Winchester, I don't think you understand the gravity of this situation. My daughter has been plagued by nightmares – she actually thinks you're going to curse her with a ... beauty mark ... above her lip – and I don't think it's funny to purposely scare children."

"I didn't threaten her with a beauty mark," I shot back. "I threatened her with herpes ... like you have."

"From the mailman," Thistle added.

"I do not have herpes," Poppy hissed. "It's a beauty mark."

"Whatever," I said. I don't have time for this. "We need to be somewhere. Unless you want me to give you a ... beauty mark ... to match on your bottom lip, you're going to want to get out of my face."

"Oh, don't be crass," Poppy said. "We all know you're all talk. You might have everyone in this town fooled into thinking you're some powerful witch, but I know the truth. You're nothing but a bitter old woman, and you're teaching these little ... hellions ... to be just as obnoxious as you are."

Well, that did it. You can call me a lot of things, but bitter isn't one of them. Bitchy? Sure. Bitter? This woman is asking for it. And hellions? Okay, yeah, that fits. I didn't hesitate, instead gathering a limited supply of power and flinging it in her direction. I didn't have the ingredients necessary to handle the herpes threat, but I made a mental note to tackle that before bed. It isn't going to be a merry Christmas in the Stevens household. I can practically guarantee that.

Poppy's haughty countenance faltered when she felt something breezy whip past her nether regions. She frowned and glanced down, horrified to find a rip in the crotch of her pants and her over-sized cotton underwear on display.

"What the ... ?"

"What's wrong, Mommy?" Lila asked, faux concern washing over her features. "I thought you were going to have Mrs. Winchester arrested. That's what you told me. Do it."

"Shut up, Lila," Poppy snapped, dropping Lila's hand and covering the spot where her thighs met. "I … what just happened here?"

"I have no idea," I replied. "Perhaps your ego got so big it ripped your pants."

"These are brand new pants!"

"Maybe you're fat," Thistle suggested.

Poppy's eyes were dangerous slits when they landed on Thistle. "I am not fat!"

"Your head is," Bay said. She tugged on my arm, drawing my attention to her. "We need to go. We don't have a lot of time before dinner."

She was right. I cast one final smile in Poppy's direction and then gestured for the girls to head toward the car. "Have a very merry Christmas, Poppy. You, too, Lapdog."

"Mommy! What is going on? You said you were going to make Mrs. Winchester cry."

"I think she's the one who wants to cry now," I said, leaving Poppy to haphazardly attempt to cover herself – and her unfortunate granny panties – while I led my great-nieces from the spectacle.

"It would've been better if she was naked," Thistle said.

"And crying," Clove added.

"Next time."

EIGHT

"Where are we?" Thistle asked, peering out the car window. She was in the back seat with Clove. Bernard's magical trail took us farther away from Ashton Lake than I would have liked.

"Traverse City," I replied, my eyes scanning the frozen Grand Traverse Bay. "We're in Traverse City."

"Why would he come here?" Bay asked from the passenger seat. "You can't even swim now."

That was a very good question. "I don't know," I said, following the trail as it led me around the bay and toward Traverse City's hospital district. The moment I saw Munson Medical Center pop into view, my heart sank.

"Is he in the hospital?" Clove asked, recognizing the building. "Maybe he is dead after all."

"I told you," Thistle said.

"You told us he would be in a ditch," I shot back. "He's clearly not in a ditch."

"He's probably dead in the hospital," Thistle argued. "I was half right."

When I realized the magical line extended past the hospital, I stuck my tongue out so Thistle could see it in the rearview mirror. "Ha, ha, little missy, you were wrong," I said. "He's not even at the hospital."

I didn't miss the relieved sigh when it escaped Bay's mouth.

"Where is he?" Clove asked.

"I don't know," I admitted. "Wherever it is, I think it's right here." I followed the trail and pulled into the small parking lot belonging to a brick building about four lots from the hospital, frowning when I read the sign over the door.

"What does it say?" Thistle asked.

"I … ."

"Bay Breeze Wellness," Bay replied, reading the sign. "Is this a mental hospital?"

Thistle may be the diabolical one, but Bay's reasoning skills are second to none. "That's what it kind of looks like, doesn't it?"

"Holy crap! Are you saying Santa is crazy?" Clove can turn nothing into something in the blink of an eye. In this case, I hoped she was being overly dramatic, as was her nature. If Bernard really had gone round the bend … well … we would be one Santa short at the town party while he was probably eight eggs short of a dozen in his mind.

"We don't know why he's here yet," I cautioned. "For all we know, he could be visiting someone."

"Yeah, maybe his sister went crazy or something," Thistle suggested.

That was a heart-warming thought.

"What happens now?" Bay asked.

"Now we go inside and find out what's going on."

"Are they even going to let us wander around a mental hospital?" Thistle asked.

"I … have no idea," I admitted. "We won't know until we ask." I killed the engine and shoved the keys into my purse. "When we get in there, you guys let me do all the talking."

"That's a horrible idea," Thistle said.

"Why?"

"Because if you do all the talking they'll try to keep you, and then what happens to us? We'll be stuck here and miss Christmas. I don't like this idea one bit."

I narrowed my eyes. Thistle's attitude is funny only when she directs it at other people. "They're not going to try to keep me." I'm almost positive that's true. "Stop worrying about things that can't possibly happen."

"Just so I know, if they do try to keep you, will I get to make a phone call so Mom can come and get us?" Bay asked. "It's like jail, right? We get one phone call so we won't be trapped here."

"They're not going to keep me."

"I hope you're right," Clove said, her expression serious. "I would miss you ... even if you are mean to me sometimes."

"Shut up and get out of the car," I ordered. "Make sure you don't talk unless I tell you to. Oh, and Clove, be ready to cry if things go bad. You know what I mean, right?"

Clove smiled. "I won't let them take you without a fight."

THE WOMAN SITTING behind the front desk looked as though she wanted to be anywhere but where she was. I didn't blame her. Tomorrow was Christmas Eve. She probably watched the clock, counting down to when she could start her holiday break. Hopefully that would work to my advantage.

The receptionist shifted her head in my direction when she heard the door shut, wrinkling her nose as she looked me up and down. She was obviously thrown by the appearance of children.

"Are you lost?"

I bit my tongue in an effort to hold in the nasty retort I wanted to lob in her direction. "I don't think so," I replied, forcing a pleasant smile. "We're ... looking for a friend."

"I see," the woman said. The nameplate on her desk read "Evelyn," although her platinum blond hair made her look more like a Tiffany. I probably shouldn't judge her before I talk to her more. Oh, fudge on a stick, who cares about that? I'll bet she's as dumb as she looks. "And who are you looking for?"

"I'm looking for my son," I said, the lie easily rolling off of my tongue. "His name is Bernard Hill. I was told he was here. That's a relief, because I've been looking for him for days. I have a weak heart, so it could give out at any time. Knowing where my son is before Christmas will help calm me."

Bay cast me a sidelong look. I couldn't tell whether she was impressed with the lie, but she wisely kept her mouth shut.

"You're Bernard Hill's mother?" Evelyn wrinkled her nose again as she checked her intake records. "He looks too old to be your son."

"It's the crazy," I said. "It makes him appear older."

"The crazy?"

What? I'm sure that's a real thing. "Can I see my son?"

Evelyn glanced at the girls, her expression unreadable. "You want to take them into the back to see Mr. Hill? May I ask why?"

I wanted to tell her it was none of her business, but I wisely kept that sentence to myself. "He's their ... uncle." Wait ... did the math add up for that?

"He's our godfather," Bay corrected, catching me off guard. "The only thing we want for Christmas is to see him, and our grandmother agreed to bring us because she doesn't want our Christmas to be ruined."

I wanted to smack her, but because hers was a better lie than the one I came up with, I let it slide. "Yeah, what she said."

"Bernard is your godfather?" Evelyn brightened. "That's so nice. Are you guys close?"

"We're closer than close," Bay replied. "That's why our Christmas will be ruined if we don't get to see him."

"We've been crying for days," Clove interjected. "We had no idea where he was. He wanted all of this to be a secret."

"We want him to know that it's okay that he's ... sick," Thistle added. "We don't want him to be sad or afraid to tell us."

"That is the sweetest thing I've ever heard," Evelyn said, her hand landing in the spot above her heart. "This is the time of year for all things good to happen. You girls are angels."

"That's what everyone keeps telling us," Bay said, shooting me a look. "Can we see him?"

"I don't know," Evelyn hedged. "He's ... kind of in a rough spot right now."

"That's okay," I said. "We're used to crazy. We like it."

"We don't really use that word here," Evelyn chided.

"Oh, I'm hip," I said. "I'm cool calling him insane."

Evelyn frowned.

Bay, as if sensing the situation about to slip away, stepped in front of me. "You should understand that our grandmother doesn't always think before she speaks," she said. "She doesn't mean anything by it. We've all been really worried about ... Bernard."

Evelyn's smile was sympathetic. "We're really not supposed to let anyone back in the treatment rooms, but you guys came a long way and ... well ... it is Christmas."

"It is," I agreed.

"Come with me," Evelyn said, gesturing for us to follow her down the hallway. "Don't ever tell anyone I did this for you."

"Your secret is safe with me," I said. I let Thistle and Clove follow Evelyn, but snagged Bay by the back of her coat and pulled her back so we were out of earshot. "I thought I told you to let me do the talking."

"I thought I told you I didn't want you locked up in this place for Christmas," Bay countered.

"I ... good job."

"I know," Bay said. "Come on. Let's find out if Santa is crazy and then get out of here. This place gives me the creeps."

She wasn't the only one.

Evelyn led us to the end of the hallway before hanging a right. There, at the second door down, she stopped. "Do you want me to go in with you?"

"That won't be necessary," I replied hurriedly. "I want the reunion to be conducted in private in case Bernard cries at the sight of his favorite girls. He wouldn't like anyone else seeing him cry."

"That's very sensitive of you."

Evelyn left us, her mind probably back on whatever magazine she was leafing through when we entered the building. She'd already moved on from our sad plight.

"Now that was a better lie," Bay said.

"I'm self-taught," I quipped. When I realized Bay didn't get the joke, I wiped the smile off my face. "Okay, you definitely need to let me do the talking this time."

"Because you understand crazy?" Bay teased.

"I … well … yes." I pushed open the door to Bernard's room, surprised to find it looked more like a regular bedroom than anything out of a horror movie asylum. There were no padded walls and there were enough sharp edges for Bernard to kill himself twenty times over should the desire arise. This didn't seem right.

"Tillie?" Bernard sat at the small table at the edge of the room, a deck of cards spread before him in a game of solitaire. He was dressed in jogging pants and a T-shirt, and despite what I expected, he looked healthier and relaxed.

"What the heck is going on here?" I asked. "I expected to find you strapped to the bed."

Bernard furrowed his brow, his white eyebrows knitting together as confusion washed over his face. "What are you doing here?"

"We came to rescue Santa," Clove announced.

I flicked her ear. "I said I would do all the talking."

Clove scowled and crossed her arms over her chest, miffed.

"You came to rescue Santa, huh?" Bernard's face was conflicted. "I … you guys know I'm not the real Santa, right?"

"We know," Bay replied. "It's just … you're our Santa. We need you to come home for the Christmas party."

"Well, Bay, I don't really think that's going to be possible." Bernard looked genuinely upset. "I … can't leave here."

"Because you're crazy?" Thistle asked.

"Why do you think I'm crazy?"

"I … ." Thistle bit her lip and then pointed at me.

"I didn't say you were crazy," I protested. Well, I kind of did. He didn't need to know that, though. "It's just ... well ... you're in a mental hospital. We weren't even sure you were alive."

"How did you find me?"

"I ... ." Crud. How could I answer him?

"We're private investigators on the side," Thistle answered smoothly.

That kid really needs to stop watching so much television.

"It's not important how we found you," I said. "We were worried. The girls wanted to see you. I ... I'm really sorry you're ... struggling."

"I am struggling," Bernard agreed. "I'm not crazy, though."

"I didn't say you were crazy."

"Yes, you did," Clove said.

"Shut up, Clove."

Bernard chuckled, the sound taking me by surprise. "You've always been a pip, Tillie," he said. "You're one of my favorite people. Do you know that?"

"It doesn't surprise me," I said. "Most people who know me love me."

Thistle rolled her eyes. "We're sorry you're ... not crazy ... but can you come home long enough to be Santa for us? It won't be the same without you."

"I can't do that, Thistle," Bernard said. "This isn't a mental hospital, no matter what your Aunt Tillie told you."

"It's not?" That was a relief.

"It's a rehabilitation center," Bernard said. "I'm trying to kick a few bad habits."

"Oh," I said, realization dawning as I glanced around the room again. Things were starting to make sense. "That's really good, Bernard. I ... now I feel like an idiot."

"It's okay," he said, waving off my embarrassment. "I'm glad someone cared enough to come looking for me. That's the reason I'm here. I realized my life was going to stay bad as long as I let the demons keep ahold of me. I'm trying to get rid of the demons."

"Not real demons, right?" Clove prodded.

"Not real demons," Bernard conceded. "They're personal demons.

They're strong, though, and that's why I need to be here. Do you understand that?"

Thistle and Clove nodded in unison, but Bay remained rooted to her spot.

"Can't you just come home for a few hours?" Bay asked.

"I'm really sorry, Bay," Bernard said, his face kind as he studied the tiny blonde. "I should have realized what my disappearance would mean for the school pageant and the town Christmas party. I honestly didn't think that far ahead. That's on me, and I apologize for making such a mess of things.

"I can't come home, though," he continued. "Not yet. I'm not ready."

"What you're doing here is more important, Bernard," I said, meaning every word. "We shouldn't have tracked you down like this. You have a right to privacy. Don't worry about us telling anyone what you're doing here."

"You can tell people," Bernard replied. "It will probably be better for me if you do. That way ... well ... hopefully people won't try to tempt me when I get home."

"Do you know you left dirty underwear on your bedroom floor?" Clove asked.

"How do you know that?"

"She has a wild imagination," I answered for her, clapping my hand over Clove's mouth before she could say anything else. "Well, I wish you well, Bernard. When you get back to town, we'll all be waiting and ready to help you."

"Thank you, Tillie." Bernard turned back to Bay. "You know the real Santa will still visit you, right?"

"There is no real Santa," Bay replied, her tone positively pitiable. "It's okay. You need to get better."

"I really am sorry, Bay."

"It's fine." Bay kept her head high as she turned and walked out of the room.

I offered Bernard a few more apologies and then dragged Clove and Thistle into the hallway. Bay was waiting and she was clearly upset, even though she was too stoic for tears. I still hurt for her. "I'm sorry."

"It's okay," Bay replied, her face drawn. "You can't fix everything."

When did that become the rule? "I'm still sorry. At least we know Bernard's okay, though."

"We do," Bay said, nodding. "We also know Christmas is officially ruined. I want to go home now."

NINE

The ride home was completed in silence. Clove and Thistle tried to keep some form of conversation going initially, but Bay was having none of it so they all shut their mouths and focused on the scenery as it blurred by.

On most occasions I'd welcome the silence. This was different.

I led the girls into the house shortly before dinner, Thistle and Clove scampering off to wash their hands while Bay dejectedly threw herself into the corner chair in the kitchen, where she proceeded to pout.

Winnie eyed her only child for a few moments, her hands busy chopping vegetables, before turning to me. "Do I even want to know?"

"Probably not." On the way home I considered how much to tell my nieces, and while I knew I could probably convince the girls to lie for me, I didn't think that was the proper message to send right before Christmas. "How much do you want to know?"

"How much do we need to know?"

That was a tricky question. "Well, I put together a tracking spell for Bernard," I explained. "We followed it through town, where I had a showdown with Poppy Stevens. I have to remember to give her another cold sore before I go to bed, by the way, so don't let me forget.

"We followed the trail out of town and it led us to a facility in Traverse City," I continued. "At first we thought it was a mental hospital and the girls were really worried Santa was crazy.

"Good news, though, Santa is not crazy," I said. "Bernard is fine. He's in a rehab facility and he's trying to dry out. He apologized for missing the Christmas festivities, but he can't leave."

Whew. I felt better after unloading all of that.

Winnie was murderous. "You what?"

Well, crap on a cracker, that's what I get for going with the truth. My first instinct had been to lie. It's always better to stick with your first instinct. "I'm not repeating all of that." I grabbed a cherry tomato from the counter and popped it into my mouth. "It's been a really long day and I don't have a lot of energy, so if you're going to yell and scream ... I'm telling you now, I'll probably only half listen."

"I don't even know what to say," Marnie grumbled, turning back to the kitchen counter.

"I do," Winnie snapped. "What were you thinking taking them to a rehab facility?"

"It was like a nice apartment complex with nurses," I argued. "Don't get your panties in a bunch. There weren't crazy people walking around drooling and collecting hair for homemade bird nests. The girls didn't see any loonies. Personally, I was a little disappointed."

"You're unbelievable," Winnie said. "I can't understand how you thought that was a good idea."

"The girls wanted to find Bernard and save Christmas," I said. "I thought I was doing the right thing. How was I supposed to know he was in rehab?"

"You weren't," Winnie shot back. "What if you cast that spell and it led you to a dead body? Did you ever think of that?"

"Quite frankly, Thistle wouldn't let me think of anything else," I said. "She was convinced he was dead in a ditch somewhere. So, for her, this was a really great day."

"And what about Bay?" Winnie asked, her gaze pointed as it landed on her daughter.

"She's a little more upset," I conceded.

Winnie threw a dishtowel at me and rounded the counter, not stopping until she was next to Bay. "Do you want to talk about what happened?"

"What is there to talk about?"

"You know that Mr. Hill is sick and he has to stay in the hospital to get better, right?" Winnie pressed. "This has nothing to do with you, so there's no reason to be upset."

"Christmas is ruined," Bay said.

"Christmas can't be ruined," Winnie argued. "Yes, you're not getting the holiday party you wanted. You still have your family. You have gifts. Heck, Aunt Tillie – although I'm really angry with her right now – even made it snow. What more do you want, Bay?"

"I … ." Bay worried her bottom lip with her teeth.

"Tell me," Winnie urged.

"I wanted as much of the Christmas we had last year as I could get," Bay admitted. "Everything changed this year. Everything is different. I wanted one thing to be the same. Is that too much to ask?"

"I think it is," Winnie replied, her tone even. "Life changes, kid. You don't always get what you want. Enough is enough, though. People have been bending over backward to make this a perfect holiday for you. What are you doing to make the holiday better for others?"

"What?" Bay was flabbergasted.

"Not everything in this world is about you, Bay," Winnie said. "I'm sorry you're not happy. I'm sorry you think the world is coming to an end. You still have a lot more than most other people.

"You have me. You have your aunts. You have your cousins. You even have Aunt Tillie," she continued. "At a certain point, your insistence on having everything you want exactly how you want it makes you a spoiled brat."

"That's not true!" Bay exploded. "I can't help it if I want the town party to be the same. I'm not trying to upset you. Not everything I do is about you."

"Well, it feels like it is sometimes," Winnie replied. "I want you to have the best this world has to offer, but you need to realize everyone isn't going to bow down to your will and make life perfect for you. You have to make yourself happy in this world sometimes, Bay. It's time you realized that."

"But ...."

"No." Winnie wagged a finger in Bay's angry face. "Now, you need to go wash your hands for dinner. When dinner is over, I think you should go to bed early and think about what I said. I want you to really think about it.

"Your Aunt Tillie did some incredibly stupid things today, but she did them out of the goodness of her heart because she desperately wants to see you smile," Winnie said. "I'm done begging you to be happy, though. We all are. If you want to be miserable, you can do it alone. The rest of us are going to be happy on Christmas, whether it's the Christmas you've been dreaming about or not.

"Now, go wash your hands and when you come back for dinner I don't want to hear a word about Christmas being ruined," she said.

Bay pushed herself up from the chair, her shoulders hunched as she trudged out of the room. She didn't look at anyone, instead focusing on her stocking-clad feet. If Winnie thought that inspirational speech would snap Bay out of it, I think she had a sad realization of her own to come.

"That was kind of harsh," Marnie said once it was just the adults. "She's just a kid."

"I know she is," Winnie said, sucking in a deep breath. "I love that child more than anything in this world, but she has got to get a grip. Nothing in life is perfect."

"I shouldn't have taken them to Traverse City," I said. "I ... it was a dumb idea. That doesn't mean I still don't think those girls deserve a great Christmas."

"Of course they deserve a great Christmas," Winnie said. "That doesn't mean they're going to get some fairy tale holiday. A great Christmas isn't the same thing as a perfect Christmas. Nothing in this world is perfect."

I licked my lips. "I'm not ready to give up."

"Well, you'd better," Winnie said. "You're out of time and Bay will have to deal with it. Apparently you will, too."

Well, we'd just have to see about that.

I MADE myself scarce early in the afternoon on Christmas Eve. I couldn't take one more second of Winnie's tough love or Bay's belligerence – and I knew both were going to be on display at the town Christmas party. Those two were a stubborn match, and I had a feeling things would explode before they got better.

I didn't want to witness it.

Instead, I made my annual pilgrimage to the town cemetery to visit my Calvin. He's been gone for a long time now, but I still feel his loss keenly at times – especially around the holidays.

Calvin loved Christmas. He liked hiking into the woods to pick out a Christmas tree. He loved decorating it. He loved shopping – spending months picking out the exact right gift for the people he loved – and then he delighted in hiding them. I'm a snoop, so we turned it into a game. I really miss that game.

I placed a bouquet of fresh flowers on his grave and dusted the snow from the top of his headstone. "I'm sorry I haven't been by in a while," I said. "Time overtakes me sometimes. I don't have teenage nieces to contend with anymore, but those little girls are a handful these days.

"Still ... that's no excuse," I said. "I'll do better next year."

"No, you won't."

The voice took me by surprise and I swiveled quickly, stunned to find Calvin's wispy countenance watching me from a few feet away. He is dead, his spirit long since passed on. "What are you doing here?" I wanted to throw myself in his arms. He is a ghost, though. He can't hug me back.

"I'm here for you."

I frowned. I loved the man, but that wasn't funny. "I'm not dying yet," I said. You tell whoever sent you for me that I have no intention of going with you. Come back in fifty years."

Calvin chuckled, the sound warming my heart even though I was still suspicious. "I'm not here to take you to the other side, Tillie," he said. "I'm here to ... see you."

"Not that I'm not happy for the visit, but can I ask why?"

"I'm your Christmas present," Calvin replied, floating closer to me so I could see the lines of his face up close. Goddess, I do miss that face.

"You're my Christmas present, huh?"

Calvin nodded, his gaze traveling down to my pink combat boots. "You still have a flair for the dramatic I see."

"It's always easier when people think you're crazy," I said. "You know that."

"I think you like the attention."

"I think you're probably right," I conceded. "It's so good to see you. How long can you stay?"

"Not long," Calvin replied. "I'm only here to give you what you need this holiday season."

"I had no idea ghosts were allowed to travel with a bottle of whiskey," I teased, causing Calvin to smirk.

"If I thought whiskey could save Christmas I would find a way to get you some," Calvin said. "That's not why I'm here, though."

"Why are you here?"

"Because you want to give Bay, Clove and Thistle the holiday they've been dreaming about, but you need my help to do it," Calvin replied.

"I ... you're going to help me save Christmas?"

"You're going to save Christmas all on your own," Calvin said. "I'm here to give you the ... inspiration ... you need."

That didn't sound so bad. "Okay. What do I do?"

"I can't answer that question for you," Calvin said.

"What can you do?"

"Tell you that life is more than perfect holidays and quaint memories," Calvin said. "You used to know that. I think you're so desperate to give those girls what you think they want you forget that you already know what they need."

"I don't remember you being this cryptic when you were alive,"

I said.

Calvin laughed, the throaty chuckle echoing throughout the cemetery. "I was always cryptic, but mostly because you talked enough for the both of us," he said. "I think death makes people forget some of the bad things about someone's personality."

"There was nothing bad about your personality."

"There was," Calvin said. "It's nice that you don't want to remind me of them, though."

I waited for him to continue, but when he didn't I narrowed my eyes and shot him a dirty look. "Aren't you going to tell me that there's nothing bad about my personality, too?"

"I'm not here to lie to you," he replied. "I'm here to help you." He glanced over his shoulder, scanning the sky to gauge the position of the sun. "I don't have a lot of time, Tillie. I wish I could spend the day with you – or even an hour – but I only have a few minutes."

"So what are you here to tell me?"

I swear, even though he didn't have a solid physical form, Calvin's eyes twinkled. "You already know how to save Christmas, Tillie," he said, blinking out of existence and then reappearing at my side. He was so close I could almost feel him and I involuntarily shuddered. "Think back to when you were their age. What made you happy at Christmas?"

I briefly pressed my eyes shut. "I wish you didn't have to go."

"I'm already gone," Calvin said. "You'll see me again, though. I'm always watching you."

"Is that supposed to frighten me?"

Calvin laughed again, though this time it was more distant. "Nothing frightens you, my dear," he said. "Have a happy Christmas. We'll be together again … someday. You have a lot left to give to this world, though. I'll be waiting."

I knew he was gone before I opened my eyes. Why did he come? What was he trying to tell me? I closed my eyes again and searched my heart instead of my brain for a change. When I reopened my eyes, I knew what I had to do. Christmas wouldn't be ruined after all. Now I just have to get all the pieces in place.

TEN

I found Terry at his house an hour before the start of the Christmas party as I had hoped. Convincing him to do what I was about to ask was going to be tricky.

"What are you doing here?" Terry asked, his eyebrows flying up his forehead when he caught sight of me on his front porch. "I ... did something happen to one of the girls? Is Bay okay?"

The fact that he immediately worried about Bay made me realize Bay's depression was taking a toll on everyone. "Bay is fine," I said, rubbing the tender spot between my eyebrows as I regarded him. "Well, actually she's not fine. She'll be fine if you do what I want you to do, though."

Terry stilled. "What do you have in mind?"

I smiled brightly and handed him the garment bag. He took it wordlessly, unzipped it to study what it contained, and immediately shook his head. "No way!"

"There's a very sad little girl whose heart will be broken if you don't do this," I reminded him. "Do you want to be responsible for that?"

"That is an absolutely dirty way to play this game," Terry warned. "You know darned well that's not what I want."

"It's not what I want either," I said. "You and I can fix Christmas for Bay … and Clove and Thistle, too. Although, to be fair, I think Clove and Thistle will be fine regardless. They have a much faster rebound rate than Bay."

"I've noticed," Terry said dryly. "I … I can't do this. I don't even know how to begin to do this."

"Now you're just being ridiculous," I said. "Everyone who has ever watched a movie knows how to do what I'm asking you to do. Now, you can say no. You can crush the dreams of the children in this town. I'm betting you're not willing to do that, though."

"You are a horrible woman."

"I'll see you in the town square in an hour," I said. "Oh, and I have a gift for you to give to Bay, Clove and Thistle when it's their turn." I pushed the box I'd set beside his door inside so he could take a gander at what I'd gotten them.

"Oh, you're going to be in so much trouble when your nieces see this … ."

"Yeah, well, they'll live," I said. "Don't be late, and don't forget the gift."

"Trust me. You don't have to worry about me forgetting the gift."

"That's good," I said, moving toward the door.

"What are you going to do while I'm doing this?"

I made a face. "Someone has to make it snow again. Sheesh."

THE TOWN practically glowed when I arrived at the party an hour later, the sound of squealing children and happy adults meeting my ears as I scanned the familiar faces for the ones I sought.

It didn't take me long to find them. Clove and Thistle were having a good time, hot chocolate clutched in their hands as they hopped up and down and pointed at the Christmas tree that was about to be lighted. Bay stood behind them, her own cup of hot chocolate resting in her mitten-covered hand, staring glumly at the tree.

Marnie and Twila laughed as they stood close to their daughters, happy to let them enjoy the moment from a few feet away. Winnie was more detached, and while she tried to pretend to have a good time, I could tell Bay's unhappiness weighed on her.

I headed in their direction, pulling up short when Poppy stepped in my path. Her second cold sore was even bigger than the first. There was no way she would be able to explain away the blimp resting on her bottom lip.

"Make it go away!"

"I have no idea what you're talking about," I replied, pasting my best "I'm innocent and there's no way you can blame me for this" smile on my face. "You look ... festive ... this evening. The red of your ... beauty mark ... really tops off the decorations nicely."

"I'll have you arrested for this," Poppy threatened.

"You're going to have me arrested for the cold sore on your lip? That's a neat trick. Tell me how that works out for you." I patted her arm as I walked past, lowering my voice so only she could hear. "If you don't rein in that monstrous thing you call a daughter, I'll give you eight more to match the two you already have." I made sure I was several feet away before I opened my mouth again. "Have an absolutely fabulous Christmas!"

Winnie, her face unreadable, watched me as I approached. "What was all that about?"

"If they still did floggings in public, I would arrange a way for Poppy Stevens to get one," I replied.

"That would be a Christmas gift for us all," Winnie said.

My gaze bounced between her and Bay. "Still nothing, huh?"

"She's decided to pout her way through the entire day and I refuse to give in and coddle her," Winnie answered. "It's a standoff."

"Do you think you'll win?"

"Probably not," Winnie conceded. "I'll probably crumble like a stale cookie and start begging in about ten minutes."

"At least you're honest," I said, patting her shoulder. "Don't give in yet. I think there's a way you can both get a win out of this, and it's right around the corner."

"Oh, yeah? What is that? Are you going to make it snow again?"

As if on cue, the flakes began falling. Unlike the quick spurt of snow I unleashed before, this was a soft smattering that cascaded to the ground in fluffy wisps.

"Oh, Aunt Tillie," Winnie chided. "You didn't have to do this again."

The children screamed in delight at the flakes, causing my heart to swell as I puffed out my chest. "I wouldn't be the wickedest witch in the Midwest if I didn't make the children happy on Christmas, would I?"

"Actually, I don't think that makes a lot of sense," Winnie said. "I thank you for the gift anyway." She leaned over and kissed my cheek, a thoughtful expression on her face as she pulled back. "You know, it occurs to me that you never told us what you wanted this Christmas."

"I'm an adult. I don't need a Christmas gift."

"You usually leave your list on the kitchen table right next to the girls' when they write their lists," Winnie pointed out.

I smirked. "I bought my own gift this year," I said. "And, well, I had another special gift waiting for me at the cemetery today."

"Is that where you disappeared to?" Winnie asked. "You know we would've gone with you, right? You didn't have to go alone."

"I wasn't alone."

Winnie wrinkled her nose. "Who were you with?"

"Santa Claus," I said, my grin widening as the sound of sleigh bells approached the town square.

"What did you do?" Winnie asked, jerking her head in the direction of the jingling. She started giggling the moment she saw the sleigh. Try as I might, I couldn't find any reindeer. Henry Hall gladly loaned me a few horses, though, so that was at least something.

"It's Santa," Clove squealed, jumping up and down as she clapped her hands.

I cast a look at Bay, smiling as she tilted her head to the side to study Ashton Lake's newest Kris Kringle.

"Who is it?" Winnie asked, narrowing her eyes as the sleigh got closer. "I ... he looks familiar."

"Ho, ho, ho!" Terry's bellow echoed throughout the square, and when Winnie realized who it was, her eyes filled with tears.

"How did you convince him to do this?"

"I didn't convince him," I said. "I ... had a little talk with him and told him Bay would cry for days if he didn't do it. You'd be surprised how easily he gave in."

"That was extremely manipulative."

"So what? He'll have a great time doing it, and you and your sisters will fall all over yourselves thanking him. This is a win-win-win situation for him."

"Still, it doesn't quite seem fair to him," Winnie said. "He doesn't have children. He shouldn't have to go out of his way for ours."

"He might not have children of his own," I countered. "He does have the best interests of ours in his heart most of the time, though. Trust me. He'll enjoy this."

Winnie smiled, watching as the sleigh stopped and Bay took a tentative step forward. Terry stared at her, his eyes bright as she closed the distance between them.

"You must be Bay," Terry said, his fake voice deep. "I hear you think Christmas is ruined this year."

Bay stilled. "I ... who are you?" She had trouble putting a real face with the voice and beard. "I know you."

"Of course you know me," Terry said. "I'm Santa Claus! You don't believe in Santa Claus, though, do you?"

"No ... yes ... maybe ... ." Bay didn't know how to answer. "If you're Santa Claus, does that mean you brought me a gift?" She was testing the big man.

"I did."

"What is it?"

"You can't have it until I'm sure you believe in me," Terry replied. "Those are the rules."

Bay narrowed her eyes. "Who makes these rules?"

"My elves."

"Aren't you the boss of your elves?"

"I'm not the boss of anyone," Terry replied, his eyes landing on me for a moment and then returning to Bay's. "It seems everyone tells me what to do and I do it."

"That doesn't seem like a very good job," Bay said.

"It's the best job in the world," Terry countered. "I'm Santa Claus. I get to bring joy to the world, even if you don't believe in me."

"Maybe I do believe in you," Bay said. "I ... ."

"If you believe in me, you have to say it," Terry prodded.

"I believe in you," Bay mumbled.

"I can't hear you."

"She said she believes in you," Clove yelled.

"Thank you, Clove," Terry said. "I know you believe. Your present will be coming as soon as Bay tells me she believes."

It was the moment of truth. Bay knew it. Everyone in town knew it. Now she only had to admit it.

"Fine," Bay said, crossing her arms over her chest. "I believe in Santa Claus."

"I still can't hear you," Terry said, staring her down. "You need to say it louder!"

"I believe in Santa Claus!" Bay practically screamed the words and Terry broke out in a huge grin.

"That's better," Terry said, leaning over and rummaging in the bag at his feet. When he turned around, he held a puppy. The black menace had a huge bow tied around its neck and it wriggled crazily.

Bay's eyes widened as she took another step forward. "Is that for me?"

"That's for you, Clove and Thistle," Terry replied.

Bay took the puppy, her eyes filling with tears. "Thank you."

"You have to take care of him," Terry said. "You girls have to feed him and walk him and love him. Do you think you're up to the task?"

"You bet we are," Clove said, rushing to Bay's side so she could pet the puppy. "Wow."

"How did you know to get us a puppy?" Bay asked.

"One of my elves told me."

"How did the elf know?"

"Your Aunt Tillie has a huge mouth," Terry replied, smiling at Bay one more time before turning his attention to the rest of the children. "Who wants presents?"

The squeals were deafening as the surged in around him. Terry didn't put up a fight as they started climbing on his lap and telling him their most fervent wishes.

Off to the side, my great-nieces were enamored with their gift. They didn't even glance at the other kids as they raced around in the snow with the puppy.

"I can't believe you got them a puppy," Winnie said, moving to my side. "You told me in no uncertain terms that a puppy was out of the question."

"I did not get them that puppy."

"Oh, really, then who did?"

I pointed at Terry. "You just saw Santa Claus give the girls that puppy," I said. "You can't possibly blame this on me."

"I'm not blaming you," Winnie countered. "I'm thanking you. Look at them. Have you ever seen them so happy?"

I hadn't. All three of them beamed and screamed as they raced around with our newest family member. "I'm glad they got the Christmas they deserve."

"Where did you get that puppy?"

"In addition to horses, Henry Hall had exactly one leftover puppy from his dog's most recent litter," I replied. "I think it was meant to be."

"You're a softie," Winnie said, smirking. "I had no idea you were such a softie."

"I am not a softie," I argued. "Santa Claus is."

"Well, you're the best Santa Claus ever," Winnie said, resting her head against mine for a moment. "Now I know we didn't get you a big enough Christmas gift."

"Oh, don't worry about that," I said. "Henry Hall also had a used snowplow and truck he was selling. I bought it for myself. We have to pick it up on the way home."

"What are you going to do with a snowplow?"

"Is that a trick question?" I asked.

"No, but … you know what? If you want a snowplow, go nuts," Winnie said. "I think you've earned whatever crazy gift you want to give yourself this year."

AMANDA M. LEE

"I have, haven't I?"

"Aunt Tillie, come and see the puppy," Bay beckoned. "Come on. You have to help us name him."

I smiled. "I'm coming."

Winnie stilled me with a hand on my arm. "Thank you."

"There's no need to thank me," I said. "You need to thank Santa Claus over there. I promised him a nice Christmas dinner tomorrow. He'll be over in the morning to watch the girls open their gifts, too."

"You invited Terry to Christmas dinner? That's a great idea." Winnie smoothed her hair as she studied Santa. "He looks hot in that suit, doesn't he?"

"You have very strange tastes, my girl," I said, patting her arm.

Apparently I took too long, because Bay raced up to me, her eyes sparkling. "You saved Christmas!"

"I told you I would."

Bay threw her arms around me, hugging me tightly. "I love you, Aunt Tillie."

The words humbled and surprised me. "I ... ."

"You don't have to say it back," Bay said, pulling away. "I can read your heart. Uncle Calvin told me you would save Christmas when he stopped by today."

"You saw your uncle?" Winnie asked, surprised.

"I didn't see him," Bay replied. "I heard him whispering. I didn't realize it was him at first. He told me I had to be nice to you and apologize for being such a brat."

"He did not call you a brat," I argued. Calvin would never say that to a child.

"He didn't," Bay agreed, glancing at her mother. "Someone else did, and I think she was right. It's time for me to do something nice for someone else on Christmas."

"What do you have in mind?"

"Can we take leftovers to Mr. Hill tomorrow so he has a nice Christmas, too?"

"I think that's a fine idea," I said, pushing Bay's hair from her face. "Maybe this time we'll get to see some actual crazy people."

"I have you," Bay shot back, smirking. "I don't need any other crazy people in my life."

"I love you, too, rug rat," I said, tugging her hair. "Now go play with your puppy and the snow. I think you've finally gotten the Christmas you deserve."

Actually, I think we all did.